THE CORPORATION

Norman Shabel

Chateau Publishing House, Inc.
Marlton, New Jersey

DISCLAIMERS:

THE CORPORATION: *A Novel*. Copyright © 2007 by Norman Shabel. All rights reserved. Printed in the United States of America. No part of this book may be used or reproduced in any manner whatsoever without written permission except in the case of brief quotations embodied in the critical articles and reviews. For information address Chateau Publishing House, Inc., 5 Greentree Centre, Suite 302, 525 Route 73 South, Marlton, New Jersey, 08053

Library of Congress Control Number: 2007936697

ISBN 978-1-60402-844-7

This novel is a work of fiction. The characters, names, incidents, dialogue and plot are products of the author's imagination and are used fictitiously. Any resemblance to actual persons, companies or events is purely coincidental.

ACKNOWLEDGMENTS:

To Arleen, my wife, who has added to the color of the places and characters depicted in the book.

To Bill Thompson, an ancient mariner with God's gift to edit wisely.

To Dawn, my secretary, who has diligently and faithfully transcribed my scribbles into a coherent text.

Other Novels by Norman Shabel

The Badger Game
The Aleph Bet Conspiracy
God Knows No Heroes

Prologue

The bright winter sun seared the paneled conference room walls. Seated alone at the head of the glass topped conference table, Jack Evans' ice-blue eyes stared across the room at the oil portrait of a distinguished looking man staring back at him. Jack Evans was Chief Executive Officer of Comtel International.

"Shit…Shit…Shit," his husky voice murmured to no one in particular. He withdrew a handkerchief from his inner suit pocket and wiped his brow. His well-manicured hands were clasped tightly on the table in front of him.

There was a gentle knock on the door. Evans' eyes didn't waver from the portrait painting.

The door opened slowly. A stocky bald headed man quietly entered the room, the door opened just enough to let his paunchy body into the room.

"I'm sorry Mr. Evans," the intruder said in a low, almost whispering voice. He put his hand over his eyes to protect his face from the invasive sun streaming through the window.

"What is it Charlie?" Evans replied in an impatient smoky voice. His hair was steel gray like a lion's mane, it framed the chiseled features of his smooth skinned face.

"The reporters are out here, sir…"

There was no reply for several seconds. Without turning his head, Evans replied, "I'm not available, Charlie…"

"But, sir…"

"I am not available, Charlie," Evans repeated in a quiet monotone.

Charlie stood in front of the double door, his hands clasped in front of his waist. Waiting. He didn't know what for.

"But Mr. Evans…"

"What happened, Charlie?" Evans asked, as he slowly turned his face toward the awkward body of his subordinate.

"I don't know, sir…The lawyers…they said we couldn't lose…"

"Never…in my wildest dreams, never…Charlie…"

"I'm sure it will be overturned on appeal, sir."

"No it won't…those bastards up there…in Tallahassee…are just waiting to cut our balls off…"

Evans paused to breathe in the hot air that filled the room. His eyes darted out to the massive window, watching the Orlando skyline just as the sun was setting into the western sky over the lakes in the distance.

"I'm afraid the verdict, if it sticks, Mr. Evans, will hurt our stock price…especially the merger with AMT on the table."

Angrily Evans shouted, "I know all about what could happen, Charlie. The merger…God, what a time to get hit with this bullshit!"

"We still have the appeal. The verdict is not set in stone yet."

"Its trouble I never bargained for Charlie." Evans' voice drifted into an almost effeminate pitch. His tanned face and neck turned beet red. He pounded his fist onto the table as he shouted, "All that money, Charlie…with interest and attorney fees for those slimy lawyers. God, those Wall Street sharks will kill our stock value."

"What about the insurance policies, Mr. Evans?"

Evans eyes darted toward Charlie who was now leaning on the back of a chair.

"Insurance won't cover the interest, Charlie. Who'd ever think?"

"Does your father…the Senator, does he know? Can he do anything?"

"Put us into bankruptcy. Maybe. I don't know…"

Charlie turned quickly toward the door as he heard a demanding knock. Loud voices seemed to pierce the heavy oak doors.

"It's the press, sir." Charlie repeated.

"There is nothing to say, Charlie. The jury said it all. What's left to say, Charlie."

Evans pulled out his silver cigarette case from his jacket pocket. He drew a large Benson and Hedges cigarette and tapped it on the case. He lit the cigarette with an initialed gold cigarette lighter and then sucked in the smoke as an asthmatic would gulp in life- giving oxygen. He then expelled the smoky residue through his nostrils. Charlie was hypnotized by the process.

Evans coughed into his handkerchief and then continued to inhale the cigarette smoke.

"Get Lowry in here, Charlie." Evans ordered in between drags of his cigarette.

"He's going to have to fight his way through the cameras, sir."

Evans suddenly bolted up from his chair and walked over to the window. The ash of his cigarette fell onto the plush carpet.

"That's what lawyers are paid to do, Charlie…fight their way through the system. Pick up the phone there and tell him I want to see him pronto...Understand? Now!"

After Charlie contacted the receptionist, Alfred Lowry, general counsel of Comtel International, appeared within minutes. His face was drawn with beads of sweat on his forehead. Lowry's slight frame stood next to Charlie as if there was an invisible boundary line daring anyone to cross to reach Evans.

"You disappeared, Jack," Lowry said as he pushed the moist wisps of thinnish hair back from his face.

"The sheriff led me out the back door of the court house." Evans replied.

"I never expected it..." Lowry stammered.

"Why would you? It's not your money, Alfred!" Evans words pierced the wisps of smoke suspended in the sunlight.

"Jack, we put three years on this case. Who the hell would expect those cowboys on the jury to believe her."

"It wasn't her, Alfred. It was those God damn lawyers."

"Lawyers don't make cases, Jack."

Evans whirled around as if he has been shocked by an electric prod, bent over the conference table and the words from his thin lipped mouth poured out. "You're an asshole, Lowry...you're a fucking asshole...What do you mean lawyers don't make cases? Who taught you that bullshit...Of course lawyers make cases and good lawyers win cases. Like you're supposed to do for your client...our client...Comtel. You know the name, don't you, Lowry. Comtel International...yours and my company...the one that has been feeding your coke habit for the last twenty years."

"The judge..." Lowry tried to answer.

"The judge bullshit, Alfred. Part of your job was to get the right judge." Suddenly a cynical smile whisked across Evans' face. He continued speaking slowly, "All you had to do was go to the Assignment Judge and ask him for the right trial judge. Don't you know we own those mothers? They owe us!" He shouted.

Evans pointed toward the oil painting he had been staring at and then continued in a quiet voice. "He put those bastards on the bench, Alfred. The Senator…our Senator…One call from him would've shut the case off. It would've been worth nada. Y'hear me, Alfred!"

"I thought Judge Gamble would be the right judge for our case, Jack."

"Well, you were fucking wrong, Alfred! Goddamn fucking wrong! He murdered us…All that sex bullshit…What the hell does screwing somebody in the executive suite have anything to do with a personal injury class action?"

"I argued that point, Jack. But he overruled my objections. The jury heard all about the sex…the dope…all that went into evidence, Jack. That's what killed us."

"How the hell did you let it be certified as a class action, Alfred?" Evans paused to drag on his wilted cigarette as he sidled into the armchair around the table. "Sit down, Alfred…you too, Charlie." Both men obeyed instantly as they sat on chairs directly across from Evans.

"Gentlemen, we have to talk this out…the future of all of us is on the line." Evans folded his hands before him, his back ram-rod straight against the back of the armchair. His body was taut, his muscles strained against the well-tailored suit jacket. His mind wondered back to Vietnam, the killing jungles of Vietnam, where nobody dared cross Colonel Jack Evans and his marine brigade. It's different now, Evans thought. 'You can't get rid of enemies with a blast of an M16. It's all so civilized. Courtrooms, judges, juries, television reporters reporting everything that went on. Nothing escaped their microscopic purview. Even though Comtel, the great and invincible Comtel, owned most of the media outlets in Florida. The greatest entertainment and hotel corporation in America brought to its knees by a crazy woman filing suit on behalf of her dead husband who wasn't worth a damn when he was alive. Class action. 'God,' Evans thought, 'I don't ever want to hear that phrase again.'

"Judge Gamble's leaving the bench soon, Jack," Lowry said, "he just didn't care anymore about, y'know…the strings…I guess he figured he'd go out with a bang…" Lowry paused and then continued, "I honestly don't know what got him going in favor of the plaintiff…Born again because of the cancer eating up his stomach…He just didn't care anymore."

"Can't happen again, Alfred. You too, Charlie. Can't happen again. Do I make myself clear? This thing," Evans spit out the words in disgust. "This awful tragedy cannot, ever happen again. No matter what happens…we must prevent anybody…I don't give a damn who it is…Anybody…never. Am I getting to you people?"

"What do you want me to do?" Lowry asked, his face contorted into a quizzical pose.

"First of all, stop using that shit you mix into the Difolation and Parathion sprays. Just to save a few bucks…" Evans declared with a scowl on his face.

"But Mr. Evans," Borden interjected benignly, "if we don't mix the inexpensive urea and other components in with the Difolatan…well…it'll cost us millions of dollars more every year."

With an angry outburst, Evans seemed to reach out for Charlie Borden's throat to strangle the paunchy effeminate accountant/CFO but suddenly calmed down and said in a low malevolent voice, "Charlie, listen and listen carefully, I don't care if it costs us millions more to avoid these fucking lawsuits. Don't you understand? If we get hit for another class action verdict like this one…we're dead in the water as far as the merger with AMT is concerned. And without the merger, Comtel cannot grow and increase our bottom line…Would you agree with me my wonderful CFO? Tell me you agree with me, Charlie."

Charles Borden sloped shoulders dropped into his chest, his flaccid face turned beet red as if he was going to have a heart attack.

"I understand, Mr. Evans," he finally replied in a squeaky voice, "but the millions of extra cost…"

"Screw the cost, Charlie. We'll dump the cost off on one of our offshore partnerships. It'll never hurt the bottom line." Evans smiled as he pulled out another long cigarette out of his cigarette case. He lit it and sprayed the smoke across the table into the faces of the two men.

"And besides you know, Charlie my boy, that if we piss off a lot of our older employees who own a lot of Comtel shares, they could just crap all over our heads by rejecting the merger. Comprenez vous?"

"Alfred," Evans directed his question to Comtel's general counsel Lowry who appeared to hide in a corner of the room until Jack Evans had finished burying Borden, "how much is the percentage of voting shares that are held by our employees, the ones over sixty and are near retirement. The ones that could possibly block the merger?"

Lowry swallowed a gulp of air and dropped his eyes to the floor as he spoke in a low voice.

"I guess about twenty to thirty employees. The ones that have been with Comtel from the beginning. They own the greatest block of shares…probably over one percent of the outstanding Class A voting shares…Enough to block the merger."

"And how many of those employees were in the class action suit we just lost?"

"A few I guess…"

"And I presume they ain't so crazy about Comtel…They might even vote against the merger…Would you say so, Alfred?"

"Maybe. I guess you're right, Jack."

"And also maybe, the employees who didn't join the class, the ones who still may claim they were injured by those toxic pesticides you idiots used, they might join the next suit…and also reject the merger because they're pissed off at Comtel for permanently damaging their lungs and bodies."

"Well, Jack…if they didn't join the class…"

"They can sue us in a future class action suit, right?"

"Maybe. I don't know, Jack."

"You don't know," Evans shouted. "Comtel pays you a half million dollars a fucking year, and you don't know!"

"I'm sorry, Jack. This is the first class action suit I defended."

"Good…that sure makes me feel good, Alfred." Evans walked around the table and stood face to face with Lowry.

"Change the fucking herbicide, gentlemen. We can't afford another suit, another massive verdict…and most of all giving our senior employees any reason to block the merger. Is that clear, boys?"

"How can we guarantee the employees will go along with the merger, Jack?" Lowry asked as he stepped back from the intimidating body of Evans.

"Be nice to them, Alfred. Kiss their asses. But make sure no more suits and no more opportunity that those very employees decide to fuck us through the nose and kill a ten billion dollar merger. That's how, Alfred."

Smiling effusively, Evans buttoned his jacket, squashed the remainder of his cigarette into an ashtray on the table, brushed his iron gray hair back with the palm of his hand, and then started to proceed to the doors of the conference room.

"I'm ready, Charlie…Let's meet the press. And fellows, smile…only losers cry. Smile. We're winners! We will always be winners!"

Evans opened the doors to face the maniacal hysteria of the cameras and reporters.

Chapter One

"He's dead, Captain. Appears to be from natural causes," the female medical examiner said as she rose up from the side of the body lying on the blood stained wood floor.

The massive head of the Captain of the Orlando Police Department bobbed up and down as if he had a crick in his neck and was trying, in vain, to get rid of it.

"Why the blood, Doctor?" he said in a deep southern cracker drawl.

"Probably fell when he died. Hit his head on the floor. See here," she pointed to the gash along the dead man's head where dried blood had caked along the forehead. The medical examiner was in her late thirties, perfect coffee colored skin surrounding her sculptured nose and mouth. Her white teeth seemed to blaze out from her face even as she talked.

"He wasn't that old…just to keel over and die…that's what his wife said…he just got up to get the paper and he just keeled over and died," the captain said in a gruff, scratchy voice.

"It happens. Any other complaints that he had?" the medical examiner asked, although she appeared to have been convinced that her primary diagnosis of death by natural causes was correct.

"The wife said he had some headaches…nausea, the last week or so.

Just didn't feel right, she said."

"Who knows, Captain. Anyway, I'll have a final diagnosis after we autopsy the body."

The captain's eyes gazed around the immaculate ranch home noting the carefully groomed lawn and bushes in the backyard. A small retention pond doubling as a lake bordered on the edge of the backyard.

"Just so strange," the captain continued, "the guy just turned sixty-one his wife said. Healthy as a horse…just keels over and dies."

"Is the wife here, Captain? Maybe I can talk to her. You never know what you can come up with."

"Yeah, she's in the living room…with her daughter…C'mon…I'll introduce you."

The doctor pulled the zipper of the body bag over the head of the deceased and followed the policeman into the living room of the small ranch house.

"Mrs. Williams," the Captain said in a respectful tone, "can you please come out to the kitchen. The doctor here would like to ask you a few questions."

The woman slowly raised her head from her cupped hands situated in her lap. She touched her white oval face with a handkerchief and then politely smiled toward the captain.

"Yes, sir," she replied in a cracked, tear-filled voice. "Can I bring my daughter?"

"Sure…" the captain replied as he led the woman and daughter into the kitchen.

The slight figure of the doctor followed the group.

"This is Dr. Pasha, our county medical examiner, Ms. Williams. She has a few questions about your husband."

The medical examiner smiled briefly as she leaned against the breakfast counter that protruded into the kitchen.

"Mrs. Williams…I don't want to add to your grief…but I just want to confirm a few details of your husband's," she paused and then continued, "fall…"

"Yes, I can't imagine Henry just falling over and…not getting up. He was as strong as a bull…a day never went by that he didn't do something physical. Every morning…he walked three miles…just before he went to work. My God, he got up at six o'clock in the morning so he wouldn't miss his morning walk."

"Did he have any heart problems? Any breathing problems?" The doctor asked.

"None…he never told me about any heart problems. Just the last few days, he was sluggish. He said his muscles' ached. Yes," she paused, "once, he said he had trouble breathing. I thought he had the flu bug or something. It's going around since the temperature dropped. His fingernails seemed to have a bluish tinge to them."

"Was he a smoker?" The doctor asked.

"Didn't touch the stuff ever. Alcohol neither. He smoked a bit when we first got married…but he stopped when the kids were born."

"Was this the first time he fell? Y'know, just fell down?" The doctor continued the questioning.

"Strangely enough, at the beginning of the week…he lost his balance. He was pale, his face was pale, but as soon as he had a few breaths at the window, the color came back to his face. He even laughed about it."

"You opened the windows?" The doctor asked.

"Yes…just opened the windows. It was a warm day and we didn't use the air conditioning much. Then…the temperature turned suddenly low…so we put the heat on…He was fine as soon as we opened the windows."

"When did you put the heat on, Mrs. Williams?" The doctor asked.

"I guess last week or so. It's been a strange winter. One day it's in the seventies and the next day it's near freezing. I don't know…I can't imagine Henry dying. He was so strong…loved his job…his boat…he was near retirement. God almighty! He just wasn't ready to die!" She sobbed uncontrollably into her handkerchief.

"When was the last physical exam…the last one he had?" The doctor asked.

"I guess about a year ago. You see…the company…Comtel…the company Henry worked for…provided good medical benefits. He took a physical exam every year."

"Anything unusual come up out of the physical, I mean."

"No…" The woman stopped suddenly and peered over at her daughter who had walked over to the kitchen door leading out to the manicured backyard.

"Heather here…my daughter," pointing to her daughter who was obviously crying as she stared out into the back yard, "she worked with Henry…in the backyard. They used to plant shrubs and trees. He was such a meticulous person. He loved everything green," she paused and walked over to her daughter and wrapped her arm around her quivering shoulders.

"Did the physical show anything?" The doctor asked.

"No, as I said…He was healthy…God, I should be so healthy. Heather and Hank worked together at Comtel…"

"What did your husband…what did he do at Comtel?" The captain asked, his jowly face reddening from the heat of the kitchen.

"Hank was supervisor of the landscaping at the Park…right next door. He loved his work…He had gone to night school and graduated with a degree in horticulture. Nobody every complained about his work… Nobody!"

The doctor smiled and then held her hand out to Mrs. Williams and her daughter. "I'm sorry Mrs. Williams. It's never easy. But you can be assured that we will do everything possible to find out what happened."

"Thank you…it was…we had been married over thirty years…I have no idea what I'm going to do…" The woman buried her head into the shoulder of her daughter as the sounds of her sobs filled the kitchen.

The police officer and the medical examiner walked out the front door. Outside the captain lit up a cigarette and exhaled the smoke almost immediately.

"What do we got, Doctor?" He said.

The cold night air sent shivers through his large body and made him wonder why he decided to wear a short sleeve cotton shirt when the water was freezing in his backyard.

"Just what I said, Captain…Nothing has changed my mind…I'd like to see the medical reports of his last physical. Maybe the doctors missed something. I grant you it's extremely unlikely for a healthy man of sixty-one to just keel over and die. Who knows? After the autopsy I can tell you more. Hold off on your police report until I finish the autopsy. Okay?"

Chapter Two

Joshua Ryan attempted to unlock the apartment door for the second time. His wife, Sosie, held the two year old Samara in her arms while her foot was lodged at the bottom of the gate of the tiny Parisian elevator, preventing it from leaving the floor with their assorted suitcases and bags.

"I got it…Hurray for the idiot! I got it," Joshua's voice rang out as the apartment door opened. He hurriedly placed the key into the alarm slot along the inner wall near the door but failing to connect in time, the shrill clanging of the alarm sounded throughout the hallway. Finally he slid the round key into the alarm slot and the piercing screams were finally silenced.

"Did you forget?" Sosie asked with a luminous smile igniting her olive skin. Joshua turned around in a flash of anger but it all disappeared as he saw his wife's face beaming with loving humor.

"You have to be a mechanical engineer to get into our apartment. It's easier for a burglar to slice through the bars in the windows."

"They hate you, Joshua," Sosie replied as she sidled past him into the warm yellow painted entry way and living room.

"Who? You mean the French? Sure…they're friends with the Germans now. So…it's got to be the Americans to hate."

Joshua rushed back into the hallway in a vain attempt to stop the elevator gate from closing but failing that, the elevator descended with several of their pieces of luggage nestled in the back of the miniature elevator.

"Merde!" He yelled as he trundled down the circular steps racing to catch the elevator before it landed on the ground floor. Missing the elusive cage on the second floor, he resigned himself to continue down to the ground floor where he knew he might encounter one or more of his French neighbors climbing over his luggage. Alas, at the ground floor, he caught up to the elevator, relieved that his luggage would be the only object sharing the ride back to his fourth floor apartment.

After finally unloading the luggage in his apartment foyer, Joshua walked slowly to the refrigerator in the kitchen. There it was. A large, unopened bottle of Orangina waiting to be devoured. He poured himself a giant jar of the orange bubbly. As he readied himself for the long awaited moment of quenching relief, he heard Sosie's voice ring out from the bedroom.

"Joshua…you have a bunch of messages…mostly from Sam…you better get over here…it sounds like Sam's voice is urgent."

Joshua gulped down the Orangina and carried the jar-glass into the bedroom. Samara had fallen asleep and Sosie had placed her in the crib in the second bedroom adjacent to the master bedroom where the phone message machine was situated.

Joshua switched on the answering machine and heard the basso profundo voice of Sam Waterman impatiently asking Joshua to call him in Florida as soon as he returned.

"You go away for ten days and the world ends," he murmured to himself. He sat his six foot three inch frame in the armchair near the phone, gulped the balance of the Orangina down, and listened to the numerous French and English messages speaking out of the answering machine.

"Joshua…call now…please…its important!" Sam Waterman's voice appealed several times on the answering machine.

"Sosie…," Joshua yelled out from the bedroom. "Sam forgot to leave his number…Do we have Sam's phone number? You would think that if it was so urgent he would at least leave his phone number."

"Look under the yellow pads near the phone," Sosie replied. "It's probably in the book...the American one."

Joshua rifled through the piles of papers on the table near the phone until he retrieved the phone book. Sam Waterman's number was under the "s" because Sosie always forgot his last name so it was easier to put Sam's phone number under the "s".

"Do you want to go out for dinner? Tell me now if you do, so I can get Malika to baby sit Samara."

"It's up to you. We've been on the road for ten days. Maybe we should go up to the market and stock up with food. Maybe a fresh baguette with ham and cheese..." Joshua's mouth watered as he ran off the items of food he savored mostly.

"Call Sam first...I never heard him so frantic, Joshua."

"He misses us. I spoke to him a month ago. He sounded like he was having fun in sunny Florida. He told me he has rediscovered sex."

Joshua dialed the multiple numbers required to reach the State side number, waited patiently until the phone rang in Florida, hearing no pick-up voice, he hung up the phone.

"He's not there, Sosie..."

"Why don't you unpack while I change Samara's diaper."

For several moments, Joshua Ryan sat back in the armchair, flipped off his loafers, and recounted the last ten days. Baden-Baden, Berlin, Prague, Heidelberg, Nancy and then back to Paris, enjoying his wife, his baby, and of course, his Mercedes. Life was good, he mused. A little writing to the folks back home, with Sosie teaching at the Sorbonne, and he still had most of the money he had saved from his last big fee as the notorious lawyer who had freed the rabbi. The infamous Rabbi and his lover. Murder for hire but not proven beyond a reasonable doubt. Joshua had had enough. He never missed it. The law, the confrontations, the money, nothing persuaded him to ever return to a courtroom. Joshua believed that dueling with sabers would be just as just as confronting the tainted judicial system of America. Sosie and Samara were all he needed. He marveled at Sosie's equipoise, her balanced happiness, and most of all, her sense of the ridiculous whenever things got a little hairy. He loved them both more than anything he could ever imagine. Fights, yes, but oh so lovely when Sosie and he settled their differences.

Joshua had never known love that was so immersed in such exhilarating sexual activity. They were married about three years now and the courting period had not ended. Each encounter with Sosie was a date with a new woman. She was imaginative as a sexual partner, but more importantly she listened and responded and listened and they talked like they were born together. Joshua knew that it couldn't go on forever. The honeymoon had to end. But when? Maybe never, he hoped. Sosie was a Sabra who could leap tall mountains and battle armed terrorists with her bare hands and feet. Joshua still couldn't believe that this sweet woman he loved so tenderly could turn into a violent machine when the situation called for it. Yet, in the three years they were married, he had rarely heard her raise her voice in anger. Other than the violent confrontation with an armed Arab when Joshua first met Sosie in Jerusalem, she eschewed violence.

Her parents would visit often. Yehuda and Zeppi Ben-Zvi, Israeli sabras to the bone. They still lived in that lovely white stoned house overlooking the Old City in Jerusalem. Joshua wondered when they would finally leave Israel to live next to Sosie and Samara in Paris. They especially loved their granddaughter. They could play with Samara all day, never returning her to her rightful parents. Joshua mused that some day Samara would disappear with her grandparents. He would have a devil of a time retrieving her from such loving kidnappers.

Yehuda, approaching sixty years old, was professor emeritus in archeology at the University of Jerusalem. His reputation had grown in stature and fame ever since he was instrumental in unearthing the Masada ruins a decade ago. Archeology students all over the world attended his infrequent classes, savoring every word of his archeologically exciting lectures. Joshua marveled at the man's depth of knowledge about the good old days in ancient Judea and Samara. Zeppi, Zepporah by birth, still directed the rehab program at the Benedict Institute in Jerusalem. Alkies and druggies of middle-eastern origin. The same all over the world. Yet Zeppi, like her daughter, never chilled out no matter what. Except for the suicide bombers. Israel had recently been inundated by the influx of youthful Palestinians literally dying to blow themselves up. Not in their own playground. Always in the Israeli city streets. Killing the innocent. For what? For a state they could never run. For an economy that would never survive. Unless Israel supported the State of Palestine. And that may never happen. Not ever, unless the bombing stopped. Forever gone. But they all agreed, Joshua, Sosie, Yehuda and Zeppi, it would never be. What will be, no one knew. Anyway, Joshua wondered when Yehuda and Zeppi had finally had had enough. Paris felt so safe. And they would be near Samara.

"Let me try again, Sosie," Joshua yelled out after his mind returned to the present. He dialed the ten numbers required to get Sam Waterman's phone in Florida. It rang several times before Joshua was startled by the cavernous voice of his old mentor and friend, Sam Waterman.

"Are you hiding from someone, Sam?" Joshua queried.

"Where the hell have you been, Joshua. Thought you carried a cell phone with you? I've been trying to get you for over a week," Sam replied in an agitated voice.

"We forgot to take the charger with us. It was diapers or cell phone charger and the diapers won out."

"I would ask you about your trip but I need to talk to you about something that I've kept inside of me for over a week."

"Speak, my great teacher," Joshua replied.

"My sister and her husband died about two weeks ago."

Joshua said nothing for several moments trying to digest the words. Then finally he replied, "Sam, say that again. You mean your sister, Helen, the one you haven't talked to in ten years…that sister."

"Yes, that sister. When I moved down to Florida we got together. She still was the same controlling bitch I so fondly remember, but she was the only living relative I have. So you know, family is family. That's what you always told me."

"Died…how? How old was she?"

"Just turned sixty. Her husband Harold was sixty-two. Both in good health. Then suddenly the cleaning woman found their bodies…dead…in the living room of their house. The medical examiner said it was death by natural causes."

"You talked to the police? The medical examiner?" Joshua asked.

"The cops told me nothing. Some fat cracker captain was conducting the investigation. He said that the medical examiner was sure it was death by natural causes." Sam paused and coughed several times and then continued, "Joshua, it doesn't smell right. Something's wrong down there in Orlando. And," he paused again to clear his throat, "they're not the only ones. Another couple just keeled over, also. Like something in the air."

"What's so strange, Sam? Maybe that's what it was…natural causes."

"Yeah…I guess you could say that, Joshua. I don't know. Maybe I just feel guilty about not being in touch with her all these years."

"Sam…I know how you feel. She was your sister…even though you have been estranged from her." Joshua stopped for a moment, saw Sosie waving at him then opened the front door to let Malika, the concierge of the building, in. Joshua waved at Malika and Sosie and then continued, "Any physical evidence, Sam? Something to show that something…anything…that somebody…maybe its some kind of Legionnaire's disease. It happened a few years ago at the Bellevue-Stratford Hotel in Philadelphia…an American Legions Convention, I remember…people just keeled over and died…They never found out why…maybe it was some kind of aerosol bacteria causing the deaths."

"Maybe," Sam reluctantly agreed, "but it wasn't just my sister, Joshua. I don't know what it is, Josh…All I know is that I'd like to have your input. The local cops don't seem to know anything."

"What the hell can I do, Sam? I'm no investigator…I'm not even a lawyer anymore. Remember, I retired…"

"Bullshit, Joshua…you're born a lawyer, you'll die a lawyer." Sam paused and Joshua could hear him blow his nose and then he continued, "I feel so goddamn guilty, Josh. Helen was my sister. We hadn't talked in years. Now she's dead. In my gut, Joshua, something ain't right."

"I gotta go, Sam…Sosie is waiting to do our shopping. I will call you back later. On your time…at night. Okay? Let's think about it. I know how you feel…Guilty…but maybe it's all gut instinct and nothing else. Okay?"

"Okay, Josh…I hope you're having a good time. It's been a long time, Joshua."

"I know, Sam. I'll call you tonight." Joshua hung up the phone, wondered why his knees suddenly developed shooting pains through the caps as he rose up to join Sosie who was just coming out of Samara's room and heading toward the front door of the apartment.

"Son-of-a-bitch," Joshua murmured in a low raspy voice, "Sam calls with a possible case…I don't know what…and my goddamn knees suddenly hurt…Son-of-a-bitch," he repeated as he followed Sosie out the front door and into the awaiting cage of the elevator.

Chapter Three

The Orlando Police Department's headquarter building was located just past the City Hall complex of buildings, within view of busy Route 4 in the near distance.

Captain Amos Parker leaned against his metal office chair which was lodged against a flaking green painted wall of his cubical he called his day home. His belly protruded over his silver buckled western belt as his burly legs extended onto the green ancient metal office desk. The phone was cradled on his shoulder as he puffed on a cigaroot that caused the tiny room to be shrouded in gray smoke. His jowly face was consumed in a reddish color as he bellowed into the phone.

"Look, Mayor Childs...there's nothing more I can do about these deaths." He paused to listen and then continued, "I know the papers are driving you crazy...here too. All they want to know is what I'm doing...well...there's nothing more I can do...She...the County Medical Examiner...she says they're all natural causes." He stopped again, listening, and then attempted to resume speaking, stopped again, and then said, "Yes, Mayor...I know she's a woman...so what? She's the medical examincr...I hcar she's a doctor also. Okay...Okay...I'll call you back after I find out something more...You too, Mayor..."

Parker dropped the phone loudly into the cradle, puffed violently on his cigaroot causing more large clouds of smoke to fill the room.

"Fucking politicians," he said angrily under his breath.

"Jo-Beth!" He yelled in his deep southern drawl. "Get your sweet ass in here."

Within seconds, a young, attractive black girl, wearing a short leather skirt walked into the office.

"You still chewing that gum?" the captain asked in an amicable voice.

"It brightens my teeth, Captain," she replied with a smile.

"Maybe you should wear your skirt a little shorter, Jo-Beth, darling." He laughed a lascivious laugh, his belly rolling up and down as the laughter increased in intensity.

"You better watch your ass, Captain…you're getting close to sexual harassment charges if you keep up with those remarks"

"Who tells you that bullshit…your lawyer friend at the Fed…what's his name, Jo-Beth, darling."

"Everett…Everett Lawrence, Captain. He's a goddamn good lawyer, Captain…so you'd better watch your p's and q's."

"Anything come in on the recent deaths?" The Captain's voice lost its laughter as he moved his chair off the wall, his legs slipping under the desk.

"The same stuff, Captain…nothing new." Jo-Beth deeply sighed and then continued, "My God…it must be in the water or something, Captain."

Parker fixed his gaze on the young woman, noted that her skin was a combination of pale bronze with a tinge of old ivory. Perfect features on her face. He wondered if she ever had her face fixed. Not Jo-Beth, he mused, a smile crossing his face. Too proud of her slave ancestry.

"The mayor is driving me up the wall," Parker said.

"Everett thinks there's something funny going on. But its not anything to do with the Fed."

"He like his job?" Captain asked.

"Loves it. Sure interferes with our sex life. That's all he talks about. I don't mind hearing about it, but not all the time…" Her voice trailed off as a lusty knowing smile filled her face.

"Hot and heavy, eh?"

"That's my business, Captain."

"I know…I know…sexual whatever…"

"Harassment, Captain."

"Everett'll have to defend me."

"Not over my body, he won't."

"And that's quite a body, Jo-Beth." She laughed a deep throaty laugh. She liked the Captain, although he stood for everything she was brought up to hate. She realized beneath that neanderthalic exterior, he was as soft as overcooked sweet potatoes.

"If it wasn't for that medical examiner's report…y'know…the autopsies on those bodies…I'd a suspected something criminal going on."

"She's a foreign doctor," Jo-Beth said.

"What's that mean, Jo-Beth? You discriminating against foreign people."

"It ain't no discrimination, Captain. Just careful of what doctors I see. She got a license?"

Parker laughed and got up from his chair.

"Where'd you say those two new deaths occurred, Jo-Beth?"

"Right there at the Lakes. At The Park…Comtel's amusement park."

"How come nobody called me to investigate?"

"Because they're going to the County Sheriff's Office."

Angrily, he replied, his heavy muscled arm tensing into round balls, "Who the fuck asked the Sheriff's Office into my bailiwick…He ain't got no right to meddle into the city's affairs."

"Give me those names, Jo-Beth…I don't care when it happened…I'm the investigating police officer in Orlando and that's what I'm gonna do. Investigate."

A fat unkempt, plain-clothes detective ambled up the hallway to Parker's office. Espying Parker, he shouted, "Hey, Captain…you still investigating those deaths out at the Lakes?"

"Yeah, so what? You got something to say, Riley…spit it out?"

"Easy, Captain…Just wanted to know because I got something off the radio."

Riley paused to glare lustfully at Jo-Beth who was bending over as she was filing paperwork into the files situated at the wall outside Parker's office.

"Stop looking at Jo-Beth's ass and tell me what you got, Riley," Parker yelled.

Riley smiled showing a bad set of teeth. "It's a free country, Captain."

"No it ain't, Riley. What do you got already?"

"Remember the lawyer, the one on the Comtel case?"

"Yeah, so what? What's that got to do with anything?" Parker impatiently replied. He pulled out another cigaroot, lit it, and sprayed the first blast of smoke into Riley's face.

"Yeah, well…he just got part of his face blasted off. They found him, naked, just on the other side of South International Drive…Way back in those swamps…way back of the Marriot. Looks like a mafia hit."

"When the hell did this happen?" Parker demanded.

"They found him about an hour ago. The body was still warm. Man, I hear that .357 did a job on his face…had trouble identifying the body," he paused and then continued, "Except for the business card left on his forehead…a nice touch…killer had a sense of humor. Hey, Amos?"

"I heard," Riley continued, "that he's the attorney for the mafia in New York…Guess he must have lost too many cases defending those bastards."

"You got the exact location, Riley?"

"Why Captain, you going out there? I think the County Sheriff beat you to the punch."

"Fuck him…who the hell reported it to the Sheriff? That's my jurisdiction."

"Yeah…well…here's the location." Riley handed Parker a paper with the milepost where the body was located.

"I tell you, Jo-Beth…something fishy is going on.", Parker repeated as he rushed pell-mell out of the headquarter building to his car.

Chapter Four

Burt and Jack's is a high priced steak restaurant just off the intercoastal in Fort Lauderdale. It draws the celebrated sports and political crowd. Anybody who thinks he's somebody finds his way to the restaurant, especially on the weekend.

It was Saturday night and Senator Evans and his son Jack were seated in a corner table. They could see the cruise liners beat a path to the ocean out of the intercoastal from their table.

"Jack," the senator's distinguished voice spoke the name with a southern lilt that only the old Southern aristocrats kept alive, "you got us in a pot of trouble...Jack. How the hell did you let it go this far?"

The senator was tall, with a cadaverous physique topped by a thick crystal white head of hair that seemed unreal. His face was almost wrinkle free, except when he smiled, causing laugh lines to form around his thin lipped smile that displayed perfect white teeth.

"Dad...believe me...if I had known...We had counsel...Lowry... a whole staff of Harvard trained lawyers...and guess what...we got beat by some transplanted Jew boy from New York."

"You should have called me sooner. I could've called Judge Gamble. And if he played hard ball, I would've called the assignment judge."

"We just never figured…Lowry said we had nothing to worry about. When the jury heard about a few of our peccadilloes…y'know what happens sometimes between the guys. Well, Gamble let all that in…the jury got pissed…then the punitive damages…that broke the bank."

"Where do we stand now, Jack?", the Senator queried, as the maitre d' approached the table with large, leather bound menus.

"Its good to have you again, Senator," the effeminate maitre d' stated in a pseudo-French accent. "Please let me know when you are ready, Senator. I'll personally take your order."

"Thank you, Charles…bring us a couple of dry, iced-cold, vodka martinis and I'll call when we're ready."

The maitre d' bowed and then backed away from the Senator's table.

"The verdict still stands," Jack said in a low whisper. "We're going to ask for a new trial…but unless the Judge changes his mind, the verdict's going to stand…except for the appeal"

"What does that do to the merger talks?", the senator asked as the maitre d' returned with the martinis.

Evans waited until the maitre d' placed the glasses on the table and withdrew.

"AMT thinks the verdict…if it stands…will kill the price of our stock."

"Will it?"

"The judgment amount goes right to the bottom line. We can't sluff it off to the offshore companies. It's too public. We'd have to include the liability on Comtel's own books. It'll drive the stock off the exchange."

"There goes our television outlets, Jack. We need those AMT outlets or we're never going to grow our profits. We need that deal, Jack!" The senator's voice deepened into an urgent drawl.

He downed the rest of the martini in his glass with one gulp. "Y'know what those cable and theatre distributors are charging us to show our television and movie products, Jack. They're killing us…they want not only the immediate profits, but also a good chunk of the residuals and global money. It could put us out of business in the long run, Jack. AMT will give us an economical distribution outlet all over the world."

"I know, Dad, I know…but what the hell can we do?"

"Talk to Gamble."

"He won't listen, Dad. The guy's dying of cancer and he doesn't give a damn anymore. We tried…believe me…we tried. I even offered to take his lame-brained son into the film business, but Gamble didn't want to talk about it. He suddenly got scruples since he knows he'll never run again for Judge."

"I'll talk to Judge Peterson, the assignment judge, Jack."

The menus were handed to them by the maitre'd. Both men ordered the porterhouse steaks and baked potatoes. The senator selected a California cabernet. The maitre'd turned after taking the menus and quickly disappeared into the kitchen.

"I don't know if Gamble will listen to him, Dad."

"He's the goddamn Assignment Judge…I never heard of a judge disregarding the A.J.'s instructions."

"You know, if the judgment on the class action sticks, Dad…Abromowitz at AMT may want too much to merge with us…or maybe even squelch the whole deal. And you know what that would mean to Comtel, Dad…We'd lose over fifty million cable customers and who knows how many movie customers. We'd never compete with Disney. Not without AMT's distribution, Dad."

The senator's eyes narrowed into slits, worry lines appearing under his lower lids as he stoked his hands through his well coiffed thick hair.

"Do we have anyone else lined up if the AMT deal disappears, Jack? What about Universal? Vivendi is looking for a partner."

"We need to raise too much cash to buy Universal. Vivendi wants to sell Universal…not merge. Besides, many of Universal's assets would just duplicate Comtel's products." Jack Evans paused to sip on his martini as he noticed a mammoth liner sailing around the inlet approaching the cut into the ocean. His mind acknowledged that that beautiful ship was one of Comtel's navy. Maybe we'd have to sell our profitable cruise ships to buy into another cable and film distributing company, he mused.

Quickly he mentally discarded that option and agreed that the AMT merger was the only way Comtel would grow into the entertainment force that could contend with it's Florida neighbor, Disney. 'We have to make it happen,' he thought with passion. 'The merger has to go through!'

"By the way, Dad, I hired a new head of security for Comtel a couple weeks ago. My old adjudant from Vietnam…Jon Paulsen…he just retired from the CIA. Lowry is going to work with him."

The porterhouse steaks and baked potatoes were brought out by a waiter followed solicitously by the maitre d'. For several seconds, both men peered at the steaks as if their hunger had suddenly subsided.

"Why the change in security, Jack?"

"Just in case, Dad. Paulsen is good at what he does. Especially during these merger talks. We don't want any loose lips sinking the deal. The case and all…Jon will put a clamp on any leaks."

"All I want to see and to hear Jack…is that Comtel and AMT are one. Merged. Married. And we come out on top, Jack. I don't care how it's done. Just do it. Am I clear, Jack?"

"Crystal…Dad. I'll make sure it happens. No matter what."

"Lets eat," the senator said with an ear-to-ear smile on his face. "I suddenly developed an insationable hunger, Jack."

Chapter Five

"You're not going, Yehuda." Zeppi pronounced with finality.

"Why not, Zeppi darling, you don't need me to watch over Samara…You have Sosie…and you know you love Paris so much, you'll never miss me," Yehuda answered with a crooked smile etched on his ruddy, burnt face.

Yehuda and Zeppi , Sosie's parents and Samara's grandparents had arrived in Paris last night after Joshua had called them at their house in Jerusalem. 'Sure,' they said with relish, "we'll catch the next plane for Paris." They didn't need any excuses to leave Jerusalem and watch over their beloved granddaughter in Paris.

Yehuda exploited his various connections with Air France to book two first class upgraded seats on the morning flight to Paris. The plane was relatively empty since there were few tourists visiting the explosions of Israel.

Yehuda peered out the window of the apartment as it overlooked the green courtyard up toward Trocadero in the far distance. Wintry rain pelted the tall windows but Yehuda ignored the sounds and just marveled at the magnificent buildings that ran up the Avenue Poincaré to Trocadero.

"You're too old to fight terrorists anymore, Yehuda," Zeppi declared, her long oval face refusing to show any signs of compromise.

"He's not going to fight anybody, Zeppi," Joshua said, as he was trying to wrap his lips around a fresh baguette stuffed with goat cheese and hand pressed cherry preserves he purchased just hours ago at the neighborhood market. Sitting in front of his chair at the dining table was a large preserve jar of juice from fresh oranges he had just squeezed. Fresh orange juice in winter in Paris was his ultimate reward, highlighting his retirement from the world of angst.

"You may be retired, Joshua, but you're a good twenty years younger than my friend here," Zeppi said, a reluctant smile growing in the corners of her still young face.

"He looks pretty good to me, Zeppi." Joshua replied in a garbled voice.

"It's sunny Florida, Zep…what could happen in Florida that could not happen in Jerusalem?" Yehuda interjected as he reached for the remainder of Joshua's baguette, and smeared it with goat cheese.

"You'll have a heart attack if you're trying to out eat your son-in-law, Yehuda," Zeppi said.

Sosie came into the dining room from the second bedroom carrying the bubbly Samara, barely two years old.

Both Yehuda and Zeppi rose from their chairs, each reaching for the baby. Zeppi's outstretched arms won the contest for possession.

"You win, Yehuda," Zeppi pronounced as she kissed Samara's cherubic face and neck.

"You'll smother her, mother," Sosie said as she sat down in the chair next to Joshua, who reached over to kiss her on the cheek with lips still edged with goat cheese and preserves.

"I'll take care of him, Zeppi," Joshua declared.

"Who'll take care of you?" Sosie asked absent-mindedly as she nibbled on the tiny remainder of the baguette on Joshua's plate.

"Sam told me he didn't know if anything was wrong, Sosie darling...He just had a queasy feeling over the whole mess," Joshua remarked.

"It's probably indigestion," Sosie said.

"Maybe, but there's been six deaths...all supposedly by natural causes...except," Joshua stopped abruptly as if his mind had thought of something important, "except the murder of that young lawyer. They attribute that death to a mafia hit man."

"What about the police?" Sosie queried in a disbelieving voice, "Why do they need you? A retired lawyer who doesn't even want to be called lawyer. Why does Sam need you? I'm sure there's enough police in Florida to find out if there's something wrong."

"He tells me that Comtel...the corporation that has all those amusement parks...they run the show in Florida. Whatever Comtel wants, Comtel gets," Joshua replied, as he rose from the table and walked out to the dining room window and marveled at the beauty of the city although the buildings and streets were shrouded in gray sheets of rain that filled the early morning air.

"He didn't even like his sister," Zeppi said still nuzzling her nose in Samara's neck causing Samara to giggle happily.

"Guilt is a tough burden to carry," Joshua replied.

"Why does he feel guilty?" Sosie asked.

"Who knows? Sam feels guilty about a lot of things. That's what happens when you come from a crazy family that barely survived in Brooklyn," Joshua said.

"Maybe she did die of natural causes. She was sixty or so, wasn't she, Joshua?" Zeppi said.

"If she were the only one...maybe...but it was her husband and a bunch of other employees...all working for Comtel...all dying after a verdict that could break Comtel."

"Sounds like Sam is gathering material for a new novel," Sosie laughed as she rose from the table and joined Joshua at the window.

"Anyway, I owe him…I have to go and see if I can help. It's probably nothing. I should be back for your birthday Sosie…A week or so…Besides I can use a little sun…Paris is beautiful, but all this rain is killing my bones."

"When do you leave?" Sosie asked.

"Tomorrow. I don't think we will have trouble getting a flight out. Not if Yehuda can still pull rabbits out of his hat." Joshua laughed as he wrapped his arms around Sosie's shoulders, marveling how tiny her body was, yet knowing how much power it contained within that diminutive frame.

"I'll miss you…We've never been apart…since…I don't know when." Her face turned toward him, her round blue eyes filled with tears.

"You have Zeppi…and Samara," he replied.

"They won't keep me warm in bed."

Joshua laughed. "I'll be back before the bed gets cold." He turned his face toward her and kissed her full on the lips. They lingered for several moments, not caring of who was watching their offerings of tenderness to each other.

"We used to be like that," Zeppi remarked soulfully, tears etched in the corner of her eyes.

"After almost thirty years, Zepporah darling, we're lucky we even say hello in the morning," Yehuda remarked as he rose from his chair to hug both Zeppi and Samara into his broad arms and chest. He kissed Zeppi on the corner of her mouth and then kissed Samara flush on her cheeks.

"Let's go to Le Dome, tonight!" Joshua announced. "Wine will flow like the Seine and the mussels…"

"To a happy and quick return," Zeppi said in a tearful voice. "And a safe one," she added with fear clearly tainting her voice.

Chapter Six

Judge David Gamble sat morosely in his car watching the ambulances race in and out of Orlando General Hospital's Emergency Room entrance. It was nightfall and the Orlando winter sun had long set in the western flatlands of Orange County and a full moon was rising sharply in the star-filled sky.

"Beautiful," he murmured to himself. He loved the great outdoors, remembering how his father would take him in his outrigger canoe, camping overnight in the Everglades. He had loved his father, but he had left the earth much too soon. "He would've been proud of me," he thought, as the traffic started to build up around his parked car. "Maybe not," he argued with himself. "All the things I've done…Good and bad," he thought. Wasn't easy to be clean when you're in the midst of Florida's politics. First a Committeeman and then a State Assemblyman, then an Orange County Commissioner. All part time…all based on the senator's support. The Almighty U.S. Senator Evans, the man who had been the political power broker in Orange County for decades. The founder of Comtel International, a megalopic corporation that actually was ceded an entire county in Central Florida. Samson County. A name of strength and religious overtones…the only government in the United States owned and operated by a private corporation. No human residents inhabited Samson County, just Comtel headquarters and The Park. A world renowned amusement park, The Park was duplicated throughout the world. It made Orlando the most visited city in America. Maybe in the whole-wide world. Only Disney rivaled Comtel in the amusement and entertainment fields.

Gamble's mind traveled back to his days at the University of Florida Law School, the carefree good old days of women, beautiful women, who were free with their bodies, the Golden Sixties…the booze…the dope…the law…the Almighty Law. He loved the law, the orderly nature of it all. No matter how chaotic his life had become as a youthful playboy, he always came back to the orderly discipline of the law. Then politics. Small town politics. Committeeman on Kissamee City Council, the youngest person to ever serve on the Council. Then he caught the eye of the only man who really called the shots in Central Florida. Osgood Evans…the governor…then U.S. Senator…nobody ever denied any wish of Senator Evans. He picked the candidates for judgeships, the legislature, even the governorship. All who wanted a piece of the Florida action had to beg the beneficence of the great Master of the Universe, Osgood Evans.

Gamble, as a part-time legislator, headquartered in Tallahassee, also operated a private law practice, had been the "collector" of the political contributions, as they were so blandly called. "Contributions" that purchased favors, all kinds of profitable favors. For re-zoned or re-constituted wet lands, or re-opened park lands for commercial development, the senator was the donor and the supplicants were the rewarded donees. Gifts from Mt. Olympus. "The Almighty Zeus," Gamble mumbled to himself.

Yet, David Gamble couldn't fault the rest of the receivers of the senator's donations; it was the quid pro quo of Florida's government. Corruption was a little used word, not around the senator, not in any of the Florida's media outlets. Never…because the senator, through Comtel, owned all the media outlets. T.V., newspapers, radio, films, whatever was produced in Florida, and points all over the United States, Comtel, and the Senator, were there.

After years of sucking at the Senator's trough, Gamble had been rewarded with a judgeship. That's all he ever wanted…to be a Florida State Judge. Hopefully to be appointed when his father was still alive, which didn't happen. Gamble's family was part Seminole, although no one ever spoke of such an ignomous past. It was like being Jewish in Nazi Germany. Hidden like a rats in the cedar closet. The Senator knew all about Gamble's ancestry; he didn't care because the Senator, like Hitler, could "aryanize" any polluted past or family heritage. Gamble smiled as his mind wandered to the days when the Senator was only the Speaker of the Florida House and was much more liberal in speaking about his inner thoughts to his disciple, Gamble. The Senator admired Hitler, not because of the insane killing spree of the German madman, but the way Hitler had re-organized the chaotic power structure of the German State in the thirties. Risen from the burnt ashes of World War I, Germany, under Hitler's domination, became the power center of the world. The Senator admired, as many others worshipped at, the Nazi Temple of meglomaniacal power…controlling every aspect of Germany, and finally, almost, the world's population.

'Now,' Gamble ruminated soulfully, 'it's all over. For me anyway.' He found out about the stomach cancer two years ago. Before the Comtel case came before him, before certification of the class, before the trial itself, and most significantly, before the shocking verdict.

Gamble knew the Comtel trial would be his legacy. He just hoped he would live long enough to help the sorrowful injured plaintiffs along…along to a shocking verdict. Gamble used all his accumulated knowledge of the rules, legal or otherwise, to steer the jury in the right direction. It was Gamble's contribution to his redemption. He had hated all his life what he had to do to become a judge. Corruption, graft, pure criminal acts, to line the corporate pockets of Comtel. Well, if he was going to die, he was going to take Comtel…and the Senator…with him. 'Redemption, said the Lord,' he murmured to himself.

Suddenly, the chemo treatment he had just undergone made him nauseous as he sat in his Lexus sedan watching the people and the cars meandering by, Gamble knew that he would never make it through another year. Never to see his son graduate from medical school, his daughter marry, his wife loving him the way they had loved each other for so many years. He had won respect, but he knew he didn't deserve any respect. Not for what he did…to the people of Florida.

'Well,' he mused cynically, 'I'm gonna make it up to them. Gonna make that verdict stick, if it takes the rest of my life,' he laughed sardonically to himself, knowing that the rest of his life would be no more than one year.

Suddenly, he felt the shooting pains down his right arm. The pain started sharply in the middle of his chest. As the moments passed the pain became unbearable, hitting him like a sledgehammer. He clutched his heart with his right hand, the pain intensifying beyond human endurance.

He tried to scream but his mouth uttered no sounds. Yet the screams were filling his brain. His eyeballs climbed into his head as he slumped forward, his forehead banging the steering wheel. The car's horn blared as his brain shut down. The pain ended as Gamble died thinking of all the things he would miss in this world.

Chapter Seven

The Orange County medical examiner's laboratory was located in a Quonset type building reminiscent of the leftover temporary buildings thrown up just after World War II. Located behind the newly built southern plantation style County Courthouse, which housed the Courts of Orange County, as well as the Orlando Police's maze of offices, the medical examiner's one story building appeared as if the County had built it as an afterthought, with no real value attributable to its forensic use. Inside the building, Captain Amos Parker was visiting Dr. Pasha, at the medical examiner's lab after she had called him about some recent developments in the Comtel case, as it was now called.

"First time I've has the pleasure to visit," Captain Amos Parker said, as he stood impatiently on the other side of the lab table facing Dr. Pasha's smiling face.

"I thought you'd be interested in seeing some slides of tissues I've extracted from some of the bodies in the ones…the ones that supposedly died of natural causes, Captain."

"Over six now, Doctor."

"The tissue seem to all have some of the same coloration…Something called hepaterization, Captain."

"Greek to me, Doctor."

She laughed a nervous laugh as she reacted to the rough hewn voice of the Captain.

"From tissues we can tell all kinds of things, Captain. Disease, age of the victim, all kinds of little pieces of forensic medical evidence that can lead one to a logical conclusion…things you can't find while performing the usual tests."

"What is hepaterization?"

"I'll show you…come to this side of the table…over here." The doctor moved slightly over from where the microscope was situated on the lab table. The Captain belying his mammoth hulk, moved agilely over to the side of the table where the doctor was standing. She was wearing a loose fitting cotton dress under the white lab smock, that still displayed a well developed body. She smiled broadly as the captain's body inadvertently touched her thigh.

"Sorry," the captain smiled as he acknowledged the touching.

"You're a big man, Captain."

"Mostly beer, Doctor."

She laughed self-consciously as she placed the slide onto the microscope's examining platform.

"Look through these two lens, Captain."

The captain peered through the proffered lens as the doctor moved the slide into different positions.

"Do you see the gray particles, Captain, in the middle of the slide?"

"Yeah…next to the red spots."

"The red spots are really gray, Captain. They look red because of the chemical solution I used to magnify the tissue."

"Okay," the captain pulled his head up from the microscope and stared into the dark brown eyes of the doctor.

"Gray hepaterization means that the tissues have been starved of oxygen, Captain. Not for a short period of time either. Usually for at least three to five days."

"So?" The Captain queried with a puzzled look on his face.

"So…my good friend, that means that somehow the victims' bodies have been deprived of the necessary oxygen to feed the cells…the blood…the brain…and the lungs. Without oxygen…the required amount of oxygen…the body shuts down. Nothing works after a couple of days. The heart stops because there is no blood with oxygen pumping through it. In other words, the victim dies."

"Caused by what, Doctor? What can cause the body to just shut down?"

"If the body is deprived of oxygen…for whatever reason…it shuts down."

"You said that, Doctor. But what causes it?"

"Inhalation of carbon monoxide is one cause that comes to mind, Captain. Also maybe certain drugs fed into the body."

"Did you find any drugs that could do that in any of the victims, Doctor."

"No. That's the mystery of it all. I found no significant amount of any drug that could cause a de-oxygenization of the victims' tissues. I took tissue from all six of the victims. Nothing, Captain."

The captain scratched his balding head and then peered again into the microscope. He lifted his head and then was silent for several moments. The doctor, whose smile seemed to be fixed permanently on her face, brushed her jet black hair back from her forehead to the side of her head. "Carbon monoxide," the captain mumbled.

"We didn't find any signs of carbon monoxide in any of the houses, Doctor," he continued.

"Its usually odorless, Captain. Unless you have some kind of CO monitor device, you would have difficulty detecting the CO emissions in a house. It is very difficult to find, Captain."

A young lady in a white coat walked up to the pair and handed a note to Dr. Pasha. She quickly reviewed it and then handed it over to the captain. He reached for a pair of reading glasses in his shirt pocket, placed the glasses on the bridge of his nose and read the message.

"I have to leave, Doctor," the Captain hurriedly said. "It seems that Judge Gamble appeared to have suffered a heart attack. Right in front of Orange General."

"I'll submit a report on my findings, Captain."

"Okay. I still can't figure out the why…the reasons for the deaths, Doctor."

"Neither can I, Captain. Maybe they are all coincidences. Stranger things have happened in my career."

"I'll look forward to seeing your report, Doctor."

Parker quickly left the lab and walked to his car at the curb.

Chapter Eight

Joshua and Yehuda flew to Fort Lauderdale to meet Sam Waterman on his home ground. Sam had a luxury one bedroom apartment on Country Club Drive in Aventura, overlooking Turnberry Golf Club's thirty-six hole golf course.

Sam picked them up at the airport in his red Porsche Coupe belying the fact that he was approaching seventy years old and suffering from sporadic prostetitis.

"How do you fit behind the wheel?" Joshua asked, as Sam led them to the parked sports car.

"You'll see…" Sam replied.

"You'll sit behind me with your legs sticking out toward the sky."

"I should have brought my limousine," Yehuda remarked, as he mechanically lodged the two suitcases and sundry small bags in the luggage compartment of the Porsche.

"I haven't seen both of you for…what…two years and all you do is complain," Sam feigned a disapproving air as he miraculously lodged his rotund belly and body behind the steering wheel of the sports car.

Joshua maneuvered into the back seat, muttering obscenities as he awkwardly crawled into the uncomfortable platform seat.

Yehuda sat comfortably in the front passenger seat.

"How's Sosie…and the little doll Samara?" Sam asked as he pulled clumsily out into the heavy traffic of the airport toward the exit to Route 95.

"You drive like you're still in Brooklyn," Joshua said ruefully.

"I am still in Brooklyn. They have more New Yorkers living here in Florida than they have left in New York."

"I could drive a limousine here in Florida," Yehuda remarked, as he turned his already tanned face toward the bright sun.

"It would probably be a lot safer than Jerusalem," Sam said with a smile that barely showed his small, uneven row of front teeth.

"So…" Joshua said impatient, "Why don't we talk about Orlando."

"When we get to the Club. We'll have a leisurely lunch and spend some time out at the pool…and look at the pretty girls in their tiny bikinis." Sam replied.

"That's the way I like to practice law, Sam."

Sam turned his round head toward Joshua, almost crashing the Porsche into a slowing school bus in front of him, and then said with quiet emotion, "Thanks…both of you…your coming means a lot to me…it's been over a week and nothing but bullshit is all I hear from cops up in Orlando. Nobody knows nothing. Died by natural causes is all I hear. And…it's been over six people already…all just keeling over and dying…in their houses, yet."

"What does the medical examiner say?" Josh asked.

"Nothing…she's one of these foreign doctors…Dr. Pasha is her name…where she got her degree only the Shadow knows."

"I got some information on Comtel," Josh replied. "They're supposed to merge with AMT, the international television and cable company, but I hear everything is on hold until the outcome of the class action verdict."

"Who knows? Biological weapons…Anthrax…bubonic plague…nobody's giving me any answers."

"When was the last time you saw your sister? Alive, I mean?" Yehuda asked.

"About a month ago. For the first time in years we were getting along. No fights…no guilt trips…just two siblings getting older and wanting to be family again. Then…she's gone…"

"Any leads at all? The cops must have something, Sam." Joshua said.

"There's an assistant U.S. attorney…name of Everett Lawrence…a black lawyer from Brooklyn who some how found his way down here to sunny Florida. He's got no jurisdiction, so he says. But he's interested. He's also a former law student of mine at Rutgers."

Sam suddenly jerked the steering wheel into the far left lane of Griffin Road almost broad siding a Mercedes 500, then pulled nonchalantly ahead of the sedan onto the entrance ramp of Route 95.

"You'd never survive as a driver in Jerusalem, Sam," Yehuda declared as his hand clutched the dashboard.

"Lousy drivers in Florida," Sam replied.

"Anyway," Sam continued as if he hadn't been interrupted by the attacking Mercedes, "he's down here now…Everett is…There's some kind of Federal Prosecutor's conference at the Fountainbleu in Miami. We're going to see him tonight."

"Sounds like you got real close to Everett." Joshua remarked, his eyes focused on the insane meanderings of speeding vehicles surrounding the Porsche convertible.

"Does everybody drive like this down here?" Joshua asked with the hope that Sam would confirm that the vehicle chaos engulfing them was isolated at best.

"It's the sun…it makes people crazy down here," Sam replied with a chuckle.

"What can we do, Sam?" Joshua asked. "I'm not practicing anymore and you've been absent from the bar for over three years."

"After thirty-five years, I still remember something about the law." Sam admonished.

"I'm not doubting your credentials, Sam. That's the last thing I would ever do. But, here we are…in a strange state…neither of us admitted to the Florida Bar…going against one of the most powerful corporations in Florida."

"Since when did you get so bashful, Joshua?"

"Since I sleep at night…all night…without worrying about some judge carting my ass off to jail for opening my big mouth. That's when, Sam."

"Everett…our prosecutor friend might need some help…That's if he decides to step in."

"Under what Federal statute, Sam?"

"Violations of the victims' civil rights, Joshua. Title 19 and all its wonderful progeny," Sam replied as he jerked the Porsche from the far left lane of Route 95 to the far right exit lane to Hallandale Beach Boulevard. Yehuda closed his eyes and mentally chastised himself for failing to take Zeppi's advice and stay put in safe and happy Paree.

"Am I missing something, Sam?" Joshua queried as the sweat from the bright sun, combined with the fear in his heart on whether he would survive Sam's unusual driving habits, saturated his forehead and hair.

"There's something wrong, Joshua. After thirty-five years I know that for a fact."

"It might be indigestion, Sam."

"Make fun if you want, Joshua Ryan."

After several minutes of fear-laden silence, Sam pulled his red Porsche underneath the canopy of the Turnberry Country Club. Sam, with surprising agility, hopped out of the driver's seat, handed the keys to the Hispanic valet, who opened the luggage compartment to retrieve the bags.

"Fancy, Sam," Joshua stated with obvious admiration.

"Only the best for my friends," Sam replied, as he helped Joshua out of the back seat.

"We're meeting Everett tonight. Here…in the Veranda Room."

"The plot thickens," Joshua remarked as they walked into the palatial lobby of the Turnberry Country Club.

Chapter Nine

"Don't, get off...not yet, Jo-Beth...not yet!" Everett Lawrence stated in ecstasy as he held on to the bouncing breasts of Jo-Beth, sitting naked on top of him.

They both came at about the same instance. Everett, the eternal prosecutor, restricted his peals of joy to a brief moment until he regained his senses. Jo-Beth's honey brown face ignited into a enigmatic Mona Lisa smile. She loved the orgasmic joy reverberating through her body but equally reveled in the fact that she had satisfied her lover and companion, Everett Lawrence, the Federalman, as she called him.

Jo-Beth slid off the sweating muscular body of Everett as he lay motionless on the big king-sized bed.

"You're gonna kill me yet," Everett said with a broad, carefree grin crossing his dark, chocolate brown face.

"That's what I'm here for, Everett darling."

He tenderly threw his arm across her breast enjoying the sensual feel of her skin on his forearm.

"I can't believe that any man would let you go," he muttered.

"Who?"

"That ex-husband of yours…you're pure ecstasy, Jo-Beth, honey. I'd a never let you go…even if you got a mouth that'd kill an army."

She laughed that deep down laugh that came out of the bottom of her throat. He loved her laugh…it was filled with lustiness and excitement. Jo-Beth took the world on her own terms. She was proud to be a southern black from Georgia. She was proud of her slavery ancestors who had survived the black holocaust of the 18th and 19th Centuries. She knew that survival was what it was all about.

"He still calls every once in awhile. Says he's calling just to talk." She laughed and then continued, "Bullshit…the goddamn son-of-a-bitch wants to climb into my pants. Never Everett…once it's over…it's over."

"You're a hard woman, Jo-Beth Washington. I sure wouldn't want to be on your shitlist."

"You're a smart man, Everett. That's what I like about you. You know where you came from and you don't want to go back. We're both from the same mold."

"And where is that?," he replied, as he reached over to light up a cigarette.

"You know where that's at, Everett. We both came from different shitholes in different places but they were still shitholes."

He raised his naked body onto the headboard of the bed and peered out the seventh floor window into the verdant lush golf course of Bayhead in the near distance.

"I gotta play that game, Jo-Beth. They say if you play golf you can get ahead in this white man's world," he said in a sarcastic voice.

"You're doing pretty good without playing the white man's game, Everett." She jumped out of the bed and stood naked in front of the window, luxuriously stretching her arms toward the ceiling.

Everett moved lithely off the bed behind her outstretched body and wrapped his athletic arms around her back onto her chest.

"I better cover you up before you start a riot out there on the golf course, Jo-Beth darling."

She turned and smiled at his sweaty face. "You want to go another round, my little chocolate lover."

He laughed and kissed her breasts and then up to her face and finally landing flush on her mouth where they exchanged soul-laden tongues.

"I can't. I have to fly out in about an hour to Ft. Lauderdale," he said as he moved away from her. "They want to talk about your boss' problem here in Orlando."

"What's the problem, Ev? They all died of natural causes."

"Maybe, maybe not."

"You talk to my boss, Captain Parker. He's an honest cop, Ev."

"Nobody's accusing anybody. Just got real interesting when the lawyer from New York got shot. We're wondering if somebody's civil rights have been violated"

"Who are you meeting?" She added.

"Sam Waterman…an old teacher of mine when I went to Rutger's Law…and another lawyer…A lawyer who just quit after he won a famous criminal case…about two or three years ago…They made a movie out of the book that Sam wrote. The other guy I don't know…some Israeli…Anyway, what the hell do I have to lose? And it's free."

"You're not picking up the tab, Ev?" she said with a short laugh.

"Can't…you have to be a member to pay…Anyway…just socializing with an old professor. I'm not giving the store away or anything. Just bullshitting…you know, that's all we lawyers ever do is just bullshit. They call that lawyering, Jo."

Jo-Beth climbed back into bed, her arms and legs spreading out toward the corners of the bed.

"One more time, lover," her husky voice invited.

"Jo-Beth…I've only got an hour to make it to the airport," he replied in an unsure voice.

"Just enough time to climb into me and make me happy, my darling," she said as a mischievous smile crossed her face.

"Goddamn you, Jo-Beth," he shouted half-heartedly as he climbed into the bed, on top of her waiting body. She closed her eyes as she felt the hardness of him entering her. She thought rapturously how much she loved this very sexy black man.

Chapter Ten

The Pissaro-like impressionist paintings on the wall meshed smartly with the silk lined draperies covering the French doors leading onto the terrace. Candlelight flickered on the rich flowered tables surrounding one side of the elliptical pool near a sparkling waterfall.

The restaurant was La Veranda, the hallmark gourmet dining center of Turnberry and probably of all of southeast Florida.

Seated at a corner table, far enough from the waterfall not to hear it but close enough to enjoy the sight of it, the four smartly dressed diners sat, three of them sipping on an Australian Shiraz cabernet properly aged and filtered

"Everett, you've come a long way since your impoverished student days at Rutgers," Sam said as his eyes admired Everett's elegant jacket, cuffed shirt and silk tie.

Everett Lawrence laughed heartily. He felt good in his Zegna white dinner jacket and light wool black pants that he had bought at Harrod's on his last trip to London.

"You look contented, Sam," he replied. "Retirement here in sunny Florida suits you."

"I was doing very well until a few weeks ago, Everett."

Yehuda was slowly drinking his wine while Joshua, a rehabilitated alcoholic, was drinking ginger ale, their minds still warped by jet lag.

"Joshua here graduated from Carlisle Law School probably one year behind you at Rutgers, Everett." "And Yehuda here is an Israeli archeological expert," Joshua declared, hoping Yehuda wasn't feeling like a stranger among a trio of lawyers.

"I was in Israel and Egypt about ten years ago," Everett said as he looked over at Yehuda.

"Next time call me," Yehuda declared, as he poured himself another glass of wine from the decanter.

"How's the ginger ale, Joshua?" Sam said with a wisp of a smile crossing his lips.

"A good year, Sam," Joshua replied, not wanting to explain his thirst for ginger ale.

After the group ordered their food, Everett leaned forward, folding his large, rough hands on the table, and asked, "So, Sam…how can I be of help? I know the back ground of the deaths pretty well. So far it all seems like a bunch of coincidences that happened all at once."

As he waited for the response, Everett smiled, took a deep swallow of the cabernet, his throat warmed by the effect of the full-bodied red wine.

"What do you know about Comtel?" Joshua asked in a staccato fashion.

"Started about what, thirty or forty years ago…by Osgood Evans…now Senator Evans…" Everett replied slowly.

"I did some checking with some of my Israeli security friends," Yehuda interjected. "It started as an neighborhood video store…something like your Blockbuster…we know about such things in Israel, too," Yehuda smiled brightly, his hands and face full of deep furrows of tanned skin. "Anyway…your Senator…Mr. Evans…built a company by buying up small radio stations here in Florida…then television…films…amusement parks…we all know of The Park in

Israel. Making it one of the largest and most powerful entertainment companies in the world."

"So?" Everett continued to play the devil's advocate, "lets say everything you are saying is true. Big is not always bad, I presume even in Israel, Yehuda."

"In fact, their books and records have to be valid. It's a publicly traded company," Everett stated. "The SEC watches over publicly traded companies with an eagle eye."

"We think they might be keeping two sets of books," Joshua replied.

"I don't understand, Joshua," Everett said. "What books are you talking about? I am an assistant U.S. attorney and nobody in my office ever mentioned that Comtel is screwing around with its numbers. You got something, spit it out, Joshua. By the way, gentlemen," Everett smiled self-consciously, "I'm not here to defend Comtel. As far as I'm concerned, if there's any evidence that Comtel or anybody is violating Federal law…I'm interested."

"What about sloughing off some of their major debts to a…lets say…an offshore corporation…maybe in Nassau or the Grand Caymans," Yehuda remarked. "By the way…most of the information I received are from some friends of mine in the Mossad…they are really intrigued by Comtel. The corporation is thinking about developing one of their amusement parks near Haifa."

Suddenly two white coated waiters appeared with several plates of signature dishes of La Veranda. Sam ordered two more bottles of the Shiraz and, of course, another ginger ale for Joshua who grimaced noticeably at the order.

"Gentlemen," Everett continued, "I have to inform you that my appointment as Assistant U.S. Attorney was nominated and supported by Senator Osgood Evans, the founder of Comtel. I just wanted to get it out on the table."

"Does that, in anyway, the fact that the Senator put you in your present position…I guess that's what you're saying, Everett," Joshua said in a voice that was insistent but not accusing, "does that compromise your attitude toward an important investigation…even if Comtel may some how be involved?"

"Not in the least…I deserved the appointment. The good Senator didn't get me appointed because of any kind of quid pro quo…He's never asked anything of me since I've been in the U.S attorney's office in Orlando."

"Is there anything discovered that would lead you to believe that the deaths were anything but natural? Josh asked.

"There are some tissue slides that I'm aware of," Everett announced, "But they just show, what I understand, that the victims has a substantial loss of oxygen from their lungs and tissues when they died."

"Those tissue slides…can we get them to an independent lab?" Sam said.

"I'll call up to my office," Everett offered. "One of my investigators could request them from the County medical examiner."

"What I don't understand…maybe I'm missing something," Joshua said, "no one is assuming that these deaths are not accidental…death by natural causes. Is that right?"

"And how? I'm used to many people getting killed in Israel…but those are by some maniac strapping dynamite to his chest…" Yehuda stated.

"Maybe it's in those slides?" Josh intimated.

"My sister had called me…about a week before she and her husband died…I didn't get back to her in time." Sam said in a melancholy voice and then added, "I wish I had…maybe I could have done something."

"I'm still not convinced in convening a Federal Grand Jury…I'll be back in Orlando on Monday, let's see what those slides show."

"This wine is delicious, Sam," Yehuda lifted his glass and then drank the glass of wine in one gulp. Finishing it, he smacked his lips and then said, "Not as good as ginger ale, I bet."

Joshua smiled and then said, "If I wasn't such a gentleman, Yehuda."

CHAPTER ELEVEN

The next morning, Joshua Ryan sat next to Yehuda and Sam Waterman on the U.S. Air flight from Ft. Lauderdale to Orlando. He had the window seat in the emergency row which Yehuda somehow managed to arrange.

Ryan's mind drifted back to the beginning of his life. How far had he really come, he mused as his eyes viewed the gray-white clouds surrounding the plane as it fought its way through the cloud barrier. Was he like all the other abused children he read about in the newspapers? Grown-up with their mental horrors still clinging to their everyday thoughts and nightmares.

The alcoholic father who showed up sporadically, his presence hallmarked by beatings and humiliation. As an only child, Joshua bore the brunt of the insane abuse of his father, and the smothering love of his sainted mother. He always though of her as a saint even though she had all the human weaknesses of an abused spouse. She had married Michael Ryan against the wishes of her Jewish Orthodox father and family. Love caught her by the heart strings when she met and slept with Michael Ryan one wintry weekend in the Poconos. Singles' weekend at Tamiment, the resort of the single swingers from New York to Philadelphia. Michael Ryan was handsome in a sort of John Wayne manner, spoke with a bit of the Irish in him, and had a smile that could light up Grant's Tomb. Within days, he had swept Eleanor Rubin off her feet, into a marriage ill considered by both of them. He didn't care if he married. He had no interest in giving his undying commitment to his bride. Michael Ryan was a user...anybody who would give to him he cherished. For a time. Until he found another provider. Which he did within weeks of the City Hall wedding. She didn't see him for over a month after the ill fated honeymoon night where he drunkenly raped his newly acquired wife.

Joshua only remembered the physical beatings his father doled out not only to him, but to his ever faithful and believing wife. She worked all her life to support Joshua as a waitress, seamstress, or a domestic, and on occasion when he showed up, gave to her unfaithful and malevolent husband. She died before Joshua had graduated from law school, yet Joshua was the only star in her heaven. She loved him from the beginning, showering him with not only love, but with praise and confidence that he was different, that he was special, he was her only gift to this cruel world.

Ryan had been a star. A football hero at Carlisle University, a law review editor at Carlisle Law School, and finally the rising star litigator of the Somerset Prosecutor's office. First Assistant Prosecutor became his celebrated position. He was respected and envied by all in the tightly woven legal community of Central New Jersey. Victorious in all of his celebrated murder trials, Joshua Ryan married and then immediately succumbed to the wonders of alcohol as depression set in. His union to the society climbing darling he married weighed heavily on his confused mind and being. The childhood poison rose slowly into his adult mindset. Nightmares of torturous beatings and death continuously filled his sleeping hours.

Ryan smiled to himself as he peered over at Yehuda seated two seats away on the aisle. Yehuda reminded him of Sosie, his caring and beautiful wife who had saved Ryan from returning to the depths of alcoholic depression. Chasing an errant client, the notorious Rabbi who was charged with the killing of his wife, Joshua had to track his client down in that inner sanctorum of Mea Shareem in Jerusalem. He then met Sosie and his life changed forever. Shangri La became his reality. He finally could see through the muddled clouds that had followed him through his younger life.

Joshua noticed that Sam Waterman, seated next to him, had fallen asleep, his head resting on Joshua's shoulder. His round, nearly bald head looked like a worn soccer ball.

Sam had been Joshua's mentor at the Somerset County Prosecutor's office. An unfavorite prosecutor because he was the only Jewish lawyer in that right wing town, Sam Waterman knew all the nooks and crannies of the trial courtroom. He taught his craft to the young, eager novitiates of the law at Rutgers Law School in Camden. Everett Lawrence had been one of his students. There were many students who now graced the judicial bench in the State as a result of the teachings of Sam Waterman. Most of all, Joshua remembered the deft maneuverings of Sam Waterman to save the life and legal career of Joshua Ryan. An almost fatal accident where Joshua Ryan, in a drunken stupor one night, almost killed a twelve year-old girl walking to a church social. Joshua would wake up in the middle of the night dreaming of the girl's face against his car's windshield on that awful, rainy night. The image of her tortured face replaced most of his nightmares filled with the childhood beatings by his father.

After a year of wandering around Europe, the bar suspension over, Ryan returned to do what he was trained and best suited to do. Practice law.

Ryan acknowledged that the rabbi's case had turned him off to the law and its unpredictable process. He had won the trial of the rabbi, but it wasn't justice that had won. It was the better lawyer that had prevailed and Joshua knew that he could not live with that kind of justice.

Here he was, flying into another legal morass although he had promised himself and Sosie that he would never venture again into the world of American law. Happy in retirement, Joshua Ryan knew that he couldn't refuse Sam Waterman's soulful request that he help find out what happened to Sam's sister.

Of course, after he learned about the multiple deaths, all seemingly from the same cause, Joshua Ryan's mind enthusiastly took up the gauntlet. Slides of tissues removed from the six bodies with the mysterious comment "loss of oxygen," confused him. 'What the hell does loss of oxygen in tissue mean? Is it some type of deadly bacteria? "What the hell is it?' Joshua murmured to himself. "Maybe it's all natural causes…what the hell am I doing here?" He wondered.

Suddenly, Joshua's mind started to resound from the song "I Love Paris" as he started to mouth the words, waking Sam Waterman up.

"I though I heard Yves Montand singing," Sam commented as he tried to find some saliva to wet his inner mouth.

"I think we're chasing windmills, Sam."

"You might be right, Joshua, but I have to know for sure what killed her…"

"And if you find out?"

"Then I can lay it to rest, Joshua. I can lay her memory to rest forever."

"You don't think Comtel has anything to do with this?" Joshua asked.

"No reason that I can think of, Joshua. All the victims were valuable senior employees of Comtel."

"This merger sticks in my mind, Sam."

"I just don't see any relationship, Josh. Probably if it wasn't for my suspicious mind, you'd still be singing, "I Love Paris" in Paris."

"He's up?" Yehuda said as he turned in his seat to face Josh and Sam.

"Just daydreaming, Yehuda," Josh answered.

"About what?"

"I don't know why I'm even here instead of in Paris having lunch at Bistro 16th"

"I like Florida, Josh," Yehuda answered. "Maybe Zeppi and I will buy a condominium right next to Sam here."

"We can visit every winter," Josh said.

"I'd have to buy a big enough place for Sammy and you and Sosie."

"Why don't you teach here?" Sam offered. "I know the president of FIU…You can teach all these old fogies about their ancestors."

"I'd like to know what's killing these people before I bring my wife and daughter to visiting sunny Florida, Sam," Joshua declared.

"We'll find out," Yehuda said, his blue eyes narrowing.

"Why are you so sure, Yehuda?" Joshua added.

"I don't know why…but my gut reactions tells me that something doesn't pass the smell test."

"Maybe you have a hyperactive nose, Yehuda," Josh said as he reached over to touch Yehuda's leg.

"Maybe, but its never failed me when I'm out digging up ancient treasures in the desert."

The stewardess alerted the passengers that the plane was going to land in Orlando International in twenty minutes and that all passengers should make sure that their seatbelts were buckled.

"I'm still mulling over those tissue slides that Everett Lawrence was telling us about. What the hell would cause the oxygen to leave the human tissues in the victims?" Josh queried as he watched the high-rise office building landscape of Orlando rushing up to meet the descending plane.

"Terrorism maybe," Yehuda said. "Some toxic bacteria floated into the air by our Moslem friends."

"But why in Orlando? And against six senior employees of Comtel?" Josh said.

"Comtel is all over the world. Who knows why Comtel? Its American and terrorists pick at anything that's American," Sam interjected.

"I don't know why, folks," Josh said as he straightened his seat up, "but Comtel worries me. They lose a big class action suit brought by their employees over some toxic herbicide that injure their employees; there's a lucrative merger in the background…I just don't know. Too much money at stake. We have to dig deeper into Comtel's books and records…maybe there's something there."

"And how do you plan on doing that, Joshua," Sam asked.

"Everett Lawrence…your assistant U.S. Attorney. We have to convince him that Comtel is not out of the picture, Sam."

The plane's wheels struck the ground with a resounding thud causing Joshua to hold on ferociously to the armrest of his seat. He feared any object that didn't actually fly with God's help, knowing full well that birds didn't offer passenger seats for humans to sit in.

As they left the plane, Joshua asked, as he walked up the gangway to the terminal, "who is meeting us, Sam?"

"Everett sent his girlfriend. We're going to stay at the Radisson near Comtel's Park. He'll meet us there tonight. Maybe he'll have some answers."

"And if he doesn't, Sam, I think we should drop the whole thing and fly back to Paris."

"I hope you're wrong, Joshua. I need some answers."

They espied a tall, shapely black girl holding a sign with Sam Waterman's name as they entered the outer part of the terminal. Their transportation had arrived.

Chapter Twelve

The B-747 took off from Orlando International Airport. The markings on the plane bore only the massive initials CI in blood-red paint emblazoned on a field of sunflower yellow. There were only two passengers on the luxuriously converted jumbo jet. The inside of the plane could easily be mistaken for the palatial lobby of a luxury liner. Massive lounge chairs lined the middle of the plane just aft of three master bedroom suites, each with its own bathroom that included a multi-headed Swiss shower, toilet and bidet. The front of the plane included the cockpit with the massive space behind it rarely found on a commercial 747. A full gourmet kitchen was situated on one side of the plane while the other side contained a zebra wood bar stocked with selected aged wines from all over the world.

Jon Paulsen, security chief of Comtel's corporate network, sat stretched out in one of the leather lounge chairs dully looking out the window of the disappearing cityscape of Orlando and the surrounding lakes.

Across his seat sat Alfred Lowry, general counsel of Comtel. He fidgeted with a tall glass of straight Canadian Club whiskey, occasionally gulping the brown liquid down his throat. His facial muscles twitched spastically after every swig of whiskey, his hand holding the glass shaking noticeably. His eyes occasionally glared at Paulsen's long, thin body stretched out in the nearby lounge chair. Every time Paulsen's agate green eyes fixed on Lowry's face, Lowry would cast his eyes downward to the floor of the plane. The atmosphere in the plane was deafening by the total absence of noise. Lowry suddenly blurted out with a fear laden voice, "Jack told me you was his adjutant in Vietnam."

Paulsen's long thin face raised up from his downward position, his vacuous eyes peered at the obviously nervous Lowry for several seconds that seemed like an eternity to Lowry, and he finally said in a low smoker's voice, "Yes…" Paulsen retrieved a tall glass of Jim Beam whiskey situated on the table near his chair and downed it in one gulp.

"Marines…Jack was a Colonel in the marines," Lowry continued in an apparent attempt to start a conversation with the silent Paulsen.

"Yes," Paulsen responded curtly, his eyes returning to its downcast position.

"Jack told me that you worked at the CIA after the Marines," Lowry continued in a deliberate voice.

"Yes."

"I was in the U.S. Attorney's office in Washington when I first got out of Harvard Law."

Paulsen's eyelids suddenly closed, the drink in his hand fell to the floor of the plane. The sound of the glass hitting the floor jolted Paulsen from his slumber.

The plane suddenly shuddered as it passed through a series of large gray clouds over the disappearing Atlantic Ocean some thirty thousand feet below.

"I don't like lawyers," Paulsen angrily blurted out, his eyes suddenly opened and glaring at Lowry. Lowry poured himself another tall glass of whiskey from the bottle sitting on the table near his chair. He again gulped down a half of glass before his eyes dared to return Paulsen's stare.

"We're not all bad…" Lowry weakly replied.

"You're fucking cowards. You hide behind your expensive briefcases," he paused and then smiled tight-lipped, "I bet you never killed a man…in combat…man to man…the one who wins, lives."

"Not in war. I was never in the Army…but I was involved in capital cases at the U.S. Attorney's office."

"Fuck your capital cases, Mr. Lowry. That's a pussy's way of killing somebody. Me and Jack Evans were a great team. Did he ever tell you about Chou Lai?" Paulsen's malevolent smiled returned as he waited for an answer from Lowry. "No, I guess not," Paulsen answered his own question. "He doesn't talk about the war. Jack Evans only talks about money now. He was different thirty years ago. He fought for this country like I did."

"I was exempt from the draft because of my heart."

"Just like your buddy Clinton. Too yellow to stand up and be counted."

Lowry shifted his gaze from Paulsen out the window of the plane noticing the blue-green waves of the Atlantic thousands of feet below the plane. His mind wandered back a month ago when he was first introduced to Jon Paulsen. Evans had made a big deal about Paulsen's intelligence credentials…as if Comtel needed a CIA outcast as head of security for Comtel.

"Jack and the senator are meeting us at the Sea Club in Nassau," Lowry offered. His fear of Paulsen was evident in the timbre of his voice, his pitch vacillating between even and high.

"Jack told me. They love that boat it seems."

"You know who we're meeting at the King Neptune?"

Paulsen smiled an enigmatic smile as he answered, "They don't tell me much, Mr. Lowry. I'm just one of the hired hands."

"You know about the pending merger?"

"Just what I hear from the scuttlebut."

"It's very important to Comtel."

"I guessed that…Even a dummy like me could figure that out."

Lowry knew Paulsen knew more than he was admitting to. Jack Evans always fed just the right amount of information to the right employee.

"It would save Comtel millions of dollars if the merger with AMT became a fact."

"Distribution of Comtel's films...cable, movie theatre, that's all I know." Paulsen smiled again as he pled ignorance of the topic of the year concerning Comtel.

"I know you know Frederick Abromowitz, Mr. Paulsen," Lowry said with an irritated undertone.

"We did a check on him."

"And AMT, also?"

"And AMT also," Paulsen admitted.

"Right now we're paying millions of dollars to the distributors and cable companies to show our products that could be Comtel's profits."

"That's what I heard, Mr. Lowry."

The slim-hipped stewardess came into the cabin carrying a tray of gourmet hor d'oevres, Lowry put several of the quiche and pate sandwiches on his plate and started eating them hungrily. Paulsen waved her by as he looked at Lowry.

"I haven't eaten all day," Lowry declared between sandwiches.

"Don't fill up, Mr. Lowry. I hear you're a guest on Mr. Abromowitz' boat tonight."

"Tomorrow night. Tonight is business at the King Neptune. We have to close the merger deal. Without fail."

"You know what's in those camp trunks we're carrying, Mr. Lowry?" Paulsen asked.

"I know...I've been here before, Mr. Paulsen."

"I wouldn't think corporate counsel would be along for the deposit."

"It's not my choice, Mr. Paulsen."

"I guess we do things we don't like to do," Paulsen said with an ear-to-ear grin. He poured himself another glass of Jim Beam straight, drank the whiskey down to the bottom of the glass. Lowry marveled how Paulsen's face or body showed no effects of the whiskey.

"Do you know Mathilda?" Paulsen asked as he stood up from his chair to walk to the window near Lowry's chair.

"Mathilda Gosling, she's our public relations person at the King Neptune."

"Do you like her?"

"She's okay."

"Did you fuck her?"

"I don't think it's any of your business, Mr. Paulsen." Lowry angrily replied.

"Everything at Comtel's my business, Mr. Lowry. Every fucking detail. And you don't forget it." Paulsen's voice was rimmed with steely anger but his voice level never rose beyond a conversational tone. He stood over Lowry, his waist directly in front of Lowry's face. "I know you fucked her. I have the videos."

"What…what are you talking about?" Lowry's voice was hysterically high.

"We video all her activities at King Neptune. Even the fucking night she had last night with Mr. Abromowitz."

"I don't understand."

"You don't? And you're corporate counsel, Mr. Lowry? Shame on you. You carry all this money that's in those giant trunks in the hold of this plane for the last ten years and you don't know about those videos? I'm ashamed of you, Mr. Lowry. I thought you were such a smart lawyer." Paulsen laughed demonically as he walked to the mahogany bar on the other side of the plane. He pulled another bottle of Jim Beam from behind the bar, opened it and then drank a seemingly unending slug of whiskey directly from the bottle.

"What do you do with the videos?" Lowry asked in a meek undemanding voice.

"We keep them for posterity, Mr. Lowry. Or when the time comes that we need to get something." Paulsen laughed again as he plopped back into his chair.

"Jack know about this?"

"Jack knows everything that goes on at Comtel, Mr. Lowry."

"I don't believe Jack would condone such…"

"Such criminal activity, Mr. Lawyer? Well, maybe he just wants the videos for informational purposes only. Who knows what goes through that genius brain of Jack Evans?"

"What about the senator?"

"I haven't had the pleasure of meeting the senator, Mr. Lowry. Maybe he knows and maybe he doesn't, I don't give a rat's ass. Jack Evans is my boss. I answer to no one else."

The plane descended slowly through a bank of clouds and the island of Nassau could be seen in the near distance. The captain announced that the plane was going to land in a few minutes and he asked his passengers to resume their seats and attach their seatbelts.

"The Inter-Island Bank next stop, Mr. Lowry. All that money stuffed into the vault. You could almost get an orgasm thinking about it," Paulsen said laughingly. "Do you get an erection thinking about it, Mr. Lowry?"

Lowry just looked away from the taunting Paulsen, out toward the landing strip of Nassau International Airport.

CHAPTER THIRTEEN

Jon Paulsen was a human enigma. No person could ever state with any certainty that they knew who he really was. He made few friends. Except possibly Jack Evans and Paulsen didn't consider Jack Evans a friend. More of an accessory to climb onto in fulfilling his goal. Self-sufficiency, without the need of anyone or anything.

Paulsen hated all people. A sociopath since he was a teenager, Paulsen would rather destroy humankind before humankind could destroy him. They tried. Well before he knew of his ability to destroy his fellow man, Paulsen suffered egregiously at the hands of his fellow schoolmates at Virginia Military Preparatory School outside Roanoke, Virginia. Not that his schoolmates considered him harmful or dangerous in any way. To the contrary. Paulsen was more effeminate as a teenager than his fellow schoolmates would allow. Beaten continuously by a sadistic father, he cowered under the skirts of his ever comforting mother. She even dressed him in some of her favorite pant suits to the revulsive chagrin of his wealthy tyrannical father.

An only child, Paulsen spent most of his early teens in a closet on the third level of his family's house in Boston. Until he was sent to Virginia Military. Unfortunately, his school associates relished in venting their degenerate excesses on the scrawny withdrawn Paulsen.

After the first year of sustaining both physical and mental beatings in terrorizing the boy, Paulsen enrolled in a survival camp for the summer.

Out in the high deserts of Utah and New Mexico. Operated by former Green Berets, the camp forced Paulsen to realize that survival could only be obtained by his own physical development. Omnivorously he absorbed the sixteen hours a day physical regime insisted upon at the camp. No mother's skirts to hide under, Paulsen built his body into a destructive force. Within three months, he had learned the ways of the sensei, karate's master teachers. Besides hours in the professionally equipped gym and weight rooms, Paulsen lingered hungrily at every karate session. Until his body and mind had evolved into a desensitized robot bent on destroying any human pitted against him.

Upon his return to Virginia Military, he immediately proved to his former enemies that Jon Paulsen would now be the punishing force. Tried in combat by two unconvinced senior students, Paulsen dispatched their bodies with such destructive force that both adversaries left school with lifelong permanent injuries. No one again doubted Paulsen's recently acquired combative skills and maliciousness to mete out unforgiving punishment to all who opposed him.

From military school, he entered the Marines at eighteen and rose quickly to Captain status before he was twenty-five. Joining forces with Jack Evans in Vietnam, Paulsen became a killing machine, without mercy. Especially at Chou Lai. Eighty women and children were discovered dead and their bodies mutilated by repeated bayonet strikes by the U.S. Marine assailants. Viet Cong supporters were the reasons given by the Colonel in charge of the operation. Colonel Jack Evans was awarded a silver star for the successful encounter with the uncovered enemy. Paulsen was awarded the Bronze Star for saving Colonel Evans's life when several of the children shot at Evans with hidden machine guns. Or so the formal written report so stated.

"You up, Siegfred," Paulsen asked as he hopped out of the king size bed onto the plush carpet of the hotel suite. The man situated on the other side of the bed mumbled a few words then buried his head in the pillow.

"Get up, man…I've got business to take care of today," Paulsen declared in an angry voice as he rolled his bed mate onto the floor.

"Fuck it, Jon! What the hell did you do that for? I was just having a wet dream," Siegfred yelled as he disentangled himself from the bed sheets on the floor.

"There's a time to fuck and there's a time to get down to business, my faggy friend," Paulsen said as he ripped open the stiff heavy drapes covering the massive window that looked out onto the Florida Intracoastal.

The small effete body of Paulsen's lover lay naked on the floor, his erection standing tall.

"What do I do with this?" the young man, no more than twenty years old, declared in a high pitched ringing voice.

"Stuff it in your fucking mouth, Siegie baby. Just like you do with mine…Now get your sweet little ass off the floor and get out of here…Pronto…Verstadt!"

"Oh I love when you talk German to me, Jonny baby. Just like my grandfather did when I was a sweet innocent baby in Stuttgart."

Paulsen bent over and lifted the slight bony body off the floor and into the air above his head. The boy lover started to scream hysterically as he tried to wiggle free from Paulsen's iron grasp. Paulsen threw the squirming boy lover out through the open double French doors of the bedroom into the lavishly decorated living room of the suite. The boy landed on his back, his head bouncing off the mahogany floor with an excruciating thud. He layed there unconscious. Paulsen grabbed a silver bucket of watered down ice from the bar in the living room and threw it onto the silent young lover.

He awoke with a cacophanous bark that sounded more like a seal's mating call.

"Why Jon? Why?" the young man stuttered as he tried to rise up from the floor.

"Because you don't know when to stop, Sieg…To you the world is one big cock and ass to lick…but it's fucking over. I got business to take care of and you ain't in that end of the business. Comprende, mon petite garcon?"

"Last night you said you loved me," the boy's voice cried out.

Paulsen laughed sardonically, his teeth barely showing beyond his pencil thin lips.

"I love everybody who gives a blow job like you, Siegie…Now up and at em…I got a bunch of Comtel people coming up for a meeting."

The young man rose laboriously from the floor, stood naked in front of Paulsen for several moments, then turned and walked back into the bedroom.

"You're not a nice man, Jon," he cried out from the bedroom as he quickly dressed into the clothes that were lying on the floor in a tangled bundle.

An Elvis Presley lyric kept pounding in Paulsen's head, "you ain't nothing but a hound dog, fucking all the time…" with the words slightly altered in Paulsen's mind.

Paulsen could never satisfy an unquenchable libido, trying all methods of erotic madness to scratch the insatiable itch. Even raping a young teenage whore in Saigon during the war. She couldn't make him come. He couldn't even get an erection. Sure he could have paid her and she would have voluntarily done anything he wanted her to do. But that was too boring. He hated all women, especially his ever loving mother. She had protected him from his maniac father but she loved her maniac lover over her son. Paulsen loved her more than anyone else on this Earth. At night he dreamed he had made love to her and she had wanted him to do it. But in real life, she despised her permutation of a son. She harbored the same revulsive sentiments her husband had…but she tried to hide them from young Jon. At times, the love dreams turned into nightmares where young Jon stabbed his father to death, cut up his body into little pieces and fed them to the crocodiles in the zoo. Then he raped his mother, having her perform all kinds of sadistic erotic acts on his body parts. He would then chop her up with a meat cleaver and toss the parts out the window of a speeding car. When he woke up, he knew his dreams would never come true because both parents were there…in the house…committing the same acts of perdition that had caused him to hate himself and all the people around him.

Siegfried quickly left the suite, not even saying goodbye to his lover.

"Maybe tomorrow night, Siegfried," Paulsen shouted after the young man, as the door slammed loudly shut. Paulsen smiled a knowing smile. They all returned, he mused. Even if you have to pay them, it was worth it. He hated the chase of new lovers. It was so boringly repetitive. Sweet words, a few drinks, an invitation to a suite of rooms at the Fountanbleu Hotel in South Beach and they were soon performing all the rites of erotic perversion that Paulsen requested.

In spite of all his degenerative trysts with boys and men, he never arrived at orgasm. Only when the ultimate act of life and death transpired, by his hand alone, did orgasm finally, mercifully, come to him.

It happened after he had been promoted to lieutenant and was a training instructor at the Quantico Marine Base. A young handsome male recruit had flirted unmercifully with him. But when they were alone, Paulsen demanding fulfillment, the young man refused and instead laughed at Paulsen, calling him a "fucking queen". Paulsen strangled the boy and then carted his body out to the ocean. Part by part, just like his childish nightmares, he dumped the recruit's body into the ocean. Gleefully, with bare hands, he dumped each bloody stump into the bouncing receptive waves. After disposing of the body, Paulsen came four times.

The suite's bell pulled him out of his reverie. The boys of winter were here, he thought, as he quickly closed the bedroom doors. After giving the living room a last viewing, he opened the front door letting Jack Evans and Alfred Lowry into the suite.

Chapter Fourteen

The B747 landed at the private hanger section of Nassau's International Airport. Lowry and Paulsen exited the plane to a waiting stretch Mercedes limousine.

Sitting in the leather surround of the back seat was Mathilda Gosling, her body draped in a revealing halter top and skirt that barely covered her shapely bottom.

"Right on time, gentlemen," her husky voice smacked of East London with a slight cockney lilt to her words.

Lowry sat next to her in the back seat while Paulsen sat on the side bench seat in the limo. Lowry noticed the sudden chill that arose between Mathilda and Paulsen.

"Hello, Mr. Paulsen," Mathilda said with a slight chuckle.

Paulsen grunted a reply as his eyes stared out the window of the limo.

Lowry's face lit up as his eyes absorbed Mathilda's face and body.

"Jack and his father are already at the Sea Club preparing for the meeting with Mr. Abromowitz tonight," Mathilda said as the limo's mulatto driver, dressed in black chauffeur's garb, pulled the stretch limo from the parking spot onto the two lane highway heading to the center of Nassau.

"It's important that we close the merger deal this weekend," Lowry declared.

"I entertained Mr. Abromowitz last night," Mathilda confessed without any emotion.

"Did you find anything out?" Lowry's voice suddenly rose with a note of urgency.

"He knows about that verdict in Orlando. I have the feeling he is going to change whatever deal Jack had worked out with him."

"Son-of-a-bitch!" Lowry half shouted.

"What does that bastard want now?" Paulsen asked in anger.

Mathilda turned toward Paulsen surprised at his sudden rush of anger.

"That he wouldn't tell me. But I'm sure the little man will exact his pound of flesh if he feels we're vulnerable."

The vehicle sped through the beach road which was saturated with hotels and newly constructed luxury condominiums. Mathilda Gosling had been public relations director at Comtel's King Neptune Hotel in Nassau for over three years now. Previously Jack Evans had discovered her in Paris where she ran a high-class escort service for lonely, wealthy business men and diplomats. After partaking of her obvious sexual charms at his suite at the Ritz Hotel, Evans offered her a proposition she couldn't refuse. She became a vital part of Comtel's entertainment program for visiting legislators and business partners that Jack Evans deemed vital to the success of his corporation. Jack Evans realized that more intimate financial information can be discovered when the prospect is nuzzling his nose and private parts in Mathilda's voluptuous breasts. Besides her own activities as an erotic Mata Hari, Mathilda had recruited a bevy of lovely ladies who had the talent of pulling important information out of their consorts during an intimate soiree. Important information that Jack Evans could use to further the interests of Comtel.

After several minutes on the heavily traveled two lane roadway, the limo pulled to the back entrance of the Inter-Island Bank of Nassau located in the middle of town.

Lowry, Paulsen and the driver got out the limo and pulled the two large camp trunks out of the luggage compartment of the limo. Paulsen and the driver carried the trunks into the bank followed by Lowry. Mathilda sat in the back seat of the limo slowly drinking a straight shot of vodka and lemon.

They walked directly to the back of the bank toward the private section housing the bank manager's office. As they approached the glass enclosed bank manager's office, the black manager peered up from his desk and with a glaring white smile walked to his office door and opened it to the trio of men.

"How's the wife and kids, Mr. Coleman?" Paulsen greeted the manager.

"Fine, Mr. Paulsen. How are you Mr. Lowry?" The manager said in a jolly voice.

"Fine, Mr. Coleman," Lowry replied, a reluctant smile crossing his face. "How's your son Douglas?"

"Great, Mr. Lowry. He's graduating Harvard this year."

"My alma mater, Mr. Coleman," Lowry replied.

"He'll be looking to go into the hotel business when he graduates."

"I'm sure Comtel can use him at the King Neptune in administration, Mr. Coleman," Lowry stated anxiously as he started to lead Paulsen and the driver toward the vaulted area behind the office.

"Yes sir, Mr. Lowry, Douglas would love working at the King Neptune. You know, he works there in the summer as a waiter."

"Good training for a businessman," Paulsen said.

"I guess you want to get back into the vault?" Coleman said as he led the trio toward the mammoth gray, steel vault.

The driver deposited his trunk at the base of the vault area and departed back to the limo.

Coleman opened the outside vault door and then let Paulsen and Lowry carrying the heavy trunks, into the inner room where Coleman opened another vault door. They placed the trunks on the large folding table located in the rectangular room.

"I presume you want to make a deposit, gentlemen," Coleman said with a knowing smile on his face.

"Yes, Mr. Coleman. The usual…then the transfer to Comtel's account in your affiliated bank in Geneva," Lowry instructed.

Paulsen opened the trunk and the three men stared hypnotically at the orderly piles of green-backs contained within.

Coleman withdrew his hand calculator from the inside of his suit jacket and started to count the piles of money. Paulsen watched every movement of the large denomination bills handled by Coleman as if he suspected the black man of taking some of the deposit for his own benefit. Lowry walked nervously around the small room, his eyes furtively staring at Paulsen's face.

Paulsen stood guard over the trunks, his arms crossed tightly against his chest. Lowry thought about the bank and Comtel's participation in creating it. Twenty years ago Comtel had created the Inter-Island Bank of Nassau in a joint partnership with several Nassau lawyers, accountants and politicians. Comtel put up the money and the native partners protected Comtel's enormous deposit of U.S. bills. The money was sanitized by Inter-Island transferring the bills through their Swiss branch located in Geneva and then funneling it back to the Evans' family through their Swiss bank accounts. With the sanitized cash, Comtel acquired radio, television, and film companies that always needed a steady available cash flow to continue their expensive operations. The vast debt of mainland Comtel was mostly shifted to the books of the Nassua "joint partnerships".

The partners in these ventures were guaranteed by Comtel a substantial return no matter what deficits the partnerships sustained. Deals and counter deals flowed unerringly from Nassau to Orlando and back to Nassau. The major accounting firm that audited Comtel's books verified each deal although as certified public accountants they should have spilled the beans to the uninformed innocent investors that gobbled up Comtel stocks with manic relish.

After about an hour of monotonous counting of the piles of bills, Coleman walked to his office to retrieve a special deposit slip reserved for Comtel's deposits.

He returned within minutes and handed the completed deposit slip to Lowry. Coleman shook hands with Paulsen and Lowry and the trio left the private vault area. Coleman would return to place the money in a special inside vault where the Comtel deposits were kept until they were transferred to Geneva for washing and re-use.

The island depositing was especially important today for Comtel since the massive verdict and possible final judgment against Comtel as a result of the highly publicized toxic herbicide class action suit would force Comtel to open its festering accounting practices and books for the whole world to see. Only the deposits of enormous skimmed cash that Comtel had completed over the last decade would be kept secret and away from the prying world.

Paulsen and Lowry returned to the limo and in minutes they were transported to the posh Sea Club located on the eastern tip of Nassau.

Upon entering the covered portico of the white pillared Sea Club, a uniformed valet, his black skin etched against the pure ivory of his creased Bermuda shorts, white collared shirt and gloves, appeared to open the limousine's rear door.

Lowry was first to exit the limo, followed by Matilda, and Paulsen. Lowry always marveled at the antebellum look of the Sea Club main building. He felt that he was entering someone's southern plantation main house, stepping back in time before the Civil War changed the world of wasteful luxury and slavery's excesses.

The lobby was marbled from floor to ceiling, aurora marble from the quarries of Tuscany. An etched glass dome covered the lobby, somehow only allowing sufficient sunlight through the glass that would not be invasively irritating to the guests below. In the rear corner stood a black granite topped cherry wood counter that surrounded brightly smiling hotel employees who generally appeared pleased that Comtel and company had chosen to visit their island paradise.

"Good afternoon, Mr. Lowry," a light cocoa skinned mountain of a man draped in black formal tails said while bowing to Lowry as he approached him.

"Good afternoon, Jerome, glad to be back…Is Mr. Evans in his bungalow?"

"Yes…I'll call him for you."

"Don't bother. I'll just go and see him. Is Mr. Abromowitz here yet?"

"I don't think so, sir. His Captain advised they were heading out to the island for some deep sea fishing."

Lowry smiled. He knew that Abromowitz hated fishing but always told the world he was going out deep sea fishing. Actually he left the shores of Nassau so that he could talk to his legions of accountants, lawyers, investment bankers and other financial wizards he employed without fear of being taped or overheard. His world was private. And it was his world that everybody lived in.

Lowry and Paulsen were led to respective white clapped bungalows near the beach of the Sea Club. Jack Evans had left a message on each of their answering machines to meet him at the bar directly located on one side of the Sea Club's gourmet restaurant. Within thirty minutes, after showering and dressing in light summer suits and open necked golf shirts, they met Jack Evans and Mathilda at the bar that overlooked the Atlantic. Evans wore a white silk sports jacket with a lavender Egyptian cotton dress shirt. Mathilda had changed into a full length silk summer gown that suggestively covered her entire body.

Evans ordered margaritas for all.

"Have you talked to Mr. Abromowitz?" Lowry asked Evans who was slowly sipping his margarita, his eyes staring out into the Atlantic.

"Missed him. He left a message for me that he'll see us tonight at King Neptune. He's out there," Evans pointed his forefinger out toward a small island in the near distance, "on his yacht talking to his world of lawyers and accountants."

"Did he mention anything about the merger?"

"Not a word. Mathilda here told me he wasn't too happy about that verdict…you know the one I'm talking about, Alfred," Evans said in a cynical voice.

"Doesn't change much, Jack. You told him that there is a good chance it will be reversed."

"Abromowitz doesn't bet on speculation, Alfred. He's going to use that verdict against us and try to get a better deal."

"We can't just walk away from the merger, Jack."

"We can't, Alfred. We need AMT's distribution resources. We always lose out to Disney or Universal because we're paying through the nose to those sharks out there. We need AMT, Alfred."

"What do we do?"

"Do? Play poker with Abromowitz. I'm sure he needs Comtel's film products and amusement parks…that's something he doesn't have. As they say in Latin, Alfred, 'Quid pro quo'".

"Maybe Mathilda here will loosen the great Mr. Abromowitz up for us," Evans added with a chuckle.

Mathilda smiled and touched Jack Evans' arm which was on the bar next to her hand. "I'll do anything to help, Jack," she said.

"I know you will, Mathilda darling." Evans laughed and brushed the back of his hand against Mathilda's face. He truly liked Mathilda. She knew her place. Who she was…and why she was there. She always reminded Jack Evans of his first experience with a woman. Like Mathilda. A paid trainer. His father had taken Jack to New Orleans for his fourteenth birthday. They never spoke of what Jack Evans experienced that night. Southern gentlemen didn't do that. But they both knew that Jack had officially entered manhood.

"A penny for your thoughts, Jack," Matilda declared as she touched the back of his manicured hand that rested on the bar.

"More like a billion dollars, Matilda," Jack answered with a slight laugh. He moved from the bar as the maître d' beckoned to him.

"Dinner must be ready," Jack said. They all followed him to a corner outside table on the terrace overlooking the quiescent midnight blue Atlantic.

Evans sat down at the table, his body facing the ocean side of the restaurant. His eyes scoured the ocean toward Dolphin Island. He smiled faintly as his eyes fixed on the lights of a large cabin cruiser no more than a mile offshore sitting between Nassau and Dolphin Island. It was too small to be an ocean liner and too large to be a pleasure craft. Unless it was the "Ruchel". Frederick Abramowitz' hundred and fifty footer manufactured just last year in the ship yards of England. Jack Evans wondered what webs the Hebrew Magician, as he was called out of his presence, was weaving. He'd find out soon, Evans thought. "The Messiah to the rescue," he murmured under his breath as he gulped down the remainder of his salty margarita.

Chapter Fifteen

The little man sat on the afterdeck of the massive cabin cruiser that was sitting idly in the Atlantic, Nassau to the South and Dolphin Island just north of the ship's position. He was playing teenage rock music on the ship's public address system, changing the CDs by hand as he grew tired of the metallic sounding music. It was Frederick Abromowitz's granddaughter's sweet sixteen party soon to be held at the Pierre's ballroom in New York. The young stewardess appeared every half hour to fill the tall glass sitting on the table in front of him with freshly squeezed orange juice.

"What do you think of the music, Joanie?" His thick accented voice caressed the words as if they were being recorded for posterity.

"Its nice, Mr. Abromowitz," the beautiful, corn haired blonde girl replied as she placed another iced glass of juice before the stocky, unsmiling questioner.

"The music gives me such a headache. How can these kids listen to this? What do you call it? Metal rockabye or something."

"I sometimes think Frank Sinatra is too loud for these old ears of mine," he continued, a wisp of a smile crossing his furrow lined face. Abramowitz still had a full head of gray-silver hair that extended from his forehead to the nape of his neck.

"I love Frank Sinatra, sir," the stewardess replied with a toothy ear to ear smile.

"Give me Mozart…Schubert…maybe even Wagner…may that Nazi bastard rot in hell…anyway, I liked his music but couldn't take the people who listened to his music."

Abromowitz lifted his head and stared out across the silent ocean, toward Nassau, toward the point of the island where the Sea Club sat majestically, on the furthest corner of the island.

The cell phone ringing brought him out of his reverie as he directed Joanie to find out when dinner would be ready. When she left the afterdeck he punched in the talk button of the cell phone. "Yes…did you get it?" He waited for a moment and then continued in a naturally hoarse, yet pleasant voice.

"I know he wants a billion dollars, Franz…Anybody can buy it for a billion dollars. But I don't buy retail…what will he take for all his stations? Yes" he paused, "the ones on the Continent also…I want everything…England…everything…Piecemeal I don't buy."

He listened patiently as the caller told his story. Frederick Abromowitz was a good listener. He learned more from listening than speaking. 'You never learn when you're talking" his sainted mother Ruchel Abromowitz admonished him when he interjected while someone else was speaking.

"Offer him five hundred…yes…million…half in stock in AMT…half in cash."

He paused to listen and then continued, "All cash is out…He has to take stock…our stock…"

Again he listened while he sipped on the tall iced glass of pulpy orange juice.

"He doesn't have the capital to finish the cable system Franz…He's just talking. If he doesn't take our offer, his companies will be in bankruptcy in a month."

"Besides," he paused again, and then continued, "If he doesn't take the offer, I'll launch a hostile take over in Luxenburg where he has his corporate headquarters. I'll steal it for less…I'll buy all the stock I can buy on the open market. Then I'll back his people out and put in my own board of directors. Tell him that, Franz."

Abromowitz clicked off the cell phone not waiting for a response from his caller. He had tired of the conversation as he so often did. Usually he either cut the caller off or went to sleep at the dinner table, depending, of course, which venue he was holding his conversation in.

Joanie returned and announced that dinner was set in the dining room located on the center deck area.

"Did you tell the Countess, Joanie?" He asked.

"She's getting dressed, sir…But she said she would be up in a minute."

Frederick raised his well muscled small frame from the chair and walked through the afterdeck to the mid section of the ship, admiring the exotic burl wood appointments that filled the walls and floors of the ship. 'Thank God I got a professional decorator to go over the 'mashuganah" choices of Marilyn,' he thought as he hand glossed over the satin wood walls of the ship. Marilyn Abromowitz was Frederick's wife of fifty years. She had taken years of decorating and art courses and she tirelessly spent enormous sums of money in buying the best art and furniture money could buy. She always over paid but that was all part of the game. Frederick bought wholesale and she compensated the world by always buying retail. And loving it. Frederick didn't mind except he hated her selections. He usually pulled out her choices of artistic beauty and replaced it with his decorator's more sophisticated selections to Marilyn's eternal chagrin. She mollified her ego by buying more useless art and placing it in areas where Frederick didn't visit or occupied for any length of time. Condos and houses all over the world…Where Frederick dropped in for a weekend and then moved on to his next part of the world. He was like a kid with ADD who couldn't get enough Ritalin to quiet his rambling urges.

The Countess was his latest acquisition. He met her in London while he was shopping in Harrod's men's shop. He loved Harrod's for their selection and ancient salesmen who knew exactly what Frederick liked to wear. He had tried the Savile Row tailoring establishments where the

Prince of Wales lingered for his clothing needs but Frederick was too impatient for the multiple fittings and tailoring. He was also intimidated by the unyielding aplomb of the clerks.

The countess was no more than forty years old but she didn't look a day over thirty. She was shopping at Harrod's for her husband's birthday gift and just happened to bump into Frederick. They quickly struck up a conversation about appropriate dress for a man going to the Queen's Garden Party, which Frederick was invited often but attended only once when he saw it was a brave showing of the tattered flag of a dying monarchy. The Countess saw in Frederick her dearly beloved departed father.

Her name was Philicia Bedminster of Surrey and she came from a long line of royalty deadbeats. She recognized Frederick as the third richest man in the world and if he continued his rapacious adventures in the entertainment/cable world he might just beat out the ancient second richest man in the world.

She found his seventy year old smile and face delightful and was totally fascinated with his frog like voice. But most of all she was surprised and genuinely entranced by his gentleness, a quality he rarely displayed.

"A penny for your thoughts," she said in a lilting voice that was almost musical in timbre.

"Ah, yes…Philicia…at least a shilling, my dear," he responded with a pleasing grin, "I've been thinking Philicia, we should pick up the plane and fly to Sicily for the weekend."

"Malcolm thinks I'm at my aunt's in Boston."

"Tell him you're going to see your uncle in Taormina."

"I don't have an uncle in Sicily, Frederick."

"How will he know, my dear. You English have relatives all over the world."

She laughed a shameless laugh that always generated an erotic urge in his loins.

"God, I'd love to make love to you," he whispered as he took her hand and kissed the back of it.

Again she laughed. They sat down at the seventeenth century oak dining room table he had recently purchased at Sotheby's. Catty-corner to each other they sat. Like teenage lovers, he brushed his knees against hers, feeling the soft skin of her leg against his knee.

"I thought you had business in Nassau, my dear," she said in her elegant clipped English accent.

"After dinner…I'm to meet my business associates at the King Neptune Hotel. Perhaps you would like to come…"

She smiled knowing that he did not want her present during his business negotiations which she apparently considered to be a duel to the death.

"I'll stay on board, darling. I have a bunch of reading I have to catch up…"

"Well, I won't be long…A few minor details to iron out."

She, of all people, knew her lover's history of combat to the death. His history was chronicled quite vividly in a book written by a ghost writer last year. The writer had left out the marks that indelibly tainted Frederick's inner soul. His driving hatred toward the "gulayim" of the world. The thugs, the murderers, the uncaring butchers of so many people. His Jewish people. He never would let up. Until he had demolished all of them. Every last one of them.

"Does your wife know we're together, Frederick darling?"

"She only claims my soul. She doesn't recognize any other women, but her, having claim over my body."

"Why not?"

"I don't ask, Philicia dear."

"You're a wonderful lover…You know that Frederick."

"Thank you, my dear. You bring out the best in me…Even at my tender age." He laughed as he reached under the table to squeeze her inner thigh.

"Malcolm considers sex a duty he has to fulfill as a marital partner…I still think he prefers little boys over me."

"That, my dear, is a misfortune." They laughed as their eyes met and locked together.

She knew of Frederick Abromowitz' violent past. From the Warsaw Ghetto he had led his mother and brother out from the devastation the Germans caused just before the end of all who had survived three years of barbaric confinement behind the massive walls of the ghetto. Through the sewer system, they followed the fifteen year old boy who had traversed the rat laden rivers flowing under the Warsaw City many times. For food. For life, he had survived though the Germans chased him and on several occasions had almost captured him. But like a greased weasel, he avoided their clutches only to disappear into the city of Catholics called Warsaw. His father had been shipped out to the labor camps the Germans propagandized to the Jewish population still alive in the Ghetto. "Arbeit macht Frei" was their theme song. 'Come with us to the summer camp of freedom' 'Work and you will be free'. Not that any Jew so selected had a choice. When you were selected, you packed your few belongings, kissed your loved ones goodbye and met down by the square of the ghetto. And then marched to the railroad depot where you were loaded onto the freight cars. Then you knew, summer camp would not be at the end of the trip. Work and you would still die. Frederick refused to accept death so passively. He led the young rebels of the ghetto to steal any kind of tool that could be used as a weapon. He learned to kill with his small bare hands. Without remorse. Without memory of who he had killed.

After the war, the young Abromowitz and his dismembered family of mother and brother escaped from the displaced persons camp in Cyprus and smuggled their way into the Palestine Mandate later called Israel. Frederick fought alongside his older brother in the Haganah after graduating from the terrorist group called the Irgun. He learned how to kill with actual tools of war, not homemade pieces of iron malfitted into weapons. Wounded in the Israeli War of Independence of 1948, Frederick Abromowitz and his family gained entry into South Africa. The little boy who survived the horrible Warsaw Ghetto finally found freedom, which, of course, allowed him to concentrate on the more important aspects of life than mere survival. Such as the acquisition of material things. He became a gold and diamond miner as he learned how to find rich deposits; then he claimed several lucrative mines with a geologist partner and soon became the youngest millionaire in Capetown.

Before long, Frederick Abromowitz ventured into the Soviet Union's illicit diamond trade and became the greatest purveyor of Russian diamonds of all. He even opened an office in Odessa, the Soviet port off the Black Sea, and smuggled the raw diamonds into Haifa and then into Antwerp for cutting and further shipment to the greatest of all consumer paradises, the USA.

Eventually, Frederick ventured into the entertainment business of Europe and purchased all the film and growing television companies he could buy. And then the cable revolution emerged with Frederick Abromowitz as the leader of the revolution. Cable after cable company fell under his ever growing umbrella of corporation captives. Then newspapers, magazines, book publishers until Frederick virtually controlled whatever was publicly sold in Europe. Control the media and you control the political power of any country. And he wanted more.

He had quietly invaded the spreading cable television companies in America and purchased many of them. Those he didn't control he had infiltrated by financial manipulation in deals of numbing complication. It was all legal and the Washington agencies, not already in his pocket, could find nothing wrong with his pyramiding cable empire. He now controlled over thirty percent of all the cable business in America. And that's where Comtel came in. They produced the entertainment but without AMT, the Abromowitz umbrella entertainment company, Comtel would only show their films in the Evans' Park basements. Without their own screen outlets, Comtel would never rise above its present position; that's why Evans was in Nassau. Without AMT's outlets, Comtel would never increase their profit margins distributing Comtel films through companies that continued to reap all the profits from theatre and cable showings of Comtel films.

Chapter Sixteen

The King Neptune Hotel was the creation of the Senator and the same power brokers that created the Inter-Island Bank of Nassau. Gambling amongst fifty thousand species of fish made for an exotic, once in a lifetime, adventure. For the plebian masses. Atlantic City with razor-tooth sharks snapping at your fingertips. The Palaces that housed the eighth wonder of the world appeared to have risen from the sea one magical night. Everyone's first visit was mind boggling because the fish seemed to course through the coral stoned hallways of the hotel. The main gambling hall was the largest free wheeling gambling hall in the world. Statuesque waitresses dressed in skimpy colorful sarongs plied the players with libations created just for King Neptune's guests. Strong, sweet and free, the drinks loosened all the inhibitions of the male player.

The various colored buildings were situated like spokes in a bicycle wheel with the giant casino hall in the middle of the wheel. Each "palace" was named after an ocean, some more luxurious than others.

Surrounding the buildings were lush, tropical palm trees and exotic flora on three sides and a multitude of intricate shaped pools on the back side leading to the white sandy beach and ocean.

Inside each palace the floors were laced with glossy marble coral floor tiles with black granite inserts that formed into painted bodies of thousands of species of sea animals.

The grand lobby of the hotel resembled a South Pacific paradise ensconced in an open aired basilica filled with giant palm trees, a massive assortment of tropical plants and jungle birds. Fountains that rose skyward to the opening in the basilica roared in timely sequence giving one the feeling that Tarzan would suddenly swing from a palm tree unto the marble floor.

The far end of the lobby, just beyond the sprawling seafood restaurant called "Neptune's Lair", floor to ceiling glass enclosed aquariums displayed a mélange of brilliantly colored species of fish and curvaceous mermaids weaving their way through the schools of fish smiling enticingly at the enthusiastic spectators joyfully lining the corridors.

In the Ronald Reagan Presidential Suite situated on the top floor of the Pacific Palace, Abromowitz faced his in house counsel who had just arrived by AMT's private jet; Evans and Lowry sat across from each other on two massive silk couches.

The suite contained seven rooms including three marbled bathrooms. The walls were adorned with early twentieth century impressionistic paintings.

The sweeping window that encased the dining room in triple paned glass allowed the guest to view the marina below, the Atlantic on the Eastern side and downtown Nassau to the south.

"I've asked Matilda and some of her closest friends to join us, Freddy," Evans declared as he sipped on a glass of Tattinger champagne.

"Frederick, Jack," Abromowitz replied in a subdued voice.

"Oh…I'm sorry…Frederick…we Americans have a habit of abbreviating first names."

"You know my counselor," Abromowitz said as he moved his hand toward the young man sitting next to him on the massive couch.

"Sure…I think we met in Geneva last month," Evans replied. "And you know our chief counsel, Robert Lowry," Evans moved his hand to his right to signify Lowry's presence.

"I have Matilda and her friends set up for later on," Evans said in a conspiratorial tone.

"Not tonight, Jack. Tonight we talk business," Abromowitz replied.

"We sent you the ten Q's and annuals for the last five years, Mr. Abromowitz," Lowry said in a voice barely above a murmur.

He seemed overwhelmed by the little compact man that sat across from him.

"Our people have looked over all your SEC filings, Mr. Lowry," Abromowitz answered.

"We're not satisfied they are as accurate as they should be," the in house counsel for Abromowitz' corporation declared in a threatening monotone.

Evans and Lowry looked over at the thin, well-dressed young man.

"If it's good enough for the SEC why shouldn't it be good enough for AMT?" Evans shot back, obviously annoyed at the young man's interference.

The phone rang. Evans picked it up and listened for a few seconds and said, "Later, Matilda…Mr. Abromowitz and I are really busy…Maybe later…Thanks," he said as he softly placed the receiver onto the telephone cradle.

"Matilda was asking about you, Frederick," Evans remarked.

"She's certainly a wonderful public relations man," Abromowitz replied. "Sorry…woman."

"Anyway, what else do you want from Comtel?" Evans asked.

"We need to look at the actual books and records, Jack," Abromowitz said in a matter of fact tone. "I don't trust the government accountants."

"We have Anderson…the best accounting firm in the U.S."

"I don't trust accountants or lawyers that don't work for me," Abromowitz replied.

"Do you have any orange juice, Jack?" Abromowitz suddenly asked.

"Sure…Alfred…call down to room service and order a pitcher of o.j. for Mr. Abromowitz." Evans paused as his long fingers adjusted the French cuffs of his shirt nervously.

"Perhaps we can get some champagne…" he added.

"No…O.J. is fine. Now where were we…Oh, yes…Jack, I like what Comtel has to offer. It's probably a great marriage. But some of the best marriages don't last. Like AOL-Time Warner. Too big and awkward. I don't need size…I need substance. We got the viewers…you have the pictures. But I can't take a chance on marrying someone with AIDS. You know what I mean, Jack?"

Evans face contorted as his upper teeth bit into his lower lip. Lowry sat stone faced waiting for a cue from Evans.

"That verdict was bullshit, Frederick…," Evans blurted.

"Not just that case, Jack…I been hearing unsettling things about Comtel. And besides, my people…Horst here," Abromowitz pointed his finger toward his young lawyer sitting by his side on the couch.

"He thinks you're cooking the books." Abromowitz paused to see Evans reaction and then continued, "Also, our financial people are afraid of the employee's stock holdings."

"We still control the stock, Mr. Abromowitz," Lowry said in a rush of words.

Abromowitz smiled as Lowry opened the door to a formally dressed waiter bringing in a large carafe of orange juice. He set it down on the glass topped coffee table in front of the four men, and poured a portion into a tall glass.

"Mr. Abromowitz," the waiter offered the o.j. to him.

Abromowitz took the glass and gulped about half of the contents of the glass.

"The best aphrodisiac in the world, gentlemen," Abromowitz said with a loud burp accompanying his words. He smiled and then said, "If your employees own more than one percent of the outstanding stock, Jack, they can block the merger. That's what my people tell me."

"Most of the employee stockholders are long time employees of Comtel. They'll listen to what we want."

"If they're still alive," Abromowitz stated quietly.

"What does that mean, Frederick?" Jack responded, his face grimaced slightly, his heart beating loudly.

"Look, Jack," Abromowitz leaned forward and extended his rough hewn hand toward Evan, "I'm not a cop…It's just that everything now happening to Comtel doesn't smell kosher. But most of all, I don't want to be part of an international scandal that I know nothing about."

"The police haven't accused anyone at Comtel."

"You own the police in Orlando, Jack. I hear the Feds might get involved. That's verboten in my book."

Evans rose quickly from his seat and walked over to the picture window facing out to the Atlantic. The seas seemed to be picking up. 'Just like my stomach,' Evans thought as he pulled a cigarette out of his case, lit up, and intensely sucked the smoke into his chest as if he was punishing himself for being alive.

"The merger of our two companies is perfect for both of us, Frederick," Evans said as he wheeled around to face Abromowitz.

"I know it is, Jack…But it still has to fit right for both of us."

"It will be. We'll do what ever has to be done to make it right. My father…The Senator…" Abromowitz rose from the couch and walked along side Evans; he put his arm around Evans shoulder.

"That's what I want to hear, Jack. The only way this marriage is going to work is if the Senator makes it happen. We got so many government agencies to hurdle. We're not going to get to the goal line if the field isn't ready for us. Understand Jack?"

Abromowitz was a fervent soccer fan. As a boy he played soccer in Europe then after the War, in Israel. His love for the game extended to his adult life. Presently, he owned a professional soccer team from Manchester, England and whenever he had the opportunity, he would be out on the field practicing with "his boys".

"The numbers are the same? The numbers we discussed last month?" Evans declared hopefully.

"I'm afraid not, Jack. The even swap is out. I'm afraid the value of Comtel has fallen too much for an even swap of stock."

Evans violently shrugged off Abromowitz' arm from his shoulders. He turned toward the little unmoving man, and with his nose almost touching the top of Abromowitz' head, he said in a raised, offensive voice.

"Nothing has changed, Frederick. Comtel is still one of the most financially stable companies in the U.S. A few set backs certainly haven't diluted the value that much. I think you're wrong. Goddamn wrong to think we're going to turn over and die for this deal!"

Abromowitz reached over to the coffee table and picked up the half filled glass of orange juice. Lowry sat on the couch, his face frozen with fear. He thought that Evans was going to rush out of the room and dump the whole deal. Stock and all. Cable systems that would never feature Comtel's productions. The word bankruptcy flashed across the front lobe of his brain.

"Two for one, Jack. Believe me…it's not me…I have a Board of Directors to answer to. And so far, they only see Comtel as a liability. As you know, we have been offered the Vivendi's Universal Studio deal also. I like Comtel's products better. But you know…I only advise AMT's board."

Evans knew that Abromowitz was lying through those large artificially capped white teeth that Frederick Abromowitz used so well. He was like a lion who was sitting down with his dinner guests that now had become the entré for the night's dinner. With Abromowitz, even a friendly merger became a hostile takeover. He never lost control over the acquired asset. Never. Control was all it was about. Without it, you might as well turn over and let your adversaries stick a spear up your ass. Although he knew even a slightly impaired Comtel was still a good acquisition for AMT, it could only be palatable if it didn't devour the assets of AMT. Debt was anathema to Abromowitz' modus operandi. He hated debt. Only when he was maneuvering his company's stock from private ownership to a public offering and then back to a private leveraged buyout had he ever considered hocking his corporation's soul for debt. Transitional debt only. Short term debt only. No more than a year and then pay off the loan sharks. He considered all creditors loan sharks. Biblically unacceptable he believed. Buying or merging with Comtel, it was going to be a debt free deal. Besides, stock swaps were tax free for the present. Of course, tax free meant tax deferred. But, as Abromowitz always theorized, you never know when that deferred tax might eventually be no tax at all. It all depended on the politicians. And he controlled many politicians. They all wanted something. He had a catalog of gifts for the power brokers. One from column A, two from column B…just like a Chinese restaurant except you don't get the won-ton soup with every offering.

"Mr. Abromowitz," the young AMT attorney said with surprising force, "you know we couldn't do any deal until we get to the original books and records of Comtel."

"I know, Horst…I know…We're just hypothesizing. We're assuming that all the records are kosher. Right, Jack?" Abromowitz smiled broadly as he resumed putting his arm around Evans' shoulders.

"Two for one won't be approved by the shareholders, Frederick. Especially the employees who hold a large share of the outstanding stock."

"Don't worry, Jack. We've examined some of your very liberal employee stockholder arrangements. Many of the shares were purchased under an option agreement, and correct me if I'm wrong, the stock reverts back to the corporation if the employees die before retirement. Am I right, Horst?"

Abromowitz turned his head to the lawyer who had risen from the couch and approached Evans and Abromowitz.

"That's what we came up with, Mr. Abromowitz. The survivor's benefits revert back to the corporation unless the employee has retired. Death before retirement. Then the benefits of the stock ownership revert back to the corporation."

Evans looked over at Lowry who seemed to shake his head in agreement.

"If we agree to a two for one deal, Mr. Evans," Lowry declared in a defensive tone, "it would substantially dilute our stock. Dramatically. A lot of our offshore arrangements would be hurt. Maybe even destroyed."

"Those offshore deals of yours are illegal, anyway," Abromowitz offered innocently belying his intimate knowledge of contract law. He knew more about the law of mergers and acquisitions than most lawyers who specialize in SEC related work. But he always propounded his ignorance of the legal tenets of "the deal" with his slight European accented voice. Adversaries were usually caught off guard by the small man with the immigrant's voice, but soon realized that the accent was camouflage for a brilliant financial and legal mind.

"They're valid deals," Lowry said in a loud voice.

"Not if they're not listed on Comtel's corporate books, Mr. Lowry," the young lawyer responded flatly.

"The accounting methods we use are approved by our auditing firm, Frederick," Evans declared.

"Not if the auditors are also your accounting firm," Horst remarked cynically. "That's an unacceptable conflict of interest, Mr. Evans."

"Gentlemen…gentlemen…," Abromowitz' deep voice echoed through the sweeping room, "lets not quibble over accounting methods. I'm sure when all is said and done the merger will be done. We all want it…and that's half the battle. Am I right, Jack?"

Evans' mind was filled with doubt, fear and death. He was approaching his sixtieth birthday and he had never thought that he would be in such an indefensible box in his later years. He loved the good things of life…art, music…great food and wine…and most of all, beautiful women. His body was strong…more like a forty year old who ran five miles each day, which he did every day. Personal trainer and all. Two hours every day, come rain or shine. Now it might all be for naught. The humiliation of failure would be too much for him to bear. Ever since he was a small boy following his father around to political meetings, celebrations and dinners, he longed for the admiration of his idolized father. If he couldn't extricate himself from this torturous box, he would just fade away on some desert island. Then he would not have to face the disappointment his father so expertly served out to him. Being on the brink of disaster was not new to him. In Vietnam, everyday was an encounter with failure, and even death. He seemed to dwell on it more than he had done in the past years. Maybe, he mused, maybe it's the years. As he got older he seemed to worry about it more and more. He hated the fear…he always ridiculed men who showed any fear during combat. Glorified fairies he would call them.

"When do you want to send your people to Orlando?" Evans asked.

"There's no rush, Jack," Abromowitz said as he gestured toward the Atlantic Ocean with his hand.

"Yes there is, Frederick. We have too much at stake to delay the merger. If it's a go, let's go. If not, we'll talk to another dance partner."

"Is next week soon enough, Jack?" Abromowitz asked.

"Just have your people make arrangements with Lowry here."

"One more thing, Jack…and it's a minor concern," Abromowitz stated as if it was really a minor concern, "What's happening to your people down in Orlando? We get reports that your older employees are dying. What is it? Somebody shipping anthrax to your headquarters?"

Evans' jaw clenched, he eyes looked past Abromowitz onto Lowry's face who was still seated on the couch. Lowry straightened his back against the couch, nervously brushed wisps of thinnish hair across his scalp, and declared with a professional tone in his voice, "We don't know what's the cause, Mr. Abromowitz. The police are investigating but all they've come up with is nothing criminal. They say it seems coincidental…so many of our older employees dying from nothing but natural causes. We have our internal security department helping the local police in trying to find a cause." He paused and looked over at Evans and then continued as if he were closing to a jury, "anyway, it has nothing to do with Comtel's operations. I'm sure we'll find it's some type of biological toxin," he paused and then continued, "the world is crazy these days."

"Well…" Abromowitz smiled as he spoke, "I don't want something to crop up and kick us in the ass just when the wedding is taking place."

Abromowitz smiled and then continued, "What about Matilda, Jack? I think I could use a little public relations about now."

Evans' face lit up. Now Abromowitz was talking his language. Showing that he was vulnerable. Showing that business would be tempered with the basic needs of men. Even seventy year old rich men like Abromowitz.

Evans laughed happily for the first time in the hour that he had been engaged in commercial foreplay with Abromowitz. He motioned toward Lowry who arose, walked to the door, spoke softly with Paulsen who was standing guard at the door and then returned. With an affirmative motion of his head, Lowry informed his boss that Matilda and her pony express riders were on their way.

Chapter Seventeen

"We should convene a grand jury, boss," Everett Lawrence softly declared to the U.S. Attorney, Henry Bartolomew. They were seated in the wood paneled office of the U.S. Attorney in the Federal Building in Orlando. It was located on the outer edge of the Orlando city center. One could view the entrance to Comtel's amusement property, The Park in the near distance.

"On what evidence, Everett?" Bartolomew dryly answered, his thick pudgy hands folded tent-like in front of his face.

"Eight deaths and I expect more coming every day, Bart."

"Besides the number of deaths, I still don't see where criminal activity is involved. And more importantly, criminal activity we should be concerned about." The U.S attorney was short, and stocky, bordering on middle-age fat; he was completely bald except for tufts of dirty blond hair growing out alongside his head. He plastered it down with a VO hair cream or something similar. He face was spotted with patches of a blonde-graying hair that made him seem that he had forgotten to shave that morning.

"Somebody's civil rights are being violated, Bart."

"Show me and I will be the first one to yell Grand Jury, Ev. We have enough work trying to find terrorists who want to blow up all of Orlando

Disneyland, as well as the rest of Florida."

Everett smiled broadly. He knew Bartolomew was a political animal and would never chance an adverse political reaction from the only man in Florida who mattered to Bartolomew. Senator Osgood Evans and company. Comtel. Bartolomew would have to witness the murders before he would act against the Senator. And even if Comtel wasn't involved, Lawrence knew Bartolomew would seek the Senator's approval before venturing forward where Comtel's name could be drawn into a potential scandal.

"Did you see the medical examiner's autopsy reports of several of the victims?" Everett persisted.

"So what?" Bartolomew gruffly replied, "some tissue findings that could have been caused by a hundred different factors…and none pointing to any criminal activity."

"I think we should at least take it up with Judge Devine…He's the senior judge…wouldn't it be his call?"

"It's my call Mr. Lawrence. Not anybody else's. We bring the case before the Court and not vice-versa." Bartolomew rapped nervously on his desk as if he were telling Everett that the conversation was over.

"Well…," Lawrence rose from his chair, smiled reflexively, and then said as he was leaving the office, "I think at least we should call in the FBI agent in charge. Maybe he can shed some light on the deaths. Y'know, Bart, if there is something going on out there, that we should be doing something about, it's gonna blow up in our faces after somebody else cries wolf. Just like September 11th. Too little, too late."

Bartolomew rose from his chair suddenly, his knee hitting the edge of his desk and said brusquely. "I'll take that chance, Everett. Just forget about things that could happen. I'm just worried about the things that are happening all around us."

"It's not because of the Senator?"

"What the hell are you talking about?" Bartolomew answered angrily, his bulbous nose turning iridescent red as he spouted the words from his quivering mouth.

"That's fucking bullshit accusing me of cowtowing to anybody."

"Okay…I'm just trying to insulate us from the criticism that the intelligence boys came under because of the September 11th thing."

"Well don't pull that bullshit in here, Everett. Nobody, but nobody tells me how to run my office. Not you…not Judge Devine…and not Senator Evans. I run my own show. Now get out of here before I lose my temper."

"You mind if I at least have Agent Smallwood poke around? Y'know, talk to the Orlando police doing the investigation?"

"Forget it…we have more important stuff to work on." Bartolomew paused and then abruptly said, "Hey…what about your investigation into that Columbian freighter…y'know the one with all that shit stuffed in its heating system."

"All wrapped up…got pleas entered into five of the defendant's cases." Lawrence's dark face glowered as he repeated his request. "I think we should at least open a file, Bart."

"What? You still playing with that? What is it? Old people dying from the air? You got nothing, Everett. And I ain't opening a can of worms until you get more than just crazy suspicions. Forget it!"

Lawrence walked out of the office into the hallway. He was more sure than ever that something was awry. Yet…he had only been an assistant U.S. Attorney for just a year or so and he certainly didn't want to jeopardize his position by going against the senior attorney's back and more importantly, ruffle the silk feathers of somebody like Senator Evans. Lawrence would deny any fear or reluctance to pursue a valid prosecution, but murder without forensic support, all circumstancial at best…and a political fall out if he was wrong. Well, that wasn't a smart move he mumbled to himself as he walked down the steps of the Federal Building to the sidewalk where Jo-Beth was going to meet him for lunch.

He smiled when he thought of her name. His mind's eyes saw her naked body prancing in front of him. Her hand beckoning toward him. Tantalizing him, and then the ensuing love making. He had never met a woman like Jo-Beth Washington. Strong-minded, witty in a raw sense of the word, yet soft as warm gummy bears when they made love.

Everett Lawrence had frequented all types of playgrounds in his thirty-five years of life. Starting on the basketball courts of Bedford-Stuyvesant, and then Sheepshead Bay, he graduated from playing with a basketball to playing with women. All kinds of women. White, black and brown women. By the time he was sixteen, his six foot four inch body was well known in New York City. He made High School All American as a sophomore at Erasmus High School and then after being recruited by over thirty colleges, he decided that the only way to achieve real success would be in the white man's world. He selected Yale University at New Haven, Connecticut, the white man's conclave that believed black was truly beautiful. And the women waited at the gymnasium doors for him after every game. His white man's facial features combined with the black sheen of his skin titilated most white college girls brought up on civil rights and being rich, white and free.

His father was a conductor on the BMT subway line that ran from Parkside Avenue to Coney Island in Brooklyn. He never missed a day of work yet was never promoted past his starting position as conductor. But Harold Lawrence wasn't angry toward the white man's system. He knew that he had made it to his highest level of achievement. But he wanted more for his boys. Both of them. Yet, only Everett survived the drive by shootings, the gangland killings, the chaos that surrounded the Lawrence world in Bedford-Stuyversant. Harold's older son was shot one day by the gangs that controlled the lawless society of Bedford-Stuyversant. He thereupon promised himself that his only surviving son, Everett, would change all that. A lawyer was what his son was going to be. Harold Lawrence knew that the only way to change the chaos, the murders, the poverty of his world, was through the law. No matter that the white police force of New York didn't give a rat's ass for the niggers of his world. That's what they were…poor niggers doomed from birth to an ignomous life and early death. But Everett would change it all; his father would preach to him almost every night before Everett went to bed.

Harold Lawrence was from Virginia. He drifted up to New York when the depression hit the hills of Virginia looking for a better life for his newly wedded wife and newborn baby. What he found was food for the table but also a lawlessness that he would never understand. A gentle man, he tried to pass on his gentleness and love for his fellow man to Everett. But he failed. Everett knew as a little boy that the gentle people were going to be eaten up by the barbarians that surrounded his world. When Harold Lawrence died just shy of fifty years old of a heart attack, the funeral parlor was filled with all the people that the kindly BMT conductor had touched during his lifetime. Everett was sixteen years-old when he died. He was so enbittered by the loss of the kindest soul he had ever known, Everett Lawrence promised himself he would never let anybody cross that line he had drawn in his mind. Trust no one and he wouldn't be the poor nigger who smiled and said thank you maam for whatever you give to me.

Everett Lawrence wanted more. Everything the white man thought he was entitled to, Everett wanted for himself. And he agreed with his father, that only through the law would he attain the kind of stature a black man could ever reach.

His mother was a seamstress at Macy's Department Store in Manhattan. She had magic fingers when it came to tailoring women's clothing. But she never wore those nice dresses she worked on for the well-to-do ladies who could afford five hundred dollars for an evening dress. She never complained. Just like her husband. They were content to be part of a society that had a place for them. Everett didn't like the place society allowed him to be in. He wanted to choose his place. Earn it by fighting for it. Whether through basketball or the law, Everett knew nothing was ever going to be given to him. Every point he scored on the basketball court was earned; every dollar he earned in the law he fought for. He learned that power came in different packages. Politics was the ultimate package. And he found Senator Evans during one of his internships in Washington during summer breaks at Yale. A black Yale student was a premium prize for any legislator in Washington. Eventually, in his senior year at Yale, he became an intern for Senator Evans' office. Then he learned what power really was, and did. The Senator was the ultimate professor of power giving and taking.

As he stood in the noonday Orlando sun, Everett wondered how far he should push the system. He was a relative stranger to the legal world of Orlando. Yet, he had always pushed to the outside of the envelope. And it had always worked. For him anyway. Either taking the last shot as the clock expired to win the game or prosecuting the powerful stock manipulator, Everett never refused to take the chance that he could lose. Big time. He had never experienced abject failure. Like the guy sitting next to him taking the bar exam. The loser would be looking around, searching for the right answer to copy. Searching for the winning answer he couldn't produce himself. Everett was different. Whatever Everett set in his mind to do, he did. Yet, here, in the sunlit microcosm of Florida's law and politics, he knew he could come out a loser. Buck the Senator and he could wind up in the backwater of the Federal legal hierarchy. Some place in Oshkosh or Salina, Kansas, someplace where the big cases were never heard. Oh sure, he thought, I could always go into private practice. There were always the opportunities that the white glove law firms afforded to the black ex-federal prosecutor. They would probably pay him $150,000 a year just for public relations. Stick him in the back law library and bring him out to show the world we don't discriminate at White, White and White.

As his mind wandered aimlessly, his eyes suddenly discovered Jo-Beth's languorous body as she glided across the street. A runner's stride, he mused. Athletic with a feline's gracefulness. He smiled as he remembered the first time he had seen her sexy walk. At Shorty's, the lounge where all the legal players wound up when the courts closed for the night. He was seated at the bar with a female associate, talking the usual shop talk, when Jo-Beth sauntered up to him and asked if he'd like to dance. Shorty's had a tiny dance floor next to an ancient jukebox where couples would move around slowly. Nothing loud or fancy. It was more like elevator music. Gave people a reason to hold each other without making a public spectacle of themselves.

Everett looked at this smiling young girl who didn't seem to care whether he said yes or no. Without a further word, he took her hand and led her out to the dance floor. No introductions, just coupling with each other. Closely. Pelvis to pelvis. Face to face. After the dance was over, they stood there, looking at each other, Jo-Beth smiling into Everett's wondering face.

They finally talked. He was surprised at her innocence but intrigued by her boldness. She had an opinion about everything. Although some of her opinions were off the wall, somehow he was surprised that her arguments supporting those off the wall opinions had some logical basis. Nothing genius, he though, but logical. Acceptable in a cock-eyed way. But then Everett Lawrence was always intrigued by reasonings offered by opinionated women. He had trouble agreeing with their arguments but often would agree with their conclusions. He wasn't a sexist. He listened to them. He tried to understand where they were coming from. Yet after the debate was over, it usually left him with a gnawing feeling that he had somehow lost his way during the discussion.

Jo-Beth was no different. Yet many of her opinions were laced with down to earth common sense. She often diffused a complicated factual scenario into an everyday solution.

"You waiting long," Jo-Beth said in a half-laughing tone as she double kissed Everett on the cheeks French style. After her first trip to Paris last year, she adapted the French cheek-to-cheek kissing welcome.

"Not long," Everett replied.

"My boss was pissed that the County Sheriff beat him to the latest "accidents" over at The Park."

"He still thinks they're accidents?"

"Until that medical examiner changes her opinion, he's still calling them accidents."

"What do you think?"

She laughed as she reached out for his hand.

"Let's go and eat. A new French place just opened down by the Square."

"My boss won't give me an opinion either," Everett said.

"Oh, I have an opinion, Ev, darling. I always have an opinion."

"So?"

"What does it matter what I think?"

"It always matters what you think, Jo-Beth darling." He laughed as he moved his hand around to her waist while brushing against her tight ass.

"They could arrest you, my big time lawyer, for fondling my buns in public."

"So I still haven't heard what you think?" he declared.

"My boss thinks it has something to do with Comtel."

"Comtel? They would have more to lose than anyone else. My God, Jo-Beth, they're losing all their experienced workers. Why the hell would they have anything to do with the deaths? It just doesn't make any sense."

"Then why don't you find out, Everett. You're the man in Orlando. Didn't you tell me you could bring down the President if that sucker doesn't watch his Ps and Qs?"

"I gotta have something to investigate." He held her hand as he waited at the corner for traffic to stop for the light.

"Besides, my boss doesn't seem to share Captain Parker's opinion that something's wrong out there at The Park."

"Sure he don't, Ev darling. He works for the man. Just like you do." She laughed as she tightened her hold on his hand.

"What's that suppose to mean, Jo-Beth?"

"You know who I mean."

"The Senator? I can't believe that any Federal Prosecutor is going to twiddle his thumbs while there is murder going on out there. Just because he is afraid of the Senator? Bullshit, Jo-Beth."

"If it wasn't Comtel involved, you would have your FBI boys swarming out there like fleas on a stray dog."

Lawrence knew she was right. He was afraid to admit to the gurgling fear that bubbled in his stomach. Frustration as much as fear. Where did he go for guidance? Not to Bartolomew…Not even to the U.S. Attorney's office in Washington.

They approached the verdant pedestrian mall that seemed to appear out of nowhere. Palm trees lined the old block walkway. Shops of all types crowded alongside the edge of the promenade. Sidewalk cafes that were dispersed amongst the shops were filled with people eating their lunch. Everett's eyes drifted skyward to the pale cobalt colored sky filled with cumulus clouds shaped like human forms. He wondered why he never took note of the sky when he was living in Bedford-Stuy. More like surviving until the next day. Was the sky ever so beautiful? Or did he fail to acknowledge its beauty because it wasn't that important to a kid worried about getting home alive from school. That same fear he knew as a growing boy now invaded his mind. Why? There are no gangs after my skin? I have the power of the Federal Government behind me. Why the hell should I be afraid of anything? Why? He knew why and the fear that he felt in the Brooklyn ghetto returned in full force. Except the danger wasn't the teenage hoodlums shouting "nigger" as he ran from the schoolyard to his tenement apartment. It was the gang politics of the Federal Government shouting after him. Leave well enough alone, he thought. 'Its not your business', his mother would always say when he ventured outside his box.

"Here we are, my great big man," Jo-Beth whispered into his ear as she led him to an outside table of a French café named "Le Petite Bistro". The waiter smiled toward Jo-Beth as he handed them menus and a wine list.

"I can't drink wine for lunch, Jo-Beth," he said with a slight chuckle.

"The French do it all the time."

"That's why they lost the war."

"Bullshit, Everett darling. If you can't think of me and my beautiful body on such a beautiful day, we might as well skip lunch."

He laughed, this time with feeling. He opened the carte de vin and selected a 1995 Medoc red.

"We both may be looking for jobs tomorrow," he said.

"Not me, darling. Captain Parker likes me drunk and silly. Then maybe he thinks he can get into my pants. But I'll never be that drunk, baby."

Everett stared at her oval face with her shiny black eyes staring back at him. When she laughed, her mouth blazed with the ivory whiteness of a comet streaking through a moonless heaven.

"Are you afraid of anything, Jo-Beth?" He asked abruptly.

For a tentative moment she paused, her thin red lips pursed tightly together. She ran her slender fingers through her short cropped hair and then replied with a smile crossing her lips, "Not any more, Everett. I used to be. When I was about five or so I lost it."

"What happened?"

"What happened? Well, it was like this. One night, all those drunken white men came and dragged my granddaddy out of the house. They just put him on top of a tree stump in our backyard. And threw that rope over the hanging branch."

"Why…why did he…"

"Because he was tired of taking their shit. Everybody told him to keep his big black mouth shut. He wasn't going to do anybody any good they said. But Granddaddy was a big son-of-a-bitch who was tired of taking all that shit. Nothing he did ever came out in his favor. Well, one day, he walked into the Sheriff's office in Altemont and told him that if those white boys ever bothered his daughter again…she was my mother, well he was going to shoot their balls right off their bodies."

"The Sheriff hung him?"

"Not himself…Maybe he was one of those white-hooded murderers. I don't know…but a couple nights later they all came…all drunk out of their skulls…flaming torches in their hands…They never found out who they were. But, I'll tell you Everett, my law abiding lover, from that night on I lost all my childish fears I had in me. There was nothing more to fear. They took my granddaddy for nothing. So why the hell should I be afraid? The most that could happen to me was that I was going to die…So what? Maybe life ain't so great. Not if you gotta give up what God gave all of us. Like my granddaddy wouldn't give up. His respect for himself. Of being a man."

"You never told me."

"There was no reason to…not until now…not until I realized that you are scared out of your cotton-picking mind to find out what happened out there."

Jo-Beth's head pointed toward The Park.

"What makes you think I'm afraid? I never said I was afraid."

She laughed loudly, her face beaming with joyous mischief.

"How long we've been sleeping together, lover boy? You think anybody I'm loving gonna escape my eyes and gut feelings. No way. When I let you get inside of me I knew you were gonna be my soul mate. What you feel, I feel. And you're feeling something terrible. A kind of fear I felt a whole lot of years ago."

Everett Lawrence had always carried a silent fear. Sort of like a great big cancer swelling up in his stomach, traveling super speed to his brain…and stayed there. He didn't know what he was afraid of. Not until now. The fear was about giving in when you had to face the devil. No one ever placed him in that position in the past. So far, he thought. Maybe now's the time he had to acknowledge the fear and battle it back. The big white man in Washington, D.C. was gonna put him to the test. The Senator from Florida…the man who had vaulted him to the almighty U.S. Attorney's office. If he shut his mouth and remained a good nigger, he was gonna be the U.S. Attorney in Florida come next presidential election. Because Senator Evans' party was going to win the White House and with that victory came the rewards of the victorious army. Yet, as he stared hypnotically into Jo-Beth's frozen face, he realized it would not be if he threw down the gauntlet at the Senator's feet. And starting an investigation into the "Comtel accidents" might just be the flame that blows the whole thing into the stratosphere. His ambitions and all. Up in yellow licking flames.

"What would you have me do, Jo-Beth?" He murmured almost inaudibly.

"Talk to my boss. He might be a southern cracker from the Panhandle but he's got a sense of right about him. And," she stopped abruptly as the white-aproned waiter stood by the side of the table awaiting their order. After they both ordered salad nicoises and bottled water, Jo-Beth continued, "greens are good for you, Everett darling."

"And what else should I do…the hell with the greens…, Jo-Beth."

"Work with the Captain. Start something. Anything…Come over to the County lab. Talk to that woman…what's her name…the foreign doctor. She'll convince you that those people falling down at The Park ain't just fainting from old age."

"Why do you think Comtel has anything to do with the so called accidents?"

"Maybe they don't…So what? At least you'll find out what's killing them. Maybe stop it."

"Would the Captain mind me bringing in a forensic engineer? Somebody that works for the FBI? And maybe an agent…Smallwood…he's a straight shooter."

"Talk to Captain Parker," she paused and then continued in a bubbling voice, "I'll tell you what…I'll set if up when I get back to the office…how's that for immediate action?"

The waiter brought over the heaping plates of salad and placed them in front of each of them. He also placed a freshly baked baquette on the table.

"My God," Jo-Beth exclaimed, "It's like being in Paris…"

Everett laughed as he reached over and held her hand in his hand. His mind still occupied with the possible dangers that lay out there if he decided to act upon his suspicions. If he found something…anything that smacked of criminal activity…he would be forced to convene a Federal Grand Jury no matter what Bartolomew or the Senator objected to.

And bringing in the FBI…Smallwood in particular…Everett had worked with him on several white-collar criminal trials and knew that he would not, in anyway, give into any political influences. Not a verbal man, but who needs another wordy lawyer by his side. Would Smallwood be intimidated by Bartolomew, and more importantly by Senator Evans? Politics were always sitting out there…like a boa constrictor ready to wrap its scaly skin around your neck and smother whatever principles and ethics you thought you had. Politics. A word rarely mentioned in the pristine U.S. Attorney's office. But everybody knew it was there. From Watergate to the Iran Contra Affair, to the corporate bullshit that was now hitting the front page of the hungry literati. It was always used for the good of somebody's political gain. And somebody always paid the price at the other end of the foul smelling stick.

As he gingerly poked at his mesculin filled plate, he remembered the words of Professor Sam Waterman, the Jewish Oliver Wendell Holmes of Rutgers Law. "Once you give in, once you let the bad guy slide by, they got you. Your balls get smaller and smaller until they disappear. And then you might as well start to dress like a woman."

Everett laughed silently, his memories of the aging mentor fresh in his mind. Fat, balding with sprouts of gray hair growing listlessly on the sides of his bowling ball of a head, his voice cracked and hoarse from the cheap Dominican Cigars he loved to chew on and occasionally smoke, Sam had been there, done it, and got burnt in the process. Ever the apostle of devil-may-care defense law, he had reaped the snake venom that the judicial system forces down the throats of those participants who dare push the rules to the outer limits. Indicted on criminal fraud charges, Waterman had barely made the morning call. But he survived, blemished and torn, he survived. And that's what it was all about, Everett mused, surviving the Huns of Hell. The rule makers who sit in judgment daring you to cross their drawn lines in the sand, and if you do, being buried in the vast wasteland you have been assigned to rot in.

"Make the arrangements, Jo-Beth," Everett declared. The sky around them had clouded up in a gray like shroud. Sheets of darkness seemed to roll in. He wondered whether it was a sign of the future. Everett knew he would know before too long.

Chapter Eighteen

Comtel owned the penthouse suite at the Fountainbleu Hotel in Miami. Between stays by visiting dignitaries and politicians, the suite was occasionally used by Paulsen who was a favorite denizen of South Beach's gay community. Jack Evans knew about Paulsen's infrequent use of the apartment but never questioned Paulsen's activities so long as he carried out Comtel's security needs.

Paulsen opened the door with a faint grin on his face. Evans and Lowry entered the suite. Lowry found a seat on the massive couch in the living room. Evans walked over to the bar and made himself a vodka martini, not offering any of the drink to his associates. It was early morning and Paulsen wondered why Evans would indulge so early in the day. Paulsen saw the heavy lines under Evan's ice-blue eyes and thought that the merger talks were surely weighing heavily on Evans.

"Who was the kid that just left, Jon?" Evans asked in a cynical voice.

"Just a friend, Jack."

"He looked like one of my kids," Evans replied, sadistically pressing Paulsen as if to vent the angry frustration welling up in his chest.

Paulsen smiled and then said, with a bit of ire in his voice, "What's up? I thought we were going to meet later this afternoon?"

Evans poured himself another martini from the decanter at the bar, swiveled the alcohol around in his mouth and then swallowed it in one gulp.

"You seem, I don't know, anxious, Jack," Paulsen remarked.

Evans walked over to the window of the living room and stared out onto the traffic building up on the A1A roadway that coursed in front of the hotel.

"It sure gets crowded early here in South Beach, Jon."

Paulsen walked up to Evans and stood by his side.

"What's up, Jack?" He reiterated.

"You know this guy Lawrence?"

"Never heard of him," Paulsen replied.

"I just got word from our people in Orlando that he's nosing around. Visiting some of our dearly departed employees' houses."

"Who is he?"

"Just the Assistant U.S. Attorney in Orlando, Jon."

"What's he after? There's nothing there to see."

"Nothing? Maybe not with the naked eye, Jon, but he's bringing out a forensic engineer, with some goddamn gadgets to detect if there's any defects in the houses."

"Like what?"

"I don't know what…"

"He won't find nothing, Jack."

"Are you sure?"

"There's nothing to find. They all died of natural causes, Jack."

Paulsen turned his head as he heard Lowry rise from the couch and walk to the bar. Lowry poured himself a double scotch and drank it hurriedly as if he didn't want anyone to see what he was doing.

"You guys are getting pretty hyped up for nothing," Paulsen remarked as he walked to the bar. The sunlight was blazing through the window covering the entire room with a yellow sheet of heat.

"We can't afford a federal investigation…especially now. Not with the merger almost completed, Jon," Evans said as he turned to face Paulsen.

"I'll look in to it, Jack."

"You have to stop it in its tracks, Jon."

Lowry poured himself another drink and again gulped it down hurriedly.

"It's kind of early for that kind of drinking, Mr. Lowry," Paulsen remarked as he roughly snatched the tumbler of scotch out of Lowry's hand.

"It's not going to work, Jack," Lowry blurted out in a confused, angry voice.

"Calm down, Alfred," Evans replied.

"It's not going to work," Lowry repeated.

"So far we're fine," Evans voice sounded weak and unsure.

Lowry moved tentatively back to the couch.

Both Evans and Paulsen watched Lowry's movements carefully. They looked over at each other as Lowry clumsily fell on the couch, their faces etched with obvious concern.

"Alfred," Evans said in a calm voice, "you have to pull yourself together."

"It's the federal…" Lowry's words stumbled out of his twitching mouth.

"The Senator will handle the federal investigation, Alfred," Evans declared.

"When will they be doing their inspections?" Paulsen asked.

"This week sometime. I got the information second hand. My father has the U.S. Attorney in his pocket...but that assistant...well, my father said he's sort of a maverick," Evans paused, walked over to Lowry and sat down on the couch alongside of him.

"But he doesn't believe anything'll become of it. He thinks he can control anybody in that office."

Lowry raised his head nervously as Evans spoke. He murmured slowly, "You can't stop a federal investigation, Jack. Not even the Senator. Once this assistant U.S. attorney starts poking around...I've been through several of them."

"And nothing ever happened, Alfred," Evans replied in an angry voice. "Nothing ever happened. Remember that and stop being such a goddamn pussy. We'll get out of it."

Lowry stared at his fingertips that were folded tent-like in his lap. He remembered the times when the Senator's power moved rivers and mountains. Literally. That's how The Park became a reality. Located on precious wetlands that was part of the water retention bed for the eastern part of Florida, the Senator induced the South Florida Water Management Commissioners to allow construction of The Park on that revered water bed in exchange for conveying an equal amount of land in the uninhabited central midriff of the State to the Water Management Board. Quid pro quo. Every one of the commissioners on the Water Management Board benefited in one way or another from their "cooperation" and voted in favor of Comtel's needs. Lowry could still feel the sweet smell of power and victory as it passed through his body. It was better than an orgasm, he thought. Lowry's need for power brought him to the Senator's inner sanctorium. A distinguished graduate of Harvard Law School, Lowry had his pick of prestigious law firms in the New York-Philadelphia legal world. But he passed it all up for the pleasure of working for the Senator's omnipotent Orlando law firm.

Lowry soon learned that the law was merely the lubricant that was used to getting things done. Nothing was impossible with the power of the Senator behind him. Now, the victories seemed light years in the past. Just exposure and denigration of whatever prestige he had built up in the fickle legal community remained. Not what his vaunted father would have wanted for him.

Lowry strived to be a writer, but his father, his all powerful father, had insisted he become a lawyer. Just like his father and his grandfather before him. Go back a hundred years and a Lowry was always before the bench and bar. Litigators all. Combatants in the wood paneled courtrooms of America. His grandfather had argued many complex issues before the U.S. Supreme Court. But Alfred Lowry was made of softer metal. Sensitive they called him as a child. He loved music and art and poetry. Confrontation with an adversary was not for him. It did not fill his heart and soul with joy. If filled him with fear. All types of fear. Most of all, fear of being found out that he was afraid, a coward, a conscientious objector. But here he was, he thought ruefully to himself, in the middle of a bloody conflagration that was surely going to burn him to a crisp. And no way out of it. Boxed in like a lion in the zoo. Caged. No place to escape to.

"If they find out how those people died, Jack." Lowry stated, his hand nervously folding his thin graying hair across the bald spot in the middle of his head.

"Look you weak-kneed asshole, those people died of natural causes. Do I make myself clear, Alfred?" Evans declared.

"I told you, I'll take care of it. Just tell me when and where the inspection will take place. That's all I need," Paulsen interjected.

"It could destroy us!" Lowry exclaimed in a near hysterical voice.

Paulsen smiled as his eyes fixed on Lowry's twitching face.

"Alfred, shut your mouth!" Evans demanded. "Jon does what needs to be done. He's a good soldier."

"He's a fucking psychopath!" Lowry shouted as he jumped up from the couch.

Paulsen strolled over to Lowry and backhanded him across the face.

Lowry fell to the ground unconscious.

"That's enough, Jon," Evans instructed.

"He's gonna be a problem, Jack. Maybe we should…"

"Leave him alone. I'll make sure he does what he is paid to do."

"It only takes one big mouth, Jack."

"I told you I'll take care of it, Jon!" Evans replied angrily.

"Okay…but you know, Jack…it's not only my ass I'm worried about…"

"He's house counsel, Jon. If he disappears now…suddenly…it's gonna look even more suspicious. Besides, if he doesn't…Well, you know…if he shoots his mouth off to the wrong people, then you will have your way. Not now."

"You're the boss, Jack."

"I'm concerned about the inspection and Lawrence. That's the black U.S. Assistant Attorney General. He's got a nationally known forensic engineer to look over the houses that they died in. It's going to happen next week."

"When next week…and where?"

"I don't know yet. It's sort of kept undercover. Lawrence, for some reason, doesn't trust his boss."

"I'll need to know when and where, Jack."

"I know…don't worry. We'll know everything by the end of the week. Bartolomew tore Lawrence apart for even doing the inspections, but if Bartolomew goes too far, Lawrence will think something's funny."

"What's the name of the engineer? Maybe I can run a check on him through my friends at the CIA."

"Bitterman. Something like that. Worked on the Princess Diana case.

You always see him on television after some plane crash."

"Can the Senator get to him?"

"Not if Lawrence has him. In fact, no one can even find where the guy is located. His own wife said he left on business yesterday and he hasn't called her since."

"I'll find him, Jack. That's what I'm good at. Finding people and then losing them," Paulsen declared with a grim smile on his face.

"Just try to scare off Lawrence. Nothing more, Jon. Understand?"

Lowry started to groan as his eyes opened. He reached for the couch to help him get up from the floor.

"You okay, Alfred," Evans asked as he reached out to grab Lowry's shoulder. Lowry shrugged Evans' arm away and slowly proceeded to climb back onto the couch. He gingerly rubbed his forehead which was reddened from the fall.

"Alfred," Evans said with a slight smile on his face, "you gotta stay with the team. Do you understand me?"

Lowry stared hatefully at Evans. For several seconds he did not respond and then suddenly he shouted, "Jack, I'm not going to stay around and watch us all wind up in jail. I didn't count on this…this…"

"What, Mr. Lowry?" Paulsen demanded as he malevolently approached Lowry on the couch. Evans put his arm out to stop Paulsen's movement toward Lowry.

"Leave him be, Jon. I'm sure Alfred knows he has to toe the mark. If not, Alfred, you won't have to worry about going to jail. Do you know what I mean, Alfred?"

Lowry suddenly rose from the couch and headed for the front door of the hotel suite.

"I need some air, Jack. Don't worry. I'll play by your rules. I don't have much choice, do I?"

"We always have choices, Alfred," Evans replied, "I hope you pick the right one." Evans walked over to Lowry and put his arm around his shoulders.

"Trust me, Alfred. After this is all over, you're going to be a very rich man. Richer than you every dreamed of. Believe me, Alfred."

Lowry's paunchy body trundled toward the front door. Evans and Paulsen watched him but both stayed unmoving allowing Lowry to leave the suite.

"He's going to be trouble, Jack."

"Maybe, but I think he's too scared to do anything stupid."

"I hope you're right, Jack. If it was up to me…"

"It's not, Jon. Besides, there's enough people out there that are more dangerous to us than Lowry. That engineer…and Lawrence. And I hear he's got a bunch of fellows sort of helping him out."

"FBI?"

"That and a couple of lawyers and some Israeli private investigator. Seems that one of the accident victims had a brother. A retired lawyer. And he brought a couple of friends in."

"I think it's maybe time to close up shop, Jack. Too many people becoming curious."

"Soon…soon…maybe next week. We're almost there, Jon…almost there."

"Get me the info, Jack. Before the inspections take place."

CHAPTER NINETEEN

Peter Anderson had married Lana Sonenberg right after they both graduated from the University of Chicago in the Spring of 1962. They had met in an accounting class which Peter had reluctantly taken to satisfy his liberal arts college requirements when they were both sophmores. Lana was a business major and accounting was one of her cornerstone courses on her way to an MBA.

After they married, Peter was called upon, in early 1963, to the National Guard and was immediately shipped to Berlin to stave off the threatened Soviet onslaught. He served eighteen months in the U.S. Army as a 1st Lieutenant in Europe rarely seeing his newly minted wife who had been hired as a trainee executive in the accounting department of a burgeoning Comtel International centered in Orlando, Florida.

After his discharge from the U.S. Army, Peter also took a job with Comtel as an assistant to the marketing vice-president. Both Andersons were rewarded with substantial and valuable stock options of the ever growing Comtel which they both took full advantage in exercising the maximum purchases of those valuable Class A voting shares.

For almost forty years Peter and Lana Anderson were faithful and dedicated workers of Comtel. They were rewarded for their good and loyal work by promotion after promotion until Peter became executive vice-president of marketing in the amusement park division while Lana became vice-president under Charlie Borden, the chief financial officer of Comtel.

In April, they had just returned from an around the world vacation. They had missed their eclectically decorated townhouse located in Comtel's Park section where Comtel had built hundreds of homes for its valued employees.

Peter and Lana were eighteen months from their allowable retirement age from Comtel. They were both looking forward, when they retired, to continue their travels around the world by staying in various world cities for long periods of time in order to get the "feel" of the natives in those selected cities.

It was Saturday in early April and the temperature had dropped precipitously below freezing that night. The Andersons had just returned from the Orlando Playhouse's production of "La Boheme", an opera they both loved dearly.

After a port wine nightcap, they languidly crawled into bed and made patient, tender love. Both of their bodies were still firm and healthy because of their strenuous, daily exercise regime they had adopted many years ago. After their sensuous lovemaking, they both decided to read before falling off to sleep. Their master bedroom was located on the second floor of their townhouse, several feet from the utility room which housed the furnace, washer, dryer, and hot water heater.

After reading for about twenty minutes, Lana told Peter that she felt a migraine coming on. Peter was now used to Lana's recent complaints about her migraines; yet he had been surprised when they started only a month ago. She had never complained of headaches in the forty years they had lived together.

In fact, Peter had succumbed to mysterious headaches himself, but they were not as frequent as Lana's and they had started only two weeks ago. He had taken several Tylenols and most of the time they had abated within the hour.

Since the weather had turned frigid within several hours, Peter has raised the heat thermostat to over 78 degrees to exorcise the chill that pervaded the second floor of the townhouse. He could hear the pounding noise of the furnace next door in the utility room as it continuously caused the dry heat to blow out from the vents in the floor of the bedroom. He usually kept a window open when the temperature was above 60 degrees to aerate the master bedroom with the fresh scent of gardenias surrounding the house.

About 3:00 a.m., Peter woke up with a start, coughing violently in successive spasms. He got out of bed, went down to the kitchen, swallowed a tablespoon of cough medicine and a half glass of water and returned to bed shortly thereafter. Lana appeared to be sleeping peacefully, her breath almost non-existent. Peter smiled at the sweet, loving face of his bride of forty years. His mind traveled back to the first time he saw her on the urban campus of the University of Chicago that wonderful spring day. She was the most beautiful girl he had ever seen in his twenty years of life. He fell in love without even speaking to her. It took another three months before she would even go out on a formal date with him. But she did, and she fell in love with the tall, gangly, straw blonde-haired Midwesterner who could never match the colors of his pants and shirt. Her natural white blond hair fell down to the middle of her tiny back, her smile as glorious as white diamonds. It had been a good forty years, Peter thought, as he reached out to touch Lana's face. Reflexively she smiled although she was still fast asleep. He suddenly thought about what life would be without her if she somehow disappeared from his life. There were no children so the world still revolved around their intimate relationship. He smiled joyfully to himself knowing that they were both healthy and with God in the heavens blessing them with long life, they would enjoy each other for many years to come. Just before he closed his eyes, Peter again peered at Lana's childlike face and then he fell asleep, warmed by her sweet smelling nearness. It was the last time Peter and Lana would ever see or feel each other again. Peter and Lana Anderson never woke up alive. Their still bodies were found the next morning by the housekeeper who arrived for her weekly cleaning of the Anderson townhouse.

Chapter Twenty

Lawrence, Ryan and Yehuda met Captain Parker and Dr. Pasha, the Orange County Medical Examiner at the Anderson townhouse that late morning after the discovery of the Anderson bodies by their housekeeper. It had rained that morning, and the frigid cold of the night before still lingered in the Orlando air.

The Anderson townhouse was surrounded by the orange ribbons of the Orlando Police Department. Two uniformed Orlando cops were stationed at the front door of the townhouse, more to keep the Orange County Sheriff out than innocent bystanders.

"I told my men to shoot that mother sucking Sheriff if he steps near the front door," Parker shouted to Lawrence as he walked into the living room of the Anderson townhouse with Ryan and Yehuda trailing behind him.

"I love the cooperation of the local cops here in sunny Orlando," Everett said to Ryan and Yehuda with a slight grin crossing his face.

"Where are the bodies, Captain?" Lawrence asked as his eyes scoured the tastefully decorated living room and formal dining room situated to its side.

"Upstairs…with the M.E. They're still warm. Got here just before that galoot of a sheriff could screw up the investigation." Captain Parker declared as he led the three men up the staircase to the second floor hallway leading into the master bedroom where the decedents' bodies were still lying in their beds. Dr. Pasha was just finishing up her physical examination of the bodies when the men walked into the room. Joshua's eyes turned to the tiny utility room as he passed it going into the bedroom.

"Doctor," Parker said as the M.E. rose from her crouched position beside the bodies on the bed, "this here is Everett Lawrence. He's a Assistant U.S. Attorney who's interested in the deaths that have happened here at The Park."

"Good morning, Doctor," Lawrence said with a bright smile, "I'm interested in how these people died." Everett then introduced Ryan and Ben Zvi to the M.E.

Pasha's dark face brightened with a hospitable smile, her pitch black eyes staring at Lawrence. She extended her hand to Lawrence, who grasped it gingerly in response. Pasha then extended her hand to Ryan and Yehuda.

"Doctor Pasha has been involved in all eight…Is it eight now, Doctor?" Parker asked.

"I think these two make it ten, Captain," she answered.

"Coincidental deaths, Doctor?" Ryan asked as he walked up to the bed to look at the immobile faces of the Andersons.

"Maybe…I don't know yet, Mr. Ryan. I don't know if the Captain told you about the tissue findings. Still…I list all the deaths as natural causes."

"Ten deaths in the same development, Doctor?" Lawrence asked in a sharp, inquisitive voice.

"It happens, Mr. Lawrence. The unseasonable cold, strep or staph, or a virus we can't discover."

"What about the oxygen depletion you found in the tissues of the victims?" Ryan asked.

"Asthmatics have the same problem, Mr. Ryan" the doctor replied. "Can't get enough oxygen into their lungs…can cause all sorts of physical problems."

"Like these two?" Ryan persisted. "They don't look like asthmatics."

The medical examiner's dark face opened up with a smile, "It's hard to determine who is asthmatic just by looking at them, Mr. Ryan."

"Could anything else cause this? What do you call it…oxygen depletion, Doctor?" Yehuda asked as he went to the doorway of the bedroom peering down the hall toward the utility room.

"Many things could."

"Like what, Doctor?" Lawrence asked in an impatient voice.

"Asthma for one, allergies to food, pollutants, a number of things. Flu, pneumonia, certain kinds of drugs."

"What kind of pollutants, Doctor?" Yehuda shouted as he walked out of the bedroom and stopped at the utility room.

"Oh, I don't know off hand…I don't usually get involved in deaths of people by pollutants," she paused momentarily and while looking after Yehuda, she continued, "gases…maybe…but what kind of gas would infiltrate into a house like this? I really don't know, gentlemen."

"Anybody check with the utility company whether there's any gas leaks in the affected peoples' houses?" Ryan asked of Parker.

"This is the first time anybody's mentioned gas leaks, to me anyway," Parker replied as he looked inquisitively into Dr. Pasha's face.

"Maybe these people were poisoned?" Lawrence proposed. "Would that cause the oxygen depletion in the lung tissue, Doctor?"

"Maybe, I don't know. I haven't studied poison and gases. It's usually not one of the causes of death in my practice."

"Ten people. What I can see from the medical reports of the other victims, Doctor, they all seem to have the same cause of death. Nothing violent listed in the reports that Captain Parker was kind enough to let me review," Lawrence declared.

"Have you explored the medicals of the Legionnaire's Disease victims, Doctor?" Ryan asked.

"No, I haven't. I read some published reports on those deaths, but I don't believe anybody has come up with a cause yet."

Captain Parker's face suddenly turned red as he said in a loud hoarse voice, "Well, Doctor, we sure better find out what's killing these people before I lose my job. I got the mayor, city counsel, and the press all on my back, every waking hour. Something is killing these people, Doctor, and we got to find out soon. Today!"

Yehuda called out from the utility room for Joshua Ryan and company to join him in that tiny space. Slowly they all proceeded toward Yehuda's anxious voice. When they arrived at the doorway of the utility room, they saw Yehuda pick up the lint trap filter from the dryer and hold it up for them to review. The filter was filled with white lint and remnants were strewn in the dryer itself. The furnace was operating full blast and seemed to suck some of the white lint pieces into the intake portion of the furnace.

"What do you think?" Yehuda asked.

"Of what, Yehuda?" Ryan replied.

"The lint. It's going into the furnace."

"So what?" Lawrence asked.

"I don't know, gentlemen. I am not a chemist or an environmental _engineer. But it couldn't be healthy for something like lint to be absorbed into a hot furnace."

Ryan's eyes washed around the six by four foot utility room noticing the vent screens and the furnace exhaust leading up into the attic.

"Something's wrong here and I can't put my finger on it, gentlemen," Ryan said.

"It looks like the same as I've seen in townhouses and apartments all over Orlando," Everett observed.

Yehuda walked around the room touching the vent leading out of the room. He peered up into the attic but couldn't see much above the opening into the attic.

"I think maybe we could use an engineer," Joshua said.

"Why an engineer, Josh?" Yehuda asked.

"Because I'm so unmechanical. I don't know what the hell I'm looking at in a utility room except that I know a dryer when I see one…a furnace, etc. etc."

Ryan walked back into the bedroom where the medical examiner was finishing up writing her notes. "Doctor, did you check the history of all the victims?"

She smiled and said, "I always do, Mr. Ryan."

"Was there anything unusual in their histories? Asthma, heavy smokers, coal dust, anything at all?"

"Some were smokers, but other than smoke scarred tissue in their lungs which didn't help them any, but, it didn't kill them either. Nothing consistent with each of them and all of them."

Ryan stared at the doctor's face hoping that she would offer a solution to the deaths. At least the common thread linking all ten deaths. His mind wrestled with the consistencies and inconsistencies of the deaths of the ten victims. A common thread. The phrase pounded inside his temples.

"Well, there's nothing more we can do," Captain Parker said as he skirted around the forensic people taking photographs of the house at the direction of Parker.

The foursome walked out the front door of the house into the sun-drenched street. The two police officers at the front of the house asked Captain Parker if they were needed any further and he told them to report back to the station.

As he stood outside of the house, Ryan muttered his thoughts out loud, "There's something here we are all missing, gentlemen. Common ground. That's what we have to find is common ground for all ten deaths." He stopped for a brief moment looking down the street and seeing an old Chevy coupe stopped along the curb, its motor running, about half a block away. There seemed to be no driver behind the wheel.

"All the decedents are over sixty, employees of Comtel, living out here in Comtel's subdivision, trusted employees of Comtel ready to retire. And they're all dead of natural causes. Where the hell are we missing something, gentlemen? There's something in the puzzle I'm missing. Healthy people just dropping like flies. Why? I just don't see it." Ryan muttered.

"Old age, I guess," Captain Parker volunteered.

"A couple of them maybe, Captain. But ten, no…just too many," Joshua replied, "in just a short space of time. No, gentlemen, something's amiss in wonderland."

The clear silent air of the development was suddenly breached by the loud crackle of a rifle shot. Captain Parker looked around as if he had been shocked by an electric prod and then his lumbering body fell backwards to the grass. The three men saw the red blotch just left of Parker's heart where the bullet had entered Parker's body.

Another shot rang out and Ryan fell to the ground with a blood curdling scream of pain emanating from his mouth. Yehuda stared down at Ryan's body lumped on top of Parker and immediately thought Ryan was dead.

Lawrence and Yehuda dropped to the grass alongside of the two inert bodies of Parker and Ryan.

Another shot rang out but it hit the grass alongside of Yehuda. Yehuda edged over to Ryan and Parker and observed that the bullet had entered Ryan's lower pelvis area and had probably gone through his body.

Yehuda crawled from the front of the house until he raised himself up behind his rented BMW at the curb. Another shot came whistling by Yehuda's head missing it by inches.

Lawrence inched his body to the front entrance of the Anderson house and then with one final leap, jumped onto the front porch into the doorway leading into the living room.

Yehuda crouched in a half bent running position and scampered around the BMW, his path crisscrossing the manicured lawns and parked cars along the curbs of the development.

As he approached the old Chevy, he saw the 30-30 shells of the rifle that had struck Parker and Ryan on the ground beside the front door of the car. As Yehuda came around the back of the car, he was suddenly slashed at by a black-hooded assailant. Barely dodging the Bowie knife thrust, Yehuda struck the assailant with the stiff side of his right hand onto the throat of the attacker. The large body of the shooter fell backwards almost falling to the ground but then he suddenly jumped up onto the balls of his feet, and violently thrust the heel of his right foot into the groin of Yehuda. Yehuda groaned in acute pain, his left hand grabbing his groin, his right hand fending off the subsequent knife slashes of the attacker. Desperately playing for time, Yehuda whirled around as he shot his left foot into the face of the assailant. Spurts of blood cascaded out of the nose area of the large man as he dropped the knife and turned to run.

Without warning, a small BMW came hurtling around the corner of the street, striking Yehuda in the back, then stopping suddenly, allowing the black-hooded assailant to climb into the back seat of the car. Instantly, it raced down the street and disappeared into the glaring setting sun.

Yehuda lay in the street, his body a wellspring of pain. But he was still alive. Climbing to his knees, he lifted himself up. Seeing Ryan and Parker's bodies in the near distance still unmoving in the grass, he limped over to where the bodies lay.

Lawrence had separated the bodies. They were lying side by side in the grass. They both looked dead except for Parker who suddenly moaned as his eyes opened up. Yehuda could see the bloody hole in Parker's shirt where the bullet had entered his chest just missing his heart.

Ryan was lifeless. Yehuda knelt down at the side of Ryan's body and felt for a pulse at the carotid artery in his neck. Feeling nothing, he started to administer CPR but stopped when he saw Ryan's left arm twitch. Within seconds Ryan's eyes blinked open several times.

Gently he lowered Ryan's head to the ground and he gingerly felt around Ryan's chest and lower body for any other bullet holes. He hurriedly pulled Ryan's pants down below his waist. "There it is," he muttered. A clean bullet hole. Just above the kidneys. The wound was bleeding unfettered and Yehuda knew Ryan would bleed to death unless it could be stopped. He pulled a handkerchief out of his pocket and stuffed it into the wound hole but the blood would not be stanched. Yehuda reached for his cell phone on his hip and dialed 911 and urgently ordered the operator to get an ambulance out to the scene.

Again he applied the blood soaked handkerchief to Ryan's wound and finally the blood flow slowed dramatically.

Lawrence ripped open Parker's shirt and they could see the bloody chest where the gunshot wound was located.

"Thank God, he's alive. The bullet missed his heart by inches." Lawrence said in a quivering voice.

"I called for help," Yehuda softly announced.

"Who did it?" Lawrence asked staring into Yehuda's ice-blue eyes.

"I don't know. We fought, but he was wearing a hood. But, I'll tell you…if I ever see him again, I'll know the bastard."

"How's Joshua?" Lawrence asked.

"He'll live. It must be the Irish in him, Mr. Lawrence."

Parker's body shuddered as if a volcano had suddenly come to life. He opened his eyes, smiled foolishly, but still was breathing with a great deal of difficulty. Lawrence took off his jacket and placed it under Parker's head.

"What now, Mr. Lawrence?" Yehuda asked as he heard the shrill sounds of the arriving ambulance coming around the corner.

"Next week I convene a Federal Grand Jury, Yehuda. Let those twenty three people find out what the hell is going on here."

Chapter Twenty-One

"Piggy...you hear me clear," the gruff voice barked over the pay phone receiver, "don't do anything but scare the shit out of them."

" I hear you, Mr. Smith," the man named Piggy replied in a southern drawl, "but my guys want to have a little fun with the pussy. We don't charge for a little fun, Mr. Smith."

"If it was up to me, I would lose them in the Everglades. But my people just want to put a scare into them. Just a fucking scare. You hear me, Piggy!"

"When are they expected to get here, at the airport." Piggy asked.

"This afternoon, about 4:00 p.m. or so. Her name is Sosie Ryan. Her father will pick her up in a black BMW convertible. It's a flight from Miami, number 232 on U.S. Air. You got that, you fat piece of shit!"

"The usual rate, Mr. Smith."

"The usual, but you and your boys better not fuck it up, Piggy or else I'll serve your filthy ass up to the niggers as barbeque pork ribs. You got me, Piggy?"

"Yes sir, Mr. Smith."

"Call me when you're finished with the job."

Jon Paulsen rammed the phone into the cradle with a loud bang and hurriedly left the phone booth.

Chapter Twenty-Two

"Ladies and gentlemen, my name is Everett Lawrence. I am an assistant U.S. Attorney for the District of Florida." Lawrence announced in a deep, no-nonsense voice which belied the warm smile that covered his face.

"You have been selected by the people of Florida and the United States to investigate a series of questionable deaths that have occurred in the last several months near and around Orlando. Our job," Lawrence pronounced as he waved his burly arms around the room encompassing all the jurors seated in the comfortable oak rimmed chairs in the panel box, "is not to indict or convict any particular person or persons for these deaths, but to ascertain whether there are suspicious circumstances that have caused these deaths. And if so, then to decide if your government should proceed to specify the particular crimes committed and the person or person who may have committed these crimes." Lawrence then stood quietly before the twenty-three immobile listeners who seemed anxious for Lawrence to continue.

"The prosecution will present witnesses and materials to you and although the presentation may not be admissible as evidence in a petit jury trial against any particular defendant, it can be used here for your consideration. One further observation. Many of you may have either been jurors in a criminal trial of a specific defendant or have seen criminal jury trials on television. Well, here you will not see or hear from a defendant or his or her lawyer. It is definitely a one-sided hearing and for a good purpose. We are all detectives…you and I…in an attempt to discover whether there is any criminal wrongdoing that should be further investigated by the federal government." He paused and stood solidly before the panel of concentrated listeners, his muscular legs astride, his shirt sleeved arms on his hips, his face and body ready for anything.

"As you have been previously instructed by the court clerk, you will be meeting here…with me or my assistants…every Wednesday for at least six months. And maybe longer. It all depends on what we find out. What all of us find out." Again, Lawrence waved his arms encircling the group into his bosom.

"If you have any questions after any of our sessions, please call my office or you can contact Agent Fred Smallwood," Lawrence pointed toward Smallwood seated at the wooden counsel table in the middle of the jury room, "who will pass on the question and answer…if it can be answered that is. But, let me say this…You," Lawrence pointed his finger toward the panel, "You and me and my staff are working together, as a team. Every one of you are essential to that team and hopefully it will result in the discovery of rational answers to the questions arising out of this investigation." Lawrence again paused and smiled effervescently and then continued in a hospitable voice, "Are there any questions, ladies and gentlemen? Anything at all? Remember nothing is to irrelevant not to question…nothing. Oh," he paused and then continued, "I will have two legal assistants at counsel table during this investigation. Their names are Samuel Waterman and Joshua Ryan, both experienced trial lawyers."

After several questions were put forth by the panelists concerning scheduling, emergencies and other personal items, the jurors left the room seemingly anxious to commence their quest for answers.

Chapter Twenty-Three

She could only secure a seat on the Concorde to Washington, D.C. and then a connecting flight to Miami and finally a puddle jumper to Orlando. Sosie Ben Zvi-Ryan looked harried as she fell into the arms of her father, Yehuda, at the Orlando International Airport late that afternoon.

Her eyes were rimmed with a dull redness that evidenced the sadness and hysteria that had filled her body the past thirty-six hours.

It was the middle of the night in Paris when Yehuda had called Sosie and Zeppi at the Ryan apartment a day and a half ago. Zeppi was asleep in the master bedroom as Sosie picked up the phone near her side of the king-sized bed nestled in the high ceiling, darkened room. Only when Zeppi heard her daughter release a brief shrill scream did she awake from her slumber. Zeppi thought, at first, she was back in Jerusalem and that a bomb had been exploded in or near their house. Looking around in the dark room, totally bewildered, her mind and eyes finally cleared to see Sosie clutching the receiver of the phone as if she were going to choke it into silence. As suddenly as she had freaked out, Sosie's voice became only a whisper as she stuttered several questions and answers to the caller's message.

"Yes…Poppa. I'll call. Air France? Who? Pierre Lamoyne? I think the main office is closed now. But when they open I will contact him." She paused momentarily, her voice catching tearfully in her throat, her hand pulling the top of her cotton nightgown to her eyes, wiping away the tears that fell unfettered down her olive skinned face. Zeppi stood by her, handed her a tissue, Sosie ignoring her, Zeppi then gently wiping her daughter's anguished face with the tissue.

"Why didn't you call earlier, Poppa? When it happened? I could have been there when he woke up." She paused again to listen to the controlled soft low voice of Yehuda as he explained that Joshua had been in intensive care for thirty-six hours and had just recently come out of it and that he didn't want to tell Sosie anything until he learned if Joshua was going to be all right. Or die. Yehuda knew, unfortunately, how to convey notices of death to loved ones. He had done it when his oldest child, Benjamin, had been executed by the Hamas almost five years ago. An experience Yehuda wished he had never learned.

"Can he talk to me?" Sosie asked in a hopeful and childlike voice.

"Okay. Tell him I love him. And?" Her voice dried up and cracked, "you tell him Poppa, if he dies before we say goodbye I'll never forgive him. You tell that crazy husband of mine. Okay Poppa. I love you too. Yes, Momma is here. I'll put her on. Yes. Go with God, Poppa. I'm glad you're safe. I love you Poppa." Sosie handed the phone to Zeppi, whose eyes were already clouded with tears that rolled down her distraught face onto her neck. Sosie uttered a tiny laugh as she saw the tearful face of her mother. Funny, she thought, how the women in this family cried so easily…like a gusher of ocean water rushing into the sand.

"Yehuda," Zeppi's voice was high-pitched and pierced the darkness of the night, "you're all right? Yes, I got the news about Joshua. He's alive. God be thanked. But you…you're an old man. What are you doing in shootouts in the Wild West? 'Vilder hyas'. I'll stay here. Yes, with Sammy. But you better stay alive until I see you. No more shootouts at the A K Corral. Okay. O K Corral. You know what I mean." She paused and finally brushed the tears from her face with the tear soaked tissue, Sosie taking it away from her and handing her a dry one. "I love you too, Yehuda. Yes forever. And give my crazy son-in-law a kiss on the cheek. No…maybe on the lips. Tell him I love him too. Go with God, my love. Until we meet again," and she reluctantly hung the receiver onto the phone trestle and sat down on the edge of the bed next to Sosie and hugged her daughter to her ample bosom, both of them crying, Zeppi caressing Sosie's head with her hands, no words being said.

The Orlando late afternoon sun beat furiously down on their heads as Yehuda pulled the BMW convertible from the curb of the airport. Sosie was seated in the passenger seat waiting for Yehuda to speak. Her head was surprisingly clear. She wore no make-up but her face still appeared fresh and unwrinkled. Except for the crow like tentacles under her chocolate brown eyes.

"He's eating already," Yehuda finally said. "That husband of yours has quite an appetite." Yehuda laughed and Sosie laughed also, more of a released breath than a laugh.

"Was it worth it, Poppa?" She asked mournfully.

"Who knows, my love? Who knows? That you'll have to ask Joshua. But I'll tell you…we're closer to the answer. I think we are. Anyway, somebody's finally doing something. They convened a grand jury. It's like an Inquisition but not, luckily, against the Jews. They call it a Federal Grand Jury. And Joshua and Sam are part of it. That's if Joshua ever pulls himself away from all the gourmet food Sam brings to hospital."

Yehuda paused and then laughed and then he continued, "He's probably going to look like Sam's twin if Joshua doesn't stop eating the food."

"What happened, Poppa?"

Yehuda drove onto the right lane parkway toward the Orlando central district where the Orlando General Hospital was located.

"We were visiting a house where two of the latest victims had died. Then suddenly somebody opens up with a 30-30 rifle."

"And you?"

"Just missed me, hit the captain instead. But I got hold of him, the shooter. Unfortunately his henchman came around and got me in the back with the car. Nothing permanent. Then they drove away."

"Just bruises? That's all you have? Just bruises?"

Yehuda's craggy, desert colored face lit up with a blazing smile, his clear eyes filled with laughter, "You're worried about me, my loving daughter?

Me? Well this body has taken worse "kanocks". Believe you me. A bruise here…maybe…nothing permanent. Bullets are more long lasting."

"You and Joshua are like a couple of kids in a sandbox, Poppa. There are people out there who mean business. Serious business."

"We know, Sosie. But…we'll find out what's going on…and then it'll be over."

"It's never over, Poppa."

"Here anyway, Sosie. Let's not talk about it anymore. Enjoy the Florida sunshine. Keep a smile on the beautiful face of yours for Joshua. He really missed you, Sosie."

The BMW convertible moved into the fast passing lane. Yehuda maneuvered the sleek black car onto the ramp leading to Route 4. Traffic was light except Yehuda noticed a battered rusty brown minivan weaving in and out of traffic following his car several yards behind.

Sosie's long blonde sun streaked hair caught in the warm air passing over the convertible and blew backwards like strands of silk ribbons caught in the back draft of a giant fan. She closed her eyes briefly, her thoughts meandering aimlessly from little Sammy in Paris to her wounded lover a few miles away in some strange hospital bed. 'Will it ever end?' She thought wistfully.

Suddenly the battered minivan pulled around several cars that were behind the BMW. Yehuda's eyes caught a glimpse of the purposeful movements of the van through his rear view mirror. The sharp rays of the intense afternoon sun blocked out his vision of the progress of the van momentarily. Yehuda noticed that the three lane highway merged into two lanes as he approached the palmetto rimmed stretch of the highway. Just palm trees and swamp land bordered on the asphalt pavement. The cars that had been behind him had suddenly disappeared. Except for the rusty brown minivan that appeared to suddenly speed up behind the BMW.

Yehuda tromped on the accelerator propelling the BMW instantaneously forward. Sosie awoke from her brief reverie and peered over at her father, whose eyes seemed to be glued to the rear view mirror.

"Poppa," she muttered. Yehuda pointed to the rear view mirror.

"Somebody's interested in where we're going."

Sosie wheeled her head around immediately noting the fast approaching minivan.

"Who are they?" She asked with a note of fear and surprise in her voice.

"Maybe nobody…maybe some bad people. We'll know in a few minutes."

The van was no more than two car lengths behind the BMW when Yehuda slowly pulled over to the side of the road and stopped his vehicle. He promptly punched in some numbers on the car phone situated on the dashboard and murmured inaudibly into the speaker located on the visor of the car. The afternoon sun seemed to hide behind a covey of gray clouds ominously darkening the roadway.

"Yes…Mr. Lawrence," Yehuda raised his voice as he noticed the van pulling onto the side of the road in front of the BMW.

"I wish I knew where I was. Just on Route 4. Probably three miles or so from the hotel. Yes…wait a second. Four men just got out of the van and I think they want to talk, or something because they are heading back here. Sosie's with me. Yes, my daughter. Okay, hopefully you'll bring in the troops before we disappear into your lovely swamps."

The four men walked nonchalantly on the traveled portion of the roadway toward Yehuda and Sosie. The leader's face was covered with a dark scrawny scrub like beard that was unevenly hanging from his fat, deeply lined face. His body was a block of muscle and fat as he waddled toward the BMW. The other three men were also unshaven, their bodies not quite as large as the leader of the pack.

As the leader espied Sosie, his mouth widened into a sneering smile that showed several missing front teeth highlighting the rest of an irregular row of brown teeth. His massive hairy head turned to his three followers and Yehuda could hear a loud chorus of bawdy laughter emanating from the approaching group.

Yehuda rose from the front driver's seat onto the pavement. Sosie also exited the car, both of them walking to the front of the BMW.

The menacing foursome stopped about five feet from where Yehuda and Sosie were standing, Yehuda and Sosie spread their legs apart, their eyes staring unwaveringly into the grinning faces of the approaching group.

"Hi folks," the leader spoke, his deep cracker accent making his words almost incomprehensible.

"How can we help you fellas," Yehuda replied, the smile on his face widening as he spoke.

"Nice young lady you have there, Mister," the fat man said in a leering voice.

"What can we do for you?" Yehuda repeated, his back straightening into a galvanized rod of steel. Sosie walked a few steps to the side of the group, her hands placed in front of her body.

"Just want to meet the young woman, Mister. Just being sociable. We're sort of like a Welcome Wagon in the Orlando area. Friendly like, you know what I mean?"

"Well," Yehuda's deep voice bellowed menacingly, "I think you fellows should get back into your car and help someone who really needs your help."

"That would be unfriendly like, Mister," one of the threesome standing close to Sosie said in a phlemy voice, his bloodshot eyes undressing Sosie's summery outfit. His hand reached out to touch Sosie's chest. Sosie stepped to the side of the man's hand and completed an inside-outside block with her left arm. Almost instantaneously, her left foot side kicked him just above his right knee, the knee sounding like it had been cracked with a hammer. As the man's head and hand dropped to the injured knee, Sosie's body whirled around into a long, back spinning kick to the right side of the face with her right foot. The man crumbled to the pavement, his body curled up into a screaming fetal ball.

The other three men immediately rushed Yehuda and Sosie. Yehuda's closed fist, acting like a scimitar, crushed the flat nose of the leader, blood gushing out of his face onto Yehuda's shirt. Sosie's right foot shot out into the genitalia area of another attacker; then, as he crumbled forward, her right knee swung upwards into his descending chin making his body fall backwards onto the asphalt.

The remaining attacker grabbed Sosie from the back as he pointed a 9 mm Glock at her head. She could feel the spit from his mouth dribbling onto her neck, as his evil smelling mouth bit into her neck.

"Back!" He yelled to Yehuda who approached the assailant cautiously. The attacker pushed the gun into Sosie's ear, his other arm around her neck in a locking movement forcing her to gasp for air.

"Don't hurt her," Yehuda pleaded. "I'll give you whatever you want. Take me instead."

"You ain't as much fun as this fucking cunt." The attacker laughed lustfully as he dragged Sosie back toward the van. His three cohorts were still writhing in pain on the ground.

"What do you want?" Yehuda said as he slowly stepped forward.

"Just a piece of ass, old man." The seedy assailant guffawed as if the whole incident was just plain fun to him.

As the man approached the van's side door, he turned his head momentarily to open the door. Sosie drove her right elbow into his fat gut, stepped violently onto his sneakered foot, whirled around as he released her neck and drove the palm of her hand upward into his adam's apple causing him to gasp for air as he tried to grab her hair. She buried her knuckled right fist into the right side of his head just above the eardrum, his head snapping back like a bent twig in a torrential storm. The Glock fell to the ground alongside his body, his hands grasping at the side of his head in a vain attempt to stem the pain and blood gushing out of his ear.

Yehuda grinned proudly as he strode up to Sosie and crushed her lithe body to his chest.

"You haven't forgotten much, my darling daughter."

"I didn't think I would have to fight my way out of Orlando, Poppa."

"There are 'gulayim' all over the world, Sosie. Its good you know how to defend yourself."

She smiled wainly, her hand straightening her hair against her head. Her eyes stared down onto the writhing bodies surrounding them.

"God forbid you should stay here much longer, Poppa. We'll have all these people trying to kill us."

"Evil is everywhere, Sosie. We must be aware."

"I should never have sent my husband with you, Poppa."

"Me!" Yehuda bellowed, his hands covering his heart. "I'm just an innocent old man in this land of Babel, my daughter. Where ever your husband goes, trouble follows him. I should stay at home if I ever want to get past my retirement."

Two Orlando police cars, sirens and emergency lights blaring, crossed the median strip dividing the highway. As soon as the cars pulled up in front of the van, Yehuda saw Lawrence, Jo-Beth Washington and three Orlando policemen rush out of the two vehicles toward them. The policemen had their guns leveled at the four fallen men who were trying to rise from the pavement.

"Sorry, we couldn't wait for you, Mr. Lawrence," Yehuda said with a mischievous grin crossing his face.

"I see, Mr. Ben Zvi," Lawrence replied as he walked around the now rising foursome.

"I guess this young lady is your daughter," Lawrence continued, his hand outstretched toward Sosie.

"Yes, and I presume you are Everett Lawrence," Sosie replied, grasping Lawrence's hand warmly.

"I'm sorry we couldn't provide you with a more hospitable welcoming committee, Mrs. Ryan," Lawrence said as Jo-Beth walked up behind him.

She smiled ebulliently, her eyes twinkling with awe as she approached Sosie.

"I'm Jo-Beth Washington, Mrs. Ryan," Jo-Beth stood face to face next to Sosie as she spoke. "My boss is in the hospital with your husband. He's the officer running this investigation. Unfortunately your husband and my boss got in the way of a couple of rifle bullets."

"Have you seen my husband?"

"This morning, Mrs. Ryan," Lawrence answered. "He's fine. He should be out of the hospital today. He was lucky."

"He would have been luckier staying in Paris, Mr. Lawrence." Sosie said with a pouty look on her face.

"Sam Waterman is the pied piper of all of us," Lawrence replied.

The three police officers handcuffed the four assailants and placed them in the two police cars. Lawrence's eyes followed the limping foursome as they were led to the police cars.

"Nice handywork."

"My daughter was trained by the Israeli paratroopers. That's before she became a wife and mother," Yehuda replied with a broad, proud smile on his face.

"I should stay a wife and mother, Poppa."

Lawrence laughed as he turned to Jo-Beth.

"Jo-Beth here has trained with the Orlando police's elite riot squad. We try not to provoke her or else she wreaks havoc on anybody disturbing her."

"Don't listen to him, folks," Jo-Beth interjected. "But, I think we're going to have to ride back with you since we didn't figure you were going to take out half the criminals in Orlando."

Jo-Beth eyed the young Israeli girl named Sosie, noticing the bronze sculptured face, the tousled blond streaked hair running down past her shoulders. The only Jews Jo-Beth ever knew as a child in Altamonte, Georgia, were the very religious Jews she saw in Atlanta when her father would take her into the big city during the Christmas holidays. Clothed in long black robes, their hair coming down over their ears, skull caps attached to the middle of their heads, Jo-Beth thought they were people from another planet. Now, as she peered at Sosie and her father, Jo-Beth wondered where these Jews came from. They were different looking Jews; their bodies were solid and they held themselves out with pride and confidence. In fact, when she was growing up, Jo-Beth was told by her Auntie Clara, that Jews were bad people. They were thieves and bloodsuckers and they were the killers of Christ. "Don't trust them", Auntie Clara would preach. "They're gonna hurt you if you don't watch out for them," she would say as she prepared the cooking in her house. Jo-Beth grew up with the same infernal prejudices all people grow up with; black against white, Christian against Jew, Muslim against the "infidel", anybody different from you, you had to distrust and watch with suspicious eyes.

But Jo-Beth moved to Orlando when she graduated from high school to attend business school. She met Jews; some she liked, some she didn't. But that was the same way she felt about colored people, or "African-Americans as the politically correct people call us," she thought. 'Skin color and religion sure got in the way of people being friends', she mused. In fact, her last year of college, she roomed with a Jewish girl from Atlanta. After a few weeks, they both forgot that their skin color was different. They studied together, double dated, and generally hung out with each other most every day of that year. The roommate moved back to Atlanta after graduation, got married to a nice Jewish accountant, and had two kids already. But Jo-Beth and her roomy still met for dinner sporadically, dished the dirt about all their former schoolmates, and never thought about how different their skin color or religion was.

As Lawrence and Jo-Beth climbed into the small back seat of the BMW convertible, Sosie offered to switch seats with Lawrence. He gladly accepted the invitation as they exchanged seats. Sosie lodged herself in the back seat. She smiled into Jo-Beth's radiant brown skinned face. Sosie's experience with people of color were more or less confined to her relations with her Arab neighbors in Jerusalem and Tel Aviv. Most were transient workers from the villages in East Jerusalem and the West Bank, their skin deeply darkened by the bright Israeli sun, their eyes full of hatred for the so-called Israeli "occupiers". Yet, Sosie had shared many exciting moments with Arab college students that she met and even lived with during her four years at Tel Aviv University. Of course, the joy of their friendships were always interrupted by the moronic bombings carried out by the insane fringe of Arab discontents. During the Israeli reprisals her Arab friends would hibernate and if sporadically seen by Sosie, would refuse to acknowledge any sign of friendship. Then the hysteria would cease and again she would have the friendship of those Arab friends. And they would carry on as if nothing had interrupted their relationship. Yet the next altercation would bring out renewed estrangement. Until Sosie decided that the stuttering friendship relations were not worth the trouble of continuing on with them.

Upon return to Jerusalem after graduation, Sosie lived in a top floor apartment with two girlfriends who worked for the Mossad along with Sosie. The apartment overlooked an Arab village within the confines of East Jerusalem. At night, Sosie would stand on the balcony of her apartment peering over into the village. The village had no indoor plumbing of any kind. There was a well where the villagers lined up to get their daily supply of water. A trench ran through the village that was used to deposit the villagers' excrement and other waste materials. On windy days, the stench of the waste would rise up from the village to the civilized mountain of Israeli daily life. Her apartment windows would have to be shuttered to prevent the egregious smell from invading the perfumed air of the apartment. Sosie wondered how those little black children that inhabited the village ever survived past their teens. But obviously some did. They were the same undernourished teens who blew themselves up in the middle of Jerusalem along with the well-nourished unaware Israeli passerbys.

"You're the first Israelis I have ever met," Jo-Beth declared, her white toothed smile highlighting her handsome face.

"Except in Paris," she continued.

"Yes, I think I met a couple in Paris. In the Louvre, I think."

Sosie smiled and said in a soft amicable voice, "We're all over, Jo-Beth. Even here in America."

"I know," Jo-Beth replied as if she had been misunderstood, "there are plenty of Israelis in Orlando, but they're Americans now. Its really hard to tell they were Israelis at one time."

"Once an Israeli, always an Israeli," Yehuda chimed in from the front driver's seat of the BMW.

"I lived in a kibbutz when I was an exchange student many years ago," Lawrence stated as all eyes of his fellow passengers sharply shifted to him.

"I never pictured you in a kibbutz," Jo-Beth said.

"Near the Lebanese border. We had to dodge Hezbollah rockets twice a day. Thank God they had a schedule or else it would have been hell for me trying to pick those grapes."

Jo-Beth laughed and reached over to lovingly touch Lawrence's shoulder.

"I never pictured you picking grapes, Everett," she said with a humorous catch in her voice.

"I've done a lot of things I never told you about, Jo-Beth, darling."

"I bet," she replied.

"Too bad you didn't stay in the kibbutz, Mr. Lawrence," Yehuda declared as he wheeled the BMW onto International Drive going south toward The Park. "We could probably use a good grape picker more than a lawyer."

"I sometimes thought of that, Yehuda. I was as happy as a grape picker. I've never really been happy as a lawyer."

"You'd have never met me, Everett darling, if you'd have stayed a grape picker in Israel," Jo-Beth said with a throaty chuckle coloring her voice.

"We'd have still met, Jo-Beth…somewhere…somehow," Lawrence replied, reaching over the front seat, tenderly touching Jo-Beth's hand.

"I met Joshua in Israel," Sosie said in a quiet undertone.

"The rabbi's case," Lawrence said.

"Yes, Joshua was chasing his own client," Yehuda declared.

"I was surprised when he left the practice. Especially after such a celebrated victory," Lawrence offered.

"Joshua thinks that justice should be meted out to the righteous," Sosie said, her mind suddenly filled with the face of Joshua.

"Sometimes it is," Lawrence said.

"He didn't think so," Sosie paused and then continued, "so he left. When it stopped being a game he told me. When real people suffered real pain and they shouldn't have," she paused and then continued again, "Well, that's my Joshua. Sometimes I think for such a hard bitten lawyer, he's like a little child. He just wants the world to be perfect. And," tears filled her eyes as she continued, "it never is…and he's the one who always seems to get hurt."

"You married an idealist, my darling daughter. Hard to believe a lawyer with ideas of right and wrong," Yehuda stated with a wide grin crossing his face.

The car sped along busy International Drive until it entered a relatively quiet and verdant stretch of a multi-laned boulevard. Glass enclosed buildings surrounded by manicured lawns and shrubbery stood majestically on the sides of the boulevard.

"We're going to the hospital, folks." Yehuda announced.

"I'll contact my office to pick us up there," Lawrence replied.

"What happens now?" Sosie asked.

"The grand jury hearing will continue Monday. I'm hoping Joshua and Sam are available," Lawrence said.

"Do you think your jury will come up with any answers?" Yehuda asked.

"Maybe…we have a forensic engineer. Bitterman is his name. Maybe he'll come up with some answers." Lawrence said as he espied the entrance to Orange County General Hospital looming in the near distance.

"Have the killings stopped?" Sosie asked of Lawrence.

"It might be the end of the deaths, or they may start again next week…next month. Until we find out if they are killings. I mean deaths caused by means other than natural causes. We are just piddling in the dark right now."

Yehuda pulled the car under the canopy of the entrance to the hospital. Lawrence exited the car, holding the door open for Jo-Beth and Sosie allowing them to exit from the back seat.

"Mr. Lawrence and Jo-Beth," Sosie announced as she held her hand out to Lawrence and Jo-Beth, "I'm going up to see my husband. I'm going to tell you now… I'm going to try my darndest to convince him that retirement from the pursuit of justice was the right option. I know he won't listen, because half of him is pig-headed Irish. But I'm sure going to try. If you'll excuse me," she said as she turned and strode into the hospital lobby.

Yehuda smiled a knowing smile and then remarked, "That's my daughter. She's had enough of people she's cared for dying before their time. Anyway," he paused as he walked around the car to where Lawrence and Jo-Beth were standing, "you can take this car if you want."

"No, I called my office. They will send a car to pick us up," Lawrence said.

"I'd like to meet Joshua and the Captain if they are out of the hospital tomorrow at the hotel. It's Sunday and I thought we could go over a plan of action to present to the grand jury. Do you think you could arrange that, Yehuda?"

"That's my job Mr. Lawrence. I'm the best arranger in Jerusalem. Tomorrow at the Renaissance Hotel. Let's say noon. Maybe over breakfast?"

"Tomorrow then. Give my best to Joshua and the Captain, if he's up and about. Be careful Yehuda."

"Au revoir, mon amis," Yehuda said as he leaned over and kissed Jo-Beth on both cheeks.

"How come you're not more French, Everett," Jo-Beth declared as she responded to Yehuda's kissing farewell by kissing Yehuda on both cheeks.

Yehuda left Lawrence and Jo-Beth, a bright smile on his face as he observed the dumb founded look on Lawrence's face at Jo-Beth's admonitions.

"Ah, the French," Yehuda muttered to himself as he entered the lobby of the hotel on his way to Joshua's room.

Chapter Twenty-Four

They lay next to each other in the hotel room, their bodies naked and facing upright, their hands, arms and feet barely touching each other.

Joshua still had a large swab of gauze covering his shotgun wound on his right side. The room was frigid from the air conditioning unit pouring waves of cold air from the ceiling vent onto the bed and their bodies.

"I'm afraid to even touch you," Sosie whispered as she turned toward Joshua.

He laughed a hoarse laugh, his voice crackling out of his parched throat.

"If you don't touch me, I might as well bleed to death anyway. The bullet didn't damage any part of my sexual equipment; just went right through my body into a tree."

Sosie laughed a fearful laugh, more to satisfy Joshua's yearning for affection than his vain attempt at humor.

"What are you doing running after cowboys? I thought you wanted only peace and quiet in your retirement, Joshua?"

"You know you didn't have to come. Your father would have told you

I was fine." He paused as he turned to reach over and gingerly touched her full rounded breast with his fingertips.

"Your fingers are so cold." She said with a childish giggle.

"That's because my blood has rushed to the lower part of my body."

"Did the doctor say we could?"

"He didn't say we couldn't."

"But so soon after."

"It's therapeutic, Sosie. It's better than penicillin."

"I don't think that we should take that chance, Joshua. You've already taken too many chances. To think that Samara could have been a fatherless child if that bullet would have hit you a little lower or higher for that matter."

He raised himself up onto his left elbow, his body moving closer to Sosie, almost touching her chest and hips.

"You know when I woke up in the hospital, my first thoughts were that I would never see you again. I thought I was dead." He raised his hand from her chest to her face, wiping the tears that rolled down from her eyes onto her high cheek bones.

"You didn't have to come to Orlando, Joshua."

"I did. You know I had to come. Sam is my friend. One of my only friends. You would have done the same thing, my love. And so would your father."

"I love you, Joshua. You know that."

"And I love you, Sosie. With everything I have. I love you more than my life. And that's why nobody can kill me. Not before we have had at least fifty years together."

"No more after this, Joshua. You promise me. After this silly game is over with, we go back to Paris. To your retirement. Am I correct?"

"Do you know the only part of me that wasn't in a coma, Sosie?" Joshua asked as he wrapped his bare leg around her leg.

"I don't want to know, Joshua." She replied laughingly. Her hand brushed over the unbandaged part of his taut muscled stomach.

"It's been over a week, Sosie."

"For what?"

He nuzzled his face onto her breasts, his hand brushing gently against her inner thigh.

"How do we do this without the wound opening up, my love," she said.

"Gently, my lovely."

Raising himself onto his arms, then pulling his body over Sosie, he lay on top of her as if all is energy had been expended into the series of movements.

"Now what?" She said as she wrapped her arms around his back, feeling the hardness of Joshua penetrate into her.

"Whatever comes naturally, my love. Whatever comes naturally," he replied as Sosie wrapped her supple legs around his thighs, the lovemaking erasing all the anguish and pain of the last few days of Joshua's mind and body.

Exhausted, they both laid there, Sosie's eyes hypnotized by the whirring Casablanca fan circling over the bed. She stroked the wet mane of hair tumbling down from Joshua's head as he nestled on her chest and neck.

Sosie closed her eyes, her mind racing back through the years and her previous lovers. To Elizea, her first love, killed so many years ago, Sosie remembering the passion and love shared between them. Other faces and bodies after that excruciating loss, just to forget the aching pain and sorrow that filled her mind and body. Until Joshua came along. The innocent lamb amongst the lions of the Middle East. How could he survive with his noble ideas of right and wrong. Justice among men. Screwball ideas that she knew would never bear any fruit.

The first time her eyes saw him, sitting across her parents' dining room table in their house in Jerusalem, she knew that he was different. Perhaps like the young David foolishly thinking that he could overcome the giant Goliath with a sling shot. His battered but handsome face surrounded by chestnut brown hair, his bedroom brown eyes staring quizzically at her. What was he thinking when their eyes locked over that dining room table? Chasing after a man that didn't want to be caught. His client. A rabbi accused of killing his wife. Or did his mind focus on her eyes, feeling the same wave of passion and excitement she felt. She remembered his shy reluctant smile that illuminated his entire face, ridges forming around his wide mouth and wrinkling his broken nose. A beauty he wasn't, she reminisced. But there was something that emanated from his eyes, something that reminded her of a child eyeing a wondrous new thing that had suddenly come into his life. The rough hewn skinned face lost its hardness and became tranquil, full of wonderment. When does a man lose his innocence, the boy transformed into the suspicious non-believing man? When did you change, my love, she wondered as he lifted his perspiring head to kiss her fully on the lips. Gently their tongues touched, her body trembling with a sudden wave of shivers.

Joshua rolled off her body, his face grimacing from the sudden wave of pain surging up from his wound to his head. They lay side by side. The only noise in the room was the waves of air rushing over the blades of the moving fan.

He moaned almost noiselessly. She turned toward him, her hand reaching down toward the bandaged wound. It felt wet. She raised her head from the bed and peered down onto his pelvis. The wound had spotted tiny droplets of blood.

"You're bleeding," Sosie remarked with fear etched in her voice.

Joshua smiled and said in a casual voice, his hand searching for the bandaged area, "Just seepage, my love. The doctor told me not to worry about a little bleeding. Besides, unless I bleed to death, you're worth every drop of blood I lose."

"We should have waited, Joshua."

"And die of starvation. Never. I will choose my manner of dying. And this is the way I want to go. In your arms and body. It's the only way to live…or die, my lovely flower."

She laughed as she slipped off the bed to go to the bathroom. Shortly, she returned with a wet face towel and started to wipe the blood from the wounded area of Joshua's body. As she cleaned the wound area, her eyes observed the red welts and scars on Joshua's abdomen.

"For such an innocent child, you seem to have taken such a beating growing up, Joshua."

"A drunken father and a bunch of unforgiving linemen in football can break any man's body into pieces."

"You speak so little of your father."

"There's nothing much to tell. He was dead drunk and homeless in a men's welfare shelter in New York City a few years ago."

"Who was he?"

"I never really found out. Except for the occasional beatings, we never really touched each other. He came and went like some kind of a phantom."

"And your mother?"

"Surprisingly, she loved him…even after the beatings. The motherfucker was always angry about something. And we were always his targets. Until I grew up…then it stopped. When he couldn't control us anymore, he never came back."

"The drinking…that's why you don't drink?"

"That's only part of it. I don't drink because one night I couldn't see a kid walking across the street. Never again, I promised myself after that accident. I'd rather kill myself before it'll ever happen again."

"Are you still punishing yourself over that accident, Joshua? It was years ago. Why do you keep torturing yourself?"

"Because you are responsible for what you do. My father never realized that obligation. He blamed everybody but himself for his failures. His dreams never came true because he didn't want them to. Failure was easier to handle than success. So he drank…just in case he might be lucky enough to succeed in what he did."

Joshua rolled off the bed and put on his underwear lying on a nearby chair. He walked over to the picture window overlooking the forest of mangroves that saturated the back lot of the hotel.

Sosie arose and dressed in jeans and a Rutgers University sweatshirt that Sam Waterman had given her. She walked over to Joshua at the window and wrapped her arms around his shoulders. He turned toward her face and kissed her gently on the forehead. She looked more like a fresh scrubbed college co-ed than a woman who has fought in two Israeli wars.

"Its time to forgive and forget, Joshua. He's dead now. It just doesn't do you any good keeping it all inside," she paused and touched his face, "I know Joshua. It happens to all of us. The pain never goes away… completely."

"For me, I can't forgive so easily, my love. Not so much what he did to me…no…more for the brutal punishment he dished out to my mother. And more so for my sense of futility when I was too young to stop him. I'll never forget that feeling of uselessness."

"Sam became your father. That's why you'll put your life on the line for him. Is that what this is all about, Joshua?"

Ryan turned away from Sosie and walked to the bed. He picked up his pants and shirt which were lying on the floor and dressed.

"He was there when I needed him, Sosie."

"Sammy and I need you also, Joshua."

"After this is over, I will always be there. You know that."

"Not if you're dead, Joshua."

He laughed as he rose from the bed fully dressed. The Orlando morning sun was drifting across the palm trees through the window of the room.

"I am invincible as long as you're behind me, Sosie darling. Come over here," he said as he reached out to embrace her small body into his burly chest. His muscular arms enveloped her ever so gently as she raised her face to kiss him.

"You're too innocent, Joshua, to roam unprotected in this "masuganuh" world. Thank god I'm here, at least to give you a chance to survive."

She laughed, her body shaking with joy in his embrace. Joshua knew that he would survive as long as this woman was there.

Chapter Twenty-Five

The Brazilian burl wood seemed to soak up the sunlight that filtered through the white shears that hung on all the Palladian windows of the immense antique filled office. Painted portraits of Senator Evans covered a part of each of the three walls of the corner office. Interspersed between the massive portraits were numerous photographs of the Senator clasping hands, rubbing shoulders or grasping the waist of various highly powerful politicians and entertainment celebrities. But the most recognizable character in one grandiose photograph was Senator Evans being hugged affectionately by President Ulysses Bancroft, the two-term president of the United States. The endorsement on the photograph in President Bancroft's incomprehensible handwriting marked Senator Evans as a close intimate friend of the President of the United States.

Senator Evans' office filled the entire east wing of the fourth floor of the Sam Rayburn senatorial office building, just overlooking the well tended bucolic campus situated between the office building and various other less pretentious government buildings. He had occupied that magnificent office for almost three decades now, ever since he became a senior senator from Florida. Democratic in name only, the Senator's policies and philosophy were right of most Republicans. Somehow, he persuaded his rather liberal voter supporters in Florida that he was the best thing that ever happened to them. And he probably was. The Senator protected his ancient voter base by making sure that their social security payments were increased yearly and paid on time, and that no one dare touch the sacrosanct pool of untouchable government insurance subsidies that were earmarked for the elderly. Since he had been chairmen of the Senate Ways and Means Committee, his power insured that his state and their inhabitants were beneficiaries of massive federal pork-belly hand outs for projects that guaranteed those Florida recipients life, liberty, and the pursuit of financial happiness. The Senator wasn't one to breach the Constitution of the United States.

The Senator sat languorously behind his period Louis Napoleon walnut desk, his clear blue eyes staring up at the ceiling of the office. Quietly, his intercom on the desk buzzed and his secretary's voice answered that Jeremy Wadsworth, the United States Attorney General had arrived and was waiting to see the senator.

His voice, soft and almost a whisper, told his secretary to let the AG wait a few minutes before she allowed him into the Senator's office. Evans played the infamous telephone and office waiting game to a scientific level, always recognizing that to wait for him was to revere him evermore.

After about five minutes, the large oak doors to his office were opened by one of the Senator's female assistants. In walked the A.G, his face reflecting the knowledge that he knew the senator had purposely kept him waiting, but what the hell could he do but offer a wide gratuitous smile as he extended his hand to the senator.

"Jerry, good to see you, you old reprobate," the senator announced in his most jocular tone of voice.

"Long time, no see, Senator," Wadsworth responded in a equally jocular voice, both knowing that the games had just commenced.

"The President must be in Republican heaven after his success in the mid-term elections."

"He is probably self effacing and uttering kind platitudes to you kind Democrats, but in public he is throwing darts at the Democrat's whip's picture," the A.G. declared referring to the Democratic congressional whip.

"Sit down, Jerry," the senator said as he pointed to the leather armchair in front of his desk. The senator made sure that the chairs in front of his desk were sunken low beneath the top of his desk. He knew that everybody that sat in those chairs had to look up to him and that's the way you fight your adversaries. And to the senator, everybody, friend or foe, was your adversary.

"I was surprised to get your call, Senator. Grateful to hear from you, but still surprised."

"Well," the senator smiled broadly, allowing his lips to part widely across his suntanned face and displaying the large even rows of sparkling white teeth to the A.G., "I always like to keep in touch with my friends in government. Especially my republican friends."

"The President appreciates your silent support in Florida."

"I am apolitical when it comes to the welfare of my people, Jerry. You know that."

"It goes without saying, Senator. But anyway, for whatever it's worth, the President sends his warmest regards and would like you to visit with him whenever your schedules allow."

"Of course…of course…especially in light of the fact that I have a small favor to ask of you people in the Justice Department."

Jeremy Wadsworth eyes lowered so he might better focus on the senator's mouth where Wadsworth knew the "small favor" would come out as a favor not so small.

Wadsworth's mind raced back six years when President Bancroft had just squeaked through as one of the few popular vote minority Presidents in United States' history. If it wasn't for his conservative friends on the U.S. Supreme Court, President Bancroft would still be president of the Houston Astros or whatever other sport teams his family bought into. But not withstanding his shaky electoral victory as President, Bancroft had proven to be a strong resilient politician more so than his doubting Democratic adversaries ever gave him credit for. He won re-election by a wide popular majority and was still running strong in the polls.

But Wadsworth's mind darted to the time President Bancroft nominated him for the U.S. Attorney General's Post. Every liberal, Democrat and Republican alike, raised up on their respective haunches, and screamed bloody murder that Wadsworth was too conservative to hold such an important legal post. Anti-abortion, gun toting Missourian, Wadsworth had been on the forefront of the religious right when he was a U.S. Senator from Missouri.

But, despite the outrageous opposition to his nomination, the President stood by his selection even though his cabinet voted to dump the nominee. And by the barest of a majority, Wadsworth was confirmed by his former brethren in the U.S. Senate. Now, six years later, Wadsworth had proven as adept at politics as his presidential mentor. Not openly singing the praises of the pro-lifers or the gun lobby, he had helped the President get good old conservatives on the federal benches, including the bench closest to God, the U.S. Supreme Court.

Yes, Wadsworth knew that his position as AG was as precarious as a clown putting his head in a lion's mouth. You never knew when your head would be unceremoniously bitten off. So, Wadsworth curried favor to all who could be instrumental in his removal as A.G. He liked the job and he wanted to stay the course.

Of all the political heavy weights in Washington, Senator Osgood Evans was the heaviest. Whatever Senator Evans wanted, you got him or else the good Senator, being the bad loser that he was, would use all the weapons at his disposal to exorcise the government functionary that didn't give the senator what he wanted. Not only politically powerful, Senator Evans controlled the largest media corporation in the United States. And he was not afraid to use every weapon at his disposal to rid the vermin, and everyone was vermin who was against him, from the face of this earth.

"As you probably heard, Jerry," the Senator started in a hoarse undertone ensuring that Wadsworth would strain to hear his words, "there has been a string of accidental deaths down in Orlando. Right in the backyard of Comtel. In fact, at The Park…where we had built a number of homes for our long term employees. Well, as you have probably heard," the senator repeated, his eyes staring pointedly at Wadsworth's face in an attempt to elicit whatever reaction Wadsworth was showing as the Senator spoke, "many of the victims…and I call them victims merely because they died and not because of any foul play. Anyway, they were many of our older employees, Comtel's employees. Nobody, as far as I know, has suggested that the deaths were caused by anything but natural causes."

"Then why did the A.G. in Florida convene a grand jury, Senator?" Wadsworth softly interjected more to see the senator's facial reaction than as a suspicious interrogator.

"That's why I called you, Jerry." The senator said in a slightly raised voice, the broad smile on his face returning, "I don't know why...my son called me yesterday...you know, Jack...Jerry?"

"Yes, I think we met in Nassau at one of Comtel's seminars."

"Well, anyway, Jack said that one of your assistant A.G.s down in Orlando decided on his own...I know Bartolomew down there...he's your chief in Orlando...and I know that he didn't convene the Grand Jury. Anyway, this assistant, I think his name is Lawrence...in fact, I think that I helped him to get the position down there, well, this jury is now meeting and there is some type of undertone to this investigation that may somehow involve Comtel."

Wadsworth knew about the proposed merger of Comtel and AMT since the legal department at Comtel had informally sent a draft proposal to the FCC and the Justice Department last month to get the feel of what the government would do or not do if the merger actually took place. Of course, Senator Evans had placed calls to the chairman of the FCC and to Wadsworth expressing his desire that the government approve the merger. But now, with a grand jury investigating a series of strange deaths in Comtel's backyard involving Comtel's own senior employees, Wadsworth opined that anything derogatory arising out of that investigation could hurt the chances of federal approval of the merger. There was little doubt that the merger smacked of anti-trust repercussions because of the definite reduction in competition in the cable and television marketplace if the two behemoths were allowed to join forces. But politics being what it is, the merger would most certainly be approved if nothing derogatory showed up in the investigation.

"Bartolomew called me a couple of days ago about the grand jury, Senator."

"What is Lawrence trying to do, Jerry? Run his own show and maybe take your job."

Wadsworth laughed, his beveled jaw opening to release a smile that barely showed his teeth.

"I don't know this assistant other than your office had strongly recommended him for the job, Senator."

"We all make mistakes, Jerry."

"Well, I don't know what he's after, but he's no dummy, Senator. His efficiency reports show a smart African-American Yale graduate who's won almost every case he's tried for the department."

The senator's blue eyes turned ice-cold as he rose from his chair and in an unexpected angry voice declared, "Listen, Mr. Attorney General, I don't give a shit if he's Clarence Darrow. I'm telling you now, get that nigger off Comtel's back or President Bancroft will be looking for another Attorney General. Am I clear, Jerry?" The senator's voice cracked as it reached into the high decibel range usually reserved for operatic sopranos.

Evans tall cadaverous body hung over his desk, his well-manicured hands cemented to the top of the desk supporting his shaking frame.

"I can't just shut him down, Senator," Wadsworth replied in a soft monotone.

"The fuck you can't…you better pull him out of there or there'll be one less mother fucking nigger in the State of Florida!" The senator suddenly leaned back from the desk and his body plopped down on his leather judges' chair causing the chair to quiver frenetically.

"I'm sorry, Jerry," the senator said in a quiet tone, his smile returning to his face.

"You know how I love that company. I built it up with my own two hands. When Orlando was just swampland. You don't know what kind of sweat and blood we transfused into that company. I can't see it fall into the swamp just because some assistant A.G. wants to make a name for himself."

"I know what you mean, Senator. But, you know, I wish I knew what he was doing before he started the grand jury proceeding. Now…well, if we just pull the rug from under him…stop the grand jury from hearing testimony. Well, you know better than me Senator, the Democrats and the media will put me on the cross. Especially the same Democrats you go to the national conventions with."

"I'll take care of the democrats and the media, Jerry. Just pull that black boy of yours in. I'll take care of the media."

The senator paused suddenly as he brushed his hand through his steel gray mane of hair that was so perfectly groomed every day.

"Look, Jerry…you're not even sixty yet. Bancroft is a lame duck president. In two years the Republicans will be looking for another winnable candidate. You've become more of a middle of the roader these last six years. I can help you get that nomination and maybe the presidency. Just play ball with me on this thing. Pull the son-of-a-bitch in and we'll talk White House in two years. Are you with me, Jerry?"

Wadsworth had longed for a crack at the White House six years ago when he ran in the Republican primaries against Bancroft. He lost and he turned down the Vice-Presidency slot because he knew that it was a dead-end position. He jumped at the chance to become Attorney General because with the terrorism scare the United States was going through, his face and voice would be in front of the American people on a daily basis. And now, with the Senator's backing, maybe he could be the next resident of the White House. It was a dream of his father who was a Senator before him from the great state of Missouri. "The White House," his mind echoed the name without words emanating from his mouth. "The White House," he repeated hungrily again in the front lobe of his brain.

"I'll do what I can, Senator. Maybe I'll fly down to Orlando to meet with Bartolomew and Lawrence. If it isn't feasible to stop the proceeding, maybe we can abort its effectiveness. As you've always said, Senator, there's a million ways to skin a cat as long as the voters don't see it."

The Senator laughed a hearty, body wracking laugh as he rose to shake hands with Wadsworth. The meeting was over. Senator Evans knew there was no more to say to each other. Comtel would survive and the merger was assured a second life.

Chapter Twenty-Six

The conference hall of the Waldorf-Astoria was overflowing with an assortment of people, all dressed in different colorful costumes as if Halloween was declared a national holiday. It was the weekend before Memorial Day and the weather had turned miserably hot in New York City. The hall was built to hold no more than four hundred people but this Saturday afternoon there were more than a thousand people, mostly standing against the walls, the rest seated in uncomfortable folding chairs.

Jack Evans was standing on the podium, his hands resting on the high table that held the microphone. Seated along side on the rest of the podium was Senator Evans, Alfred Lowry, Jon Paulsen, Charles Borden, the CFO of Comtel, and Frederick Abromowitz of AMT. Their hands were folded on the white linen covered table adjacent to the dais holding the microphone.

Sam Waterman stood quietly in the rear of the hall waiting for the Comtel shareholders' meeting to commence. As his eyes roamed down the hall, he observed that many of the attendees were older people, many dressed in Bermuda shorts and golf shirts. It appeared as if all the elder citizens of Orlando had flown in for the meeting on the same charter flight.

Evans pounded the high table with a gavel and announced that the annual shareholders' meeting of Comtel would come to order. Slowly and reluctantly the murmuring crowd quieted down until the silence was almost palpable.

"Ladies and gentlemen, fellow shareholders of Comtel," Evans announced in an expansive friendly voice, "I welcome you to the annual meeting of Comtel shareholders. It's been a long and exciting year for our company and I have our executive staff here today to tell you about Comtel's progress in the past year and of our dynamic plans for the future. Also," Evans directed his arm toward Frederick Abromowitz, a glowing smile crossing his face, "I would like to present the Chairman of the Board of AMT, Frederick Abromowitz, who will discuss with you the upcoming merger of Comtel and AMT. We have passed out the annual prospectus and a brochure which outlines the enormous benefits to Comtel and Comtel shareholders when the merger with AMT is finally concluded. First, let me introduce my father, Senator Osgood Evans, the founder of our great company who will speak to you about the future of Comtel as the result of the merger with AMT. And finally, I will take great pleasure in introducing Frederick Abromowitz, Chairman of AMT, and one of the pioneers of cable television in our world."

The senator rose from his chair and walked over to his son and warmly embraced him. He approached the microphone slowly, waited a few seconds until the audience had quieted down. Sam Waterman, from his back of the hall vantage point thought the senator resembled a symphony conductor awaiting perfect silence from the audience before he raised his baton to start the concert. Waterman saw the entire proceeding as a well organized concert, the Evans as conductors assuming that the audience would rise up at the end of the concert to give the Comtel orchestra a standing ovation.

"Ladies and gentlemen," the senator's deep mellifluous voice flowed out to the massive audience, his famous ear-to-ear smile enveloping his devoted followers in the audience, "most of us have been together these forty years. It's been a long, hard trail that you, and I, have forged since the beginning of Comtel. I remember in those early years we couldn't even afford a secretary, no less computers and all the other mechanical things that complicate our lives today. From that corner store on International Drive in Orlando, we have built an entertainment corporation that takes a back seat to no one. After this very profitable year, Comtel is ready to advance to the next plateau. That is the merger with a great cable and television company, AMT.

As you can see from our annual prospectus, Comtel exceeded the previous year's profits by almost twenty percent. But we all know that a company that sits on it's laurels will never maintain its prominent position in a field as changing and evolutionary as the great entertainment and leisure industry is. And," his voice stopped suddenly as he sucked in a draft of air into his lungs before proceeding, then he raised his arms outward to the vast throng of people beneath his position, "Comtel will continue its rise above the pre-eminent position it now maintains. Only through the merger with AMT can Comtel sustain that pre-eminent position as one of the leading corporations in America. We will all profit from that success!"

Jack Evans felt the electric tension that permeated the audience of Comtel's shareholders. Normally at a shareholders meeting, the 'common folk" as he loved to call his shareholders, would sit quietly in their chairs soaking up all the good financial propaganda the executive staff would transmit. Everybody felt rich if their favorite corporation was doing well. It was a well planned Broadway production with enthusiastic shills sprinkled throughout the audience to generate a feeling of wellness and security.

Today's meeting was different. In order to guarantee that the meeting go according to his plan, Jack Evans had his army of security men under the direction of Paulsen standing along the fringes of the audience. They were all dressed in sport shirts and khaki pants and seemed to blend nicely into the audience.

After the senator completed his sermon and absorbed the applause generated more by the security men than the shareholders, Jack Evans rose and introduced Frederick Abromowitz to the audience.

Abromowitz slowly rose from his chair and confidently strode to the microphone. He shook hands warmly with Senator Evans and with the microphone in his hands, spoke ever so softly so that unless the listener strained to hear his words, his words were incomprehensible. The lowered voice resulted in the people of the audience to cease their talking in order to listen to the indistinguishable words spoken by Abromowitz. Within seconds, the silence was deafening and universal.

"...and like any good arranged marriage, love doesn't necessarily have to come when the partners first meet. Respect, necessity and eventually affection will emerge in the final stages before the marriage is consummated. And so will the Comtel-AMT marriage produce the offspring of success for all the shareholders of the partner companies.

Using the resources of both companies efficiently, the result will be overwhelmingly beneficial to all of you.

We, at AMT, are ready, willing and able to devote not only billions of dollars in investments, but also the human resources to capture the attention of the entire world with the 21st century products of the evolving giant.

Therefore, ladies and gentlemen, shareholders of Comtel, I ask you to review the merger prospectus and I'm sure, that after review, you will be as confident as I am that the benefits of the merger far outweigh whatever difficulties we face or will face in the future!"

Abromowitz turned to shake hands with the Senator and Jack Evans and then proceeded to his chair.

Jack Evans returned to the podium and asked if there were any questions from the audience. Sam Waterman strode from the back of the room to the middle of the aisle between the chairs where the shareholders were seated. As he came forward, he grasped one of the microphones situated at the outer rim of a row of chairs.

"Yes, Mr. Evans. My name is Same Waterman. I am a shareholder in Comtel and would like to know what benefits you and your fellow board members will receive that are not outlined in the merger prospectus. And further, why hasn't the substantial verdict amount of the class action suit that was lodged recently against Comtel not contained in the prospectus and annual statement?"

As quickly as Sam's words sailed out of his mouth, the public address system went blank. Suddenly a crowd of the ordinarily dressed security men surrounded Sam and forcibly guided him from the room. The entire action took no more than a few minutes leaving the shareholder audience shaking their heads from side to side wondering what the hell was happening. The lights dimmed almost throwing the room into complete darkness and when they returned to its full brightness, Sam Waterman had disappeared from the room.

Jack Evans was still standing at the podium, a bright confident smile on his face. He raised his arms skyward appearing more like a victorious Dick Nixon than a concerned executive, his voice booming out of the revived public address system. "Ladies and gentlemen, thank you for your patience and support to your local board of directors and executive staff of Comtel. I'm sure when the merger is completed, all of us will reap the benefits of a great new company serving the world. Thank you again,"

Lowry moved that the shareholder meeting be concluded and the motion was seconded by Charles Borden.

The shareholders sat there for a few moments wondering what had happened to that cherubic, bald headed man who asked those questions. Getting no answers, the shareholders rose, almost as one, and left the room to enjoy the rest of the weekend in the Big Apple.

Chapter Twenty-Seven

"Ladies and gentlemen, I would like to welcome you back," Lawrence said as he stood in front of the oak railed jury box in the massive federal courtroom. Portraits of long gone federal judges hung on the walls surrounding the recently finished portrait of President Ulysses Bancroft. It reminded Joshua Ryan of Madame Tussaud's wax museum in London. He was seated alongside a wooden table left of the grand jury box. Sam Waterman and FBI agent Fred Smallwood sat to the far left of Joshua. Lawrence's chair was to the right of Joshua and closest to the jury box. Although there was a judge's bench in front of the courtroom, it remained unoccupied during the pendency of the grand jury proceedings.

"We will present two witnesses today," Lawrence continued, "they are considered expert witnesses who will not only inform you of the facts involved in this investigation, but also will submit their respective opinions on the whys and wherefores of the mysterious deaths happening out at The Park. If during their testimony, you have any questions, please raise your hand and we will try to have the expert witness answer your question. Remember, again, as I told you when we started this proceeding, we are a team in this investigation. Your input is vital to the outcome of this investigation. So don't be bashful, ladies and gentlemen. We want you to participate fully so we can get some intelligent answers to some very thorny questions. Okay?" Lawrence paused as his ebony eyes peered at each juror in an attempt to read their minds.

The foreman of the jury raised his hand and Lawrence motioned for him to ask his question. He was a hulky white-haired former lumberjack who had a grizzled face with sharp piercing eyes. His voice was deep and throaty as if the sound failed to pass through his nasal passages.

"Yes, Mr. Robertson," Lawrence said.

"Well, Mr. Lawrence, I'm sort of new at this…this investigation thing. So I don't want to sound like a jerk…but, can we ask any question of the witnesses…even if its outside of the box. You know what I mean? We ain't lawyers so we don't know what's important…you know what I mean?"

Lawrence smiled and replied in a patronizing manner, "You don't have to worry about whether its relevant, Mr. Robertson. You people should ask any question you feel is important. You…this grand jury…are also the judges of what the facts are. So you decide what is relevant and what is not. Forget I'm here or any of my associates." Lawrence pointed to Waterman, Ryan and Smallwood seated at the counsel's table.

"Does that answer your question, Mr. Robertson? Or anybody?" Lawrence's eyes searched for any of the other jurors' questioning looks but seeing no other questions, he proceeded to call Dr. Indiri Pasha to the stand. Smallwood rose from the table and walked to the giant double doors leading into the courtroom. After motioning to Dr. Pasha, who was seated outside the courtroom, Smallwood followed the tiny dark figure of the doctor into the courtroom. The court reporter was stationed just below the empty judge's bench recording all that was said at the proceedings on her steno machine. Her eyes were vacant as they looked straight ahead out the courtroom window onto Central Avenue of downtown Orlando.

Within seconds of Smallwood's entrance, several men bearing marshall badges on their shirts suddenly burst into the courtroom.

The lead marshall, a thin, lanky figure of a man, no more than thirty years old rushed toward Lawrence. The other marshalls surrounded Waterman and Ryan as if they were going to make an arrest.

"Are you Everett Lawrence?" The thin marshall asked. Lawrence could see a .357 mm in the shoulder holster of the marshal.

"Yes. Yes, I am. What the hell is going on here? Who the hell are you? I'm an Assistant U.S. Attorney conducting an investigating grand jury hearing. What right do you have to burst in here and surround my assistants?"

The grand jurors appeared shocked and frightened by the invasion of armed men into the courtroom. They had concluded that the attackers were terrorists.

The lanky marshal handed Lawrence a federal cease and desist order seemingly signed by an a judge whose signature Lawrence couldn't read.

"What is this? How can anyone issue a cease and desist order stopping a duly organized grand jury hearing?" Lawrence shouted at the marshal.

"It's signed by Judge Stuyvesant, sir. A U.S. District Court judge."

"I don't care if it's signed by President Bancroft himself. What right does any judge have in stopping a grand jury investigation?"

"I don't know, sir. But I was ordered to serve the order by U.S. Attorney Bartolomew. I believe he's your boss, Mr. Lawrence."

Another marshal handed Ryan and Waterman arrest warrants. Ryan looked at the legal documents and noted that the charges specified were the illegal practice of law in Florida and obstruction of justice. He also looked at Waterman's warrant and concluded that both of them were being charged by some federal judge who had also issued the cease and desist order.

The marshals roughly pulled the arms and wrists of Waterman and Ryan behind their backs and handcuffed both of them. Lawrence rushed over to them, shouting at the marshals to immediately release Ryan and Waterman. Instead the marshals brusquely pushed them toward the courtroom doors completely ignoring Lawrence.

Lawrence turned and walked to the jury box. The faces of the jurors were aghast, fear apparently covering their faces.

"Ladies and gentlemen, please forgive this intrusion. You will be called back after I straighten out this obvious misunderstanding. You are discharged for today. My assistant will call you when we reconvene. Thank you so much for your consideration and patience."

The jurors slowly filed out of the jury box, past the armed marshals and into the corridor. Suddenly a phalanx of media cameras and reporters appeared just outside the courtroom doors. Questions were hurled at the jurors, who covered their faces as if they were criminals instead of investigating grand jurors.

Lawrence followed the marshals, Ryan and Waterman out the doors into the hysterical atmosphere that existed in the courtroom corridor. Questions were thrown at Lawrence, who kept saying "no comment" as his eyes followed the marshals prodding Ryan and Waterman down toward the elevator leading to the jail below the courthouse. His mind was cluttered with a mixture of emotions filled with anger, fear and frustration that such an illegal act could happen on his watch. It was inconceivable that a federal judge would interfere in a legal grand jury investigation. He knew in his heart of hearts that somebody higher up, probably in Washington, was manipulating the judicial process in Orlando. Bartolomew wouldn't have the balls to stop a grand jury proceeding, Lawrence mused, as he quick-stepped down to Bartolomew's office.

Chapter Twenty-Eight

Bartolomew had refused to see Lawrence until the U.S. Attorney General himself had arrived from central headquarters in Washington. The sun had faded in the western sky and black clouds appeared to envelope the Orlando urban area.

Lawrence called Jo-Beth to see if Captain Parker was up and about and to tell her what had happened. She was noticeably surprised and told Everett not to do anything he would regret. The Captain had left the hospital and was on his way back to his office.

Lawrence told Jo-Beth to get the Captain to call him on his cell phone. He also told her that he was trying to get in to see either Bartolomew or Judge Stuyvesant, the federal judge who signed the cease and desist order and the arrest warrants. Lawrence wanted Captain Parker to visit Ryan and Waterman who were temporarily being held in the Orlando Municipal jail until they could be transported to the federal facility at Elgin Air Force Base in central Florida. For some reason, the marshals were trying to move Ryan and Waterman out of the Orlando area.

About 6:00 p.m., Lawrence's cell phone rang and Bartolomew's secretary was on the phone. She told him that Bartolomew had called a meeting, at his office for 6:30 p.m. and would Lawrence be so kind to attend. The U.S. Attorney General himself would be there.

Lawrence knew that only one man could get the A.G. himself to interfere in a grand jury investigation. Senator Osgood Evans' political stamp was all over the entire incident. Well, if they forced him to do the dirty deed, he would call a news conference to reveal the grimy tid bits of the chaotic nightmare. "Nobody," Lawrence thought, "can get away with this shit. Not even the President of the United States. Nobody…"

Arriving at Bartolomew's office on the second floor of the federal courthouse, Lawrence waited outside the office until he had gathered himself up. He hadn't eaten all day and was dying for a cup of coffee to open his mind to the verbal assault he knew he would be subject to once the meeting started. Facing the A.G. was frightening in itself, but more so because Lawrence knew that if he didn't relent in his investigation he might be the patsy taking the fall. He knew being right in politics doesn't mean you are tagged the winner. Only the strong survive in a political struggle that Lawrence knew was enfolding around him.

The door of Bartolomew's office suddenly opened and Smallwood appeared, his tight muscled face barely showing a reluctant smile.

"How are you, Mr. Lawrence?" Smallwood greeted Lawrence as he opened the door of the office to allow Everett in.

"Missed you, Agent…when the shit hit the fan in the grand jury room."

"I had to hit the head, sir. Nature called."

"I bet…you knew all along what was coming down the pike, Agent. Isn't that so?"

Smallwood's facial muscles started to twitch as he allowed Lawrence to pass him into the office. Bartolomew's secretary was still at the reception desk; she smiled graciously as she pointed to Bartolomew's office. "You can go right in, Mr. Lawrence," she sweetly announced. She had been with Bartolomew when he was a political hack in New York and she followed him down to Orlando when he was appointed the Florida U.S. Attorney. She was more than sixty now, but she still had a youthful face and smile.

"Thank you, Ms. Conover. I presume the Attorney General is also here."

"Yes, I believe he arrived a few minutes ago. Nice to see you again, Mr. Lawrence," she said ever so sweetly.

Lawrence felt he was being led to the guillotine by his grandmother. That great paying job he was offered in the white glove firm in New York started to look really good. A little house in Long Island, Jo-Beth waiting for him when he came home, maybe a kid or two, a new Mercedes every three years. No aggravation, just boredom curdling his brain into mush. 'Ah, what the hell,' he thought, 'you only live once. God,' he almost shouted to himself, 'how I hate these fucking politicians.' As he walked toward the inner office of Bartolomew, he thought of Ryan and Waterman being held in some city jail, just because they wanted to see justice done. "Justice," he murmured to himself, "there ain't no justice in this here land. The judge gave a divorce to my old man, but I sure laughed at his decision; he gave him the kids, and they ain't even his'n." a humorous statement that roamed around in his head that was more true than funny.

After Lawrence was ushered into Bartolomew's office, he immediately saw Wadsworth, the U.S. Attorney General, standing in front of the office window, silently looking out onto the green campus behind the federal office building. He kept extending his arms and noisily cracking his knuckles. Although he knew Lawrence was in the office, he failed to acknowledge his presence by turning around to face him.

Bartolomew sat in his leather swivel chair, leaning tensely against the wall. His short-cropped hair seemed more disheveled than usual, Lawrence mused. 'Probably got his ass reamed out by the A.G.,' Lawrence thought.

Lawrence sat down in the armchair in front of Bartolomew's massive desk. No one spoke for several moments. Smallwood stood guard over the office door.

"Illegal practice of law, obstruction of justice!" Lawrence suddenly bellowed out. "Give me a goddamn break, Bart. They were my assistants, duly appointed by me. You might as well have me arrested for obstruction. What kind of bullshit is this?"

"You didn't have the department's authority to convene a grand jury, Mr. Lawrence." Wadsworth said in a threatening, yet well modulated voice.

Lawrence turned in his chair to look at the side of Wadsworth's well-groomed figure. The A.G. was wearing a pin-striped dark blue suit with a blue bow tie against his Turnbull and Asher hand tailored white on white shirt.

"I didn't think I needed prior approval before I did my job, sir."

"I told you to stay away from this case, Everett," Bartolomew interjected loudly.

"Why this case, Bart? I thought this office…your office…didn't stand for any political bullshit."

"We don't need to use foul language, Mr. Lawrence," Wadsworth admonished as he quickly turned around to face Lawrence.

"I did what I thought was right, sir. That's what I was sworn to do…Prosecute criminals. Murderers. Anybody who breaks the law."

"Not without the department's prior's authorizations, Mr. Lawrence."

"You said that already. I've never needed prior approval to convene a grand jury before this case." Lawrence paused to stare at Bartolomew's face, who had partially covered his face with his clenched fist.

"This is a state matter, Mr. Lawrence. We stay out of state matters," Wadsworth announced as he walked over to where Lawrence was sitting and stood directly over him. Lawrence could smell the expensive Dior men's cologne discreetly coming from Wadsworth's face.

"Violation of the victim's civil rights is a federal matter, sir."

"Whose rights?"

"The poor and unfortunate victims who were strangled by some heinous son-of-a-bitch."

"Strangled? What do you mean strangled, Mr. Lawrence? Do you mean there is a serial killer loose in Orlando and only the Justice Department can assume jurisdiction. What do you think we have the Florida State Police for. We have no federal jurisdiction over murder,

Mr. Lawrence."

"Murder is a violation of the victim's civil rights, sir."

"Technically, maybe…but we don't get involved unless the state boys screw-up. And as far as I know, the Orlando police are on top of the situation."

"It's been three months since the killings started, sir. And still no one has been arrested. There aren't even any suspects."

"You're to stay out of it, Lawrence," the A.G. warned as his eyes locked with Lawrence's eyes.

Lawrence stood up and directly faced the A.G. No more than inches apart, Lawrence spoke in a deliberate tone, "I don't know what this is all about, Mr. Wadsworth. All I know is I have two assistants, duly appointed, sitting in a municipal jail. Men of untarnished reputations. And," Lawrence's forefinger came up as he pointed it at Wadsworth nose, "if they are not released post haste, this whole ridiculous can of worms is going to hit the media. No holds barred, gentlemen, because I think somebody up there is really interfering with a duly appointed grand jury investigation. And I'll tell you, gentlemen, you can strip me of my badge, take my gun away, take me off the payroll, but I'm still going to blow this whole kettle of fish to kingdom come. Bare ass and all, the department will think it's Watergate all over again!"

The attorney general and Bartolomew stared at each other as Lawrence voiced his threats.

Bartolomew nodded to Smallwood who quickly stepped up behind Lawrence, his government issued .357 out of his shoulder holster and pointed it behind Lawrence's right ear. Lawrence heard the click of the safety pulled back releasing the gun's mechanism to fire.

"Put that gun away, agent!" Wadsworth shouted in a phlemy voice to Smallwood.

"Bartolomew, have you lost your fucking mind!" Wadsworth added.

Lawrence's face broke into an effusive sweat as he felt the cold metal of the gun touch the side of his head and the overwhelming relief when Smallwood withdrew it.

"You said…" Bartolomew sputtered.

"I know what the hell I said, Bartolomew! I didn't say you have to shoot your deputy in the head. Mr. Lawrence is a reasonable man. I'm sure he understands the necessity of discretion in this matter." Wadsworth paused, smiled at Lawrence, then walked back to the window.

The overhead light of the office chandelier burned a hole in Lawrence's eyes as the life threatening fear that permeated his body slowly dissipated. His body felt drained, his mind delirious that he was going to live another day. 'But,' he thought, 'at what cost?'

"Mr. Lawrence, all we ask is for you to step back and consider the situation in a rational manner. Consider the big picture. You know what I mean?"

"The big picture, Mr. Wadworth, is to lay off Comtel and the senator. Is that what you mean by the big picture?" Lawrence replied, his face filled with a wave of sudden anger.

"The senator is a very powerful man, Mr. Lawrence."

"No one gets away with murder, Mr. Attorney General. Not even the President of the United States."

Wadsworth smiled at the innocent fervor of the large, black man standing in front of him. 'When does the innocence disappear and the reality begin,' he thought.

Wadsworth had been the law review editor of Stanford Law many years ago. The late sixties was a cauldron of world shattering innocence; when your vision of right and wrong and justice for all were so clear. The war was wrong and the killing of innocent civilians were wrong. Protesting the rule of law was right and defending those who protested was right.

Political power was never considered by the young defenders of the faith. Until they realized that political power was the only consideration.

It was a lubricant that made the wheels of justice turn. There was no law school course on political power. You had to learn it first hand. From the street level up to the very pinnacle of power, the White House. And so Wadsworth became the ideal student. A Nixonite from California, Wadsworth was a fast learner. Until he became the power broker. The student, after years of toiling in the backyards of the power brokers, suddenly woke up one morning and realized he had graduated at the head of his class. The student had become the teacher. Yet, he felt the sense of loss of that innocence, of that pure goal seeking, of the search for right and wrong, of discovery that there was justice to be had for even the lowest class member of our great democracy. 'Great democracy,' he thought. 'Was it ever?" he questioned.

"No matter what you do to this present grand jury," Lawrence warned as he turned to leave, "the investigation will go on. And if you order me to cease and desist, Mr. Wadsworth, I will resign from the U.S. Attorney's office and pursue the investigation as a private lawyer."

Lawrence walked quickly out of the office, both men's eyes following his disappearing body.

Wadsworth knew that the Lawrences of the world have become the real enemy. The innocents who would not realize that only through power, political power, only then could the wheels of our great country operate. And of course, he would have to be destroyed because some people would never learn.

Chapter Twenty-Nine

The Orlando City jail was located in the basement of the Orange County courthouse. Ryan and Waterman were moved from a holding cell in the Federal Courthouse facility to the city jail within an hour of their arrest and detention. Bartolomew wanted their confinement whereabouts kept secret to avoid any statements to be made by them to the searching media teams.

Jo-Beth was notified by the lieutenant on duty at the jail that Ryan and Waterman were guests of the city. Jo-Beth called Everett Lawrence on his cell phone and also notified Captain Parker, who was resting at home watching the replay of last year's Florida State-Miami football game.

At the request of Jo-Beth, the lieutenant moved Ryan and Waterman out of the crowded common drunk tank into separate cells for each of them. It was about 11:00 p.m. when the transfer was completed. Neither Ryan nor Waterman had eaten anything since they were arrested in the early afternoon.

"I knew I would wind up in jail, Joshua, if I kept hanging around with you," Waterman said with a cynical chuckle as he sat on the thin mattress cot that folded down from the wall of the cell.

Ryan paced nervously around his cell until he found his final resting place leaning against the barred cell door.

"You would think that I would get used to getting locked up," he replied.

"It's a shame that Sammy has a convict for a father, Joshua."

"So I'm not the perfect father. It'll make her a better person, Sam."

"Why ain't we more concerned about our present environment, Joshua? Maybe we figure this is where all lawyers wind up anyway."

"I'd rather be a visitor than a resident, Sam."

"You know, Josh me boy, when I visited one of my innocent clients in one of these spas with bars, I could always smell the sweet scent of Lysol and urine that would clog up my sinuses for a month. It must be the perfume that is manufactured only for jails."

"They must be desperate, Sam, to stop the grand jury proceedings. It's just never done."

"Florida has its own rules. The senator makes them and everybody blindly follows them. I think he created his own rule book."

"Well, the president must be beholden to him. He finagled the presidency into Bancroft's corner six years ago. Chad ballots and all."

Sam rose from his position on the cot and walked over to the bars closest to Joshua's cell.

"I could use a cigar just about now."

"Not with your heart, Sam."

"Its cigarettes that kill. Not cigars. Cigars only give you lip cancer. You can lose your lips but not your life, Joshua."

"You know, I could sure use a gyro just about now. Like the ones they make in Paris. You know where I'm talking about, Sam. The Marais…that place where the lamb is covered with the greatest sauce this side of Tel Aviv."

"Do you think they'll hang us? You know Florida executes more prisoners than any other state in the union, Joshua."

"Information like that I don't need, Sam. Why don't we talk about the weather."

"Florida doesn't have any weather, Joshua. It's always the same weather, so what's to talk about."

"You know, I somehow feel we should take this more seriously, Sam. The U.S. Attorney's office appears to be serious about blocking the Comtel investigation. It could make Watergate look like a walk in the park."

"Is that meant to be a double entendre, Joshua."

"The Park? Yes, I guess it is." Joshua paused to walk back to his cot and sat down on the edge of it, as he put his head in his hands, "I wonder how Sosie is? You know she wasn't crazy about me coming to Orlando, Sam."

"But you did it, and I appreciate it, Joshua. You did a good thing coming to my rescue."

"I haven't done you much good so far, Sam."

"Yes you have. At least something is happening. We stirred the pot, Joshua, and the soup is boiling like crazy. Anyway, they let me make my one phone call and I called a lady friend of mine. Used to be a judge in these here parts. Her name is Helen Walsh and she's already working on getting us out of here on a writ of habeus corpus. She knows the federal magistrate real well. Used to party with him at these judge's conventions. Since Judge Stuyvesant, the federal judge who filed the arrest warrant is sleeping, the magistrate can sign the release order before Stuyvesant wakes up. Then I think they will leave us be or else we'll tattle to the media."

"We need to get into their books, Sam." Joshua announced.

"I got a feeling the books will be more interesting than a Jacqueline Susan novel."

"Do you know anyone? Like a good CPA, Sam."

"I got the perfect accountant for this job. He used to work for the SEC and now lives next to me at Turnberry. Bored shitless and he would welcome a little adventure in la-la land."

"Who is this lawyer, Helen Walsh?"

"I met her at the Comtel shareholders' meeting. The one you wouldn't come to with me."

"Did she leave the bench voluntarily? Or was she..."

"No she wasn't, you suspicious little bastard. She had had enough, she told me. Now she takes whatever cases she wants. Believe me, she doesn't need the money. Besides, her husband was one of The Park victims."

There was a small barred window high up in Joshua's cell that allowed darting moon rays into the cell. If Joshua stood on the cot, he could see the skyline of Orlando lit up like a Christmas tree. He could hear the sounds of nighttime Orlando going about their business, obviously not concerned about the plight of two foreign lawyers incarcerated for getting their testicles hammered by Florida politics.

'Did anyone really care?' Joshua mused. 'Does anybody really care if it doesn't affect themselves or their loved ones?' He was chastising himself for getting involved again in a system he couldn't control. 'Sosie was right' he thought painfully, 'I should have stayed down on the farm in Paris'. "Sosie must be as mad as a nest of hornets," Joshua said, not caring if Sam heard him or not.

"She'll forgive you, that's after she kicks some ass in getting you out of here. I'm worried she'll intentionally forget about me for bringing you to Orlando."

"It's getting late, Sam. I don't think your friend is going to get us out tonight. The last time I spent the night in jail was three years ago when I represented the rabbi. Didn't like it then and I ain't enjoying it now."

"I'm hoping she gets to the magistrate before morning. Once he signs the release order, the federal judge will think twice before putting us back here."

As the nighttime passed into early morning, Joshua and Sam were sleeping in fitfull starts in their respective cells. Joshua dreamt he was being thrown into the air by several mean looking men and never coming down to earth again. He felt like throwing up but remained asleep while his body was racked with fear and nausea. He didn't know when his acute claustrophobia would kick in making him do things that would destroy him. Like banging his head against the bars.

Sam slept silently until he suddenly arose from the bed and started to scream out at the phantoms that existed in his mind. He remembered being in prison while he waited for his trial on statutory rape to begin. Two weeks of eternal hell that stayed within his brain all these years. Even though he was acquitted of the frivolous charge brought by his live-in consort who was pissed off at him for throwing her and her ugly fifteen year old daughter out of his house in Camden. 'A woman scorned,' he muttered often to himself.

With the early morning rays filtering through the barred window, Joshua's eyes were shocked opened by the intense light. He woke up with a start thinking he was still in Paris. But the nightmare was still with him. Paris was light years away. The smell of piss and Lysol reminded him that he would not be getting fresh brioche and raspberry jam this morning.

As Joshua was washing his face from the water in the rusted sink in the cell, Captain Parker appeared outside the cell. Sam was just rising and barely settled on the edge of the cot when he saw Parker.

Parker opened both cell doors and walked into Joshua's cell.

Helen Walsh appeared dressed in a well tailored suit. She was a woman in her early sixties with salt and pepper hair pulled back into a bun. She smiled maternally at Sam.

She showed him the habeus corpus writ. He looked at it for a moment and then handed it back to her.

"Can't read without my glasses," he said.

"We have to appear before Judge Stuyversent at 1:00 p.m. today, Sam."

"What for?"

"He has to decide whether to make the writ permanent."

"Thanks for coming to the rescue, Helen."

"What are friends for, Sam."

He laughed briefly, the pain in his chest spreading down to his stomach. "I'm too old for this shit, Helen." He said as he gently rubbed his flaccid chest.

"Maybe you should quit playing Zorro."

Sam rose from the cot and walked out of his cell into the corridor. Joshua had already left his cell and was waiting outside in the waiting room of the facility.

"Come on Helen. Lets go have breakfast. I also need a shower. Maybe you will join me?"

Helen Walsh followed Sam out of the cell and placed her arm around his stooped shoulders.

"I've already showered, Sam. Maybe next time…if you still want me to join you."

They both laughed as they walked out of the cellblock door into the waiting room. Joshua Ryan was surrounded by Sosie and Yehuda. Sosie turned and walked over to Sam and hugged him to her chest. He noticed the tears in her eyes as she kissed him on the side of his unshaven face.

"Are you okay?" Sosie whispered to him.

"Fine…How's Joshua?"

"Joshua says he's alright. I don't believe him. He thinks that all this is his fault."

"He still thinks he's a quarterback."

"It's not a game anymore, Sam."

"Tell that to Joshua. I know him all these years Sosie, and he thinks the first half is over, but he can't wait to get back at them in the second half. I hope they don't kill him before the end of the game."

"Is it all worth it, Sam?"

"You should know better than to ask that question, Sosie."

"I know. But when will it all end? When I come here to pick up my husband's body? I been through enough of that."

Sam smiled his crooked tooth smile as he put his arm around Sosie's shoulders and marched her out of the jailhouse door. Everybody followed.

"Lets talk about it over pancakes and eggs, Sosie. I think better on a full stomach."

CHAPTER THIRTY

Federal courtrooms reminded Joshua of third century Roman coliseums where one expected to hear trumpets blaring as the Christians were released into the arena full of lurking lions. Majestic beyond belief, this federal courtroom had antique brass chandeliers hanging from the ceiling. The walls were covered with wainscoting and ornate dark woods meshing harmoniously with the wooden benches and jury box.

As Joshua, Waterman and Helen Walsh stood at the defense table awaiting the arrival of Judge Peter Stuyversant, Bartolomew sat quietly at the prosecutor's table scribbling notes on a yellow legal pad. He had a female legal assistant sitting by his side seemingly reviewing case law in several law books on the desk. Lawrence was seated behind the railing, just behind the defendants and their lawyer. He was whispering into the ear of Jo-Beth, who was smiling occasionally as Lawrence talked.

The clerk came out of the back door of the courtroom along with a court reporter who set up her steno machine in front of the judge's high bench. The federal courts in Florida still clung to the vestiges of the old reporting system revolving around the use of human stenographers instead of mechanical recording machines.

The court clerk stood up from his chair alongside the jury box and announced that the "Honorable Peter Stuyversant is entering the courtroom, God save these United States."

Everybody in the courtroom stood, as the tall, angular body of Judge Peter Stuyvesant strode quickly into the courtroom from a side door that led to his chambers. He stood for several moments looking out into the courtroom as if he were searching for a particular person and seeing none, he sat down in his high-backed, black leather judge's chair. Everybody then sat down.

"Now let me see," the judge barked in a deep voice that resounded off the deep paneled walls of the large courtroom, "we are here for what?" He looked over at his clerk who handed him several white sheets of paper.

"The United States vs. Ryan and Waterman...Are they in the courtroom?"

"Yes, your Honor," Helen Walsh rose in front of the counselors' table, "I represent Mr. Ryan and Mr. Waterman, Your Honor."

"What are they here for, Mrs. Walsh?"

"Well, Your Honor, that's a good question. I'm in as much of a quandary as you are."

Bartolomew bolted up from his wooden arm chair, his face ashen white as he spoke quickly to the court. "These men are charged with the illegal practice of law in a federal courtroom as well as obstruction of justice, Your honor."

"Are these federal offences, Mr. Bartolomew?"

"Yes, your honor, they are. I cite 42 U.S.C. Section 2711 making the practice of law in a federal courtroom reserved for lawyers admitted to the Florida bar. Neither of these gentlemen are, your honor."

"Where are they practicing law, Mr. U.S. Attorney?" The judge asked somewhat irritated. His face was long with a sharp aqualine nose that pointed comically out from his high check boned face. 'He almost looks like Cyrano de Bergerac,' thought Sam Waterman.

"Right here in our courthouse, your honor. As legal assistants to my deputy, Everett Lawrence."

Suddenly the secretary to the judge appeared from the door leading to his chambers. She handed him a note which he read for several moments, his half glasses almost falling to the end of his nose as his angular head bobbed up and down as he read.

"Mr. Bartolomew," he bellowed out, "it seems your boss has a different mind set than you have. I think you should all join me in chambers."

Judge Stuyvesant jumped up from his chair and bolted out the door leading to his chambers. Helen, Sam and Joshua looked quizzically at each other and slowly followed the judge out of the courtroom. "Do you want me to join you folks," Lawrence asked.

"Might as well," Waterman replied. "You know as much about these charges as we do."

Bartolomew rose quickly from his chair and walked sullenly past the defendants out to the judge's chambers.

"Rude son-of-a-bitch," Waterman said as his eyes followed the pear shaped body of Bartolomew hurrying through the side door of the courtroom.

They marched out of the courtroom into the anteroom of the judge's chambers. The secretary asked them to sit down for a few moments until the judge was ready for them. The anteroom had four secretaries' desks, each equipped with several computers.

Bartolomew came rushing out of the Judge's inner office, his face twisted with frustration.

"The judge wants to see all of us," he announced as he turned to walk back into the judge's inner chambers.

The foursome followed Bartolomew. Joshua again marveled at the grandeur of this federal judge's enclave. Gold bound legal volumes adorned the cherry-wood bookcases that ran from one end of the room around to the far other end. A portrait of Chief Justice Rehnquist was prominently situated on the wall behind Judge Stuyvesant's elegant gold trimmed mahogany desk. He sat behind the desk, his black leather judge's chair lodged against the wall. His eyelids were closed and his hands were folded tent like on his belly.

"Bartolomew," he shouted, his eyes still closed, "hand these gentlemen the note received from the Attorney General."

Bartolomew handed the note bearing the U.S. Attorney General's stamp at the top of the paper to Walsh. She quickly read it and handed it to Sam who handed it to Joshua because he didn't have his reading glasses with him.

Joshua quickly read the note, handed it to Lawrence who read it and then handed it back to Bartolomew.

"What is your wish, Mr. Bartolomew? In light of the A.G.'s request, do you have a motion for this court?"

Bartolomew peered down at his shoes. He brushed his buzz-top hair back but was unsuccessful because the hair was not long enough to do anything but stand up on his head.

"I have no choice, your honor," he finally muttered.

"I guess not, Mr. Bartolomew," the judge replied. "Gentlemen," the judge addressed Ryan and Waterman, "if you want to represent anyone, including the people of the United States in any courtroom of Florida, I'd strongly suggest you file your pro haec vaec application for admission in that particular case and for that particular courtroom. Because of the kindness of our wondrous attorney general, the charges will be dismissed. Although, I'm curious to find out the basis for the obstruction charge. No matter…I have enough to do than hear the basis for frivolous charges. Besides, you all may be before me again. That is if you're involved in anyway with that Comtel billion dollar plus class action verdict. My office just received a motion by Comtel's lawyers to remove the case from the State Court to the Federal Court. Unusual motion, since the verdict is in on the case, but…I guess…if the State did not have original jurisdiction…and I hear the trial judge is dead…well, it may still wind up in my courtroom."

Helen Walsh knew of Judge Stuyvesant. She had appeared before him on several occasions. His pomposity and arrogance was shop talk among the lawyers appearing in federal court in Orlando. His disdain and dislike for lawyers many times translated into punitive and public monetary reprimands under Federal Rule 11, which allowed sanctions against lawyers at the discretion of the federal judge.

Stuyvesant, as his name suggested, was the last male member of the famous New York family that had literally founded the city. Rich, powerful and all right wing democrats, the Stuyvesants had been serving in the nation's judiciary and political hierarchy for over three hundred years. A product of the Choate-Princeton-Harvard academic chain, Peter Stuyvesant was the end product of intermarriages between the Dutch families that had come over to the shores of colonial America in 1664. Older and richer than the Rockefellers, the Stuyvesants had left the "trades" as they so disparagingly called business activities, to administer the rich rewards of owning a good piece of Manhattan Island.

For almost ten years, Peter Stuyversant had sat in Orlando, until he was now the senior judge on the Florida U.S. District Court bench. Still waiting for the politicians to elevate him to the Fifth Circuit Court of Appeals sitting in New Orleans, Stuyvesant and his family pulled all their unheralded strings, but no politician would dare push his nomination to the Appellate bench for fear of the people's back lash.

Stuyvesant, as Helen Walsh knew personally, was a sexually active man in his late fifties. On several occasions, he had propositioned Helen, although he was married to his third wife. Helen had politely rejected his advances, keeping Stuyversant at a distant arm's length. They had had dinner once during one of the judicial conventions in Washington, D.C. but she told him she would not be interested in anything further.

"Who is prosecuting the plaintiff's case in the Comtel matter, your honor?" Walsh asked the judge, her mind returning to the present situation.

Stuyvesant smiled, his brown eyes narrowing into tiny slits, as he said, "Who knows, Mrs. Walsh? Seems that the original lawyer got his brains shot out. He was also an out of state lawyer. I am sure some avaricious lawyer will take up the cudgels of that plaintiffs' suit. Perhaps you, Mrs. Walsh."

Helen looked around at the other lawyers in the room. She smiled and replied, "Perhaps, your honor. I'm sure Mr. Ryan and Mr. Waterman could be interested in representing the class, especially in light of the fact they'd be protecting a number of people who have rightfully been awarded a large sum of money against Comtel."

"Perhaps," the judge replied, "but they'd better get approved to represent anyone in Florida…or else…I might have them back in the lovely jails we have in Florida."

Lawrence cleared his throat as he spoke, "Your honor, I had convened a grand jury in the investigation of numerous mysterious deaths at The Park. Comtel's Park. Seems that Mr. Bartolomew aborted that hearing when he arrested Mr. Ryan and Mr. Waterman. I plan to continue that hearing next week. Does the court have any objection to me reconvening that grand jury?"

Stuyvesant stood up as the lawyers observed that the judge was over six feet five inches tall. His stooped shoulders belied his real height. His narrow chinned face broke out into a half smile, half sneer. He had long incisors that made him look draconian.

"Nobody has presented to this court any motions dealing with your grand jury, Mr. Lawrence. But, of course, that's between yourself and Mr. Bartolomew. And I guess he wins since he's your superior. What is your wish, Mr. Bartolomew?"

Bartolomew's face lit up with instant gratification as he replied, "There will be no grand jury hearing, your honor. There is no probable cause for a hearing. Mr. Lawrence has abused his authority in convening one."

"Under the administrative code which the U.S. Attorney's office is bound, your honor, it is clear that any U.S. attorney, and I am so designated, can convene an investigative grand jury if there is probable cause that a crime has been committed. And there is very little doubt that several crimes have been committed, your honor." Lawrence declared with obvious answer in his voice.

Stuyvesant walked around his desk to stand near Helen Walsh. He said with a flirtatious smile on his face, "What do you think, Mrs. Walsh? Is Mr. Lawrence or Mr. Bartolomew right? I always have had confidence in the distaff side of our wonderful profession."

She returned the smile to Stuyvesant as she replied, "I couldn't say, your honor. If you would like, I can brief it for the court."

"No, No, I am not ordering any sua sponte activities by battling U.S. attorneys. I would suspect that Mr. Bartolomew has the final say in the matter. Maybe we will get some answers when I hear the motion for a new trial in the Comtel case. I have set it down for the next motion day, my learned friends. So if nobody shows up for the plaintiffs, I might have to dismiss the whole mess."

Stuyvesant's eyes stared hypnotically at the four attorneys wondering if any of them realized that he had already decided the outcome of the upcoming motion for a new trial and/or dismissal of the plaintiffs' case against Comtel.

'Politics', he mused to himself. 'A necessary evil? Especially after Senator Osgood Evans had promised him the long desired appointment to the Fifth Circuit Court of Appeals. Judge Stuyvesant, a southerner at heart, always loved the bordellos of New Orleans. All he had to do was dismiss a billion and a half dollar verdict against Comtel. He smiled as he walked past the lawyers out into his reception area and then back into his courtroom to mete out justice on the cases listed on the calendar before him that day. Peter Stuyvesant's justice.

Chapter Thirty-One

The one hundred and fifty foot yacht was docked about a mile off Palm Beach. Even among the giant pleasure boats standing majestically, side by side, the 'Ruchel" stood out as the most opulent of all the floating palaces. The dining room was ablaze with the lights of several Baccarat chandeliers extended over the long dining table with plush silk brocade chairs.

Frederick Abromowitz was seated at one end of the table. Senator Evans was seated at the other end, while Jack Evans, Alfred Lowry, and Horst Steingut, AMT's general counsel was seated between the two white haired patriarchs. No one spoke as the blond haired stewards and stewardesses dressed in immaculate white uniforms adorned with the personal white dove insignias of Frederick Abromowitz, as they served Christophe crystal flutes of Tattinger champagne to the assembled diners. When all was served, the wait staff disappeared from the room.

"Gentlemen," Abromowitz announced in his deep, stentorian voice, "we don't have menus during the ship's dinners. My chefs, the head chef is the three star Michelin former chef of Paul Bocuse's restaurant, will serve you four courses including several dishes in each course. Some you may enjoy, others you may not. Please feel free to reject any dish in any course, but I hope all of you will enjoy all the courses. Also, my wine steward on board, has selected several wines of various origins and vintage dates. Enjoy all of them, some of them or none of them. Any liquor you desire, please feel free to order. I'm sure we will be able to find it on board. We have a temperature controlled wine cellar on board and if your selection cannot be found, then it must be unobtainable.

Further, I have invited a friend to dine with us tonight. Philicia, her title is the Countess of Surrey. She prefers to be called Philicia or Phil by her closest friends. I'm sure you will all enjoy her company."

The Senator raised his champagne glass as he stood up at the end of the table with his trademark smile ablaze on his face. He declared joyfully, "To the coming marriage of two giants in the entertainment industry. Frederick, I have lived for the day that Comtel out does our Florida rival, Disney. And with the birth of the Comtel-AMT Corporation, we will have far exceeded the breath and width of any other corporation in the cable, film and television industries."

As the senator finished his toast, the countess appeared from the staircase leading to the master cabin. She was wearing a Chanel evening gown made of diaphanous silk that seemed to cling to her body. Her dark hair was swept up on her head leaving one to see the sparkling diamond earrings that hung from her ears. Her face was tiny and fragile; and appeared as if she had applied no make-up. Every feature of her face was perfect. Most of all, her radiant smile illuminated the room as she entered.

"Good evening, gentlemen," her voice purred with a clipped royal English accent.

Smiles ignited on every face surrounding the dining room table.

Abromowitz pulled out the vacant chair to his left at the table. She floated into it effortlessly, gently touching his hand. She smiled up at him, her dark green eyes obviously filled with affection for him.

"I'm glad you can join us, Philicia my dear." Abromowitz said as he sat down. "I've told my friends here that you would certainly add excitement to our dinner conversation."

"If it's business talk, please continue on. I love to talk about money."

Everyone laughed at the comment, not so much because it was funny, but rather more to show the countess their collective admiration for her serene beauty.

"Gentlemen," Abromowitz announced, "please feel free to discuss anything at all in front of Philicia. She's on the AMT Board of Directors as well as one of our major stockholders."

"You might also add the fact that I have an MBA from Wharton, Frederick."

All the men around the table continued to smile and shake their heads in the affirmative. Frederick recognized that she was a decided asset when men were involved in a business deal.

Before any further discussion could be held, the wait staff brought out the various appetizers which included escargots en croute, fois gras infused with truffle shavings, grilled longastinos, and, miniature steak tartare with accompanying rare mushrooms in a port wine sauce. Each diner could select whichever appetizer or appetizers his or hers eyes desired and the steward would place it in front of the diner. Another steward brought out hot loaves of various types of bread on a tray and each person would select his or her choice and then the selected bread would be cut fresh by the waiter on a cutting board located on the massive antique buffet against the wall of the dining room. About the same time, the wine steward brought out a brass trolley with an assortment of wines and liquors which the diners could choose from. None of the various wines were later than 1997 vintage because Frederich Abromowitz knew exactly which year the great wines were made and he believed no wine bottle should be opened that didn't have at least three to five years to mature. Occasionally, his aged wine steward politely disagreed with Abromowitz in the wine steward's belief that you really needed five to seven years for a good red wine to mature, but, of course, the wine steward obeyed the final decision of Abromowitz when it came to the ultimate decision of the wine served at dinner. Abromowitz not only enjoyed good wine as an oenophile, he also owned and occasionally participated in the operations of two large wineries located in the Barossa Valley outside of Adelaide, Australia.

After the staff had served the bread, the appetizers and the wine selections, they again withdrew, leaving the diners in privacy.

"Do you always eat this well, Frederick?" The senator asked as he sampled each appetizer.

"I pick a lot, Senator. But I try to sample everything," he paused and smiled at the countess, "as I do in life. What good is wealth unless you can try everything this earth can provide."

"Frederick is always growing, Senator," the countess said while reaching over to touch the back of Abromowitz' arm.

"Only in the twenty-first century can a poor Jewish boy from Poland meet such a wonderful lady like Philicia here." Abromowitz said with a large grin on his weathered face. As suddenly as the smile appeared, it vanished as Abromowitz spoke in a measured tone, "We are at that time when we either have to go forward with the merger or not, Senator…Jack. Do you have enough of the shareholders votes behind you to go forward?"

Jack Evan nodded toward Lowry who was clearing his throat to answer Abromowitz.

"Mr. Abromowitz, we are in the process of tallying the votes. The only problem…and its not such a problem that it can't be resolved in a few days…is tallying up the proxies. Many of our shareholders are overseas and we need to wait three more days to receive those votes. Also, if I may mention, Senator…Jack…bothersome judgment…"

"You mean the one for a billion and a half dollars? That is decidedly bothersome." ThatAbromowitz interjected.

"Yes, that one."

The senator's voice interrupted Lowry, "Frederick…we have found a solution in that matter. It's been told to me, and Alfred, correct me if I'm wrong, the senior federal judge in Orlando has granted Comtel's permission to remove the entire class action suit into the federal court. I believe he's reviewing the documents now. And," the senator paused to smile and then continued in a conspiratorial tone, "and I believe he will rule in our favor."

"You mean what?" Horst Steingut, AMT's counsel asked in a suspicious voice.

"Tell him Alfred," the senator ordered.

"We think our motion to dismiss has merit because the class certification that was granted by the State judge was erroneously approved. Secondly, I think that because of the differences in the individual damage claims, among other problems, the Federal Court will most likely reverse the decision to certify the class and the verdict itself, and dismiss the case entirely."

"How do you know that for sure if the court is still reviewing the papers?" Abromowitz asked.

The senator finished a glass of excellent shiraz before he answered. "The federal judge…the one deciding the case…he's one of my appointees to the federal bench. Lets just say, he's an ambitious man and he can't get what he wants unless I get what I want."

"So the judgment will disappear?" Abromowitz asked as he wiped his mouth with the linen napkin after he devoured an escargot en croute.

"I think so, Mr. Abromowitz," Lowry answered.

"Are we sure?" Horst questioned in a disbelieving voice.

"I am as sure, counselor, as I opine that this shiraz is the best red wine I've tasted in years," the senator replied.

"What about the one percent or more of the shareholder votes that your employees hold?" Horst asked.

"Many of those employees, unfortunately, have passed away," Jack Evans said.

"As you know Frederick, the option clause where most of the employees' stock was purchased under, compels the employees' estates to sell the stock back to the corporation upon the death of the employee before retirement. And that's been done in the ten incidents."

"You mean the employees who have died by natural causes?" Abromowitz asked in a cynical tone.

"Yes. Those employees held the greatest amount of stock among all of our employees. Since they held a large portion of the one percent of the voting shares needed to block the merger, I think we're home free with the rest of our voting shareholders."

Abromowitz smiled and continued to finish off the escargot in front of him. Then, Abromowitz washed a slice of bread down with a glass of white Sancerre wine.

"What about the under-financed employee pension plan?" Horst suddenly asked, his voice unrelenting in its intensity.

Lowry looked at the senator and Jack Evans with a quizzical look. His eyes closed into slits as he awaited the silent nod from his Comtel superiors.

"What do you mean Mr. Steingut?" Jack Evans inquired innocently.

"Well, Mr. Evans, our auditors have reviewed your books and records and they have determined that your employees' pension plan is acutely underfinanced. Which, of course, means that when the FCC and SEC and the Justice Department review our application for the merger, they will conclude, as our people have concluded, that Comtel is probably over five hundred million dollars in the red in financing employees' retirement plans."

"Have you considered the employees that did not reach retirement…the ones that died…their retirement plans are substantially reduced," Jack Evans replied.

"We have taken all that in to account, Mr. Evans." Steingut stated with finality. "You're still five hundred million in the red."

"Well," the senator said, "I'm sure we can come up with the difference. Can't we Jack? We have reserves."

Jack Evans looked over at Lowry who was looking down at the top of the table.

"We'll make up the difference, Mr. Steingut," Jack said.

"And I'd be careful about those offshore partnerships," Abromowitz stated in a whisper. "Because of the Enron fiasco, your IRS is looking at all corporations who have offices in the islands. I believe Comtel has an office in Nassua. Isn't that so, Horst?"

"Yes, sir...and a sizable interest in the Inter-Island Bank there."

"When will AMT shareholders meet to vote on the merger?" Jack asked of Abromowitz.

"We have scheduled an emergency shareholders meeting in Paris in two weeks. I'm not concerned about our shareholders, Jack. Fortunately, a simple majority of voting shares will allow AMT to satisfy its commitments in the merger. Isn't that so, Horst?"

"Yes, Mr. Abromowitz. And because of your family's shareholder interest in AMT, we can be assured of a majority vote in favor of the merger."

The stewards and stewardesses cleared the dishes from the table. The wine steward brought new wine glasses and placed them in front of the diners. Patiently, he went around the table with his golden trolley and poured the selected wine into the diner's large globe glasses. The countess requested a 1989 Dom Perignon champagne and it was quickly brought up from the wine cellar by a young stewardess. The countess tasted a small amount, held it briefly in her mouth and then swallowed the champagne. She nodded to the wine steward to leave the bottle in the side ice bucket.

Shortly there after, the staff brought out the entrees consisting of grand veneur de chevreuil (roasted leg of venison) served with a rich brown velvety sauce flavored with braised chestnuts, escalope de veau aux morilles (veal cutlets surrounded by morel mushrooms, served in a sauce of pan juices, Madeira wine and meat essence), and poulet de Bresse (sautéed chicken from Bresse served in its own juices). After the dishes were brought out and each diner selected his or her entrée, the quiet at the table was broken only with the Christophe silver forks and knives touching the Limoges plates and into the discerning mouths of each of the diners.

The senator regaled his dining companions with stories of the idiosyncrasies of famous politicians and celebrities. Since he had been in the limelight for almost five decades his stories included every name since the time Greta Garbo married up to and including the Clinton/Lewinsky under the table affair.

The countess laughed and spurred on the aging raconteur. She was one hell of a listener, Jack Evans noted. He had always admired a woman who can listen to a man bare his life and soul and still seem to be participating in the conversation. Her emerald green eyes were alive and sparkling as the senator went from one story to another addressing his tales directly to the countess. Jack noticed that this elfin-sized beauty drew the attention of the men all around her without contributing any revelations of her own.

Finally, when the senator had tired from his story telling, a quiet enveloped the dining table. The countess then said, with an ebullient smile on her face, "Frederick, when we become one…I'm referring to our intended merger…we must make the senator a star. Just like Larry King, Senator." She addressed her words to a beaming Senator Evans. "Has anyone told you what an exciting personality you have? I could sit here and listen to you all night. Isn't that so, Frederick?"

Abromowitz smiled knowing that the countess could make a frog into a prince with one of her smiles and kind words so elegantly spoken.

"You missed your calling, Senator," Abromowitz said.

"I was on the stage when I was a young man, Frederick. But alas I got caught up in the awful tentacles of politics and I succumbed to the wiles of power and greed."

"I don't imagine you're an easy conquest, Senator," the countess remarked as she leaned over to touch his hand.

"Why thank you, Countess. I've been called worse, believe you me. But you develop a rather thick skin when you are in the public eye. Not like my son here." The senator nodded toward Jack Evans seated next to her at the table. "He likes to run things behind the scenes."

"Well obviously you and your son make a good team, Senator," the countess said looking directly at Jack Evans.

Jack's face displayed a knowing smile as he listened to her flattering remarks. He knew his father's vanity was probably the senator's only vulnerable spot, but fortunately Jack was always there to protect the senator's soft underbelly.

The wait staff removed the entrée plates as the head steward rolled out a three level trolley into the dining room upon which cheeses such as brie, camembert, roquefort and assorted other goat cheeses were placed. After the cheeses were selected and devoured and the plates removed, the trolley returned with an array of desserts. The orders for espresso coffees, cappuccinos and exotic teas were taken and quickly served along with the desserts.

Again a peaceful quiet settled over the table as the desserts and coffee were enjoyed and consumed by all.

Then came the after dinner drinks of either well-aged port, homemade grappa, or an assortment of various liquors presented on the rolling cart brought out by the wine steward.

It was midnight before the dinner had finally run its course. Everyone was cheerfully satiated by the food and wines and pleasant conversations, especially after the hard business talk had been explored early on in the dinner. The business talks were understood that they would be continued but Jack Evans was satisfied that the terms of the merger had been tentatively agreed upon.

The full moon floated directly above the massive pleasure liner, its rays softly gilding the vessel below.

Frederick and the countess bade farewell to Senator Evans, Jack Evans and Alfred Lowry who debarked into a sleek launch manned by two crew members of "The Ruchel." Although the parting was extremely warm and amicable, Jack Evans somehow couldn't exorcise the gut feeling he had that no deal was done until the deal was done. And the merger deal was not a done deal. Not yet.

After their guests left the boat, Abromowitz, Steingut and the countess sat out on the promenade deck sipping their port wine, watching the motor boat make its way to Palm Beach.

"Have you notified your contact at the SEC about the accounting discrepancies we found in Comtel's books?" Abromowitz asked in a sharp voice to Steingut.

"It's done, Mr. Abromowitz. I don't think Senator Evans will be able to repair the damage."

"Then we can buy the Comtel stock at a much lower price if the scandal forces it into bankruptcy. Would you agree, Horst?"

"Even if it doesn't go bankrupt, Mr. Abromowitz, I think those Comtel employees who own substantial stock holdings and make up the remainder of voting shareholders that could block the merger will want to sell to us. Why would they sell to a board of directors who don't give a damn about them?"

"Well, make sure nothing of this gets back to the Evans. Understand?"

"Yes, sir. It won't."

"We have to be discreet…also, Horst retrieve the tapes from the ship's recording machine. With proper editing the Evans might consider a hostile take over bid for Comtel by AMT"

"I'm sure the Evans would be surprised that the whole evening's conversation was recorded on our ship's audiotape, Mr. Abromowitz."

The countess smiled an enigmatic smile and said, "You play very rough, Frederick. Just like your soccer team."

"That's business, darling. No quarter can be given if you want to win," Abromowitz said as he looked over at Steingut. "Go to sleep, Horst. You're going to have a busy few days setting our traps for the Evans and Comtel."

"Yes, sir," Steingut smiled with effort. "Good night, Countess. I'll see you in the morning."

The countess and Abromowitz were left on the promenade as the countess brought out a large Havana cigar and clipped off the tip. She then lit the cigar with a gold engraved lighter, handed it to Abromowitz who puffed luxuriously on the cigar. They sat there, content that they were holding the world in the palms of their hands.

Chapter Thirty-Two

Ryan had contacted the plaintiffs' committee who represented the class of employees of Comtel that had won the class action suit in the Florida State court. It appeared that the out of state firm that the original winning trial attorney was a partner in, wanted to withdraw as lead counsel because of the removal of the suit to the federal court and the death of its partner who had won the original suit. The partners felt that the present state of the suit in federal court would tax the limited resources and efforts of the New York law firm representing the class. Of course, the partners still wanted a pro rata share of any attorneys fees awarded by the federal court, but certainly would take less if Ryan and his associates were to assume the legal mantel for the plaintiffs and, of course, win the suit.

Ryan and Lawrence met at the coffee shop of the Renaissance Hotel. Except for a few late breakfast diners, the cavernous café was empty. Most of the staff seemed to be busy preparing for lunch. Lawrence's eyes looked blood shot and there were wrinkling bags growing under them.

They ordered coffee and juice and an array of bagels and toast.

"Do we really want the aggravation, Ryan?" Lawrence said as he sipped his hot coffee, almost spilling the black liquid on his golf shirt.

"If we don't take it, Everett…well…none of us except me has ever handled a class action suit."

"Have you actually handled a class action suit, Joshua? Especially in the federal court."

"I handled a small one but the case was never certified, Everett."

"The federal courts are different than the state courts, Joshua."

"A court is a court, Everett. You read the rule book and presto, you know the procedure. What's to be afraid of?" "Except," he continued, "Sosie, my wife, will bury me alive if I spend anymore time than I have to here in lovely Orlando."

"It could be over sooner than you think, Joshua," Everett replied as he nibbled on a toasted English Muffin.

"Yes…," Joshua said, "it will be over if that federal judge throws it out…and with the senator pulling the strings…"

"I can't help you folks out," Lawrence said, "but I have to agree with you. I think Stuyvesant wants to be on the appellate bench and the only way he's ever going to get there is if the senator paves the way. So…I agree that you might have a short lived case."

"Then we appeal," Joshua shot back. "I'm sure the senator doesn't control the appellate court in New Orleans."

"He was powerful enough to influence some of the Supreme Court judges six years ago during the presidential election." Lawrence said.

"Nobody can be that powerful," Joshua said.

"If you lose in the U.S. District Court, you'd be hide-bound to file an appeal…and that takes time and money and all your efforts," Everett replied.

"I think Mrs. Walsh can help us out there. Sam says she knows her way around the courts in Orlando…even the Federal Courts.

"Comtel plays rough, Joshua," Lawrence said with a worrisome look his face.

"Sam says Walsh sat twenty years on that Orlando bench and she supposedly faced the best lawyers in the state. I'm hoping she can handle whatever Comtel throws at us."

"We still have the grand jury hearing, Joshua," Lawrence said

"The trouble is, Everett, that even if you find out there is probable cause to bring an indictment against who…whatever…is it going to hold up if the A.G. tells you to forget about it." Joshua said.

"If that happens, we still have the media."

"If Comtel is in the case, the senator controls the media."

"Not the nationals."

"He will if the merger with AMT goes through," Joshua said.

"They'll control fifty percent of all the national television outlets…and most of the print companies, also," he added.

"Then we have to stop the merger, Joshua." Lawrence said.

"And how do you propose doing that, Everett."

"I don't know yet." Everett replied.

"I wouldn't bet on getting any indictments," Joshua warned. "But maybe," he stopped momentarily, his face screwed up in what looked like painful thought, then said in a rush, "I still think that Comtel and the Evans are screwing around with their books." He paused again and looked over at Everett. "Everett, isn't it rather unusual, for the SEC to conduct this investigation on certain accounting practices of Comtel but yet keep it under wraps. They usually love to leak out all kinds of juicy tidbits to the public. What the hell are they hiding, and why?"

"The chairmen of the SEC is beholden to…"

"Let me guess," Joshua said with a flourish, "the senator. Doesn't this guy ever let the process work without his influence?"

"It's been over forty years." Lawrence said. "That's a long time to be in Washington. He makes a call and the country turns around for him. I know," Lawrence said. "One call for me and suddenly I was the Assistant U.S. Attorney in Florida. Just four years out of law school, no experience and whammo, I'm the second most important lawyer in the federal legal world in Florida."

"I happen to know a lawyer who's near the top of the SEC," Everett suddenly added in a low voice.

"Maybe that's the answer," Joshua said.

"What is?" Lawrence asked.

"The SEC has been investigating Comtel for months. Ever since the Enron fiasco blew apart. They surely weren't so quiet with the Enron investigation. Why are they so suddenly discreet with Comtel?" Joshua asked.

"Maybe I should take a trip to Nassua," Joshua added.

"What's in Nassau?" Everett asked.

"My information…Yehuda's people in the Mossad who stick their noses into everything…"

"Why would the Mossad be interested in an American company?" Everett asked in a suspicious voice.

"Comtel and AMT want to open in Haifa…anyway that's what they told Yehuda. Also, Comtel and the Evans have been salting away million of dollars in their Nassau bank. The Inter-Island Bank of Nassau. And from there it goes to their Swiss corresponding bank… Geneva International…and then back into the Evan' private Swiss accounts. They put in the money, then skim it off the top and it comes out freshly cleaned and smelling like real tax free money."

"Can you find any evidence in Nassau?" Everett asked.

"Yehuda's friends in the Mossad know the manager of the Inter-Island Bank real well. A Mr. Coleman. Even well enough to get his son, he just graduated from Harvard, a job at one of the Mossad's Israeli corporations that have offices in New York. Computers or something. Anyway, he's been kind enough to let our people look over the bank records of Comtel's deposits…cash deposits for the last ten years or so. Very enlightening reading, Everett."

Joshua's eyes stared blankly out the restaurant's picture window and then suddenly he continued absent mindedly, "What do I do, Everett? I take on the class action representation or not? I have to tell the plaintiffs' group in the next few days. A reply brief is due in federal court to Comtel's motion to dismiss the suit in two weeks. Time is of the essence."

The two men looked at each other, no one saying anything for almost a minute. Each man occupied himself with either another bite of a bagel or downing another gulp of coffee or juice.

Joshua finally declared, "I guess I can answer my own question. I'm committed. It was Sam's sister, and even though they weren't the best of friends, I feel I have to do this thing for Sam. Besides, I think the stink from The Park is so strong, I couldn't breathe the air in Miami if I didn't do something to clean it up."

"I'll help you as much as I can, Joshua. But, don't depend on it. I'm fighting my own battle…and I hope it's not a losing one."

Joshua lifted up his coffee cup and toasted, "What the hell, Everett. You only live once. Let's play ball! All we can do is lose the game."

"I hope that's all we can lose, Joshua," Everett replied with a grim look on his face.

Chapter Thirty-Three

Yehuda and Ryan were picked up at Nassau International Airport by a chauffeured limousine that Yehuda had arranged.

They walked through the empty terminal with the black chauffeur, passed the custom officials who didn't seem to care who they were, into the sun-drenched street outside. Numerous black vendors were hawking an assortment of straw baskets, hats and clothing items. The chauffeur led them to a limousine parked along the curb on the far side of the circle drive situated in the front of the terminal.

"You're booked at the King Neptune, Mr. Ben Zvi," the chauffeur said as he led them to the limo at the curb.

On the way to town, Yehuda informed Joshua that they were to stop at the Inter-Island Bank of Nassau. It was a meeting with the manager, a Mr. Coleman, arranged by Yehuda's Mossad friends.

In the center of town they exited the limo and walked down the main street which was filled with native hawkers stationed along the sidewalks in front of the many retail shops which mostly sold gold and jewelry items to the tourists. The rays of the hot sun enveloped every part of the town. The buildings reminded Joshua of the buildings he had seen in Key West. Pastel clapboard buildings with porched verandas on the second floor, retail shops filling the street level. The next street over, the main drag,

Joshua could see the mammoth cruise ships parked alongside the concrete piers patiently awaiting for the return of their passengers.

They arrived at the bank with in minutes. Yehuda and Joshua walked into the bank directly to the high counter in the middle of the marble floored main level. Yehuda completed a deposit slip and then they walked to a woman seated at a desk off the corridor, handed her the deposit slip and asked to see the manager. She led them back to the manager's office.

Coleman got up from his desk to greet the two men by shaking each of their hands.

"Good to see you, Mr. Ben Zvi," Coleman said in a not so anxious to see you voice. He looked past the duo through the plate glass window that faced the main hallway of the bank. After inviting the two guests to sit down in the chairs in front of his desk, he returned slowly to his chair behind the desk.

"I understand your son Douglas likes working in New York?" Yehuda asked in a knowing voice.

Coleman smiled a gapped tooth smile as he replied, "He loves the people he works for. Mostly Israelis. But they are nice people…"

Yehuda smiled and said without any irritation, "Some of us are, Mr. Coleman."

"You know what I mean. My son never met Israelis before. You know you hear such stories about them. The bombings…and all."

"We know what you mean, Mr. Coleman," Yehuda said in a conciliatory tone.

"I understand Comtel owns part of the bank," Joshua said.

Coleman anxiously peered over their heads for a moment as if he was trying to determine if anyone could see or hear what was happening in his office.

"Yes, that's true," he absentmindedly replied.

"We want to know about the cash Comtel's been depositing here, Mr. Coleman." Joshua stated, a broad friendly smile crossing his handsome face.

"I can get into a lot of trouble, Mr. Ryan."

"Your son likes his job, Mr. Coleman?" Yehuda asked pointedly.

Coleman deliberated for a moment, his hand nervously brushing the side of his face, his other hand beating a rapid drum beat on the desk. "I've been here ten years."

"And in those ten year, Mr. Coleman…how much cash has Comtel deposited and transferred to Geneva International in Switzerland?" Joshua asked.

"Something like three hundred to six hundred million dollars," Coleman replied in an incomprehensible whisper.

"Do you have the specifics in writing, Mr. Coleman? Records, books, transfer slips…the paperwork that backs up those numbers," Joshua asked.

Coleman opened the bottom drawer of his desk and pointed to several accordian files of documents.

"Is it three hundred or six hundred, Mr. Coleman?" Yehuda insisted.

"Six hundred and forty-seven million dollars." Coleman blurted out.

The two men looked at each other. Ryan's mouth seemed to be taking in massive gulps of air as he absentmindedly rubbed his nose with his thumb.

"And what happens to the money after it's deposited here by Comtel, Mr. Coleman?" Ryan asked.

"We transfer it to our Swiss correspondent, Geneva International. What happens after that, I don't know."

"That's not true, Mr. Coleman," Yehuda declared with a lurking grin on his face. "You get copies of the transfers and deposits of the money from

Geneva International to other accounts in other banks, don't you? Like the Evans' personal accounts."

"We have those. But I don't know how accurate they are."

"Who deposits the money here? For Comtel?" Ryan asked.

"Usually Mr. Lowry. And lately we've seen Mr. Paulsen."

"Are there any affiliated companies, partnerships, whatever…to Comtel that your bank does business with?" Ryan asked, his mind narrowing to the guts of his inquiries.

"Several. Besides the money deposited into the Comtel account…there are about four of five partnerships that Evans puts money into those accounts."

"Are the individuals listed…the ones that are the partners?" Joshua asked.

"Mostly the Evans family. Also Lowry and I think somebody named Borden."

"He's the CFO of Comtel," Joshua added.

"How much money in cash has been put into the partnership accounts?" Joshua persisted.

"I haven't added it all up. But I guess probably over another hundred million dollars."

"And that money also goes to Switzerland?" Yehuda asked.

"Some of it goes into investments in the island. Like those condos you saw on the way from the airport."

"Can we get a copy of these records you have in your desk, Mr. Coleman?" Yehuda asked as he pointed his finger down to the bottom drawer holding all the documents.

"I'd get in a lot of trouble if I do…It's against the law in Nassau to give out confidential banking information."

"I hear your son is up for a promotion," Yehuda said in a friendly voice.

"I'll see what I can do, Mr. Ben Zvi."

"Just put the files on your desk and leave us alone for about twenty minutes, Mr. Coleman." Yehuda instructed.

"I'm afraid for my family." Coleman stated

"If anybody threatens you or your family, Mr. Coleman, we'll protect you," Yehuda offered.

"How?" Coleman replied quickly.

"We deal with bad people every day, Mr. Coleman," Yehuda said as he rose from his chair.

"You can have them for twenty minutes, Mr. Ben Zvi. I'll leave my office for twenty minutes. Please, no longer."

Yehuda and Ryan stood up and shook Coleman's hand. Ryan could feel the sweat on Coleman's palms as he observed the fear in his eyes.

Coleman said nothing as he left his office. Yehuda pulled out a small Minolta camera and immediately photographed the documents on the desk which Ryan had extracted from the accordion files. They were finished in less than twenty minutes as Coleman returned to his office.

Chapter Thirty-Four

The café was located in a corner of a fortress-like amphitheatre surrounded by sixty thousand or so of various species of fish swimming contentedly in the floor to ceiling tanks of the first level of Nassau's King Neptune Hotel.

Seated in a secluded booth in the far corner of the café were Yehuda, Ryan and Matilda Gosling. Her voluptuous body was enwrapped in a sarong type ensemble which barely covered her overflowing breasts. She wore almost no makeup accept for a little eye shadow that emphasized the greeness of her eyes. Ryan thought her innocent face belied the exuding sensuality of her body. Yehuda had told him the background details of Matilda Gosling's worldly young life. From the attentive gaze that she showered on Ryan's face, it was apparent that Matilda Gosling knew how to attract any man. She slowly sipped the white wine in front of her.

"Is this the first time you gentlemen have been to the King Neptune?" She asked with a captivating smile.

"First time we've been to Nassau," Yehuda answered, his eyes fixed on her bosom.

"Do you spend most of your time on the island?" Ryan asked.

"Some. My job takes me all over the world, Mr. Ryan."

"For the hotel?"

"Yes. A good part of my job is for the King Neptune…but…anyway, I want to hear more about you gentlemen." Her natural red lips opened to a sparkling brace of perfectly aligned white teeth, her tongue sensually licking her lips and teeth.

Ryan was surprised at the electricity this woman generated just by opening her mouth and smiling.

"I'm a retired lawyer," Ryan declared. "And Yehuda is an archeologist studying island formations in the Carribean. Isn't that so, Yehuda."

"Retired also?" Mathilda directed her question to Yehuda.

"Semi-retired. All depends on the formations I'm searching for."

"You're very young to be retired, Mr. Ryan."

"Yehuda is my father-in-law and he supports me and my family. Isn't that so, Yehuda?"

Yehuda laughed a boyish laugh. "He should live so long. Joshua is independently wealthy. A rich father…Isn't that so, Joshua?"

"Well, it's nice to be in the company of independently wealthy men, gentlemen."

"And you?" Yehuda asked of Mathilda, whose long, red colored nails covered her wine glass as she lifted her glass to her mouth.

"I have a small nest egg. Nothing of any consequence. But, I hope to have a lot more in a few months."

"Comtel?" Yehuda asked innocently.

"Perhaps," she replied equally innocently.

"The merger?" Ryan asked.

Matilda's eyelids opened up wide as Ryan mentioned the merger. "You know about the merger?" She asked, apparently surprised.

"We're stockholders of Comtel," Yehuda answered.

"Really?" She asked.

"I guess you know about AMT then," she added.

"Sure," Ryan interjected. "We know about Frederick Abromowitz, also."

She smiled at the mention of the name, "Yes, I have met Mr. Abromowitz."

"We need your help, Ms. Gosling," Ryan said in a quiet needy voice.

"Sure, how can I help you, gentlemen?" Matilda replied as if she really wanted to help.

"We think Comtel may be involved in the mysterious deaths in Orlando." Joshua stated.

"You've heard about those deaths, Ms. Gosling?" Ryan added.

"Yes. Yes, I have. But I never heard Comtel was involved."

"It may not be," Ryan interjected quickly. "But the victims are all Comtel employees…older employees. Employees that seem to own a great amount of stock in Comtel. Voting stock."

"So what?" She replied with a tinge of anger filling her voice.

"Its probably nothing, Ms. Gosling." Yehuda said. "But if Comtel is involved…Well, for all the shareholders…you, me and Josh here…well it sure could kill the value of our stock especially if this merger falls through."

"Gentlemen, you're wasting your time. If you think I'm going to give you damaging information about Comtel…well, you've got the wrong girl." Matilda slid out from the booth table and stood alongside Joshua and Yehuda.

"There is a grand jury investigation going on, Ms. Gosling," Joshua offered.

"I don't know anything about grand juries or whatever. You want information about Comtel, call Jack Evans up. I'm just a poor working girl. I know nothing, gentlemen. Nada. Do you understand?"

"You could be dragged into this investigation, Ms. Gosling," Joshua stated.

"Me?" She laughed as she placed her hand on her chest, "I'm a peon, gentlemen."

"Not from what we hear, Ms. Gosling," Joshua's voice tightened.

"Well, fuck you, gentlemen. Excuse my French…but I just follow orders. Nothing more, nothing less."

"You could be subpoenaed to testify before the grand jury, Ms. Gosling," Joshua added.

"So, I'll tell them the same thing I'm telling you. I don't know nothing," she half shouted as she straightened her skirt and turned away from Joshua and Yehuda. She strode purposely through the restaurant into the wide corridor holding the floor to ceiling fish tanks.

"I don't think she would voluntarily testify against our friends at Comtel," Joshua said as he slowly chewed on the straw dipped into his lemonade drink.

"At least we got the records. Let's see what Sam's friendly ex-SEC accountant says the records show, Joshua."

"At least, lets have dinner here…I hear the seafood is great," Joshua said with a smile across his face.

Chapter Thirty-Five

Everett Lawrence knew that he would never resume the grand jury investigation by going through the normal channels of the Justice Department. His own immediate superior, Bartholomew and the A.G. himself were dead set against having Comtel and the Evans implicated in The Park deaths. Senator Evans had his hands around the A.G.'s throat as well as the SEC investigators. Or it certainly appeared so. There was only one man who could countermand the A.G., Judge Stuyvesant and Bartholomew. The President of the United States. But Lawrence knew Bancroft, the Republican president, would never intercede in a local matter, especially one involving his good friend Senator Evans. Everything was "a local matter" if the politicians in Washington wanted to avoid interceding in those affairs. An old political axiom was that hot potatoes were only dealt with in a cooking class. Everett knew he would never get near the president without an intro from someone more powerful than Senator Evans.

As Lawrence deliberated on his options, he sat across from Jo-Beth in The Palm restaurant, a newly opened Orlando steak and lobster eatery. It was Saturday night and the restaurant was packed with local politicians and celebrities. Only Jo-Beth Washington, utilizing her bravado and charm could obtain a prominent booth in the popular restaurant.

As the massive porterhouse steaks surrounded by the equally massive steak fries were served by the butcher aproned waiter, Lawrence's mind was miles away. As far as Washington, D.C. Into the office of Simon

Warner, confidant to presidents, no matter what their political persuasion might be. Pitch black in skin color, Simon Warner had no fear in revealing the obvious to the presidents he counseled with, that Warner's skin was indeed black and he would use that blackness for his own advantage any way he could. No politician wanted to mess with Simon Warner because they knew that Warner had substantial credibility with not only most of the millions of black voters in the U.S. but also most of the millions of white left-leaning liberals who took pride in conforming their allegiance to Warner's politics.

Warner had been Mr. Inside in Clinton's administration, even to the extent of sleeping in the Lincoln bedroom's king size bed (perniciously rumored alongside Hillary). Yet, he still retained enough power to be called for advisory sessions with President Bancroft and his Republican cabinet.

Warner was Lawrence's black mentor. Not publicized in any of the scandal sheets, Warner saw Lawrence as a probable successor to his Mr. Inside position in Washington politics.

"Your mind is a million miles away, Everett dear," Jo-Beth said in between hungry bites of her steak.

"About one thousand miles is more like it."

"Eat your steak, Everett. You'll grow up to be a big strong colored boy who can fight the big bad white slaver." Her accent was inflected with the flavor of the poor black southerner of the distant past.

"That's what I'm trying to figure out, Jo-Beth darling. How to fight back against the evil oppressors of our people." He laughed. The banter between them was ongoing; Jo-Beth, the revolutionary black and Lawrence, the integrated black who argued that the white man's world had accepted him into it's bosom.

"If you don't eat your steak, I'm going to take it home with me and eat if for lunch tomorrow." She paused momentarily from her eating and reached out over to touch Lawrence's hand. "You haven't said a word in about an hour. What's got you going, Everett?"

"I need to get that grand jury hearing going again. And I'm trying to figure a way to bypass the big boys."

"Who the hell is Simon Warner?"

With a perplexed look on his face, Everett asked. "How'd you know about Simon Warner?"

"You talk in your sleep. That's all I heard from you last night."

"He's an important man in Washington."

"How important?"

"He talks to the president everyday"

"That important. Well maybe he can get you to talk to the president also."

"That's what I've been thinking about the last couple of days."

"President Bancroft is a Republican. Why would he help a black politician?"

"Cause even Republicans need black folks."

"You're going to get yourself hurt, Everett if you step on the Man's toes."

"Somebody has to do it, Jo-Beth." Everett said with a chuckle. He started to bite into his platter sized steak after pouring A-1 and Worcheshire sauces all over the steak.

"You're gonna drown that steak, Everett."

Everett's mind spiraled back to the summer after his second year at Rutger's Law. He had been invited by Simon Warner's law firm to work in their office in Washington, D.C. After a month of fourteen hour days stuck in the back of the firm's massive law library doing research, Simon Warner himself appeared like some kind of a black wraith.

Everett's head was buried in a case book when he looked up to see

Simon Warner's giant body hovering over him. He jumped up from his chair and was ready to salute the giant black man standing so quietly before him.

"So you're the new black law student they have hidden in the backyard of our liberal law firm. Do they feed you once a day or do you brown bag it?"

"Brown bag it, sir," Lawrence's voice cracked as he sputtered the words out.

"They say you're pretty smart for a black boy. They usually got them affirmative action niggers to show off their liberal bullshit."

"No sir…I graduated Phi Beta Kappa from Yale undergraduate."

"Come with me," Warner paused and then said, "what's your name, boy?"

"Everett, Everett Lawrence, sir."

"I'm going to take you to the U.S. Supreme Court today, Everett Lawrence. I want you see how all those white folks on that bench cow-tow to me because they know I'm black and they know I know they know I'm black and that they better be nice to me because I'm black and I tell the world that's what I am…black as the black of Ace of Spades. Remember also, Everett Lawrence, that your black skin is not to be ashamed of… because as long as you know it, and you let the world know you're proud to be black, the world will tell you to your face that it's great to be black but in their heart of hearts them white folks hate you for being such a miserable nigger."

Lawrence, at that time, didn't know what the hell Simon Warner was talking about. Within a summer spent along the side of the black giant, Everett finally understood what his adopted padrone was talking about. Racial discrimination had not disappeared from American's heart and soul. It merely was buried beneath the outer layer of skin of America, never to be raised above the skin by the white politician. But when the black leader wanted something the white majority wouldn't give him, he, himself, raised the horrific specter of racial discrimination. And the white politician knew there was no logical nor acceptable response to such an egregious accusation.

The backlash of two hundred years of racial discrimination in America left no room for the white politician to maneuver when he was charged with being a racial bigot. He might as well hang himself from the same tree that his bigoted predecessors hung innocent colored people in the twenties, thirties and forties in the deep intolerant south.

Yet, Simon Warner had a lust for life unequalled by any of his black brothers who led the charge for civil rights. Lawrence accompanied Warner on his mentor's night crawling adventures into deepest Washington. With envious wonder, Everett witnessed Warner's insatiable sexual appetite. Within the period from dusk to dawn, Warner would fornicate with no less than three women; skin color, of course, was no object. And after a night of lustful fucking and drinking, Warner would arrive at his office refreshed and prepared to meet his obligations for the day.

Of course, as Warner's aide-de-camp, Lawrence was allowed to partake of the women Simon had no time or desire for. Within a week, Everett's sexual hormones were gratified, nay, completely spent…until, of course, the following week.

Most of all Everett Lawrence learned the meaning of black power. Without riots, without revolution or killings, the savvy black leader got whatever he wanted. Without even changing the system.

"I hear Simon Warner is a real ladies man, Everett," Jo-Beth said. She had completely ravished the one and half pound porterhouse steak and was eyeing Lawrence's half eaten steak.

"He's married, Jo Beth."

"That didn't stop your boy Clinton."

"How do you know all that juicy gossip?"

"I read the scandal sheets."

"That's just bullshit, Jo-Beth."

"I better not see your name in those papers doing what Simon Warner is accused of doing."

Everett laughed as he pushed his steak platter away from him. "Do you want dessert, Jo-Beth? They have a great strawberry cheesecake."

"I'm on a diet, Everett. No carbs. Just meat."

Again he laughed at the tiny girl sitting across from him. She had a body with a twenty-two inch waist and a thirty-six inch bust. Except for her breasts, her body was devoid of any excess fat.

"You don't have to lose any weight, Jo-Beth."

"I'd rather lose weight than lose you." Her eyes and her voice were suddenly serious, unquestionably sincere.

"Jo-Beth, I've been thinking," his hand covered hers on the table.

"About what?"

"If I ever get out of this mess, why don't we get married?"

"Careful, boy, you're going to get into another mess!" She paused and then continued, "But I do love you, Everett."

Lawrence reached into the pocket of his suit jacket and pulled out a small ring case. He opened it and showed it to Jo-Beth. The ring was centered by a large, clear green emerald surrounded by three small diamonds that sparkled under the spotlight situated above the booth.

Momentarily the smile disappeared from Jo-Beth's face. "Tell me why I should marry you, Everett?"

In a surprised voice Everett said, "Because I love you, Jo-Beth."

"Everett, you know, if we get married, the only way you can get rid of me is to kill me."

Everett smiled and reached out for her left hand. Adeptly he pushed the engagement ring onto her appropriate finger. "I bought the ring for you, Jo-Beth. If you don't want to get married, then keep the ring as a souvenir, but it'll be the biggest mistake you ever made."

Jo-Beth released a hearty laugh that made several people turn around and look at her. "Sure I'll marry you, Everett Lawrence. And bear your children and love your black ass when the world is dumping crap all over you. I'm your partner for life, Everett…as if you couldn't tell already."

He bent over the table and kissed her full on the mouth. All eyes and faces in the restaurant bore affectionate smiles as Everett and Jo-Beth turned to them and bowed their head graciously in response to their sudden out pouring of congratulations. Jo-Beth bowed her head graciously and then held up her hand to her fellow diners, and pointed at her ring.

Chapter Thirty-Six

The stretch limo picked Everett up at Reagan International Airport. He hadn't been back to D.C. for over six months. It was humid and hot, almost typical of early May in the Washington area.

Lawrence had opted to taxi into D.C. from the airport but Simon Warner had insisted on sending his personal limo to pick him up. "Nothing is too good for one of the brothers" Simon would say. He particularly wanted to show Lawrence that political power brought all kinds of goodies to the broker. Warner wanted to know if Everett would join him on the town after the meeting at the White House. Lawrence opted out knowing that Jo-Beth would somehow know if Everett had even looked at another pretty woman.

It was only yesterday that Lawrence had spoken to Warner about his problems. Within several hours of Lawrence's conversation with Warner, Warner called and told Lawrence to catch the morning flight to D.C. the next day. His appointment with the president was for that afternoon at 3:45 p.m. sharp. Lawrence had ten minutes to explain his problem and hope for a remedy from the President of the United States.

The limo was recognized easily by the White House Police and immediately allowed entry into the circle drive leading up to the west wing of the White House.

Simon Warner himself met Lawrence at the door of the west wing.

He placed his muscular arm around Lawrence's shoulders. His face was illuminated with the world famous Warner smile as Simon Warner led Lawrence through the marbled corridors of the West Wing of the White House. At some of the checkpoints in the White House, Warner and his guests were waved through. Still most of the checkpoints required metal detector scanning and identification passes displayed on the outside garments of Everett and Warner. Lawrence thought that Warner really appeared to be the chief resident of the White House instead of Bancroft.

"I had a real night on the town planned for us, Everett," Simon said as he led Lawrence into the reception area outside the oval office of the president.

"Thanks, Simon. But Jo-Beth…my lady…thinks that adultery is a capital offense."

Warner laughed loudly as he nodded to the several secretaries seated in the reception area.

"Hi, Ms. Ellstone," Simon said to a very white haired lady seated at the desk closest to the president's office.

"Hello, Mr. Warner…give him a couple of minutes. I'll let him know that you're out here."

Within minutes, Lawrence and Warner were ushered into the truly oval shaped office where President Ulysses Bancroft sat poring over some documents on his large leather top desk. Lawrence was surprised that the office looked exactly like the set of the television show about the White House. Two aides were seated on the couch in the middle of the room.

President Ulysses Bancroft was a small man with a small square face that was centered around very round brown eyes that stared laser-like into the face he was observing.

"Simon…I haven't seen you…in what, twenty-four hours. How are you?" The president said in a high pitched distinctive voice that sounded like it came from a Texas rodeo jamboree. "Let me introduce you fellows to my right hand people. Mr. Wright and Mr. Sloan," the president pointed his arm to the two young aides who quickly rose from the couch to shake Everett's and Warner's hands.

"Fine, Mr. President. May I introduce my former law clerk and friend, Everett Lawrence." Everett walked toward the president who had extended his hand to Everett.

"So you work for my old friend, Jeremy Wadsworth. How is Jeremy doing lately?"

"Well, sir…Mr. Wadsworth is the A.G…as you know…I rarely get to see him."

"He's doing one hell of a job over at Justice."

"Yes sir. I wouldn't know. I'm based down in Orlando."

"Well that's great. I love Florida. That state put me over the top in the last election, you know."

"Yes, I know sir."

"Senator Evans was a big help…You know Senator Evans, Mr. Lawrence?"

"Not very well. He was helpful in getting me into the Justice Department."

"Good man, Osgood. Even if he's a goddamn Democrat." The President laughed huskily, the laugh sounding more like a guffaw to Lawrence.

"Okay, Mr. Lawrence. May I call you Everett?"

"Yes, sir, please do."

"Simon here filled me in on your concern with the, what are they… accidents. Whatever is happening down in Florida. I'd love to help but I don't want to interfere with a situation being handled now in a proper manner."

"Mr. President, if we don't find out what's happening down there, it could turn into a situation that will need much more than handling."

"Why is that, Everett? Why can't we let the state boys handle the investigation? Isn't that what Justice normally does?" The President's voice hardened as he rattled off the questions to Lawrence, but his eyes included Warner in the questioning.

"Mr. President, Senator Evans and his company could be involved," Lawrence blurted out.

The President's face turned sour and he curled his upper lip to the left of his mouth. His eyes took on an angry dreaded glint.

"Have you talked to the Justice about this? Isn't it procedure to go through Justice? You know Wadsworth is a thorough, stick-to-the-book, Attorney General, Mr. Lawrence."

"I have, Mr. President. Justice doesn't want to touch it."

"Then why should I, Mr. Lawrence?" Everett noticed the president was no longer calling him by his first name.

"Because I think the killings of Comtel's senior employees and substantial shareholders are deliberate and may involve the contemplated merger of Comtel with AMT."

President Bancroft retreated back to his desk. "Gentlemen, please sit down." Bancroft pointed to the two armchairs in front of his desk. He turned his swivel chair around to face the window behind his desk. Nothing was said for several moments.

"Simon, you and your friend are asking me to jeopardize my party's position with a powerful friend and crucial ally."

"Sir, respectfully, Senator Evans' actions may do much more damage to your party if he's allowed to continue what's been going on," Everett warned.

"Mr. President," Warner interrupted, "if the shit hits the fan… Comtel will make the Enron scandal look like getting caught throwing a spitball in a baseball game."

"What would you have me do?" The president repeated in a half hearted voice.

"All we ask, sir, is that you let the grand jury investigation continue." Lawrence replied.

Bancroft raised himself from his chair and walked back and forth in front of the office window looking out to Pennsylvania Avenue. "Clinton had more trouble in his last two years than he had in the first six years of his administration. I don't want to follow in his footsteps."

"Mr. President," Lawrence said in a pleading voice, "if we don't continue with the investigation and it comes out later that Comtel…the Evans…were responsible for ten deaths and maybe more to come, just to eliminate any obstacles with their merger with AMT…well, sir, the fall out for your administration and your place in history would be devastating."

"Mr. Lawrence, there's no evidence."

"There's a great deal of evidence, sir," Lawrence persisted as he rose from his chair to face the president.

"I don't have it, Mr. Lawrence…nobody has shown me anything," he angrily replied.

Warner also arose from his chair. He towered over both men as he said, "Mr. President…you know me, how many years now? Have I ever steered you down a dead end. If what Everett has told me is true, probably true, well, I just don't see how you can disregard it."

"What evidence do you have, Mr. Lawrence?"

"Forensic evidence that the houses where the victims lived had been tampered with. Vents had been sealed to produce fatal doses of carbon monoxide in the homes where these employees lived…and died."

"So what? Why would Comtel…Senator Evans want to kill their employees? It doesn't make sense."

"On the face of it, you're right, Mr. President. But when you tie in the stockholdings of those employees, they almost held enough shares to block the merger with AMT."

"Who would benefit most from the merger, Mr. Lawrence?" The president asked.

"The Evans family, the large shareholdings of the executives, the merger would have allowed them to make billions. For the little guy, well, his stock value would be so diluted that he'd be better off selling out before the merger."

Everett's stomach was noticeably growling. He felt beads of sweat forming on his forehead. He wiped the sweat off with his handkerchief.

"Why was the grand jury investigation stopped and who stopped it?"

"It was on a cease and desist order signed by Judge Stuyvesant."

Bancroft's face glowered red when he heard Stuyvesant's name. He walked back to his desk and sat down, his body leaning forward as he rested it on his elbows planted on the desk.

"How far did you get in the hearing, counselor?" Bancroft addressed his question to Lawrence.

"The hearing was stopped by federal marshals before any witnesses could take the stand."

"But you didn't link Comtel or the Evans to the deaths?"

"Not yet, Mr. President. We were just getting to that part of the hearing."

"What evidence do you have against the Evans…against Comtel?"

"The ten victims were all senior employees of Comtel, Mr. President. Each one of the victims was the holder of thousands of voting shares of Comtel. All it would take to quelch the Comtel merger with AMT is one percent of common A stock which is a voting stock. If enough of the original senior employees voted against the merger, the merger would die stillborn. Comtel had a written provision in each of the stock option plans that the stock would revert back to Comtel if they died before retirement. And all of the victims were over sixty and close to retirement. Lastly, Mr. President, we had concrete, scientific evidence that each one of the victims died from the same cause. Lack of oxygen in the lungs and tissues of the body was found by the County Medical Examiner after the victims' bodies were autopsied. Dr. Pasha, the medical examiner, would have testified at the grand jury hearing that she concluded that the cause of the oxygen depletion arose out of a gaseous emission in each of the victim's houses. All built by Comtel. She further concluded that the probable toxic gas that filled these people's lungs was carbon monoxide emissions in the house. We think the carbon monoxide was caused by somebody's intentional act in cutting off the ventilation in the utility room of those houses. Through the further investigation by the Orlando Police Department and a forensic engineer named Bitterman, testimony elicited at the grand jury hearing would have proven that the cause of death in each incident was caused by carbon monoxide poisoning emanating out of an intentional act like shutting off the venting in the utility rooms of subject houses."

"That still doesn't link Comtel or any of its employees, Mr. Lawrence," the president stated with a voice mixed with anger and doubt.

"Comtel had the most to lose, Mr. President. If these employees had survived,as well as other senior employees that were still alive...well, they could have voted against the merger and succeeded in killing the merger. Some of the victims had also been members of a class action suit against Comtel. That's the billion and a half plus verdict Comtel is trying to set aside. Mr. President, the pieces of the puzzle were in the process of being put together when the grand jury hearing was aborted. And only Comtel would benefit if the grand jury stopped it's investigation."

Bancroft stared at Warner and Lawrence. His mind, as usual, was going in many different directions. Cause and effect. Do something, anything, and he knew there would be an opposite reaction. Bancroft now only cared to preserve his presidency for the sake of history. He had made many mistakes during his presidency, but somehow he and his administration had weathered the political storms accompanying the Bancroft administration. Now, at the end, he had nothing to gain by striking out for justice.

"I understand your position, Mr. Lawrence...Simon...I'll have to think about the situation and make a few phone calls. It's been a pleasure, gentlemen."

Bancroft rose from his chair, came around from his desk and extended his hand to Lawrence. They shook hands as Lawrence and Warner rose from their chairs.

Bancroft put his arms around Warner's shoulder as he led them out of the office into the reception area.

"Call me, Simon. I'll let you know what I decide."

With that farewell, Bancroft turned quickly around and re-entered into the oval office. He nodded angrily to his two aides, who were now standing mute in the middle of the oval office.

He then had his secretary call the Justice Department. Particularly Jeremy Wadsworth, the U.S. Attorney General. When Wadsworth came on the phone, Bancroft said in a stark, angry voice, "Jerry, what the hell's going on down there in Florida? I want you to get your ass up here pronto. Understand?"

He then violently hung the phone up, turning his chair towards the window as his eyes followed Warner and Lawrence's limo drive down the road to the White House gate.

Chapter Thirty-Seven

Captain Amos Parker sat across the dining room table from Indira Pasha, the medical examiner of Orange County. They were sipping kir royales that Ms. Pasha had prepared as pre-dinner cocktails. Centered in the ceiling of the brightly colored dining room was a Venetian chandelier that sprayed soft rays of light over the room. The dining room was small, filled with tasteful European antiques, including a 19th century wood dining room table.

"Do you still want a beer, Captain?"

"No, this will be fine, doctor," he shyly replied.

"Please call me Indira, Amos,"

He smiled that gruff broken toothed smile that caused his rough facial skin to wrinkle up like the face of a mammoth pug dog.

"Indira," he muttered the name, "the drink, what do you call it? It's fine."

"Kir royale. Champagne and a small amount of cassis. Just to sweeten the champagne."

"Pretty, isn't it?" She added.

"I'm just a beer and shot guy. But this is good."

"Let me fill your glass up again, Amos. Drink it slowly. I have to go into the kitchen and finish up the chicken masala. You'll love my chicken. Amos, do you like Indian food?" She rose from her chair and stood momentarily for his answer.

"I've never had it, doctor."

"Some people find it a little spicy, but I'm sure you'll like it."

She left the table to go into the adjacent kitchen. Amos Parker, dressed in a bright tan sports jacket and a sport shirt, gulped the fluted glass of champagne, then refilled it from the bottle sitting in the ice bucket by the side of the table. His eyes drifted around the delicate flower wallpaper in the room, his mind wondering how the hell he got roped into going to dinner at the medical examiner's house. Indian food to him was something you feed to your pet snake, if you had a pet snake. Amos Parker was a meat and potatoes man, with an occasional ear of corn thrown in during the corn growing season.

Dr. Pasha had visited him in the hospital after he had been shot, and they had talked about this and that and before he knew it he was accepting her invitation to dinner at her house. Not that he didn't fancy the pretty dark Indian woman, but Amos Parker's selection of women bordered on the barely educated, earthy women who hung around the Western bars that surrounded the Orlando area. He was a farm boy, raised in the rural boon docks of Kissamee in Central Florida where you learned about the opposite sex by rolling in the haystack with Cindy Lou or Betty Jane or whoever he could entice into his Poppa's massive barn. Sex was something you learned by watching the male sheep jump on the rear of the female sheep and hump his brains out while the female squealed herself into animal ecstasy.

Amos Parker had been married once, to a gal from Paduka, Kentucky who had drifted down to Orlando to waitress at one of the Western bars along the strip just outside of Kissemee. They had had a series of sexual encounters and after a weekend of straight banging and drinking, they both decided, in their drunken state, that marriage would be good to try. So they went to the nearest Justice of the Peace, who disregarded their obvious drunken state, and married them until death do them apart. Amos was married to Edith for about a year until he came home early one night to find her in bed with two drunken cowboys, in his trailer no less. They were all naked and the cowboys were in the midst of filling Edith's orifices with their organs, when Amos came into the trailer with his .357 standing right out there in front of them. The two cowboys sobered up real quick and with no further persuasion lit out of that trailer as if they had been attached to fiery rockets up their assholes. Edith did not object to the divorce.

Gentle, educated women, like Indira Pasha, were not what Amos Parker was used to socializing with. But she had insisted on making him wonder what the hell was wrong with this very civilized woman who had taken such an attraction to a cowboy like him.

Indira Pasha brought out the fired kulcha bread filled with onions, a yogurt dish filled with bits of cucumber, and spice filled deep fried shrimp rolls that burnt your lips as you swallowed it.

Amos Parker, at first, was wary of these strange dishes but after several exploratory bites, found himself enjoying the hot spicy tastes of the appetizers. Dr. Pasha also brought out a large pitcher of a mango based drink with a bit of rum in it. Parker knew that he had discovered a world that had nothing to do with Kissamee, Florida.

After the appetizers were eaten, Pasha refilled Parker's glass with straight champagne. His head started to buzz as it often did after he had gulped down a six-pack of beer.

"You like Indian food, Amos?" Pasha asked with a benevolent smile.

"I guess I do."

"Don't fill up yet. We still have the main dishes. They're favorites of my home in India."

"I think I flew over India on my way to Vietnam."

"You were in the Army?"

"The marines. I served two tours of duty in Vietnam. Saw a lot of my buddies die in front of me. It was a bad war."

"No war is good, Amos."

"Some you have to fight. Like my Pa did in World War II. But not in Vietnam."

"We were against the war."

"Didn't matter if I was or not. I had to go no matter what." Parker pulled out a cigar from his inside jacket pocket and asked if he could smoke.

Pasha smiled and asked him if he minded not to smoke. He smiled and put the cigar back into his jacket.

"My father was killed by the Japanese in World War II," she exclaimed.

"I'm sorry."

"It was a long time ago. I was no more than a baby."

"I saw enough killing in 'Nam to last ten life times."

"Let's forget about the wars. I'll bring out my chicken masala and shrimp tiki that will make you cry like a baby, Amos."

"That bad?" He chuckled as he spoke with a piece of onion kulcha bread still in his mouth.

She rose from the table and walked into the kitchen. Amos Parker's head was light and joyous. The succulent after taste of the spicy appetizers remained in his mouth. 'Forget about the war, she said,' he thought as he remembered the blood and gore of the Tet offensive or was the Tet defensive; he couldn't remember because the battle swung back and forth, no side claiming a victory until the bodies were counted. The shrapnel that was still buried in his body kept reminding him of the nightmare of those two years in the steamy jungles of Vietnam.

Coming back to the Orlando Police force was like coming back to a summer camp for girls. No horrific crime committed in Orlando matched the horror of those thirty some days in the Asau Valley in the central part of 'Nam. Names like Quan Tri, My Lai, Dien Bien Phu and of course, Chou Lai, especially Chou Lai. Parker walked into that village after the First Calvary had attacked and then butchered those women and children. His patrol had stumbled upon the village and the bodies because they had lost their way to Division headquarters. Every man in his platoon spilled their guts out onto those barren fields surrounding the village. Later, Master Sergeant Amos Parker had learned that the First Calvary was led by a Colonel Jack Evans and Captain Jon Paulsen who had subsequently been awarded medals for bravery in the Chou Lai offensive. For some reason, the ensuing inquiry into the massacre at Chou Lai had fizzled like warm beer. Amos Parker now understood the reason for the aborted investigation. 'Senator Osgood Evans no doubt,' he mused.

Dr. Pasha brought in the large platters of shrimp badami, chicken marsala and a heaping mound of hot white rice with raisins.

As they ate the steaming food, Pasha's eyes occasionally stared at the big burly man at the other end of the table. She had never been in the company of such a bearish man. Her ex-husband was small and lithe, more like a young girl than a man like Amos Parker.

"Do you like being a policeman?" She asked.

"It's the only real job I've ever had. Went right into the police force out of high school. Than the Marine Corp. Besides those two jobs, I've never had any other jobs." He paused in between bites of the chicken and shrimp and than continued, "Do I like it? Yes, I like being a cop…There's a code of rules that lets you know what's right and wrong. My daddy believed in the bible…the rules that are set down there…and he told me if you follow those rules, you'll die an honest man…you'll die without regrets."

"Are you an honest man, Amos?" She asked, her eyes fascinated by Amos Parker's weather skinned face that contained features that were all disproportionate to each other. A flattened nose that spread over the middle of his face, located just over his thick lips that covered two rows of irregular teeth. 'Yet when Amos Parker smiled, it made you want to return the smile,' Pasha thought.

"I think so," he replied, setting his fork down on the table.

"There sure is a lot of dipsy-doodling around Orlando but I just keep my nose clean and I can sleep like a baby at night."

"Even when it comes to Comtel?"

"Yes, even Comtel. I know they're mighty powerful in this state. What with Senator Evans telling everybody what to do. It don't bother me much who I bother…if they don't like it…well, I'll hand them my badge and go fishing down at Lake Ochochobee and collect my retirement checks."

"You receive the latest forensic report, Amos?"

"Yes, I did, Doctor."

"You saw the DNA results on the sputum found on the rifle that shot Mr. Ryan and you."

"Yes, I did. Jon Paulsen, my favorite butcher of Vietnam. Yes, maam. I sure did."

"He might be the killer of all these people, Amos."

"He might…and he might not. But right after dinner, I have an arrest warrant sitting in my office. It's made out for Mr. Paulsen."

"Please be careful, Amos. I'd be very disappointed if I lost my favorite dining guest." She smiled a forlorn smile.

"I don't think he knows anything yet. But if he does…well, I have the bullet proof vest in the car. It can stop any type of bullet."

"You're a very nice man, Amos."

"You're a nice lady, Indiri."

"I'd like you to come again, Amos. Many times."

He reached over to touch her tiny outstretched hand. For several moments they held hands together. Then he rose from his chair and came over to her, bent over and kissed her ever so gently on the lips. "I'm over fifty years old, Indiri," he said as his rough hewn hand touched her face.

She reached up to caress his hand.

"I want to be your friend, Amos."

He smiled and then returned to his chair. She rose and went into the kitchen. Shortly, she returned with two dishes of rasmali (a dessert of cheese and rose water) and placed them in front of Amos Parker.

"How about you, Indiri? I don't want to make a pig of myself."

"I love to watch a big man like you eat. I've had enough, Amos. Enjoy."

After the desserts and the after dinner drink she served to him, he kissed her full on the lips and he left her small, one-story rancher located on the back of the ninth hole of the Bay Side Golf enclave. Parker couldn't remember when he had had such a great meal with such a lovely lady. And, who for some strange reason, liked him for what he was. His mind echoed the warm fuzzy feeling generating in his stomach. There was a spring in his step as he walked down the path of Indiri Pasha's ranch house.

Amos had parked his car just across the street from Dr. Pasha's house. He couldn't wait to see her again. 'Maybe,' he thought 'he wouldn't die a bachelor after all.'

The shot was muffled as if a silencer had been placed over the snout of the rifle. Amos Parker's body hit the pavement of the path. The bullet had passed through his left shoulder and the shock of the rifle bullet hand had thrown his burly body to the ground with a resounding thud.

Indira Pasha happened to look out her front window when she saw Captain Parker lying still on the ground. She called 911 and rushed out to the Captain, crying quietly as she administrated CPR to ensure her friend would not be another dead victim.

Chapter Thirty-Eight

"I've been subpoenaed to testify in front of the grand jury next Wednesday," Lowry declared as he stood in front of Jack Evans who was seated at his desk in his office atop Comtel's forty-five story headquarter building overlooking The Park.

"I thought that was dead in the water, Jack," Jon Paulsen said as he stood behind Evan's desk looking out over the vast greenlands of The Park and onto downtown Orlando.

"Lawrence got to Bancroft," Evans replied in a sullen voice.

"I thought the Senator controlled the situation," Paulsen said.

"Lawrence somehow got to the president," Evans repeated.

"I heard he used his old colored mentor, Simon Warner," Paulsen replied.

"My father called yesterday and told me the good news. He's supposed to see Bancroft sometime this week. Maybe something can be done to kill the investigation."

"We have to kill more than the investigation, Jack," Paulsen stated with a sardonic smile elicited on his pencil thin lips.

"Jack," Lowry half shouted in a pleading voice, "no more…if they ever find out about…"

"What, Mr. Lowry?" Paulsen threatened as he walked over to tower over Lowry's smaller body.

"Look, Jack," Lowry disregarded Paulsen's nearness, "I've had enough. If there's anymore, you know what…I'm out."

"Where would you go?" Evans' voice was a mere whisper. "To Lawrence?" Evans added.

"I'd never do that, Jack!" Lowry replied.

"I think Mr. Lowry doesn't understand the situation, Jack. It's too late to turn back, Mr. Lowry."

"Sit down, Alfred." Evans ordered.

"I have two kids in college, Jack."

"Nobody's after your kids, Alfred." Evans said.

"My family's reputation, Jack. They'd uncover all the shit."

"They won't, Alfred, unless you tell them." Evans said as he stood up to tower over the seated Lowry.

"Why can't I just retire, Jack."

"You know what happens to employees who want to retire, Alfred."

The three men seemed frozen in place as their words created the intense, emotional vibrations filling the room. Lowry's unshaven face was near tears as he buried his face in his hands.

"Jack," Paulsen said as he walked behind the seated Lowry.

Evans held out the palm of his hand to Paulsen.

"Leave him alone, Jon. Alfred is a team player and he knows if he causes the team to lose, well, Alfred, you know I hate to lose. Don't you?"

Lowry's head suddenly bolted up from his hands, his eyes bleary and crazed with fear. "I'm subpoenaed, Jack. Under oath! What do I do when Lawrence questions me about. You know, everything. The deaths of our own employees…the stock transfers…the money in Nassau…and I'm general counsel to Comtel!"

"Tell them nothing, Alfred." Evans replied as he reached into his desk and withdrew an English Rothman cigarette.

"How can I tell them nothing, Jack? That would be perjury. I would go to jail for lying. You know I would never last a day in jail."

"You'd never last a day out here, Alfred, if Jon here does what he wants to do."

Lowry's small beady eyes stared insanely at Paulsen who was standing directly over him.

"Jack, I never signed up for this kind of deal! You never told me that I could go to jail!"

"Didn't I Alfred? I'm sorry I forgot to tell you that you can't get the brass ring unless you lunge out for it."

"The corporation has also been subpoenaed to produce their books and records to some independent auditor. He used to be with the SEC, Jack. We can't let him see the real books."

"Show him the books and records we base our quarterlies and annual reports on, Alfred. Its passed muster in the past."

"This guy is good, Jack. I don't think he wouldn't see through them."

"Can't we get to him?" Paulsen asked.

"Pay him off?" Lowry replied. "Not this guy. He had been with the SEC for over thirty years. The head of their criminal audit division."

"Then maybe we should make him disappear, Mr. Lowry?"

Lowry's small body lurched forward in the chair and then suddenly jumped up in the air as if he had been shot in the ass with a shotgun of pellets. He turned to leave the office but stopped in his tracks when Evans shouted after him, "Alfred, if you leave this fucking office without telling us what you're going to do in front of that grand jury, well, I'd have no choice but to let Jon here handle any future relations with you. Do I make myself clear? Comprenez-vous, mon ami?"

Lowry turned slowly, his shoulders slumped forward, his hand brushing away the tears running down his cheeks, as he said in a sputtering cadence, "Jack, I've taken all the shit I'm going to take. If you're going to kill me…there's nothing I can do to stop you. But I can't live with myself if I have to go on knowing what you're doing and me not doing anything about it." As the words rushed out of Lowry's quivering mouth, his voice gained a certain air of resolve. As if Lowry had decided life as it existed wasn't worth saving. All his life, Lowry had cow-towed to his so-called superiors; his father, his grandfather, Evans, judges, anybody who appeared to be better than him. But the pervasive fear that filled his mind and body all his life had somehow disappeared at this moment. Like letting go of the rope that is holding you to the mountain precipice; falling freely down the mountain without restraint, not caring if you lived or died anymore.

"Jack, all my life, people like you have scared the shit out of me. From my father to my ex-wife, to everybody who bullied me around. But I'll tell you, the last few months have been the greatest hell I've ever been in. And for me, today, it's over. I'm leaving here, and you can do what you want. But I'll tell you now, no matter what the consequences, I'm going to tell that grand jury the truth, so help me God. So help me God." Lowry repeated as he turned and strolled out of Evans' office. Paulsen started after him, the 9mm Glock suddenly pressing against his shoulder where it was holstered, but he stopped when he heard Evans yell to let Lowry go. Lowry left the office with a resounding slam of the doors. Paulsen turned to look at Evans, who had sat down in his chair.

"Jack…" Paulsen said in a high-pitched voice.

"Sit down, Jon. Let's get organized so we don't get caught with our pants down. We can tend to Alfred later. Let's talk about the grand jury and this accountant."

"We'll have to take care of Lowry, Jack. Before he takes the stand."

"I told you we will do that. But he's not testifying for at least a couple of days and maybe more and there are more important things to talk about."

"Like what?"

"The corporation was served with a Bill of Particulars from the U.S. Attorneys' office. Lawrence to be exact. And it includes a request for the stock holdings of the employees who died, the ten people. Plus, they want to know about the partnerships we formed in Nassau. And also all the particulars about the merger with AMT. They want it all by Wednesday."

"And if we don't give it to them? What's next?"

"They will have to go to a federal judge. Probably Stuyvesant to get an Order Compelling Production."

"He's on our side."

"Yes, but if he's too one sided, they could appeal to the Fifth Circuit Appeals Court in New Orleans."

"That will all take time, won't it?"

"Sure, but it might hold up the merger. We need approvals not only with AMT's Board of Directors, but also the Justice Department, the FCC and the SEC."

"Matilda called," Evans added. "To add to our problems, she sounded scared."

"Of what?"

"She was visited at the hotel by Ryan, the lawyer helping Lawrence out. I also hear that he and his buddy Waterman are going to take over the class action suit."

"Maybe I should take care of this Ryan fellow, Jack."

"Not right now. The civil case is now in front of Judge Stuyvesant. We're hoping he dismisses the case on a technicality. Then we will only have to worry about the grand jury investigation."

"The way Lowry is, Jack. I don't think he can handle it."

"Look, we're going to bring in outside counsel. It's the firm that handled the Microsoft trial. My father's very friendly with their chief litigator and he is very friendly with Judge Stuyvesant. They went to the same law school. Fraternity brothers to boot. Anyway, unless President Bancroft himself interferes with the court proceedings, which I don't think he would even try that, we should be home free with the civil suit."

Evans pulled out the cigarette case and lit another Rothman cigarette. Paulsen noted that Evans was smoking more than usual in the last week or so. The former wrinkle free face of Evans started to line, especially under the eyes.

"I got a call yesterday from our underwriter…the guy handling the merger paperwork. He said that for some strange reason, there has been a lot of activity on our stock. Somebody is out there buying up a whole lot of shares. Not only on the public exchange, but he said that some of our employees have been selling their shares to that same entity."

"Who is it?"

"He doesn't know. More likely a shell corporation. Probably a front for somebody who's interested in taking over our voting shares. Maybe an attempt at a hostile take over of Comtel."

"What would happen to the merger with AMT?" Paulsen asked.

"Probably kill it for now. More importantly, Comtel would be worth less in a hostile take over, especially if it kills the deal with AMT."

"Do you think?"

"Yes, I do. Abromowitz has done this before. Make a friendly offer to a corporation. Then while they're counting their chickens…attack it by buying up the corporation's shares and replacing the Board of Directors.

He'd own the corporation for half the price he would have to pay on a friendly acquisition."

"What do we do if it is him?"

Evans smiled as he dragged heavily on his cigarette. The Grand Canyon Suite was playing on the office stereo and it momentarily filled his mind with the clean and peaceful air of Utah's mountains.

"We still have the video...the one with Abromowitz and Matilda...don't we Jon?"

Paulsen smiled as he repeated Evans' words, "We still have the video."

"It might make him think twice about fucking us, Jon."

"He'd fuck his own mother. They're all like that."

"Well, let's not jump ahead of ourselves. We don't know if it is Abromowitz."

Evans rose from his chair and walked to the window.

"We have built such a beautiful world to live in, Jon. Just so damn hard to keep it like it was."

"What do we do about Lowry, Jack?"

"Lets see if he shows up at the hearing. Follow him. See if he strays from the farm. If he does...well, you have my permission to correct the problem, Jon. Oh," Evans added, "Matilda was served with a subpoena also. It seems that Lawrence's reach is further than we think."

"How the hell can they get her in Nassau?"

"Well, I guess if she doesn't come voluntarily, they could charge her with some bullshit charge and extradite her. You know what pussies those Nassau police are. Especially if it's the U.S. government involved. She'll come. But we'll talk to her before she sets foot in that courtroom. Meanwhile, let me call Bartolomew and see where he stands on the investigation. The lawyer from New York is due to come in tonight. The one that's going to handle the civil action motion before Judge Stuyvesant. And if need be, the grand jury testimony of any of our people."

"Do you want me to do anything?"

"Just stay loose. I'm sure there'll be plenty to do once the hearings start. Meanwhile, let's stop at the Bayville Club for a round of eighteen holes. Okay?"

They both walked out of the office, confident that Comtel would prevail against all that the world would throw against it. It was a company formed to survive a thousand years, just like all the other entities the world had seen that are formed to survive a thousand years.

Chapter Thirty-Nine

"It's really very difficult to tell what they're really doing with the records they produced." Harry Sharon was a bald headed man in his early sixties whose voice resembled a foghorn blowing in a tunnel. His eyes were pale blue and as clear as glass.

"I told you, Joshua my boy, they'd never produce the real records. It's like a Greek diner owner keeping two sets of books. One for the IRS and one for his partners in Athens," Sam Waterman thundered as he sipped on the pineapple and vodka highball that he had set on his extended belly while he sprawled out on the lounge chair. Ryan was seated at the round, glass top dining table, munching on the crispy tostados dipped in salsa, sour cream, meat sauce and a crushed vegetable sauce he couldn't rightly name. The entire concoction burned his lips and the roof of his mouth as he devoured them with gusto.

"You'll have a heart attack eating those so quickly, my love," Sosie said as she drank her green tea.

They were seated on the outside terrace of the tower-penthouse floor of Turnberry's recently constructed high-rise condominium overlooking the glass-like intercoastal and the million dollar estates of Golden Beach which bordered on the ocean. Yehuda was seated at the far end of the round table directly opposite from Joshua. He was eating from a platter of freshly cut carrots and peppers that he dipped in hummus and a yogurt cream sauce.

"You should eat the fresh vegetables, Joshua. It's good for a growing boy. Instead of that Mexican who knows what you're eating. You've got to keep your arteries open and I'm certain that stuff you're eating is closing them off for good," Yehuda mumbled.

"Harry, how do you know these records aren't the real Mc Coy?" Joshua asked as he pointed a tostado at the bald headed man.

"Because I spent thirty years examining all kinds of financial records at the SEC. Everybody lies a little. Exaggerates profits…or losses… depends on what the corporation is trying to show. But these numbers are pure bullshit."

The night air was a little chilly for North Miami in May but the smell of bouganvilla and hibiscus growing below the terrace on the impeccably landscaped grounds surrounding the luxurious complex of towering condo buildings somehow gave off its own heat. The four of them were dressed in summer shorts and shirts except for Sam who was wrapped in a tattered City College sweat shirt that barely reached down to cover his protruding belly.

"Why would they lie to the SEC?" Joshua asked.

"Why? Who knows why, Joshua?" Harry Sharon answered as he sat next to Sam on a lounge chair, both staring out at the ocean which was dotted with the blinking lights of the ocean liners wending their way out to the islands of the Caribbean.

"Maybe," Harry continued as he turned in his lounge chair to face Joshua, his body thin and scrawny compared to Sam's globular form lying next to him, "they wanted to impress the market. They usually do that by exaggerating profits and hiding debt or losses. Comtel is probably shifting a great deal of debt to those partnerships they formed in Nassau. Suddenly their financials look squeaky clean. Little debt and skillions of profits. That's what it's all about. Exceed the prophetic projections of the market gurus and your stock goes through the roof. Nobody is the wiser, especially if you can fool the SEC watchdogs. It's like getting the FDA to approve your miracle drug that cures cancer, heart disease and herpes all at the same time without human trials."

"How do we get the real numbers, Harry?" Waterman asked.

"From the real books and records. Probably the ones that AMT reviewed. I'm sure Fredrick Abromowitz knows what's real and what's bullshit."

"Abromowitz has a clever little German lawyer named Horst Steingut." Yehuda declared.

"So how does that help us?" Waterman asked, now sitting up in the lounge facing Yehuda.

"There's no doubt that the general counsel of AMT, Steingut, knows what's really going on at Comtel," Joshua declared.

"Can we subpoena Steingut?" Waterman asked.

"Maybe, but if he hides under the lawyer-client privilege, he'll tell you nothing."

"Of course," Waterman smiled as he said, "the best witness to get the numbers we want would be the general counsel of Comtel."

"Alfred Lowry."

"Wouldn't he hide under the same privilege?" Sosie asked. Her mind had drifted out over the Atlantic to Paris and her never forgotten offspring, Sammie. She caught the tail end of the discussion which prompted her question.

"Not if he's being charged with a crime. Sure, he could refuse to testify at the grand jury hearing if he was a defendant, but the rumor I heard was that he was buckling under the strain," Joshua said.

"By the way, Harry," Waterman interjected as his eyes wandered around the luxuriously decorated apartment, "how can you afford this?" Waterman's hand pointed to the living room located just inside the terrace's doors. "I thought you were just a retired government employee?" Sam added.

Harry Sharon smiled brightly, lighting up his hang dog face.

"Franny…" Harry replied. "Well, when she was alive she believed that real estate, Florida real estate was the only sound investment. For me, after looking over the shoulders of those Wall Street sharks for so many years, I couldn't disagree with her. And you know, Sam…her father was a real estate broker down here…way back in the seventies and eighties. So she'd take what we both made, and what her parents left her, and bought up half of South Beach. That's how I can afford this apartment, Sam."

"I'm sorry about Franny," Sam said in a soulful voice.

"She was a good woman, Sam," as he spoke of his late wife, Harry Sharon had a glimmer of a smile and a glint of light in his eyes.

"Remember how we would sit on Eastern Parkway, Sam…just outside of Dubrows…the three of us."

"Yeah, right after the dance was over at the Jewish Center we hightailed it to Dubrows for our midnight snack. Fanny drank coffee as she watched her two favorite boyfriends make pigs of themselves."

Harry looked over at Yehuda, Sosie, and Joshua as he spoke. "Sam, Franny and I all went to Jefferson High School in Brownsville. We both fought over Franny and she didn't commit to either one of us until we all graduated from City College. Then, of course, Sam was drafted, the U.S. Army didn't want me because of my flat feet. Well, I guess, Franny decided it was time to get married and have a family. And there I was, flat footed and fancy free. We were both twenty or so…but in those day, everybody got married earlier. Forty years of a good marriage and then she dies on me. I told her the husband was supposed to die first, but she kissed me on her death bed, and told me to shut up and made me promise that after she was gone, I would marry again."

"I could never find another woman like Franny," Sam said soulfully, his eyes brimming with tears. "So I married a Russian immigrant who only wanted my body so she could get a green card."

"Fran loved you all through her life, Sam." Harry said.

"I know, that was the trouble, Harry. You married the only woman I could love, and where the hell did that leave me?" Sam laughed as he reached over to clap Harry on the back of his neck.

"I should have invested my money with Franny instead of your goddamn stock market, Harry," Sam added.

"What I saw at the SEC, Sam, I wouldn't put a nickel into the market. Everybody had a "schtick" going. The brokers and the mutual funds wouldn't tell their clients about hidden commissions and management fees and the corporations would bury the bad news in long term capital losses or pass debts onto offshore entities that weren't governed by the SEC and wouldn't show up in the corporation's annual statements."

"Just like Comtel," Joshua said.

"Just like Comtel, Joshua, and a thousand other public corporation," Harry replied with a slight note of anger in his voice.

"Harry, did you get a chance to review the list of shares held by the senior employees who were terminated?" Joshua asked.

"Sure…that they had to show…you can't hide shareholder's interest in a public corporation."

"Did those employees have enough voting shares to block the merger with AMT?" Joshua asked.

"Almost, Joshua. They held almost one percent of the outstanding voting shares. They're called Class A Stock. And from what I read about the merger…no one but the top echelon of Comtel would benefit from the merger. The little guy, well, his shares were diluted since it was a two for one exchange in the merger. Two shares of Comtel for one of AMT."

"So by eliminating those ten or so senior employees," Yehuda interjected, "those employees holding almost one percent or so of the voting shares, they could have, maybe, with the help of a few more senior employees not happy with Comtel, hold up the merger."

"For sure," Harry confirmed. "The Evans family combined with Comtel executives held the largest block of Comtel stock. The only other way the merger could be thwarted, if those senior employees you just mentioned were eliminated, would be if the public stockholders voted against the merger but they usually voted with the Board of Directors and the executive staff."

"So by terminating those ten or so employees…shareholders…that more or less ensured the merger." Joshua stated rhetorically. "Just one percent of the voting shareholders would have killed the merger. Now how do we take that fact and prove who killed those people?" Joshua added.

"It's all circumstantial, Joshua." Sam declared.

"It's tough…no, probably impossible to prove criminal guilt beyond a reasonable doubt based on circumstantial evidence."

"What we need are inside witnesses, Sam." Joshua muttered.

"The ones who are going to dime out the Evans…Paulsen…Comtel."

"Getting the real books and records wouldn't hurt either, Joshua." Harry said.

Yehuda stood up and walked to the railing of the terrace. He leaned over and placed his elbows on top of the railing and peered out into the dark blue night filled with city lights and the smell of flowers wafting up from the bucolic grounds below.

"I might have a way. To get Lowry…It'll mean using Sosie, Joshua."

"Forget it, Yehuda. Sosie is finished risking her life for anything like this," Joshua answered angrily.

"I hear Lowry is ready to fold, Joshua. Wouldn't take much to bring him over to our side. Here's my plan. If you and Sosie don't like it…we'll try something else. Just listen. Okay?"

Yehuda turned around and faced the foursome. They listened for fifteen minutes without interruption. The moon was slowly descending into the far horizon when they all left Harry Sharon's apartment, all agreeing, reluctantly, to Yehuda's plan.

Chapter Forty

She walked confidently into the dark, somber lit lounge of the Renaissance Hotel. Dressed in a dark silk business suit, the skirt conservatively reaching her knees, Sosie stopped for a moment to see if the man she was supposed to meet was there. The jacket was tailored seductively to her lush upper body but yet no one could criticize the tastefulness of her attire.

It was 7:00 p.m. and the Orlando sun was setting. That morning, Waterman had contacted Comtel's legal office and had persuaded Alfred Lowry, general counsel of Comtel, that an immediate meeting was necessary to discuss legal strategies with Nicholas Beals, the famous litigator from New York whose firm had been engaged to represent Comtel and it's executives in all legal procedures arising out of the civil class action suit and any possible criminal actions eventuated by the grand jury investigation orchestrated by Lawrence.

Waterman, acting as the administrator of Beals' prestigious law firm, instructed Lowry to meet with Beals' chief assistant at the Renaissance Hotel lounge at 7:00 p.m. that evening in preparation for a conference with Beals himself later on that evening. Lowry asked very few questions of the authoritative voice on the phone, exhilarated that Beals would finally remove the monstrous cancer off his devastated mind and body. Not seeing anybody remotely appearing lawyer-like, Sosie requested a corner booth in the lounge. She ordered a vodka tonic, placed her black leather briefcase on the table and slowly sipped on the whiskey glass. She opened her briefcase and withdrew a long yellow legal pad and placed it on the table in front of her. She wrote a few notes at the top of the page. Mechanically, she reached into the briefcase and withdrew a business card with the endorsement display noting that Angela Latrobe, Esquire was a senior partner at Beals, Crawshaw, Bookbinder, Fullbright and Latrobe, the central office of the multi-national law firm located at 434 Park Avenue, New York City. The simple inscription in gold raised letters on the business card evoked a gripping respect and prestige of one of the leading litigation firms in the world.

Sosie Ben Zvi-Ryan had engaged in the art of deception on many occasions before this night. Trained not only in the martial arts required by the elite Israeli paratroopers, Sosie had six months of intense espionage training at the Mossad school located just outside of the desert city of Beersheba.

She had served the Israeli intelligence agency all over the world. Her innocent face and quiet demeanor pierced the shells of the most suspicious enemy targets. After two years, she had had enough. Coincidently she had met and fallen in love with Joshua Ryan.

As she sat in that dark, secluded booth waiting for her quarry, her mind wandered back over the many assignments that were filled with danger and boredom depending on who she was engaged to deceive. From the banal market places in Beirut to Cairo to the sophisticated elegant world of Paris, she successfully carried out her assigned tasks. She had to overcome her basic sense of honesty but like every great deceptor, her mind was cut into two parts. The shrinks called it schizophrenia if the mind was unaware of its two sided position. But Sosie knew who she was and what part she had to play...to survive the assignment.

She spoke Arabic as if she were schooled by a coterie of muslim clerics.

The Mossad language school mostly had Arab scholars teaching the many dialects of the Arab world. Inflections and accents were emphasized whereupon the Mossad agent could easily pass in Beirut or Damascus as a native educated citizen of that society. To fail was to die. As many of her closest friends had suffered excruciating deaths.

Although Sosie had weathered each demanding assignment with a blasé attitude and mind set, yet after the episode was over, after the cumulative effects of the withheld emotions had finally and tumultuously surfaced, she was placed in a secluded rehab center for alcoholics and drug addicts administered by Zeppi Ben Zvi, her mother, who was also a director of the facility in Jerusalem. The Benedict Institute was privately funded by the wealthy friends of Israel who were cognisant of the life-giving needs of the residents of the gated cluster of three story brick buildings located near the King David Hotel. Sosie had suddenly, after two years of constant participation in one dangerous assignment after another for the Mossad, had mentally collapsed-virtually on her parent's doorstep. No advance warning was noted by anyone, including Sosie. Her demeanor had always been cheerful and even tempered. Then one night after returning from a particularly dangerous assignment in Beirut amongst the Hamas and Al Fatah terror groups centered there, she was attempting to unlock her family home's front door overlooking the Old City in Jerusalem when she collapsed on the porch leading to the front door of the house. Yehuda found her unconscious body stretched out in a fetal position, her face contorted with a crazed fearful look, her mouth bubbling with saliva dribbling down to her neck. Although seemingly unconscious, her lips moved frenetically, muttering incomprehensible words and sounds. As Yehuda lifted her tenderly from the cold ceramic tiled front porch, her eyes suddenly opened as she lurched out of Yehuda's arms onto her feet. But her legs caved in, her body falling forward down the steps onto the gravel pathway leading to the porch. She screamed, the words muddled by the saliva filling her mouth and lips, her face striking the tiny stones filling the pathway. Her fragile nose was broken in three places, as well as her left cheek bone.

After almost a month of surgeries repairing her nose and checkbone, and the drying out nightmare of ridding her body of the alcohol and tranquilizers she had been using to survive, she finally remembered the words that bubbled out of her crazed mind that hot August afternoon on the pathway of her parents' home. She was praying to a God she had denied existed; she was praying for her brothers and sisters who were dying in the streets around her. And she was praying for herself, knowing that she could never do enough in her espionage role to change the terrible world surrounding her loved ones. She realized her efforts were inconsequential and meaningless. Yet, she felt compelled to continue on. As if to discontinue would be to let her people die. A betrayal she could not live with.

"Eretz Yisreal, adonoi elehano, adononoi echod," the words of the prayer to Jehovah to save Israel and its people were the incomprehensible words she had repetitively muttered in a cathartic state of mind as she was held in her father's arms. Sosie had sought forgiveness for what she had done but more importantly had asked the God she denied existed to save her Israel. But, of course, when she had recovered her sensibility, she realized that the God that may not be at all, could not deliver deliverance to her nor her long suffering people. They still died in the streets of Tel Aviv, Jerusalem, Haifa, Hebron, and the many other little towns and settlements scattered through that tiny country where insane children were released from all reason by their masters to blow themselves up and whomever may wander near them to kingdom come.

As her eyes recovered their sight, Sosie saw Alfred Lowry's gangly figure walk into the lounge. She recognized him from the photo her father had shown her. He asked the maitre d' something and the man directed Lowry to Sosie's corner booth. Lowry walked quickly over to Sosie, held his hand out as he neared the booth. Sosie raised herself from her seat and firmly grasped Lowry's hand, holding it for several moments. Her wide eyes focused sharply on Lowry's thin, heavily lined face. The whites of his eyes were streaked with spindly red lines, almost touching into the brown pupils.

Lowry nervously sat down on the seat on the other side of the booth from Sosie. He wasn't used to dealing with attractive female lawyers as equals.

"Have you been waiting long, Ms…" he asked.

"Call me Angela, Alfred. May I call you Alfred?" She replied with a coy smile on her bronzed face.

"Yes, please, Alfred will be fine. I'm sure glad your firm is in the litigation now. Believe me, the last few months have been hell trying to keep the hinges from falling apart."

With a smile still on her face, Sosie replied, her hand reaching out toward Lowry's hand as he absentmindedly placed them on the table in front of him. Although the lights above the booth were dim, he could easily see the lovely face of Sosie. Although she intentionally rejected giving off any lustful vibrations for fear that Lowry would unmask her lawyer's persona, Sosie naturally exuded a subtle erotic charisma. Her husky voice, her deliberate stare, the way she languishly moved her upper body as she spoke, sent never ending shivers through Lowry's mind.

"When will Mr. Beals arrive, Angela?" Lowry asked in a whispering undertone.

"Oh…probably before 9:00 p.m. His plane is due to arrive at 8:00 p.m. so I guess 9:00 p.m. would be about right. Anyway," she smiled broadly as her hand reached closer to Lowry's hand on the table, "Nicholas wanted me to get some background on the class action suit…and anything more on the grand jury investigation. We've received the package of documents you sent up to us, but there are legal insights that only you can give us, Alfred."

"Yes, yes…I'm sure I can provide you and Mr. Beals with some of the innuendos that you can't get from the complaint and the discovery documents."

"And just to fill you in on our review so far, we didn't have time to go through the transcript of the testimony of the class action trial, Alfred. So whatever you can detail for us would save us an awful lot of time."

Lowry suspiciously peered around the lounge before he continued his conversation and then he quickly turned his head toward Sosie who noticed Lowry's eyes ticked every time he spoke. "Now Angela, since your firm is Comtel's new counsel, we can agree that whatever I tell you…that everything that is said here is protected by the lawyer client privilege. You would agree with that, Angela?"

She released a confident laugh and reached over and touched Lowry's hand. As he had been shocked by an electric prod, he pulled his hand back and placed it on his lap under the table.

"It goes without saying, Alfred. The privilege extends to whatever information you reveal to me, or for that matter, anybody at our firm who participates in Comtel's representation."

Lowry released a deep sigh as his mouth opened up to an irregular smile.

"You don't know how much your firm's taking over the reins of this case means to me, Angela. It's been sheer hell these past few months."

"Well, that's why corporations call on us. We take the difficult cases and win in court."

"Beals did a hell of a job on the Microsoft case."

"He always does."

"Well, Angela, our case is much worse than Microsoft's position. The government was only going after them because of an anti-trust violation."

"Only," Sosie laughed knowing that Microsoft was threatened with dissolution by the U.S. government.

"Well," Lowry laughed, his face reddened as he continued, "I know what you were facing there…but let me tell you, Angela. Here, in our situation, we're talking murder…a series of murders that that the deputy U.S. Attorney is trying to hang on us with…"

"Wait a second, Alfred. From what I read, we're talking about a civil complaint. Allegedly Comtel knowingly utilized herbicides…poisons, whatever in maintaining their amusement parks. Am I missing something, Alfred?"

"I don't know if I should talk to you about it, Angela. Maybe we should wait for Beals."

Again, Lowry swiveled his neck around the lounge to determine whether anyone could overhear their conversation. It being mid-week and after supper time, the lounge was virtually empty. Except for the two bartenders behind the bar and the maitre d' who was stationed at his desk in the opening area of the lounge apparently working on paperwork. Nobody seemed to care about their conversation.

"Look, Alfred…I know there is always some reluctance to reveal sensitive corporate information to a woman, but, I'm Nicholas Beals' right hand man. I sit second chair on any trial he tries. Whatever you're going to tell him…well, he certainly wants me to hear about it. We're a team, Alfred. It's been like that for over five years now. You don't tell me everything, and I mean everything, Alfred, well, I think Comtel is wasting its money on us. Do I make myself clear, Alfred?"

Lowry released a loud phlemy sound as he cleared his throat, then removed the linen handkerchief from his back pocket of his suit pants and blew his nose with a deafening noise. His eyes moved down to his lap as he spoke, "I wish it was a simple as that, Angela. There are complications that could…well, let me say this…if you knew the whole story, your firm might withdraw from the case. And there's also another problem," Lowry paused as he purposely lowered his voice to a bare whisper, "Comtel's head of security is a man named Paulsen. Jon Paulsen."

"So?"

"He's not just the a normal head of security one might expect."

"Tell me," she laughed in order to ease Lowry's reluctance to reveal this intimate corporate information, "Nothing could surprise Nicholas Beals or myself. Not after Enron and Worldcom. The corporate world has changed dramatically, Alfred, in the last couple of years. Nothing surprises us anymore."

"Enron is nothing compared to what's happening at Comtel."

"Okay…what are we talking about? Skimming a little bit off the top, sexual harassment. What Alfred? I've heard it all in the last couple of years."

"Murdering its own employees," Lowry mumbled almost incoherently.

"What? I didn't hear the last statement, Alfred. Could you repeat it?"

Reluctantly Lowry raised the volume of his voice, his eyes skirting around the lounge room. The tick in his eyes increased noticeably as he spoke. "Murdering their own employees."

"Well, Alfred, let me understand you…Are we talking about the civil action where Comtel knew about the possible danger of the chemical fungicide injuring their park employees. That I don't think constitutes murder, Alfred." She paused to catch her breath and then continued. "Am I missing something, Alfred?"

"Do you know about the merger with AMT? We sent you the prospectus along with the civil action docs."

"Yes we read it, all of it. So what? It appears that the merger will help both companies."

"Not if it never happens, Angela."

"Wait a second, Alfred. What does the death of several employees…"

"Over ten," Lowry interjected loudly, his reluctance seemingly disappearing as they spoke.

"Over ten?" Sosie repeated and then continued, "There are many cases involving allegations of thousands of employees being injured. Dying because of the egregious omissions…whatever…that the corporation refused to acknowledge and remedy…like your Johns Manville, the asbestos claims. Our firm was involved with some of that litigation, Alfred. But those actions were omissions by the corporations which certainly doesn't constitute murder."

"Paulsen and the Evans, both Jack and the Senator, either planned or knew about the murders…by Paulsen and his so-called security staff. The out and out killings of over ten senior employees of Comtel."

Sosie's face was ostensibly paralyzed with shocked disbelief as she heard the words coming out of Lowry's mouth.

"I knew you wouldn't believe me…I didn't think anybody would."

"What you're saying, Alfred….well, you're accusing the CEO of Comtel, Jack Evans, and the largest individual shareholder and founder of Comtel, Senator Evans and this Paulsen fellow of some kind of conspiracy. I still don't understand why, Alfred?"

"Those senior employees, besides possibly filing subsequent class action suits for the same reasons as the plaintiff's in the billion dollar verdict case, well they held enough voting stock in Comtel to destroy the merger with AMT. And," he paused to catch his breath as if he were undergoing an asthmatic attack, "Comtel needs that merger with AMT to grow…and maybe…even survive."

"Why?" Sosie questioned in a disbelieving voice. "I've looked at the quarterlys and the annual filings...Comtel seems to be prospering more every year."

"That's what Evans wants the SEC...the market place to believe. But if you look at the actual books of Comtel, well you'll find a different story."

"Then why isn't the SEC investigating Comtel?"

"Talk to Senator Evans about that. The SEC started an investigation but it died on the vine. He's the head of the Senate committee that supervises the SEC."

"So what are they doing? How do they pull profits out of the air?"

"They're forming partnerships in Nassau that absorb billions of dollars worth of Comtel debt. It goes right to the bottom line. To the profit side of the ledger."

"Wait a second, Alfred. I'm not an accountant, but what I know about accounting, if the partnerships absorb Comtel's debt, well, how do they stay afloat."

"Simple...Comtel awards lucrative contracts to these partnerships and when they run a deficit...Comtel shores them up by issuing Comtel preferred to the partnership. The value of the Comtel stock issuance more than offsets any deficits the partnerships absorb. Comtel guarantees those partners a twenty-five percent annual return on their investment. And those partners are all friends and relatives of the Evans."

"You too?"

"Yes, me too, I'm a partner in one of the companies. Anyway, Comtel guarantees at least a twenty-five percent return on the investments to the partners...the transfers of Comtel's stock add substantial value to the partnerships and puts them solidly in the black. And the parent Comtel has very little debt on its books."

"I still can't believe that the Evans...Comtel would plan the deaths of all those employees. Wasn't the merger good for all the Comtel shareholders?"

"Just the Evans, me, Paulsen, mostly the executive staff and the board of directors. We each received special class A shares in the merged company. But the ordinary share holders, those long term employees, well they got the shaft. Their shares would have been diluted substantially. Enough to wipe out most of their investment…and probably their pension plans as well."

"Still, murder, Alfred?" Sosie repeated as if she were spurring Lowry onto reveal all the ugly inside corporate information he had purposely hidden in a corner of his brain for so long.

"There is more…much more, Angela," Lowry's voice suddenly sounded purged of fear and guilt as he spoke. It was absolution for the sinner, Sosie thought, as she observed his face, the lines of tension slowly being erased as he confessed.

"Comtel is underfinanced for over five hundred million dollars on the employees' pension plans. AMT brought that up. Abromowitz is no fool. He's the head honcho at AMT, you know. He told Evans that before the merger could be completed, Comtel would have to fully finance the pension plan or the SEC, the Justice Department, the FCC would never approve the merger."

"Where could Comtel get five hundred million dollars?"

"The Evans have it…in Nassau, Switzerland. All the monies they have been skimming off Comtel, over the last thirty years. Cash deposited in the Inter-Island Bank of Nassau. That's where they would get it."

"Does anybody else know all this?"

"Probably Abromowitz suspects. He's no fool. I heard from Jack Evans that maybe Abromowitz is trying to undercut the merger by attempting a hostile take over. By buying up, for cheap, all the shares from the senior employees or on the open market. It would save him billions of dollars if he tried it and succeeded."

"Are there any documents. Anything, writings that reveal all this?"

"There are. I have some, but most of it's in Evans' wall safe in his office. The penthouse office on top of Comtels' forty-five story headquarters."

Sosie could hear the twinges of jealousy and envy now so apparent in Lowry's voice. The fear of disclosure had suddenly disappeared as he expunged the long retained poison from his mind. Absolution had suddenly filled him with a spirit of courage he had not felt in twenty years. Before he started working for Comtel. Before he became paralyzed with fear every time he thought about Jon Paulsen.

"Could you produce those documents, Alfred? I'm sure Nicholas will want to see them before we proceed."

"Maybe. It all depends on what you think about all this."

"Well, I know Nicholas Beals won't proceed with representing Comtel unless we get the documents, Alfred."

"If I have to, I will. But I want some kind of immunity."

"Well, that you'll have to take up with Nicholas. It would probably be a conflict of interest for us to represent both you and Comtel. I just don't know. But anyway," Sosie smiled her most lured smile as she tenderly stroked Lowry's hands that were clasped on the table in front of him. He smelled the expensive French perfume she was wearing; he ogled the swell of her full breasts against her jacket and the come hither smile directed salaciously at him. He felt like a hero after his expungement of the cowardly fear that had absorbed his life for so long. Here was a beautiful woman that seemed to beckon him forward.

"Look, instead of waiting for Nicholas here, why don't we go up to the suite we have in the hotel. I can order us some champagne. Maybe some hors d' oeuvres. After what you've been through, Alfred, you probably can use a little relaxation."

Lowry held her hand within the palms of his hands. Whatever shyness he retained when he was attracted to a beautiful woman disappeared.

'Why not?' he thought to himself. 'Angela Latrobe was a fellow lawyer. A beautiful woman who happened to be co-counsel with him.' A wave of sexual confidence pulsated through his body; he could feel himself getting hard as he sucked in the lustful aura this beautiful aggressive woman cast toward him.

Sosie moved up from the lounge chair, around the table, awaiting Lowry to follow. She left a twenty dollar bill on the table for the drink, took Lowry by the hand, picked up her leather briefcase with the other hand and led the willing target to her bedroom suite located at the top of the Renaissance Hotel.

Chapter Forty-One

They had rented the penthouse presidential suite at the luxurious Renaissance Hotel. Nothing was too good for the Grand Inquisitors of Orlando. They had placed a large round bridge table in the master bedroom hidden from the enormous living room. The suite had a balcony that surrounded it, allowing the occupants to clearly observe Orlando and many miles due east toward Melbourne Beach.

Yehuda, Sam Waterman and Joshua Ryan sat around the table playing black jack for pennies or whatever change they had jingling in their pockets. They had been playing for over two hours, Ryan the big winner at eighty-seven cents. Cans of ice cold ginger ale sat before each of the players. Each player alternated who the dealer would be for that hand. Waterman was the big loser. Over one dollar of loose change he had contributed to the big winnings of both Joshua and Yehuda.

At the sound of the front door of the suite opening, they laid their respective hands down on the table and waited. Within seconds Frank Sinatra's romantic voice swept through the suite. Several minutes passed as they listened to the clinking of ice dropped into drinking glasses situated on the corner horseshoe bar in the living room.

Except for murmuring sounds coming from the living room which they could not understand, the trio waited, hoping that they would not have to forcibly interfere in the well rehearsed playlet.

The bedroom doors slowly opened and Sosie entered, her jacket off and her blouse opened enough to see the hint of cleavage of her breasts. She smiled at the waiting trio knowing where they were located back against the wall near the bathroom. Lowry followed her into the bedroom, his face full of lustful expectations, his hands groping at her waist and rear end.

Then as his eyes lifted from Sosie's shapely bottom toward the bathroom, Lowry saw the smiling trio of card players. Sosie thought they appeared like models for Cezanne's favorite portrait study of "The Cardplayers", except for the Floridian assortment of clothing they were loosely wearing.

"Good evening, Mr. Lowry," Sam Waterman's voice barked out toward the stupefied face and body of Alfred Lowry, general counsel of Comtel.

"Please," Waterman's friendly voice invited as he pointed to the chair at the end of the table directly opposite where Sam was seated but next to where Yehuda was seated.

"What is this?" Lowry's voice stumbled as he turned to look at Sosie who had her back against the bedroom door blocking Lowry's exit from the bedroom.

"Who are you guys? Ms. Latrobe..," Lowry's angry voice was directed at Sosie who was now buttoning up her blouse to the top of the blouse.

"Mr. Lowry," she said in an amicable voice, "let me introduce you to these three gentlemen." She rattled off the introductions as if the trio were actors in a play just completed and they were absorbing the applause of the audience.

"And my name, Mr. Lowry," she added, "is Sosie Ben-Zvi-Ryan. Mr. Ryan here is my husband and Yehuda, the paunchy gray haired fellow there," she pointed her finger to Yehuda, "is my father. Mr. Waterman is not related except by friendship."

"Mr. Lowry, please sit down," Ryan politely ordered.

"Look, I don't know what your people are trying to do, but I'm leaving," Lowry threatened as he turned to leave the bedroom. Sosie stood firmly against the door, her hands behind her back holding the knob.

Lowry raised his right arm to strike her across the head with his fist. Sosie moved to the right as her left arm blocked the oncoming blow, her right clenched fist shot out and struck Lowry in his solar plexes. His body crumbled to the deeply carpeted bedroom floor. Ryan moved forward, but Yehuda put his arm out to stop him.

"Sosie can take care of herself, Joshua my boy," Yehuda said with a smile.

"I know that, Yehuda. I'm not worried about Sosie. I'm worried about Lowry," Joshua replied with a quiet laugh.

Sosie stood over the prostrate Lowry as he tried to rise up from the floor. His face was twisted with the pain and shock of being waylaid by the unexpected force from such a beautiful diminutive woman, one he had great hopes of making love with instead of doing battle with.

Joshua and Yehuda walked slowly over to Sosie. She smiled demurely as if she were a purring Cheshire cat caught intimidating the family dog.

"Mr. Lowry," Joshua Ryan said after he placed his hand on Sosie's shoulder, "we would like your help in solving the mystery of The Park murders."

Lowry rose to a sitting position on the floor, the waves of pain surging through his abdomen up to his brain. His eyes darted hysterically around the room, glistening beads of sweat forming on his furrowed brow.

"I have nothing to say," his voice cracked and sputtered as the words barely left his parched lips.

"Why should you take the fall, counselor?" Sam Waterman said as he shuffled the deck noisily on the table in front of him.

"Those deaths were accidents," Lowry said.

"Really, Mr. Lowry?" Josh declared, "that's not what you told this lovely woman." Joshua pointed to Sosie who was opening up the top buttons of her blouse. The black wire that ran across her bosom was clearly evident.

Yehuda helped Lowry up from the floor. He dusted phantom dust from Lowry's body, Lowry wincing from the cleansing blows of the open palm of Yehuda's hand.

Sosie went into the bathroom and after a few moments returned to the bedroom with a tiny recording machine and an attached wire clearly evident in her hands.

"Mr. Lowry, we feel that you were forced into doing some of the things…some of the acts you participated in…" Joshua said.

"I did nothing…I was not involved in any of those…" Lowry shouted.

"Murders?" Waterman said, his hands still noisily shuffling the decks of cards.

Lowry straightened his tie and suit jacket in an attempt to organize himself from the sheer fear of the total destruction of his life that his mind clearly envisioned.

"Whatever I said on that…" Lowry said as he pointed to the microscopic recording device now sitting on the table where Waterman was absent mindedly shuffling his cards.

"Nothing I said there is admissible in any court," Lowry added.

"And why not?" Joshua queried.

"Why…you know Mr. Ryan…you're a lawyer. Whatever I said to this lawyer…" He pointed to Sosie who was seated next to Sam at the card table, her fingers playing with the recorder.

"She's not a lawyer, Mr. Lowry," Joshua admitted.

"Then who is she? She said that she was with Nicholas Beals. He's Comtel's new counsel. Anything I said to her is covered under the privilege. The lawyer-client privilege."

"If she was a lawyer, you'd probably be right, Mr. Lowry. But since she's not a lawyer; by the way, she's my wife, there is no privilege as to what you confess to her that's on that recording."

"I want to see a lawyer…" Lowry blurted out in a high pitched frenzied voice.

"We're not the police, Mr. Lowry," Waterman said as he rose from the table and strode slowly over to where Lowry, Ryan and Yehuda were standing. "You're not entitled to a lawyer. We could beat the shit out of you and whatever you confessed to would be admissible in court. But of course, you know that, Mr. Lowry. You're a lawyer, aren't you?"

"If we present your confession that's on that little disc," Joshua said as he pointed to the recorder on the table in front of Sosie, "I can assure you, Mr. Lowry you can kiss your career…no…not only your career, but your life away. Even though I am sure you didn't have a hand in the killings, you certainly were an active conspirator with your buddies at Comtel."

Lowry's mind could only think of escape. To anywhere. Maybe death. He knew he could not bear the ignominy of trial and conviction. He had been through that heart stopping experience once before when he was six years old. He had stolen a can of cranberry sauce at the local grocery store and then been caught by the proprietor. His father, one of the most respected lawyers in Vermont, as his father before him, took young Alfred to the mammoth barn located on the family farm outside of Rutland. With a switch from an old oak tree in the back yard, his father had beaten little Alfred until his screams stopped into an unconscious stupor. Bloody and scarred on his back and legs, his father had left him in that desolate barn all night. Alfred's mother finally came to help him the next morning. Not that his mother hadn't sympathized with her first born son, but he knew that she only did what she was permitted to do by her husband, his father. Alfred's father had threatened to publicize Alfred's earth shattering theft of that can of cranberry sauce to all of Alfred's friends and teachers at the local Lutheran school. Alfred Lowry never again stole a can of cranberry sauce or any other items of worth for fear of the lash and scandal of his father's discipline. Even after his father had died, Alfred Lowry knew that any transgression on his part could be met with his father's wrath reaching from somewhere beyond.

Now, in this hotel bedroom, Lowry knew that the punishment for his knowing conspiracy in the multi-layered Comtel crimes would be more devastating than the blinding pain of a switch from an old oak tree meted out by the father he had feared and hated all his life. Worst of all, Alfred Lowry realized that his father's repetitive prophecy that Alfred would never 'cut the mustard' would become a reality. His mind kept thinking that maybe his thoughts of suicide were the only suitable way out. And, yet, Lowry's brain was not ready to give up. As if it was an independent organism, his brain sought refuge in blinding hope. Maybe it could get out of this situation without shutting off the flow of blood and oxygen to his cells and tissue. Maybe…maybe…were words that criss-crossed the lobes of his brain; survival at any cost.

"What do I have to do?" Lowry asked, his hand wiping the sweat from his face.

"Tell your story to the grand jury, Mr. Lowry," Joshua said.

"And what do I get for my cooperation? You know the Evans, Paulsen. They'll never let me live if I testify against them."

"I'm sure the U.S. Attorney's office can offer you safety in its witness protection program, Mr. Lowry," Waterman declared.

"And what if they can't?" Lowry rebutted quickly.

"You wouldn't be safer in jail, Mr. Lowry," Joshua offered. "You'd always be a threat to Evans and their people."

"Can you guarantee me immunity, Mr. Ryan?"

"I wish I could. But Mr. Waterman and I will strongly recommend immunity if you fully cooperate."

"But there is no guarantee?" Lowry asked with a voice that denoted his complete retreat.

"None, Mr. Lowry. You have to be ready to do the right thing. No matter what the consequences," Waterman said harshly.

"My experience as a prosecutor, Mr. Lowry, would lead me to believe that the government would be foolish to turn its back on your full cooperation," Joshua offered optimistically.

"And Paulsen? Whose going to stop Paulsen?"

"There's already an arrest warrant issued for him," Waterman said.

"Lot a good it'll do me if he kills me before he's arrested, Mr. Waterman."

"Well," Sam declared in an offensive manner, "when you sleep with lions, Mr. Lowry, you should expect to get your head bitten off." Sam paused and with a cherubic grin on his face continued, "an old Russian prophecy that my dearly departed wife left me with."

Lowry knew there would be no easy way out. He could clam up and risk jail and maybe more punishment. Or testify and risk possible death by Paulsen. But if Paulsen was caught, destroyed…maybe there was still hope.

"Okay…whatever I said to Ms…whatever her name is…I'm willing to testify in court."

"And provide whatever documentation you can secure? Or tell us where to get them? Is that your understanding, Mr. Lowry?" Joshua asked.

"But before I do anything I want assurances from the U.S. Attorney's office of immunity and protection after I testify. If I get those guarantees, I'll give you whatever is within my power to give."

Ryan looked over at Waterman and Yehuda and his wife who was now shuffling the cards at the table. Her face was illuminated with a mysterious smile that reflected Sosie's feeling of satisfaction. Maybe we could be out of here in a week, she thought. And with my husband and father in the seats beside me on the plane that heads home to the safety of Paris.

Chapter Forty-Two

Upon the directive of the senior judge of the U.S. District Court of Florida, Peter Stuyvesant, the parties were to appear before him at 9:30 a.m. sharp at the Federal Courthouse in Orlando on that Tuesday.

Nicholas Beals, the hired legal gun of Comtel, had arrived in Orlando the night before and had met with the Senator, Jack Evans, Alfred Lowry, and Jon Paulsen. He told the Comtel group that he was ready to argue the various motions before the U.S. District Court on behalf of Comtel in the class action litigation. At stake was the merger of Comtel and AMT and most probably the very survival of Comtel itself.

Nicholas Beals was over six feet five inches tall although he weighed less than 180 pounds dripping wet. Joshua Ryan first saw him when Beals entered the Federal courtroom that morning. He thought that Ichabod Crane had ridden into Orlando that very morning. Beals' face was razor thin, with high jutting cheek bones that hovered over hollowed out cheeks. His piercing eyes were extremely large for the narrow face and extraordinary wide mouth that held two reed-like colorless lips. When he smiled, which was a rare event, Beals showed two rows of very wide and large teeth, his smile signifying more of a display of animal ferocity than human laughter.

On the plaintiff's side of the courtroom was Helen Walsh, Sam Waterman and Joshua Ryan. Sitting directly across from the plaintiffs' counsel table were Nicholas Beals and Alfred Lowry at defendants' counsel table. Behind defense counsel were two female legal associates of Beals sitting at one long table filled with federal statute and case books piled high in front of the two young lawyers. Both of the associates were scribbling madly on yellow legal pads that reminded Ryan of voracious law students attempting to finish up the bar exam before the examiner called "time's up." The associates were dressed in dark suits and with their uniform short-cropped hair could easily pass for two male lawyers. Both wore small rimmed eyeglasses.

Lowry occasionally peered over at Ryan and Waterman but quickly returned his eyes to the defense area lest someone accuse him of showing any weakness or fear to plaintiffs' counsel.

Judge Peter Stuyvesant appeared promptly at 9:30 a.m., his black robe swirling around him as he entered the courtroom from his chamber's door. Waterman thought Judge Stuyvesant had literally leaped from the side door leading into the courtroom up the three steps to the judge's bench in one Olympian leap. Beals' and Stuyvesant's physiognomies were fraternally similar, both men thin and gaunt and deadly serious in their facial demeanor.

'They could almost pass for brothers,' Waterman thought as he slowly rose from his chair upon the entrance of Judge Stuyvesant into the courtroom. Stuyvesant stood in front of his judge's table for several moments looking out at the array of lawyers standing nervously in front of his bench. He appeared as if he were enjoying the discomfort of these subservient petitioners to his judicial throne.

After he sat down on his high-backed leather chair, he clasped his well manicured bony hands in front of his nose and nodded to the court clerk to call the list for that morning.

The court clerk rose from his table and chair located in front of the judge's bench and to the right of the court reporter's chair and machine and called off the list of cases that were scheduled that morning before Judge Stuyvesant. After about fifteen minutes of colloquy between various lawyers representing parties in the cases before the court, Stuyvesant dismissed all the other lawyers not involved in the Comtel case for another scheduled day.

"Now we come to the stars of the show, counselors," Stuyvesant barked cynically as his body leaned forward as he spoke.

"Your honor…" Helen Walsh stood quietly up from her chair, her legs leaning against the table, her legal pad full of notes held in her hand.

"Yes, Ms. Walsh. All of you must assume I've taken the time to read your briefs and attached exhibits. So, instead of wasting my time…let me start with Mr. Beals, attorney for the defendant, Comtel."

Beals quickly rose and his face broke into an accommodating smile as he addressed the court. "Good morning, your honor. For the record, my name is Nicholas Beals. My firm is the attorney of record for the defendant, Comtel."

"Yes, Mr. Beals…welcome to my humble courtroom. It is a rare occasion to have the luxury of such eminent counsel before me."

Waterman didn't know whether Stuyvesant was kissing Beals' ass or sticking a sarcastic pencil up the same orifice of Beals. He looked over at Ryan who had the same quizzical look on his face.

"Well," Beals said in a smiling voice, "It's always a pleasure to appear before your honor."

"Mr. Beals," the judge said, his voice dripping with obvious respect, "there are really only two issues before this court. One involves the jurisdictional issue, more simply said, does the federal court have original jurisdiction over this suit and the parties thereto. And if so, does the criteria set down by Federal Rule 23 and all the case precedents concerning certification of a class compel this court to actually grant or deny certification to this class of plaintiffs. It's as simple as all that…Would you agree with me, Mr. Beals?"

Joshua Ryan knew by the colloquy passing between the judge and Beals that this performance had been rehearsed and scored before this fateful morning. It was obvious Stuyvesant was covering his large judicial ass on the record knowing full well that the matter would be appealed to the Fifth Circuit Court of Appeals if Stuyvesant was going to do what Ryan knew he was trying to do.

'The fix is in. All they needed were the horses to finish the race,' Ryan thought as his stomach started to growl, his mouth parched from the sudden dryness always accompanying Ryan's reaction to being fucked by the judicial world. He well knew that Oliver Wendell Holmes' purity of law and justice was controlled by the robed monks who administered that justice.

Ryan rose from his chair and began to speak. "Your honor, for the record, my name is Joshua Ryan. I am one of the new counsel representing the plaintiffs."

"Yes, Mr. Ryan…we've met before. I believe you were before me as a defendant. Brought on by the U.S. Attorney's office. If I remember correctly, you were charged with practicing law in Florida without the proper license. Am I correct, Mr. Ryan?"

"That is correct, your honor. But if you review the documents presented to your honor…you will find an order from Judge Richards of the Florida Superior Court admitting both Mr. Waterman and myself pro hace vice to represent the plaintiffs in this particular case."

"I believe you, Mr. Ryan. It would be foolish for a young man of your obvious intellect to lie to a Federal judge. Wouldn't you agree, Mr. Ryan?" Stuyvesant paused to push his thinnish brown hair back, rub his sharp beaked nose with his forefinger and then to continue his colloquy with Beals as if Ryan had failed to intervene.

"Now, Mr. Beals…"

"Your honor," Ryan interrupted Stuyvesant again. "I'd like to be heard before Mr. Beals answers the two questions posed by the court. I think the plaintiffs have the right to be heard."

"Mr. Ryan…we are not in some New Jersey courtroom where you can fly off the seat of your pants." Stuyvesant's voice flared loudly out at Ryan, his face twisted with controlled rage, "Sit down, Mr. Ryan…you will have plenty of opportunity to be heard."

Ryan continued to stand in direct defiance of the order of the demanding jurist.

"Sit down, Mr. Ryan. If you don't sit down, I will call the bailiff and have him run you down to the cell beneath the courtroom until you learn some needed manners. Do I make myself perfectly clear, Mr. Ryan?"

Waterman reached over and pulled Ryan by the bottom of his suit jacket forcing Ryan to either punch Waterman in the mouth forcing him to release his jacket or sit down in his chair. After looking angrily over at Waterman, Ryan slowly sat down in his chair.

"Now, Mr. Beals, could you kindly answer my previously stated question?" Judge Stuyvesant had regained his benign composure and even flashed a smile at Beals who was still standing at the defense table.

"Yes, your honor," Beals stood straight, his shoulders arched backwards as if he were on a military parade ground reviewing his troops, "I think your honor, as usual, has directed his inquiry to the meat of this suit. The nitty-gritty…because everything that has transpired…the trial, the verdict…it's all superfluous to the foundation premise that must be answered in the affirmative by the plaintiffs.

Firstly…and probably most importantly…since the substance of the complaint deals with federal law, employment safety laws, this case should never have been filed in state court. Therefore our petition for removal of the entire case to federal court must be approved. This court…the federal court is the only court that can readily decide this case."

"Well, Mr. Beals," the judge said in an approving undertone, "let's say I remove this case to my court…please proceed to the real question. Should this case be certified as a class action? Isn't that the real issue?"

Beals smiled and looked over at plaintiffs' table. Helen Walsh, who had been silent while Beals and Stuyvesant were patting on each others' legal backsides, stood up at plaintiffs' table.

"Your honor…for the record my name is Helen Walsh. Along with Mr. Ryan and Mr. Waterman, I am co-counsel on behalf of the plaintiffs in this matter. As I stand here listening to your honor's automatic acquiescence to defendant's wishes…"

"Wait a second, madam," Beals interrupted as he stared malevolently at Walsh.

"Please, Mr. Beals...I think it would be proper for you to respect my right to represent my client. And besides, a gentlemen never interrupts a lady when she's speaking." Walsh smiled demurely, her face irradiating with feminine indignation. Beals sat down abruptly.

"As I was saying, your honor...the federal laws governing employee safety and discrimination against the disabled is not the gravamen of our complaint in state court. If anyone," she emphasized the word dramatically, "If anyone reads the complaint, the discovery transcripts and docs, and the trial testimony, any blind man can tell that the complaint is based on product liability, gross deception and egregious conduct by Comtel against their employees. It has very little to do with federal law." She paused and looked at her notes for a moment and then continued, "The plaintiffs had the option of filing in federal court or state court and they decided that state court was where they wanted to be venued. Besides, in order to meet federal jurisdiction criteria, each class member must have a minimum of $75,000.00 of damages before the federal court would accept jurisdiction. We couldn't say we had that jurisdictional amount for each prospective member of the class. Anyway...the plaintiffs chose the state court and that's where the case should stay."

Beals rose slowly from his chair awaiting Walsh's final words of her argument. He knew that the decision to retain jurisdiction of the case in Federal Court before Judge Stuyvesant had already been made. The deal was described in detail to Beals by Senator Evans the night before. As all savvy lawyers know, more final decisions are made in the backroom of some of the finest courts in the land. Deal making is a national pastime for the American judicial system. And Judge Stuyvesant had made the deal of his aging lifetime. A place on the magisterial Fifth Circuit Court of Appeals; all he would have to do is subvert the law by dismissing the Comtel suit.

"Mr. Beals," Stuyvesant leaned securely back in his chair, his hands held bridge like in front of his mouth, "I presume you disagree with Ms. Walsh's argument."

"Yes, your honor, I respectfully do. As the court is aware, the federal courts have superior jurisdiction over any matter which falls within the purview of federal law. Especially when we are talking about class action matters. I bring to the court's attention the Johns Manville suit which also involved injuries to employees of Manville. There was little doubt that Manville and the case before this court were ripe for Federal jurisdiction."

"Anything else, counselors?" Stuyvesant ordered in a gasping breath signifying he had heard enough on this particular motion.

"Well…if that's all we have, I think there's little doubt that this matter should be removed to the federal courts. I doubt that the minimal jurisdictional amount per class members applies since I am exercising jurisdiction not under the diversity statute but on the specific federal law dealing with employee safety in the work place. The latter federal statute does not need a minimum jurisdictional amount for each potential class member. Now," Stuyvesant leaned forward in his chair, his hands rolled into clenched fists placed on the table before him, "Do we really have to argue the class certification issue? It seems so apparent to me that damages for personal injuries claimed by class members herein do not clearly fit under Rule 23 or any other relevant federal rule. The damages are all different for the individual employees which would destroy any claim of uniformity or commonality that is required in any class action certification. In fact, Mr. Beals' briefs clearly point out the legal precedents of the U.S. Supreme Court as well as other lesser esteemed appellate courts' rulings."

Beals sat down, his head bobbing up and down in agreement with Judge Stuyvesant's opinion.

Ryan quickly arose and with his hands wafting through the air as a prologue to his fervent disagreement with Stuyvesant's opinion, he said in slow articulate words, "Your honor, although I usually have great respect for the court's opinion, I must respectfully and emphatically disagree with the court's opinion in this case. This court would have to sit as an appellate review panel to Judge Gamble's decision in the state court certifying the class. No trial court…and this court is the trial court under the federal system…can not take the decision of another trial court as the law of the case. The defendant, Comtel, has seen fit to appeal not only Judge Gamble's decision on certification but also various other claimed errors of that trial court. To undo what the Florida judicial system has deemed the law of the case would be to unravel the entire legislative and constitutional mandates of Florida legal precedents. No federal court is authorized to order that done unless there is some claimed constitutional breach which none is claimed in the case before this court. If that order is issued, if this court usurps it's definitive authority by removing the case to federal court and dismissing the case, after trial and judgment entered against the defendant Comtel, that would be an enormous injustice visited upon these many injured employees in this case. Therefore, we would have to file an immediate appeal of the court's order with the Fifth Circuit Court of Appeal in New Orleans."

Ryans words seemed to hit home. Judge Stuyvesant's turkey neck jiggled noticeably as he moved his head toward defendant's table and back to where Ryan was standing.

Beals said nothing in reply. He sat erect in the wooden arm chair, his legs crossed under the table. He knew that Stuyvesant would order the case dismissed and that an appeal would have little chance of succeeding. Most appellate courts hate to disturb the status quo of any order of the lower court unless that appellate court wishes to make a statement for the world to heed. And although Ryan spouted the magic words such as "breach of the constitution" and "usurping state law," the federal appellate courts have little regard for their brethren state courts, treating them similarly as state courts treat their subordinate municipal courts. It was the pecking order of the law courts of the land. Every good lawyer knows that only ten percent of all lower court decision are ever reversed on appeal. And the lawyers in that courtroom were all good lawyers.

"Mr. Ryan, I appreciate your admonitions to this court. You certainly have the right…no…the obligation to do what is best for your clients." Stuyvesant paused and smiled as he directed his gaze toward Beals. Ryan noticed the slight smile crossing Beals face as Beals turned to his two associates. Stuyvesant suddenly left the bench and courtroom signifying his order was final.

"The deal was done before we walked into the courtroom, Josh," Waterman said as he helped Ryan shovel in the legal books and documents from the desk into two large briefcases.

"What now, Helen?" Josh asked of Walsh who stared at the retreating figure of Judge Stuyvesant as he jumped the three steps from his bench to the door leading to his chambers.

"We go to New Orleans, gentlemen. That's after we prepare the petition and briefs for the appeal."

"What chance do we have in overturning Stuyvesant, Helen?" Waterman asked.

"Maybe none. But we still have to file it, Sam. There may be a chance we could get an expedited hearing. You see," she smiled as she walked alongside Waterman and Ryan out of the courtroom, "I know the chief justice of the Fifth circuit. He's a Brooklyn boy…just like you, Sam."

"How the hell did a Brooklyn boy get to New Orleans?" Sam asked with a rasping chuckle.

"Who knows? You Brooklyn boys turn up everywhere. Like bad pennies. We met at NYU law school a hundred years ago."

"God save us from past lovers, Helen."

She laughed and hugged Sam Waterman around his sloping shoulders. They were outside the courthouse in the bright morning sunlight of Orlando.

"We're just friends, Sam. You don't have to be jealous of an old flame like Dominic Florenza."

"Another Jewish boy from Brooklyn I guess?"

"The same…Italian through and through. Just like you, Sam."

"I guess you won't need me for any of these fun and games, Helen." Josh declared as he placed the briefcase at his feet when they had descended the courthouse steps to the sidewalk.

"You bet your sweet "tuchas" we will, Joshua my boy," Sam acknowledged. "Who the hell is going to write the brief? Not me. I haven't written a brief in ten years."

"Don't worry, Josh," Helen said as she kissed Joshua on the cheek, "I'm good at brief writing. Together we'll overturn that wasp son-of-a-bitch Stuyvesant."

"Even if we lose here, we still have the grand jury hearing to get these mothers," Joshua said, his voice turning hard and bitter.

"That's if it ever goes forward, Joshua," Waterman warned.

"We'll know in a couple of days. I guess we'll be busy for the next week or so, Sam," Joshua said, his face opening up with a boyish grin.

Yehuda and Sosie drove up in the SUV. They all decided that they had had enough of the courts of the land and therefore they would spend the rest of the day in Disney Land eating hot dogs and riding the bumper cars and roller coasters where at least they knew when the ride was over. Never so in the judicial system of America.

Chapter Forty-Three

"Beals called, Dad," Jack Evans said to Senator Evans who was seated across from him at a corner table reserved for very important diners at Le Cirque, the celebrated New York restaurant located in the courtyard of The Palace Hotel on Madison Avenue in New York City.

"And…"

"Stuyvesant dismissed the case."

"As planned, Jack."

"As planned…"

"What about Abromowitz? Have you heard anything further about AMT and the merger, Jack?"

"Unsettling news, Dad."

"Like what?"

"Like I think Abromowitz is trying to double deal."

"How so?"

"The underwriter called this morning. Just before I flew up here.

He said that there is no doubt someone is trying to buy up enough shares of Comtel to grab the majority seats on the Board of Directors. He said most of the purchases are coming from some corporation in Luxenbourg."

"Luxenbourg is close to Paris, Jack."

"I know, Dad. Very close."

"Can't you find out who's behind the corporation?"

"Tough to do. They don't freely give out corporate information in Luxenbourg. I'm having our European people checking into it."

"Now that the suit is dismissed, Abromowitz should have little to complain about."

The senator paused long enough to order from the extensive menu and wine list handed to him by the formally dressed waiter. Jack ordered the same as the senator.

"I think he's greedy, Dad. He wants the whole pie and he doesn't want to pay for it."

The waiter served the champagne cocktails and placed the basket of hard baguette rolls on the table. Jack Evans absent-mindedly chewed on the corner of a baguette roll while he sipped his champagne.

"What do we do, Jack? I don't want to die a poor man."

"Abromowitz has to go, Dad."

"How so, Jack?"

"The same way all greedy people go."

"Do you think it's wise. Abromowitz is a very important man, Jack."

"He's already bought up over a million of our shares, Dad. More than enough to stop the merger."

"Why would he stop his own merger?"

"To renege on our deal, Dad. He saves about three billion dollars if he kills the merger and buys the shares on the open market."

"Our three billion dollars?"

"Our three billion dollars, Dad," Jack Evans repeated.

"What can we do to stop him, Jack?"

"Kill him. Literally kill him."

"Isn't that a bit drastic, Jack?"

"Its him or us, Dad."

"And how do you propose doing the dirty deed, Jack?"

"Paulsen."

"Its different killing Abromowitz than some aging employees, Jack."

"Abromowitz is not the only problem, Dad."

"We have more? I thought with the dismissal of the suit and I've taken care of the SEC investigation…What else is there, Jack?"

"Lawrence has subpoenaed Lowry and Matilda for next Friday's grand jury hearing."

"Lowry has as much to lose as we do, Jack."

"In his present mental state, Dad, he's unpredictable."

"What can we do?"

"I don't know. Paulsen has prescribed his usual medicine but I don't know."

"Do we have something to worry about with Lowry? I thought he was on the team, Jack."

"Something is bugging him the last couple of days. He's always been a pussy. But lately, honestly, I don't know, Dad. He knows everything."

The waiter appeared and served the foie gras with shaved truffles spread liberally over the delicacy. The wine steward also appeared and opened a bottle of 1994 Haut Medoc red, the senator tested the blood red liquor by swirling it around in his mouth, then affirmatively waved for the wine steward to fill their glasses. Silently, Jack Evans and his father drank from the wine glasses, each wondering if their comfortable life would change over night.

"Do what you have to do, Jack. I'm too old to make those hard decisions anymore. I've always been against that type of violence, but it seems the world has changed too much for me to care."

"Dad, if we can get rid of Abromowitz, we save Comtel and maybe launch our own hostile take over of AMT. Without Abromowitz, AMT is a headless horseman. He runs the show there."

"What about his right hand man Steingut, the little kraut lawyer?"

"Whatever happens to Abromowitz happens to Steingut."

The foie gras was eaten quickly as if each of the diners hadn't even tasted the appetizers. Theirs minds seemed many miles away preventing them from focusing on their food.

"I got a call from the A.G., Jack."

"What did he have to say?"

"He apologized for what his Deputy is doing in Orlando. He said he couldn't stop the grand jury hearing because it came right from the President. Bancroft is deathly afraid of antagonizing Simon Warner…even though he's out of office in two years. I guess Warner is his Lowry…knows too much for his own good."

"What happened to good old fashion loyalty, Dad?"

"Went out with Watergate. Nixon tried to save Halderman and Mitchell and got his balls singed off."

The waiter removed the foie gras plates and immediately returned with the porterhouse steaks, blood red rare. There was a delicate sauce béarnaise dolloped on the side of the plate as well as sautéed onions sprinkled over the steaks. Father and son ate voraciously as if attacking the massive steaks would save their world.

Nothing further was said until the steaks were devoured. Except for the eyes of each of the men, communicating the unsaid plan of destroying anybody that could topple their safe and warm worlds of opulent luxury.

Chapter Forty-Four

The Concorde flew into Paris' Charles De Gaulle airport at 6:00 p.m. Paris time. Paulsen had slept throughout the three and half hours flight. After touchdown, he was shuttled over to Air France domestic terminal and was seated in first class on the flight to Nice. After about an hour flight, he disembarked in Nice about 8:00 p.m. He picked up his small piece of luggage which contained plastic pieces of his automatic rifle.

A Rolls Royce limousine and driver was waiting for him at Nice International. He was driven to Monte Carlo over the high mountain road and deposited at the Hotel de Paris' entrance. Quickly he was led to an enormous suite overlooking the harbor.

Sitting at the desk for him was an envelope marked personal and confidential. He unwrapped the envelope in his suite and three hollow, poison tipped bullets fell onto his bed.

He unpacked his leather bag onto the bed. The plastic pieces of his rifle scattered amongst his personal clothing items.

Sitting at the edge of the bed, he pieced together the plastic barrel, the firing mechanism, the gun stock, the gun sight and various other little pieces that formed the complete automatic rifle. He placed a bullet into the loading mechanism, and clicked it shut. Placing the rifle's gun sight up to his right eye, he aimed the rifle out the picture window onto the boat filled harbor. The lights of the Monte Carlo Casino filtered through his window giving off a carnival like atmosphere.

Paulsen disassembled the rifle into its original pieces and placed them into a dark leather carrying case. The complete rifle case appeared as if it were a saxophone carry-on.

Paulsen ordered a roast beef sandwich and a Heineken beer from room service. He flicked on the remote for the television set located in the bedroom and lodged himself against the padded head board of the king-size bed. His feet and body lay full on the bed. He absentmindedly watched a French talk show which he minimally understood.

There was a quiet knock on the suite's door. Paulsen slid quickly off the bed and opened the door to the room service waiter. After the waiter set up the table with the sandwich, French fries and the Heineken, he withdrew from the room.

Paulsen picked up the baguette sandwich and the Heineken and went back to the bedroom. While laying on the bed, he ate the sandwich and drank the bottle of beer while intently watching the talk show. His eyes darted to the clock on the table and he noted it was approximately 10:00 p.m. He looked at his Rolex watch on his right wrist and then adjusted the time on the watch to the bedroom clock's time. For complete accuracy, he called down to the front desk for the exact time.

Paulsen laughed at some of the antics of the talk show host with three beautiful singers who were being interviewed by the clownish host.

After finishing his sandwich and beer, he looked at his watch again. It was approaching 10:30 p.m. Adeptly, he arose from the bed and started to undress. He reached into the bottomless bag and removed a dark t-shirt and dark pants, and a pair of black Addidis running shoes.

He again opened up the gun case, pieced the elements of the automatic rifle together, tested the rifle by clicking the trigger and peering through the gun sight, and then again disassembled the rifle into its original pieces and placed it back into its carrying case.

Within five minutes, Paulsen was dressed and with his carrying case exited the luxurious lobby of the Hotel de Paris.

The night had a little chill to it although it was late May. There was a full moon centered directly overhead illuminating the harbor and the casino square.

Paulsen walked down the hilly street to the end of the harbor. The area was filled with closed warehouses as he arrived at the end of the pier.

His eyes noted a small twenty-two foot skiff that was tied just below the pier. He opened up the gun carrying case and pieced the rifle together quickly. He jumped into the boat with the assembled rifle and after placing the rifle to the side of the boat's control board, lifted a rubber mat on the floor. After searching around for several moments, he found a lone key under the mat; he placed the key into the ignition and the boat's motor sputtered for several moments and then finally kicked over. Paulsen untied the boat from the pier and placed the throttle into drive. With a sudden surge, the boat sprang forward, the wind and the ocean spray lifting above the windshield blowing into Paulsen's face. Like the ship's pilot in the Wagnerian opera, "The Flying Dutchman," Paulsen stood erect against the pounding sea waves, his face barely flinching from the attacking ocean. His mind always prepared itself for the ultimate assignment. Death. The final erotic emotion. Orgasmic. Paulsen wasn't ever motivated by hate, personal or otherwise; execution was totally impersonal. Every fiber in his body was tingling with the anticipation of the kill. The hunter and the quarry. The battle of life and most enjoyably, death. Paulsen remembered the execution of all those women and children at Chou Lai. An orgasmic dream come true.

The skiff jumped from the top of each wave into the abyss of the next wave and then to the top of the next wave. His eyes suddenly saw the lights of the hundred and fifty foot pleasure craft lying quietly at anchor just off an ocean shoal no more than a thousand feet from the jutting land mass extending out from Monte Carlo. The music of a Verdi opera flew through the air as it blasted out from the "Ruchel".

Paulsen grabbed the assembled plastic rifle and inserted one of the hollow poison tipped bullets within the firing mechanism. Shortly thereafter, Paulsen pulled alongside the uninhabited starboard side of the "Ruchel". Paulsen saw three people sitting around a card table on the backside promenade deck of the boat, faint flickers of cigarette and cigar ash wafting through the air like fireflies.

Paulsen checked the pocket of his pants for the other two bullets. After confirming the presence of the bullets, he sidled the skiff alongside the "Ruchel". Paulsen could see that the only movement of people on the ship was on the backside of the promenade deck.

He threw a rope with a metal hook over the railing of the "Ruchel". With the rifle slung over his shoulder, Paulsen climbed up the rope onto the ship. He then drew the rifle from his shoulder and carried it in his right hand against his hip.

With cat-like stealth, he ran along the port side of the boat until he could see the three card players on the promenade.

He loaded the other two shells into the firing mechanism of the automatic rifle.

With balletic grace, he sidestepped onto the promenade. Abromowitz saw him first. Fredrick Abromowitz' small athletic body attempted to leave his deck chair. But Paulsen shot him right between the eyes from the hip position of the rifle. Abromowitz' body fell forward onto the card table, blood immediately spurting from his head onto the table.

Steingut's face immediately lifted up from the cards that he was holding in his right hand, his eyes staring directly at the smiling Paulsen. Steingut threw his arm across his face as if to ward off the next bullet but Paulsen shot him cleanly through the heart instead. Steingut's hand clutched his wounded heart, his eyes still staring at Paulsen's exhilarated face. Then Steingut's head fell forward onto the table sending the table crashing to the deck.

The countess had time to jump from her chair and started to run toward the pilot's deck. Paulsen raced after her, caught her by the hair before she left the main deck, throwing her to the ground. She was wearing a casual white evening dress that Paulsen ripped from her shoulders, her bare breasts immediately became exposed.

The petite beautiful face immediately twisted into a fearful ugliness as she pleaded with Paulsen, her body sinking to her knees in front of Paulsen's erect body.

Paulsen uttered a hideous cackle as he stood over the crying, prostrate body. He raised the rifle from his hip, and clubbed the tiny head with the plastic gunstock. The countess' body fell face down onto the deck, her pleas mingling with the gurgling tears that filled her mouth and nose.

Paulsen raised the rifle to his shoulder and shot her through the back of her well coiffed head. The garbled pleas stopped almost immediately.

Suddenly, Paulsen saw three crew member emerge from the cabins below. He turned and ran to the promenade deck. His mouth was open to a sneering grin as he jumped off the "Ruchel" into the dark sea below. All he could hear were the shouts of bewilderment coming from the deck of the "Ruchel". He dived below the roiling waves to deposit the plastic rifle under the sea and lodged it amongst a row of ocean boulders that had not moved for centuries.

Within one hour he was on his way to the Nice airport, sipping a Jack Daniels' whisky in the back seat of the Rolls Royce. The joy he felt in his pounding heart was overwhelming knowing that he had done his job well. Even his damning father couldn't have criticized Paulsen's success now.

Chapter Forty-Five

"He did what?" Lawrence shouted at the three people sitting in front of his desk in his small office located in the back of the fifth floor of the federal office building in Orlando.

"I received the orders hand delivered this morning," Helen Walsh said in an unemotional voice. She was dressed in a sand beige business suit with the skirt conservatively knee length. Her dark sparkling eyes gave Sam Waterman a surge of erotic sensation for this late middle-aged female lawyer as his own eyes enjoyed the natural beauty of this newly discovered "friend".

"What the hell is Stuyvesant ruling on a criminal investigation that's not even before him?" Lawrence continued angrily as his clinched fist pounded the desk. He wore a light blue linen suit and white shirt unbuttoned at the neck. It was clear that he was agitated.

"Beals submitted an ex parte application without even telling us about it," Ryan said as if he expected anything to happen in the wild west carnival of justice in Orlando.

"He also submitted this order dismissing the civil case, but that we expected." Helen Walsh declared.

"Now what?" Ryan asked his mind cluttered with the frustration and anger at the act of unexpected injustice and being pissed off at himself for being surprised at anything that comes down from a tainted court.

"I called Dominic Florenza, Joshua," Helen Walsh announced.

"Would he buck the Senator, Helen?" Waterman asked.

"Dominic is ready for retirement, Sam. He doesn't give a damn about politics and politicians. Not even when he was a young renegade federal prosecutor in the days of Lyndon Johnson."

"I wonder if President Bancroft knows anything about this," Lawrence mused aloud.

"Bancroft knows everything," Helen said knowingly. "I knew Bancroft when he was a councilman in New York City decades ago. He does whatever is expedient for Bancroft and I guess Senator Evans told him about his life after being President. Just like Clinton. Bancroft wants a wealthy retirement plan and I bet the Senator offered it to him in spades."

"Call Judge Florenza, Helen," Joshua said in a mild but demanding voice.

"When can we go to New Orleans if he's amenable to a conference?"

"Today, tomorrow, now, Helen," Lawrence insisted. "All I need is to put on my tie and I'm off to the races."

"Then gentlemen, get your overnight bags packed. We're off to New Orleans," Helen said as she rose from her seat, kissed Waterman on the cheek and proceeded to leave the room. On her way out she said, "I'll be calling Everett here within the hour…all we need are plane tickets."

Waterman and Ryan rose from their chairs as Walsh left the office.

"Everett," Ryan said, "you know Stuyvesant wouldn't have enjoined the grand jury hearing without the blessings of your superiors at the A.G.'s office."

"I know that, Joshua. I'm going to let the chips fall where they may. If I lose my job, so be it. Maybe Jo-Beth and I can open up a coffeehouse in Miami. Just for fucked on lawyers…There should be a steady flow of customers." Lawrence laughed. His body releasing all the pent up hatred that had poisoned his mind and body these past several days. He couldn't believe in his still innocent mind that injustice could prevail in that wonderful legal world he so much worshipped. Maybe Jo-Beth was right…give it up and retire to the Bahamas. At least black is beautiful in the islands.

"Come to Paris, Everett. The French would love Jo-Beth." Ryan offered.

"Maybe…let's go to New Orleans first and fight the Civil War once more." Everett replied as he offered his hand to Joshua with a broad toothsome smile on his face. He liked these white folks. Somehow they must have had black blood in their geneology. Everett had never been close to white people, although his roommate at Yale was a white, anglo-saxon wasp. Was Simon Warner right about how the white folk thought? 'Trust them as far as you can kick 'em,' Warner warned his protégé. 'They'll fuck you as soon as look at you,' he would go on and on. 'Scare the shit out of them and then maybe you'll get justice,' Warner further lamented.

'We'll see,' Everett thought as he noticed Ryan and Waterman leave his office.

"Ah," he muttered to himself, "maybe the coffeehouse wasn't such a bad idea." He laughed to himself as he dialed Jo-Beth's office to tell her the latest news flash. He knew she would throw a tirade and want to come along to New Orleans. Maybe that wasn't such a bad idea. "We'll see," Lawrence repeated as he waited for Jo-Beth to pick up the telephone receiver.

CHAPTER FORTY-SIX

Their American Airline Flight had landed at New Orleans airport at noon sharp. It was the first time that Ryan, Yehuda, Sosie and Jo-Beth had ever been to New Orleans. Waterman and Walsh had been to the fabled city of jazz attending an American Bar Convention several years ago, but at that time they did not know each other.

It was late May and the city was filled with conventioneers of all color, trade and perversity. If you couldn't satisfy your lust for life in the city by Lake Ponchontrain you might as well sign up for the local Trappist monastery.

They booked rooms at the Hyatt Hotel which faced the lake and downtown New Orleans. Since everybody was paying their own way, the rooms were rack-rated, although Yehuda had convinced the manager of the hotel that Jo-Beth was Whitney Houston's sister and that she was forging ahead for her sister's next concert in New Orleans. To the surprise of them all, each member or couple of the Lawrence tour were blessed with an upgraded junior suite overlooking the lake.

Sosie and Jo-Beth were not going to be part of the conference that afternoon with Chief Judge Florenza. They had planned to take a walking tour of Bourbon Street and parts therein and report back to the hotel at 6:00 p.m. They would also attempt to reserve a large table at one of Chef Emeril Lagasse's restaurants, since Jo-Beth watched him on the food channel at least once a week.

The meeting was scheduled for 3:00 p.m. New Orleans time. Judge Florenza had verbally ordered Beals and Judge Stuyvesant to attend this emergency conference. Stuyvesant had first balked at the idea of being compelled to explain himself to the chief justice citing pressing judicial matters on his home front, but Judge Florenza threatened an undisclosed warning to the senior judge of the U.S. District Court in Orlando. Besides, Stuyvesant knew that if he didn't appear at Judge Florenza's invitation, his chances of ever being appointed to the Fifth Circuit Court of Appeals' bench was nil.

Beals had contacted Senator Evans and Jack Evans when he got the call from the clerk of the Fifth Circuit Court of Appeals inviting him to the conference in New Orleans. Senator Evans contacted the A.G. but the A.G. said he could do nothing about canceling the conference. When Evans called the president's office, Bancroft's secretary told him that the president was attending the NATO conference in Brussels and wouldn't be home for several days. She said she would pass on Senator Evans' request that President Bancroft call him as soon as possible.

The Fifth Circuit Court of Appeals courtroom was located in the antebellum white columned courthouse in downtown New Orleans. It had been a working courthouse since just after the Civil War. There had been many petitions to tear it down and build a new federal courthouse but the Yankee hating powers to be in New Orleans killed all efforts to destroy one of the last symbols of confederate allegiance still present in New Orleans.

Seated around the large oblong conference table were Judge Peter Stuyvesant, Nicholas Beals, Joshua Ryan, Samuel Waterman, Helen Walsh and Everett Lawrence. Present also was a court reporter with her trusty stenographic machine now computerized and backed up by an audio tape.

They all waited for the appearance of the eminent Chief Judge Dominic Florenza. He had been touted to become the next appointee to the U.S. Supreme Court but he had his name withdrawn from consideration because he knew his liberal decisions on the Fifth Circuit Court would subject him to voracious and vindictive cross examination by the Republican led Senate. And besides, President Bancroft had no love for the judge who had written the basic opinions on the subsequent progeny cases of the pro-choice, pro-abortion Roe v. Wade decision that had originated in Florenza's jurisdiction decades ago. Further, many other of his opinions had been adopted by the moderate but closely split U.S. Supreme Court and President Bancroft and his fellow Republicans knew that if Florenza was appointed to the U.S. Supreme Court, the Court would definitively swing laterally and firmly to the left. Anyway, Dominic Florenza looked forward to retiring in a year or so and returning to his roots in New York City. He maintained an apartment in Manhattan where his daughter practiced entertainment law and lived there. His wife had died over five years ago and Florenza missed her terribly. Whenever he had an opportunity he would fly to New York City and revel in the theater, opera, ballet, and the general cosmopolitan atmosphere of the city of his birth.

Before his wife of thirty years had died, she had pulled him out of his provincial mindset and he had learned to love the antiquities and luxuries of the European world. They had traveled extensively throughout Italy and France, enjoying the hallmarks of history brought so delicately into the 21st Century. His parents came from Naples and he had been born on the ship that brought his parents to America.

Judge Florenza reveled in his immigrant beginnings as well as the love for the richness of his family's provenance. His parents had lived to see their youngest son become the Chief Judge of the Fifth Circuit and his mother had held the bible when he was sworn in two decades ago. Now that they were gone as well as his loving wife Paulette, his loneliness was buried in his legal work and his daughter's life in New York.

The small figure of a man, his hair full but silver, his face grizzled but highlighted by dimpled cheeks giving him a boyish aura, walked sure-footed into the wood paneled conference room. He was wearing his black judicial robes but it was evident he wore no tie nor suit jacket under the robes. He briefly smiled at Helen Walsh who was seated at the other end of the table between Ryan and Waterman. Florenza nodded to Beals who he had known for several years as a result of their joint participation in the American Bar Association's committee on revising the Federal Rules of Court.

"Good afternoon, everyone," the judge said in a lilting voice still tinged with the flavor of New York.

Everyone uttered a replying greeting to the robust, barrel chested judge who pulled his arm chair flush to the glass topped mahogany conference table.

"Ms. Walsh requested this meeting…this emergency meeting…because of some of the things she highlighted which caused me great concern. That's why I've asked Judge Stuyvesant to appear here and I must thank him for coming on such short notice. I know how busy you are, Judge…"

Stuyvesant nodded in the affirmative and released a token ingratiating smile to the chief judge.

"Ms. Walsh has submitted a brief memorandum of what has transpired in the last few days in Judge Stuyvesant's courtroom. Unfortunately, I couldn't insist on a reply memo from Mr. Beals or even any comments by Judge Stuyvesant. But, I must say, I have known Ms. Walsh for over thirty years, we were law students together," Florenza smiled at Helen Walsh who returned a demure smile, "I have always found her to be candid and direct. So, if I take her memo at face value I am extremely disturbed by the rulings of Judge Stuyvesant…especially in light of the ex parte application of Mr. Beals' in dismissing the grand jury hearing called by and held by Mr. Lawrence here." Florenza nodded to Lawrence who was seated at the other end of the table.

"Let me direct my first question to Mr. Beals. Why did you submit an ex parte application to Judge Stuyvesant to enjoin the grand jury hearing? And the follow up question to Judge Stuyvesant is simply why in the hell did you grant it, Peter?" Florenza's voice became angrier as the words came out of his mouth.

"Well, your honor…if I may," Beals inpleaded, "the ex parte petition was submitted because Mr. Lawrence here did not have the permission and authority to continue on with his fishing expedition into my client's internal activities. He was carrying on a witch hunt, your honor and there is no probable cause to drag my clients through the mud of a politically motivated grand jury farce of a hearing."

Lawrence and Ryan both started to speak but Florenza put the palm of his hand out to stop them.

"Well, Mr. Beals, we know that the grand jury hearing was held in secret session…were there any leaks to the press about what Mr. Lawrence had discovered? I saw nothing in the press."

"Not yet, your honor…but Mr. Lawrence had subpoenaed massive quantities of internal records of Comtel and some of their key employees. And there was no probable cause to do all that."

"My understanding of the attorney general's power in this country, Mr. Beals, is that he has the power to convene a grand jury to find out if there is probable cause that a crime or crimes have been committed. Isn't that your understanding of the law of the land, Mr. Beals?"

"Well, yes…but Mr. Lawrence was told by his superiors not to convene the grand jury. His own bosses at the Justice Department clearly instructed him to cease and desist in continuing the grand jury investigation."

"Judge," Lawrence said as he rose from his chair. Florenza motioned him to sit down and continue with his reply. "As an assistant A.G., I have the power without prior approval of anyone, including my superiors, to convene an investigating grand jury. The only reason Mr. Beals objected was because we were getting close to some very embarrassing and inculpatory answers to why and how ten or so Comtel employees were murdered. Right in their own houses, your honor. Several expert witnesses were ready to testify that those victims did not die of natural causes. They were murdered by someone or someones who had intentionally blocked off the ventilating outlets in those homes which caused high levels of carbon monoxide gases to be admitted into the houses. The same houses that Comtel itself built for its senior employees. Further, those deaths were perpetrated not only because Comtel wanted to ensure that it wouldn't be joined again as a defendant in another class action suit, but more importantly to ensure that those senior employees would not block a potential and very necessary merger of Comtel and AMT, a major international cable transmission company. Particularly…both Senator Evans and his son Jack Evans and other top level executives of Comtel stood to benefit in the sum of billions of dollars if the merger was consummated. Those ten or so victims could have stopped that very lucrative merger. That's why I convened the grand jury, your honor. We were just getting to the testimony and evidence of our expert witnesses, as well as the general counsel, the CFO and the public relations director of Comtel along with the presentment of scores of internal Comtel documents which could have revealed the reasons behind the deaths and other egregious corporate acts of Comtel's executives.

We think that the Evans and certain of their executive staff were directly involved in the whole sordid mess, your honor. Only because of Judge Stuyvesant's injunctive order in stopping the grand jury hearing, which the court had no basis in issuing, could the reasons and evidence behind all these criminal acts be destroyed."

Florenza stroked his hair back with the palm of his hand. His azure blue eyes stared hypnotically at Lawrence. Then he moved his stare to Beals and Stuyvesant, who was drumming his bony fingers nervously on the table. Beals was raising his hand to reply to Lawrence's accusations but Florenza held his hand out as he said to Lawrence, "Look, Mr. Lawrence...I thoroughly agree with you. You certainly had the power to convene the grand jury. But Mr. Beals is somewhat correct; if the grand jury was called in some kind of fishing expedition against Comtel and the Evans...well, I think Judge Stuyvesant would have the power under Rule 11 or a host of other court rules that give the trial judge discretion in ordering the termination of that hearing. I've read the reports and testimony of your two experts and they certainly spell out that the deaths were certainly not caused by natural causes. There was, and your experts are clear about it, an intentional act by someone and that's the rub, Mr. Lawrence. I saw nothing in the testimony of these experts that definitively pointed to the someone who committed these serial murders."

Ryan motioned to Judge Florenza by raising his hand slightly that he wished to be heard. Judge Florenza nodded to Ryan to proceed.

"Your honor, my name is Joshua Ryan. Mr. Lawrence had deputized me to act as assistant counsel along with Mr. Waterman here," Ryan nodded toward Sam Waterman seated next to him, "to aid in the investigation and presentment of the evidence to the grand jury. Mr. Waterman's sister and brother-in-law were two of the victims so he had more than a passing interest in finding out what happened here. Anyway, besides the medical reports of Dr. Pasha, the medical examiner of Orange County who clearly said that carbon monoxide poisoning was the root cause of all ten deaths, we have the report of Dr. Bitterman, a well respected forensic engineer who clearly maintains that the carbon monoxide was created by someone who cut off the necessary ventilated outlets in each of the decedents' homes. In the construction of these Comtel homes the utility room held all the major appliances of the home. The dryer, the furnace and the hot water heater. By cutting off the ventilation of these heat generating appliances, especially when the furnace was absorbing excess lint from the dryer into its firing mechanism, it would then cause an incomplete combustion in the furnace. From that reaction, the furnace would emit carbon monoxide…enough to injure or even kill the residents of that home.

Normally, one would conclude that the defect itself…the appliances in a small utility room with inadequate ventilation…would be the cause of the carbon monoxide induced death. And certainly it was a partial cause. But the final coup de grace was the purposeful shutting off of the vents located inside of the houses that normally would vent the CO, at least to the extent of diminishing the amount of CO below the danger level. That someone…or somebodies…is what we were ready to prove to the grand jury, your honor."

"Your honor," Beals interjected as he impatiently waved his hand in the air as if he was swatting flies from his face, "This is all speculation…nothing that we know…and we have been privy to the investigation reports of the Orlando Police Department and also the Orange County Sheriff's office, there is nothing in those reports to even vaguely implicate anyone at Comtel. My client has voluntarily and enthusiastically participated in the investigation of those deaths. Nothing but nothing can vaguely implicate anyone at Comtel. My God!" Beals declared with a gasping breath, "Who in heavens name would even think of perpetrating such a horrendous act or acts?"

"Your honor," Ryan persisted as he reached into his briefcase and brought out a small tape recorder which he placed on the table. "I would agree with my eminent adversary that not discovering a person or persons that committed these horrendous acts would be a waste of the court's valuable time." Ryan pointed to the little black tape recorder sitting in front of him on the table, "We have brought with us a tape of a conversation we had with Comtel's general counsel, Alfred Lowry. After you have heard that testimony, your honor, I'm sure you'll be a convinced as we are that Comtel…and its top executives…participated in the deaths of those many employees."

Beals shot up from his chair as if he was reaching across the table to grab Ryan by the throat. Almost hysterically, his speech garbled as first, he sputtered out his words as if he was forced to stop to take a breath he would be silenced by some outside force.

"Your honor, this is all hogwash. Counsel is trying to blackmail my client into paying the ridiculous verdict amount on a case that's been thrown out by the court. I don't know what's on that tape but I do know that if Alfred Lowry is saying something against Comtel...well, your honor, I would certainly have to vociferously object under the lawyer/client privilege."

"Your honor," Ryan quietly replied as he arched his back against the back of the armchair, "the lawyer-client privilege does not come into play here. Mr. Lowry, who will probably be a defendant in a criminal indictment, cannot hide under the lawyer-client privilege. A lawyer, as your honor knows, cannot use the privilege if he, himself, is a participant in a crime. If need be, we can brief the issue for the Court in twenty-four hours."

Florenza's eyes burned at Beals, knowing full well that the celebrated lawyer was getting his balls cut off and was trying to snow the court with his bullshit charade. Anyway, Florenza wanted to hear what was on that tape, whether admissible later at trial or not.

"Play the tape, Mr. Ryan. We'll worry about admissibility at a later date...if even there is a later date."

Ryan switched on the tape and the entire audience in that conference room sat transfixed by Lowry's and Sosie's voices. Beals was tapping his pen against the table, louder and louder as Lowry's words buried his client deeper and deeper into the soft Louisiana dirt. Even Stuyvesant, knowing all that was a stake for him personally, couldn't wait for the words to shoot out from that microscopic tape.

There was no doubt in anybody's mind in that large conference room that Lowry was sealing the doom of himself, the Evans – the Senator and Jack – Paulsen and probably even good old Charlie Borden, the CFO of Comtel.

Everything came out that early afternoon. The money laundering, the phony accounting methods, the murders, the merger, and most of all, the reasons why all these horrendous and illegal acts were being done. For billions of dollars. For the Evans, for Lowry, for Borden, for all the directors on Comtel's board. The AMT merger was the pot of gold at the end of the rainbow.

After the tape had been played and digested by all the listeners in that room, Judge Florenza looked toward Judge Stuyvesant and said in a slow monotone, "Peter, why did you enjoin the grand jury hearing? I haven't seen anything before me which would lead me to believe the reasoning behind your order in this matter."

Stuyvesant moved nervously in his seat, his left eye started twitching as he spoke, his voice extremely high and effeminate.

"Chief Judge, I issued the order at the bequest of the Attorney General…Wadsworth. He submitted a certification to my court stating that he had not authorized any grand jury hearing. Therefore, I had no choice but to order the cessation of the grand jury hearing."

"Was this certification and the petition submitted by Mr. Beals ever transmitted to Mr. Lawrence? Did you ever schedule oral argument so Mr. Lawrence could oppose the motion by his own superior?"

"No, Judge…I did not. And maybe that was my error. I just didn't think I needed any other documents to issue the injunctive order."

"Was it because of any deal making, Judge Stuyvesant? There are rumors that Senator Evans is pulling no punches in Washington to get you nominated as a judge in my court?"

Stuyvesant's bony white face colored a bright red as the twitching of his eye became even more noticeable.

"Judge Florenza, on my oath as a judge…never did anything Senator Evans promise me ever come into play in my decision to enjoin the hearing. Never in a million years!"

Florenza knew Stuyvesant was lying through his large teeth. He always knew when somebody was lying. He could smell the mendacity and the fearful sweat emitted by the liar. Florenza had been surrounded by liars all his life. He was an oasis of truth in a desert of intractable liars.

"Well folks, I think we've had quite a day. Ms. Rogers," Florenza said to the reporter, "please get a transcript of today's proceedings to me by tomorrow morning. I want to consult with my fellow judges to see what should be done. At the least, I will let the appeal of the civil action dismissal go through the normal channels of appeal. But, I'll tell you folks now, my first impression is to let the grand jury hearing continue. And if it does, there certainly will be a number of people indicted. And ladies and gentlemen, I don't care who is indicted…Senators, the CEO, the CFO and heads of state…Let the chips fall where they may."

Florenza rose sprightly up from his chair almost knocking it backwards. He gathered his robes about him and walked toward the door of the conference room.

"All of you…please make yourself available at 10:00 a.m. tomorrow. I will have then rendered a final decision on this matter."

Florenza smiled broadly at Helen Walsh and said to her, "Helen, could you join me for dinner tonight? I haven't had the pleasure of dining with a beautiful woman since Paulette died."

Walsh looked over at Waterman who nodded affirmatively.

"I'd love to, your honor. As long was we go dutch."

Florenza laughed a deep laugh and tipped his head toward Helen. "What ever you say. May I select the restaurant?"

"I wouldn't have it any other way, Dominic," she replied as everybody rose from the table and left the room.

Chapter Forty-Seven

At exactly 9:30 a.m., the twenty-three members of the grand jury filed into the almost empty federal courtroom. Orlando had rainy weather, the black clouds covered most of the city all morning. It had been almost three weeks since these same twenty-three people had met and sat in the jury box. Their collective wonderment clearly showed on each of their faces as they waited for Lawrence to speak to them.

Seated at the defense table was Nicholas Beals, dressed in a dark shark skinned suit, his eyes fixed on each of the jurors as they moved cautiously into their seats. A friendly smile filled his face as he nodded to each of the jurors. Alongside of him he had his two legal assistants who were passing notated yellow pads to Beals who didn't even bother to look at them. His attention was concentrated on the grand jurors.

Lawrence, Ryan, and Waterman sat at the prosecutor's table.

Lawrence had agreed to allow Beals to attend the grand jury hearing although that was an unusual allowance for defense counsel to sit in at a grand jury hearing. Seated behind Beals were Alfred Lowry, Matilda Gosling and Charles Borden, the CFO of Comtel. To the side of the prosecutor's table were six boxes of documents delivered by Comtel's attorney's office the week before on Florenza's court order. Ryan, Waterman, Lawrence and Walsh and Harry Sharon, the independent auditor, had combed through the volumes of documents and ledger sheets of Comtel's and had pulled the most interesting and damning documents to present to the grand jury.

Lowry's face was lined with deep furrows, his eyes more redlined than usual. He kept licking his fingers as if they had dried out completely.

Matilda Gosling smiled innocently, only her eyes displaying the fear she felt through her mind and body. She wore a dark brown cotton dress that disguised her voluptuous body.

Charles Borden, an overweight, dark haired accountant, kept whispering into Lowry's ear. Lowry appeared to disregard whatever Borden was telling him, his eyes fixed on Ryan and Waterman.

Lawrence rose from his chair and faced the jury panel. He smiled, his eyes wandering from one juror's face to another. With a deep homey voice he started to speak, "Ladies and gentlemen, thank you for appearing on such short notice. I know you still remember the unfortunate interruption you witnessed several weeks ago. I promise you, that will not happen again." Lawrence paused to take in a deep breath and then slowly exhaled the air from his chest. He walked slowly from one end of the jury box to the other end, his body moving sideways so his face was always in front of the jury. 'Never move too much or too quickly before a jury,' his moot court mentor, Sam Waterman would always preach from his Rutgers law pulpit. 'They want a show but don't let the show drown out your words.'

"As you can see, there is a defense attorney present in this courtroom. I told you in my last conversation with you that neither defense lawyers, nor defendants would be sitting in this grand jury hearing.

For this hearing, the court has made an exception. Therefore, let me introduce Nicholas Beals and his associates who represent Comtel and several of their executives."

Beals stood up and buttoned his suit jacket in the process. His smile was emblazoned across his long, thin face as he bowed his head ever so slightly toward the jury. Graciousness was the hallmark of Nicholas Beals' success as a trial lawyer. He rarely raised his voice in front of any jury, ensuring that they knew that a nice guy like him would never represent anybody but another nice guy.

"Without further adieu, ladies and gentlemen, I want to present our first witness to you. His name is Alfred Lowry, the general counsel of Comtel." Lawrence turned his body and lowered his head toward Lowry who was slowly rising from his bench seat in the audience section just beyond the cordoned off litigation pit where the lawyers and the reporter were seated.

As Lowry slowly trod through the swinging wooden gates leading to the witness chair in front of the courtroom, Ryan noticed Smallwood, or a man who certainly looked like Smallwood enter the courtroom and take a seat at the rear of the courtroom. He had Smallwood's marine brush cut hair and a long thin face that surely resembled Smallwood. The only difference Ryan noticed was the uneven malevolent smile that appeared on the man's face. Ryan turned around to face Lowry who had just been sworn in by the clerk of the court.

After Lowry took the oath, he fiddled around in the witness chair looking very uncomfortable and uneasy. His beady eyes stared down at his shoes as if he were to lift them toward Lawrence, he would be cursed with blindness.

"Good afternoon, Mr. Lowry," Lawrence greeted him with a benign smile and voice.

"Yes, hello," Lowry replied as he raised his face toward Lawrence.

Suddenly, Lowry jumped from his chair, his hand pointing toward the back of the courtroom. A resounding shot rang out from the back of the courtroom and instantaneously all eyes followed the phantom path of the bullet toward the front of the courtroom. The bullet was directed to the witness chair where Lowry had risen to his full height, his face transfixed into hysterical fear. Except Lowry's face now showed a bullet hole through his forehead, his body slumping to the witness chair, his screams dying into nothing as his body crumbled to the witness stand's floor.

As quickly as the shot was emitted toward Lowry, Ryan saw the man resembling Smallwood, rush up to the back of Matilda Gosling and Charlie Borden and blow the back of their heads off with bullets from a machine gun pistol. Bang, bang, were the only sounds Ryan heard as he saw both Borden and Gosling fall like torn and bloody rag dolls to the floor of the spectator row where they had been seated. Blood and gore filled the entire spectator section of the courtroom as well as the blood leaking out of the witness stand area where Lowry had been shot.

Ryan tried to jump from his chair in the well of the courtroom and stop the shooter from leaving the courtroom. By the time he got to the swinging doors of the well, the shooter had disappeared out of the courtroom into the hall corridor. Ryan and Lawrence quickly followed the escaping shooter out into the corridor but by the time they entered the hallway, they saw the shooter leap over the entrance guard's barriers out the front door of the courthouse and down the long flight of steps in front of the courthouse.

Yehuda and Sosie were just entering the building as the shooter ran past them almost knocking them over.

Yehuda saw Ryan and Lawrence running toward him, so he immediately turned and started to run after the fleeing man. The escapee jumped into a waiting car, a BMW, Yehuda noticed, and the car squealed noticeably out into the street and disappeared around the next corner.

Ryan and Lawrence stood alongside Yehuda as they watched the black car disappear from their sight.

"What happened?" Yehuda yelled as he tried to regain his breath.

Ryan and Lawrence were puffing and bending over as if the air had been knocked out of their bodies. Ryan sat down on the curb of the sidewalk, his head between his legs.

Sosie sidled up to Ryan, sitting next to him on the sidewalk, her arm around his shoulders.

"What happened?" Yehuda repeated, his eyes staring at Lawrence who was just recovering from his seemingly asthmatic attack.

"That guy shot Lowry." Lawrence finally uttered.

"And Gosling and Borden," Ryan added in a whisper.

"All three?" Sosie asked in a credulous voice.

"All three." Ryan replied.

"How did he get into the building with a gun?" Yehuda asked in a shocked voice.

"I don't know," Ryan replied as he ran his hand through his wet, sweaty hair.

"I thought he was Smallwood, the FBI agent when he walked into the courtroom. But it couldn't be Smallwood," Ryan paused as he thought momentarily and then continued as if he was talking to himself, "Why would Smallwood kill Lowry and Borden? Why? It couldn't have been Smallwood."

"Maybe somebody dressed like Smallwood," Lawrence offered.

"Everett, he looked like the spitting image of Smallwood. That marine brush cut Smallwood has."

"There's no way he could have brought that automatic into the courthouse. The metal detectors would have picked the gun up when he entered. Only if he convinced the guards he was FBI could he get the gun into the building."

"I haven't seen Smallwood for days, Everett." Ryan said.

"Neither have I…and he's usually in my face at least once a day. Checking up on me I guess."

"It must have been our friend Paulsen," Yehuda declared.

"Sure didn't look like Paulsen, Yehuda," Ryan replied.

"Have you ever seen Paulsen, Joshua?" Yehuda asked.

"Just a picture…"

"I saw him when we fought out at The Park. Just a glimpse of his face. That guy that ran by me didn't look like Paulsen."

"Who the hell else could it have been?" Lawrence wondered aloud.

"What now, Everett?" Ryan asked as he pulled himself up from the curb. Sosie followed as she helped her obviously fatigued husband up from the sidewalk.

"You're out of shape, my dear." Sosie said with a relieved smile on her face.

"We can't get the Lowry recording into evidence without Lowry testifying, Joshua. And the testimony of Gosling and Borden sure would have helped our case against the Evans."

"What about the docs?"

"Well you saw what they were all about. We can crucify Lowry and Borden and Comtel itself…but there's nothing in the Evans hand that inculpates them in all this mess. Jack Evans and the Senator were smart enough to let Lowry and Borden sign all the docs. Unless we get somebody inside to testify against them…I just don't know, Joshua."

"Maybe we don't have any criminal actions against them but I sure damn well know that a class action suit on behalf of those ten victims would put Comtel into the poor house."

"Hate to agree with you, Joshua…but unless we can catch Paulsen and he spills his guts out which I don't expect him to do…we don't have anything against the Evans as far as the murders are concerned."

Yehuda grabbed Joshua around the shoulders and hugged him to his barreled chest.

"You're still alive, my 'masigunuh' son-in-law. I was afraid that the 'gulayim' had shot you too. And then I would have to support your wife and child until they put me into an old age home."

"He's part Irish, Poppa," Sosie reached over to kiss Joshua on the lips, "he has nine lives."

"A cat has nine lives, my love," Joshua replied as he kissed his wife tenderly on the lips.

Waterman wobbled down the steps and walked up to the quartet standing on the sidewalk.

"You didn't catch the son-of-a-bitch?" Waterman chastised angrily.

"He got away, Sam," Joshua replied.

"There goes our case," Sam declared, his round face dark red from the effort in getting down the massive steps of the courthouse.

"We better let the jury go," Waterman said as he started to walk up the steps. "We still got one hell of a class action suit against Comtel for the deaths of those ten innocent people."

"Did you hear about Abromowitz?" Yehuda queried.

"No, what?" Joshua replied.

"Somebody shot him and his lawyer in Monte Carlo. I got an e-mail from my Mossad buddies in France."

"This guy has really been busy," Waterman said.

"Well, we still have a shot at the Evans if we can catch Paulsen alive. Right, Mr. Lawrence?" Yehuda asked to the departing Lawrence.

"Only if you catch him alive and he's willing to dime out the Evans. I just don't think he's the type to rat on his buddies."

"I got a feeling he's heading back to Comtel's headquarters. And The Park," Yehuda declared as he started to walk to his BMW convertible parked along the curb.

"Where are you going, Poppa?" Sosie asked with obvious concern etched in her voice and face.

"I need some amusement, my daughter. I'll be alright."

"Let me send a couple of my agents with you," Lawrence offered.

"No, sir. Maybe one of your FBI boys shot all these people up there. No, I'll be all right, besides, I have a little pea shooter attached to my ankle. Just in case somebody wants to use me for target practice."

"Here Poppa, use my cellphone and if you find anything, call. Will you?" Sosie pleaded. She handed him the miniature cell phone.

Yehuda took the cell phone and walked quickly to his parked car. A bright smile lit up his craggy face and Yehuda suddenly felt he had something worthwhile to do. With a little danger thrown in. 'Lucky Zeppi is not here,' he thought whimsically, 'she would have a fit and carry on like a banshee.'

He entered the BMW and drove toward The Park and the Comtel headquarters building as the remaining quartet looked on, all concerned that Yehuda might be biting off more than he could chew.

Chapter Forty-Eight

Yehuda sped along I-4 until he saw the turnoff to The Park. It was approaching noon and the hot summer sun was directly over his head nearly blinding his vision although he was wearing his ultra-violet polarized desert sunglasses. He reached down with his right hand and felt the bulge under his sweat socks. "Little Fannie" he called his trusty pea shooter that could expel three shots and strike its target twenty feet away. His mind wandered back to the battles he had fought in the last three decades. 'God must be with me,' he mused to himself with a cackle. 'Even though I believe it's all bullshit.'

Yehuda loved life like no one else on this earth. He was healthy, loved his wife and family, his grandchild most of all, but he had decided that if he had to go where ever we go when we die, he was ready. He just wasn't going to sit back in a rocking chair and think about his past glories. Every day was going to be an adventure or else he didn't want to live in boredom and complacency.

His body was strong. He exercised at least two hours a day including running a minimum of five miles every day, rain or shine. His neighbors in Jerusalem thought he was crazy to run in East Jerusalem or wherever he wanted to run no matter who lived there, but he knew once you gave into the fear in your belly, you should give up your life as well.

The exit to The Park came up and he turned the car into the exit lane. Within five minutes he was parked across the street from the Comtel headquarter building waiting for Paulsen. Yehuda knew that the killer would return to his masters who ran him for whatever reasons Paulsen had to kill for the mighty Evans family.

After about an hour of patiently waiting in his car, the sun beating down on his head and body, Yehuda saw Paulsen exit from the Comtel building.

Paulsen was dressed in a white t-shirt with Army infantry pants. Yehuda could see the holster bulge under Paulsen's t-shirt.

Yehuda slumped into his seat as Paulsen walked to the parking lot of the building.

As Paulsen entered his car, Yehuda started up the engine of his car. Paulsen pulled his black sedan out of the parking lot toward the amusement park itself. He glanced around and evidently saw Yehuda in the BMW. With a spastic burst on the accelerator, Paulsen's vehicle shot ahead toward the massive parking lot of Comtel's amusement center. Yehuda followed within two car lengths of Paulsen's vehicle knowing that Paulsen knew he was right behind him.

Paulsen suddenly stopped his vehicle and jumped out and headed full blast toward the entrance of the amusement park. He flashed a badge at the guard at the entrance who let Paulsen through the gate.

Yehuda parked in front of the entrance gate, jumped out of his car and ran furiously toward the entrance gate. He could see Paulsen openly running toward the center of the amusement park.

Yehuda leaped over the entrance gate, pushing the guard to the side while flashing his honorary Jerusalem police badge at the guard who probably thought that Yehuda was an American cop.

Paulsen wheeled around to see where Yehuda was. Espying Yehuda running after him, Paulsen ran through the gate leading to the enormous ferris wheel called "The Top of the Universe" allegedly the largest ferris wheel in the world.

As the ferris wheel carriage came around, Paulsen pushed two young girls to the side and leaped into the carriage.

Yehuda flashed his badge at the ferris wheel attendant as he grabbed the next carriage also pushing the two angry girls to the side. Yehuda smiled at them and said in a mollified voice, "Sorry, police, young ladies." They smiled back at him and seemed to be satisfied that they were performing a civil duty allowing this nice policeman to go ahead of them.

Yehuda could see Paulsen in the second carriage in front of him. Fortunately, most of the carriages on the wheel were empty.

Paulsen suddenly turned around in the carriage and pointed the machine pistol at Yehuda. Yehuda dropped to the bottom of the steel carriage as he heard the pop, pop of Paulsen's pistol, the bullets bouncing off the steel back of the carriage.

Higher and higher, the two carriages rose. The passengers in the other carriages turned toward Paulsen and Yehuda when the gunshot sounds reverberated loudly throughout the wheel.

Yehuda heard a girl's scream behind his carriage as one of Paulsen's successive gunshots struck her in the arm. As in a Greek chorus, hysterical screams and cries were filling the air.

The operator of the ferris wheel started to order the other passengers off the wheel. One by one the carriages were emptied of non-combatants.

Paulsen continued to shoot his hyperactive automatic weapon at the crouching Yehuda.

Then, as suddenly as the shots commenced, Yehuda heard the clicking of the hammer of Paulsen's automatic. Paulsen frantically searched though his combat pant's pocket for additional bullets. His face reflected his frustration when none of any additional bullets were found.

Paulsen threw the pistol at Yehuda who was now climbing out of his carriage along the steel lines that held the carriages together.

Yehuda hated heights especially on a moving carriage. His carriage rose higher and higher following Paulsen to the top of the mountainous wheel. Mystically, Yehuda envisioned the smiling face of his departed son Benjamin in front of him. Yehuda moved courageously, with out fear.

Yehuda's mind filled with thoughts of death as his mind's eye saw his body flying to the cement below the ferris wheel. He wondered whether he would feel any pain as he hit the ground. Dying…is it painful? He asked of his ghost son. Benjamin only smiled and encouraged his father on. Yehuda smiled back at his son, as the thought of death crossed his mind. 'Whatever will be will be, Poppa,' Benjamin said to him.

Yehuda edged his way toward the carriage next to the one Paulsen was trying to climb out of.

Paulsen slipped at the edge of the carriage as he dropped back into the well of the carriage just as Yehuda reached the edge of Paulsen's carriage.

Paulsen slammed his fist against Yehuda's clutching hands which were clinging to the rim of the carriage, his body caught between carriages.

Suddenly Yehuda's left hand painfully released from the rim of the carriage, Yehuda holding on by his right hand only. His body dropped into the air, the carriage still a hundred feet off the ground. Yehuda looked down to the ground, a mass of people gathering at the base of the ferris wheel. Screams of several women were uttered when Yehuda dropped one hand off the rim of the carriage and his body just hung from the carriage like a disjointed rag doll.

Paulsen was now clubbing Yehuda's right hand with his clenched fist. Without warning, the ferris wheel screeched to a halt, throwing Paulsen back to the front edge of the carriage.

Yehuda quickly lifted himself up to the lines holding the carriage and with a Herculean effort, started to climb into the carriage itself.

Paulsen regained his footing and rushed at the unsteady body of Yehuda who was still trying to get a firm foot hold inside the carriage. Paulsen jabbed the bottom of his booted right foot into the genitalia of Yehuda. Yehuda grimaced and fell forward as the boot heel caught him right above his groin.

Paulsen then brought his right fist up into Yehuda's jaw as Yehuda quickly turned his head to the side to avoid the blow. The fist partially caught him on the side of his face, throwing Yehuda against the side of the carriage.

Paulsen jabbed his other booted foot into Yehuda's stomach, but this time Yehuda brushed the assaulting foot away with the swipe of his arm.

Yehuda turned swiftly and completed a three hundred and sixty degree turn and drove his right foot into Paulsen's chest, throwing Paulsen to the edge of the carriage onto the floor.

As Yehuda rushed toward the falling body of Paulsen he could see the sun streaked glint of the Bowie knife that Paulsen had pulled out of the sheath on his pant's belt.

Yehuda lashed his left foot into Paulsen's face, crushing Paulsen's nose as Paulsen rushed at Yehuda with the point of the knife.

The knife dropped to the ground as Yehuda lifted Paulsen to the edge of the carriage with his right hand grabbing Paulsen's pant belt. Paulsen threw his clenched right fist at the face of Yehuda, Yehuda hearing the crack of his cheek bone being broken. As Paulsen struck Yehuda, his body pitched violently forward and over the rim of the carriage. Yehuda turned to see Paulsen's body falling to the ground below, the crowd of spectators parting to allow the body room to land. Paulsen hit the ground a dead man.

Yehuda sat down on the seat of the carriage, his hand trying to stop the blood from gushing out of his face.

From below he heard Ryan's and Waterman's voice shouting to the operator to start the wheel again. At that time, Yehuda really didn't care if he ever landed on Earth again.

When his carriage hit the ground, Yehuda was sitting patiently in the seat, smiling at Ryan and Waterman. Yehuda could see Sosie running from the entrance of the park to the ferris wheel.

"What took you guys so long?" Yehuda said with a glint in his bloody eye. He remembered nothing else until he awakened in Orlando General surrounded by reporters and of course Ryan and Waterman and Sosie.

Epilogue
One Month Later

The Everett Lawrence-Jo-Beth Washington wedding was held in the grand ballroom of the five star Plaza Athanee in Paris, located on Avenue Montaigne, near the American and Canadian Embassies. Across from the apartment in the building where Marlene Dietrich spent her final decade as a recluse. Two blocks from the Place D'Alma and the bridge over the Seine to the Left Bank. It was catered by the chef of the year, Alain Ducasse, who was a three star Michelin honoree. The wines were selected by Simon Bouvier, the celebrated wine steward and the author of "Wine for the Very Rich."

All of these bacchanal luxuries were paid by Samuel Waterman, a recently minted millionaire who had also recently become a part time resident of the Paris' 16th arrondisement, across the hall from his protégé and friend's apartment in the same 1930's apartment building. Joshua Ryan, the protégé, and his lovely wife Sosie and their adored child Sammie all had benefited substantially from the fees earned by Joshua Ryan as co-counsel in the two class action suits against Comtel. Millions of dollars in fees. Unfortunately the verdict amounts, which totaled in the billions, were severely compromised by the Chapter Eleven bankruptcy of Comtel some six months earlier.

Just to back track a smidgen, the reader should be brought up to date as to the happenings of the last twelve months before this glorious wedding of Everett Lawrence and Jo-Beth Washington was taking place.

After Paulsen's fatal fall from grace and the traumatic deaths of Lowry, Gosling, Borden and the discovery of Smallwood's body in the swamplands just off International Drive, a rifle bullet through his forehead, Lawrence was forced to terminate the grand jury hearing. No criminal charges were ever brought against Comtel or the Evans. But, the Fifth Circuit Court of Appeals presided over by Chief Judge Florenza, overturned Judge Stuyvesant's order dismissing the civil class action suit against Comtel and restored the verdict and judgment including interest and attorneys fees of just over two billion dollars. Since Helen Walsh, Joshua Ryan and Samuel Waterman were counsel of record when this fortuitous event occurred, they recovered the bulk of the fees awarded to class counsel.

Soon after the institution of the class action suit on behalf of the ten or so victims of Comtel's murderous acts against their senior employees, Comtel filed for Chapter 11 bankruptcy protection.

The insurance carrier for Comtel had decided it would be fruitless to defend that suit and appeal the earlier class action herbicide poisoning verdict against it's insured, Comtel, and therefore settled with the two classes for the hundred million dollar limits of the policy.

Attorneys fees in both of those civil litigations, and included in the settlement amounts, totaled ten million dollars, split equitably amongst counsel. Joshua Ryan received two and a half million dollars, Helen Walsh and Sam Waterman received similar amounts and the balance was awarded to the original law firm who handled the previous herbicide suit for the original class action members who had been injured as the result of Comtel's intentional, harmful and deceptive employment practices.

Sam Waterman also derived an additional million dollars as the sole beneficiary of his sister and brother in-law's estate that had benefited from the twelve and some million dollars settlement on behalf of the ten or so decedents' estates which was the subject matter and claims of the wrongful death class action suit against Comtel. Generous to a fault, Sam decided to foot the bill for his former student's wedding (Lawrence) and he decided Paris should be the forum where that proceeding should take place. Waterman hired a private Canadair jet holding sixty people comfortably and in first class accommodations to transport his most favorite friends and the bride and groom's relations and friends to Paris for the wedding.

After the filing of the bankruptcy petition for Comtel, Senator Evans had a combination stroke and heart attack and was in a coma for over three months. Jack Evans filed for personal bankruptcy, but no one ever found the millions of dollars skimmed off Comtel's earnings these many years. Under Florida law, Evans' ten million dollar estate in toney Lake Evans' gated community was safe from the greedy clutches of the many-shafted creditors of Comtel including the plaintiffs in the two class action suits.

Lawrence was fired in the subtle ways lawyers are terminated from sophisticated law firms such as the U.S. Justice Department. Instead of accepting a transfer to the hinterland U.S. Attorney's office in Minot, North Dakota, Everett decided that the government of the United States didn't really want him around anymore. So after one call to his mentor Simon Warner, Lawrence became a named partner in Warner's law firm. He now traveled extensively between Washington, D.C. and Europe, heading the international commercial legal department of the esteemed international law firm now partially bearing his name. Although he didn't benefit from the lucrative fees that his white lawyer friends partook of in the class action suits, Lawrence now commanded upwards of five hundred thousand dollars a year as his base salary plus, of course, a piece of the action of whatever fees he originated as a rainmaker for the firm. And with Warner's connections, Lawrence created lots of rain.

Jo-Beth Washington left the Orlando Police Department and now was entered in the graduate program in film production at George Washington University. She figured she would either become another Halle Berry or Steven Spielberg depending on which side of the camera fate had in store for her.

The wedding was the event of the year for the American colony in Paris. She chose the recovered Captain Amos Parker as Everett's best man. Everett joined in her selection joyfully.

Waterman, the eternal impressario, hired seven of the coolest expatriate American jazz musicians in Paris whose lead female singer sounded like Sarah Vaughn yet had a body like Jennifer Lopez, to entertain the intimate hundred or so guests. Simon Warner, himself, arranged for the U.S. Ambassador to France to officiate at the wedding. Jacque Chirac planned a brief appearance at the reception but he stayed over three hours eating and drinking and flirting with the gorgeous bride's maids flown over from the States, all friends of Jo-Beth who were as beautiful as the final five of any national beauty contest.

The wedding reception lasted until four in the morning, the early June Paris sun barely setting before it again rose in the East. By midnight, the jazz ensemble had turned the wedding's solemnity into a rip-roaring, hip swinging jam session with Jo-Beth belting out several Ella Fitzgerald be-bop songs that certainly could bring old Ella back from the dead.

Ryan, his mind filled with alcoholic joy, danced with everyone, including Sam Waterman.

The spirits of long dead friends and lovers hovered over the happiness of the occasion. Ryan thought, as he saw the magic of Everett and Jo-Beth dancing as one, that life could be good and wondrous sometimes.

Waterman clung to Helen Walsh, the superb wine turning him into a bloody romantic. He proposed marriage at least twice and she turned him down twice because Helen wanted her singleness to explore. She indeed loved Sam Waterman but she had had enough of marriage. 'Maybe in a couple of years,' she mused. 'Maybe never.' She wanted to look out of her suite at the George Cinq Hotel and deliberate on the historical magnificence of Paris or sit on the Spanish steps of Rome or visit the pyramids of Egypt without feeling obligated to do or feel or be there for anybody. Only for herself.

Simon Warner had invited all the bridesmaids to his penthouse suite at the top of the Plaza Athenee for a post party celebration. They all accepted knowing full well the reputation of their host as an omnivorous but magnificent lover. They all bet Warner could not take on all five at the same time. Warner won gloriously.

As Ryan, Waterman, Helen, Sosie, Yehuda and Zeppie sat around a large round table, their stomachs and minds filled with food, wine and love, the band finished up their musical entertainment, the clock was speeding toward the 4:00 a.m. mark, they lifted their champagne glasses to the ceiling for one last series of toasts.

"May we always be together." Waterman toasted.

"May we always be friends," Ryan toasted.

As Yehuda stood to give his toast, Jo-Beth and Everett danced over to their table. Yehuda lifted his glass high above the table and flashed the most magnificent smile Zeppie had ever seen on Yehuda's face, as he declared for all to hear, "To life…Le Chaim…May our wonderful new friends be as happy as we all are…right now. Forever."

They each drank the champagne down in one gulp as they surrounded the newly married couple exchanging loving kisses and hugs, all knowing that the magic of this moment could never be duplicated. Forever and ever they hoped they all would feel like this and most of all, love each other as friends.

Joshua, his mind sloshed with champagne, put his arm around Sosie's shoulders as he drew her near to him. The tears in his eyes cascaded down his face merging into the crooked grin planted on his face. The gnawing fears that had consumed him these many years mysteriously disappeared. As he stared at the beautiful loving face of Sosie, he knew that he had come close to nirvana. Reborn to a better life.

She kissed him on the lips, tasting the salty tears of her boyish looking husband. The panic she felt for the future of all her loved ones evaporated in the hazy lights of that majestic ballroom. No matter what happened she knew her lover and husband would be there. That was enough to erase the nightmares of the past and fill her with the hope that the yet unfilled future held.

"I love you, Joshua Ryan," she said in a tearful voice.

His bleary eyes looked up from her shoulder and with the most mischievous little boy's smile she had ever seen, he said, "I couldn't even spell the word before I met you. LOVE," he spelled and then said before his eyes closed, "I love you, Sosie. Forever."

They all left the Plaza Athenee as the sun rose in the far east of Paris. Down Avenue Montaigne to the Champs knowing that life didn't get any better than it was right now. Never.

As Ryan slowly walked up the Champs Elysee, his arm around Sosie's shoulders, her head leaning against the nape of his neck, he saw an unusual heavenly vision. The dawn's early sun was barely rising from the east, when the descending moon appeared to overtake it. And then the small moon disappeared. As if it had been consumed by the hungry sun.

Abreast of Joshua and Sosie was Sam Waterman and Helen Walsh, walking arm and arm. Alongside Sam were Yehuda and Zeppie, their hands locked together. The wide sidewalk of the boulevard was empty, except for a lonely sanitation man scooping up the debris of a busy Saturday night on the Champs.

Ryan's eyes hypnotically focused on the top of the majestic Arc de Triomphe looming in the near distance. It filled center stage of the wide boulevard. AS the sun's rays pierced and shunted aside the gray, cumulus clouds, as if it was a heavenly groundskeeper clearing a verdant jungle of leaves and branches, it centered suddenly on the top of the magnificent Arc. Joshua saw the words that symbolized the meaning of freedom for all: Liberte, Fraternite et Equalite illuminated by the darting rays of the sun. To Ryan, the words together meant justice for all.

He repeated the words in his mind. Justice for all. Did American law give justice to those many people who had been murdered so violently? Can you get away with murder? Did the Evans commit murder and remain unpunished? Or is there a higher law that punished Senator Evans where he now lay dormant in a coma waiting for death to arrive? What about Jack Evans? Was bankruptcy punishment enough for his crimes?

As he did three years ago, Joshua Ryan promised himself that he would never return to the practice of law. He did for a friend. Now, as he walked shoulder to shoulder with his family and friends in that early Paris morning, he resolved that he would not return to a practice that produced little justice. He was richer now, but the money was irrelevant. It provided comfort, but not salvation.

"Oh, the hell with it," he muttered in a whispery voice that only

Sosie heard. "I'm in Paris with the only people that matter to me. That's enough."

He turned his head and kissed Sosie on the cheek and walked on toward the waiting Arc.